DISASTER AT BUSHEHR

REGINALD NELSON

To order additional copies of this book, contact:
Bookwhip
1-855-339-3589
https://www.bookwhip.com

To my wife, Donna, and my best friend
Walter who have given me wonderful love
and support over the years.

PROLOGUE – THE IRANIAN DESERT

HAMID LOOKED DOWN at the rocky, barren ground as he led his mule up the precarious path. His throat was raw from all of the dust he had ingested. It even hurt to swallow. He remembered a trick from his youth while trekking in the Sonoran Desert landscape of southern Arizona and reached down to grab up a small, smooth edged stone. Hamid examined the stone, turning it over in his hand and then placed it in his mouth. The foreign object would stimulate his salivary glands and provide some moisture to his dry tongue and parched lips.

The path he was following led from the border of Iraq, the place of his training, into Iran, Hamid's birthplace and his final destination. He had studied the route well in the months preceding his trek. He carried a GPS locator in one of the packs tethered onto the back of his mule, but he had not needed to use the device up to now. He had already crossed what used to be the wetlands of Iraq, an area full of thriving wildlife and exotic plants at one time only to be drained by Saddam Hussein as part of a reclamation project southeast of Bagdad. He could tell by the length of the journey that he had probably crossed into Iran. He knew that the border town of Abadan lay forty kilometers off to his right, to the southeast. He would continue east until he would pass south of Ahvaz and then continue southeast skirting the coastal waters of the Persian Gulf for about two hundred kilometers until he would approach his destination…the nuclear reactor seventeen kilometers outside the town of Bushehr to the southeast.

Hamid was alone. He was not a part of the many caravans which criss-crossed the border between Iraq and Iran. He knew that he may encounter others and that some may be hostile, but he also knew that he was prepared for any trouble. Hamid had trained long and hard and felt blessed by Allah to be the chosen one to complete this mission. Oh yes, there were others of his group involved with other aspects of the mission, but he believed that his role was the pivotal piece to the puzzle.

He worked hard to limit his trek to ten hours each day. Hamid avoided the hottest part of midday and sought shelter for his mule and himself. Only when he stopped did he treat his furry companion to some water. He also partook only during these forced periods of rest. He knew from his past training that at best he and the mule would average a walking speed of four kilometers each hour. Hamid also knew that if he averaged forty kilometers per day that he would easily reach his destination within the week he had allowed for the journey.

Hamid looked up into the sun and decided that it was time to seek shelter. He found a rocky outcropping which offered some protection and he bedded down the mule. After sharing some of his water supply with the mule, he nestled up against the hot boulders, pulled his ghutrah over his eyes and closed them. Sleep did not come instantly. His mind began to play games on him.

He first jumped back to his early childhood. Hamid had begun his life as the fourth born, but first boy, to a lovely Iranian couple during the years of relative calm under the Shah of Iran. They chose the name Hamid because it meant 'Praiseworthy', and they had so desperately wanted a boy. His mother and father moved to America by the year of his sixth birthday. By now there were five children and all of his four siblings were girls. His father had secured a teaching job at the University of Arizona in Tucson. His parents felt blessed with this opportunity and the chance to escape Iran. They had watched the religious zealots operating under the Ayatollah Khomeini take over their beloved country and drive it back into the dark ages. Many of their well educated friends had simply 'disappeared' at the hands of Khomeini's rabble. Pursuing higher education was surely not going to be a part of the coming Theocracy in Tehran.

The environment around Tucson reminded Hamid of Bagdad, where he had trained for this mission. He remembered that these early times in his life were carefree and fun. His mother and four sisters spoiled him rotten. On occasion his father would let Hamid attend his classes at the college where he taught the youth of America about his version of world history. Hamid wondered how it was that the teachers around the world could not teach a subject like history without editorializing on the facts. Twisting the facts often to fit their version of the truth.

Hamid's father once showed him a textbook on geography in the Middle East. There was no mention of Israel in the text. Just a black area where Israel should be. Everyone knows where Israel is! Who did they think they were kidding? Obviously the leaders throughout the Middle East influenced the writers to eliminate any mention of Israel. So backward and shallow.

At the dinner table all seven would gather around the table and listen to stories told by Hamid's father about his great birth country. He puzzled at times why his parents always referred to that land as Persia, and to others they spoke of being Persian. The Persian Empire existed between the years of 550 BC until 330 BC. There was no Persia in modern times! His family wasn't Persian…But his parents called themselves that. Was this more of that 'twisting'? Were they embarrassed to be Iranian? That was a question for his father once Hamid was older.

His mind then jumped to Hamid's high school days at Sunnyside High School. He loved wrestling and lettered each of the three years he attended high school. His team, the Blue Devils, won three state championships while he was competing. Hamid contributed by winning all of his bouts at his weight classification. Wrestling taught Hamid the discipline to maintain weight restrictions for competition. He learned how to starve himself, avoiding liquids and food, before a weigh in. Sometimes he even had to learn purging techniques to void his body of any excess waste to lower his weight.

He also remembered his first love at Sunnyside. Her name was Beth and she waitressed at the local Denny's. One night she showed Hamid the Denny's' menu which included a breakfast called, "Moon over My Hammy". From that moment on she and all the kids at school nicknamed him, "Hammy". Beth was also credited with taking Hammy's virginity one night on a drive home after her shift at Denny's. All he remembered from that first time, besides the awkward fumblings of a first timer, was that she smelled like bacon, and pork is a bad thing for Muslims.

Hamid's musings then took him to his college days at Arizona State University in Tempe. This is where he met Farroukh. They met during

Hamid's freshman year. The Muslim community was quite small in Tempe. Farroukh turned out to be active in a student protest group, called CARAMA, and recruited Hamid into the group. CARAMA stood for Coalition of Arabs and Muslims in America. Hamid originally felt that a group to pull together Arabs and Muslims would be a good thing. He had felt isolated as a Muslim growing up in Tucson and missed the camaraderie of others with similar pasts and religious interests. Hamid felt at home with this group and he enjoyed their monthly meetings. He also became more militant in his beliefs during his early college years.

By his senior year at ASU Hamid had joined a cell of six Arab Muslims dedicated to the eradication of Israel from the planet. They called themselves the 'MADEI'. The anagram was short for Muslim Arabs Dedicated to the Eradication of Israel. The MADEI group was loosely associated with other extremist groups around the country, but never did much other than protest against Israel whenever possible.

Hamid spent several years as a lost soul after college. He rarely worked, and when he did they were menial labor type jobs. He maintained his involvement with the MADEI. One night the six met as usual, but had a guest in their midst. The man spoke to the group for two hours. He was an eloquent speaker. This man gave Hamid's life a purpose, a focus, a drive and a mission.

A vision of the mission was compassionately laid out that evening. All six young men saw how the mission could work.

Two members of the group, Hamid and Farroukh, immediately committed their lives to this man and the others would help out with the necessary behind the scenes activities to pull off their mission.

All six would immediately relocate to Iraq. That's where their training and indoctrination would take place under the guidance of Al Qaeda in Iraq, a combination of Osama bin Laden's Al Qaida group and the Al Jihad group from Egypt. All costs for relocating the six and living expenses would be borne by this man. All of the MADEI group's energy would be focused on the eradication of Israel.

Hamid then thought about the plan. It was simple and the timing was perfect. Iran's new government was 'thumbing their nose' at the US and defying pleas to back off of their nuclear program. They had completed the first nuclear reactor of any Arab state in the Middle East with Russia's help.

The reactor was begun in 1975 with guidance from Germany. Construction stopped in 1979 when the Shah was overthrown in the Islamic Revolution of Iran. Construction commenced again in 1995 and stalled in 2007. A new agreement was reached with Russia's Atomstroyexport and there was a launch ceremony in August, 2010. During the renewed phase of construction there was much saber rattling by the United States and Israel that a nuclear reactor would never be allowed to be completed on Iranian soil. Airstrikes from Israel were the most likely way to take out the reactor.

The MADEI group was to blow up the reactor and make it look like it was the work of the Israelis. World support of Israel would vanish and the Arab states would once again focus all of their energies on the removal of Israel from Palestinian lands that it had occupied since May, 1948.

Hamid had one last thought before he slept…in less than one week he would be with Allah with all of the gloried of martyrdom. He drifted off to sleep dreaming of the seventy two virgins soon to be his.

On the fifth day of his trek Hamid spied the buildings of the Bushehr nuclear reactor off in the distance. He knew that he had two days to dig in to the sand hills surrounding the facility and to find a high ground from where he could aim his laser. He worked his way closer in to the facility and searched the surrounding terrain for the highest terrain point. He maneuvered his way so that he was positioned northeast of the reactor site and leading the mule to what he chose as the best location. Hamid unloaded all of the gear that had burdened the mule for the last five days. He fed and watered the mule for one last time and then shooed the animal off into the desert. As the mule ambled away Hamid felt a sense of loneliness.

Hamid spent the day digging into his temporary encampment and setting up all of the equipment that had been packed away on the mule's back. His location was north and east of the nuclear facility. All of the gear was stolen from Israel and had Israeli identification and markings. There was a satellite phone and case to communicate with his comrades. There was a tripod upon which the giant laser pointing device was mounted. He packed away in the sand the remaining food and water supplies and placed his prayer rug so that he would be kneeling to the east during his five daily prayer sessions.

A hard cover version of the Torah was unpacked and placed at the head of the prayer rug. Some of this book may survive the blast and reinforce that there had been an Israeli at the site. Hamid kept a tattered paperback version of the Koran inside his belt. He knew that this book would vaporize at the right time. There were high powered binoculars, also stolen from Israel, so that he could observe the goings on within the nuclear facility.

The main buildings and outbuildings were just as he had studied them from the satellite photographs that were supplied during his training in Iraq. He found the building where he would focus the laser. The round, domed structure was the building that housed the main reactor and it was this building that he would 'light up' with the laser beam.

Hamid completed his preparations and dialed a number into the satellite phone and waited for an answer. After several moments the phone clicked to a live connection and he talked with his other cell member, Farroukh, who was also soon to become martyred. Farroukh was holed up at the air field on the eastern end of Kharg Island.

Kharg Island lay twenty five kilometers to the west of Bushehr. The boat that brought Farroukh to the island was tied up to the pier a short distance from the airfield. There were a couple of dozen boats tied up to the pier or anchored a short distance from the pier.

A heavy tarpaulin covered up the instrument which would catapult the two of them into martyrdom. A stolen AGM-129 ACM cruise missile made by the United States was ready on the launch platform beneath the cover. The missile was painted with Israeli markings. It would not be a long stretch to assume that this missile followed a 2,000 kilometer path from a launch site in Israel. The Advanced Cruise Missile designed by the United States had a range of 3,000 kilometers. No one would suspect that its flight path began only thirty kilometers northwest of the nuclear facility, launched from a stolen boat tied up at an almost deserted Kharg Island.

There were no planes at the airfield. This once thriving oil terminal was now a ghost of an island. Iraq bombed the oil terminal out of existence in 1988 and the island never recovered. Hamid's comrade had no trouble hiding out in the airport terminal until shortly before the appointed hour. His environment was much more accommodating than Hamid's. They prayed together and arranged a time to talk the following evening.

On the final day Hamid checked and rechecked all of his equipment. He thought many times about his family and almost reached for the satellite phone to call his mother to say, 'goodbye'. But his training was better than that. He knew the dangers of placing any extraneous calls.

And then it was time.

He switched the laser on and checked that its fiery red beam danced on the side of the rounded, domed building in his sights. He placed one last call to his friend who had moved to the boat. He confirmed that the laser painting was active and accurate. His friend shouted into the phone, "Allah Akbar", and Hamid heard the roar as the missile's engine ignited. He calmly placed the satellite phone in the sand and watched.

Within minutes he saw the missile fly into the side of the building. Very shortly there was a blinding white flash. Hamid had time to mutter his own "Allah Akbar" as he watched the fireball reach into the sky... within seconds the concussion reached his position and he was gone. Hamid, his martyred friend and one million unknowing souls vaporized into the atmosphere.

PART ONE

CHAPTER ONE

Dubai, UAE

TOOK MY FRESHLY brewed French Roast coffee out onto the back patio of our Dubai home. I breathed in deeply as the aroma coming from my mug reminded me of a happy time from my childhood. The smells wafting up the stairs, emanating from the kitchen beckoned my brothers and me to breakfast. My mother's coffee percolator and her numerous sizzling pans on the stove provided the symphony of smells and sounds that promised a wonderful beginning to our day. As my brothers and I padded downstairs for breakfast, our senses were tuned to the wonderful creation issuing forth from the kitchen. The saliva flowed freely as we smacked our lips in anticipation.

On occasion I had helped my mother measure the coffee grinds into the percolator basket and never noticed much smell from the grinds as I scooped them out of the metal can and placed them in the percolator basket. I would finish assembling the contraption and place in on the electric stove burner. Soon I could hear the water begin to make noise as the hydrogen and oxygen molecules absorbed the heat and became more agitated. Once the water was hot enough, you could see it erupt into the clear dome and cascade down over the coffee grinds in the basket. Now I could begin to smell the aroma and it was rich and powerful. A smell that has been a delight to my nose ever since my childhood.

It was only the aroma that I enjoyed as a child. I hated the taste of coffee! It wasn't until college that I began to drink the steaming dark liquid. I remember that it was so bitter that I had to use cream and sugar to make it palatable. The caffeine was supposed to help with those late night studies, but I still fell asleep in the middle of them. I never was able to pull an 'all nighter'.

It was after Dental School that I weaned myself off of the cream and sugar. I liken the process to the enjoyment of wine. In college I bought the sweetest wine available. The closest thing to soda pop! Now, I enjoy the driest wines…Chardonnay for white and Cabernet for red. My dental team has come to love the taste of my coffee, but they know it will be really strong!

I thought about those times and the new coffee drip machines and wondered to myself if anyone still used percolators. The aroma just wasn't as powerful coming from our drip coffee maker.

I made a course around the outside of the patio, enjoying the colorful flowers that were blooming along all three sides of the patio. I looked out onto the Persian Gulf and made note of how calm the waters were. All of the homes on Jumeirah Palm Island had ocean frontage due to the ingenious design of this man-made island. The island was the shape of a palm tree with a trunk and sixteen palm fronds, and a protective surrounding crescent. All of the homes are placed along each side of the sixteen fronds. The Jumeirah Palm Island is the self-declared 'Eighth Wonder of the World'.

This first man-made island was such a success that the engineers in Dubai have designed a Palm trilogy…three man-made island projects! People can now inhabit the Palm Jumeirah, and soon the Palm Jebel Ali or the Palm Deira. We lived on the first, and smallest of the three island projects.

The Arab visionaries are also working on a project called, "The World". The project was originally conceived by Sheik Mohammed bin Rashid Al Maktoum, the ruler of Dubai. The final outcome is to give the appearance of our world as seen from outer space as shown in the artist's conceptual drawing below.

The World or World Islands is an artificial archipelago of two hundred and sixty small islands constructed in the rough shape of a world map, located 2.5 mi off the coast of Dubai. The World islands are composed mainly of sand dredged from Dubai's shallow coastal waters.

The ambitious vision was unveiled in 2003. As with most of the construction in Dubai, development halted in 2008 when oil went south. Right now, though, it is just a series of sand islands pumped up from the seabed that don't resemble much of anything! I shot the picture below from my phone's camera as I flew over 'The World' on a return to Dubai's airport. Now that oil is trading at an acceptable level for the Middle East, 'The World' will march on to its eventual completion.

I then took my place, seated at the patio table to watch the sun rise from the east. I have always enjoyed my solitary time in the mornings as the earth awakens.

As I watched the fiery red and orange clouds reflecting the sun's energy as it rose over the horizon, I contemplated about our new endeavor, I.N.C.I.S.O.R. I had coined the phrase just before a breakfast meeting with Ashonte' Black and Lance Wood in Abu Dhabi at the end of a roller coaster ride that found us chasing a Saudi Arab terrorist cell around the world. We all lived through some harrowing close calls to be sitting together for breakfast in this Abu Dhabi restaurant. The three of us had decided that we enjoyed working together and that we were a good team. We enjoyed each other's company outside of the work that we were now involved in, and our wives got along famously well, at least for this first year that we were involved so closely together.

Maybe we could form an organization to fight against the world's terrorists?

Our other option was to split up and go our separate ways, returning to lives we knew before we met in Colorado Springs. For Lance this meant to return to his duties as a CIA operative, duty station and destination unknown. Ashonte' would return to Colorado Springs and his karate dojo, possibly providing independent contractor duties for the CIA, as he had in the past when his unique abilities were needed by our government. I would stay in Dubai, running my American Dental Clinic. My life in Colorado Springs where I had practiced dentistry for so many years was over now. Becky and I had fallen in love with all that made up Dubai. This would be our home for the foreseeable future.

As we awaited our meals I had explained to Ashonte' and Lance what the anagram stood for, "**IN**ternational **CI**vilians for a **S**afe Society **OR**ganization".

I also reflected back to how we three had come together. Colorado Springs, Colorado now seemed so far away.

A dental patient had mentioned a new athletic club opening not far from my dental practice. I needed desperately to work on my physique! I went to check out the new club and met the owner, Ashonte' Black. Ashonte' was also a Karate instructor, and I had a history, going back to my high school days, of fighting competitively in Karate. I knew immediately that this would be my key to getting back into shape. I hated just 'exercising', but tying those efforts to a sport would make the effort palatable.

Ashonte' and I hit it off from the beginning, and shortly into our new relationship I had told him about an invention of mine. Ashonte' was a thin, wiry mass of well sculpted muscle that had been a CIA operative. He performed 'Black Ops' for the CIA, which was a kind way of saying that he was a trained killer. Ashonte' was older, as I was, and his handlers had, for the most part, put him out to pasture. He now performed contract work for them in really 'dicey' world situations. That's how I had met Lance Wood.

Lance was a CIA operative. Lance was a big man with a military style haircut and no neck. He shook hands like he meant to break something! Lance had that no nonsense air that said loudly that you didn't want to mess with him. Looking at him reminded me of all of the virile young men that the military builds up into these beautiful physical specimens only to place in harm's way, many to be sacrificed in one world conflict or another.

It was Lance's input to the CIA that carried my invention so that it became the latest in covert technology aimed at thwarting terrorism in the Middle East.

A year earlier, I had come up with a dental invention that had catapulted the three of us into an international stage involving espionage, a world-wide chase, encounters with Arab terrorists, close encounters with a Russian hit squad and a near world-changing disaster involving a nuclear weapon on American soil. We also became close friends during that intense year. The CIA embraced "Project Loudmouth", which was the name that Lance had coined for my invention at one of our first meetings in Colorado Springs. A terrorist plot to destroy America's oil reserves was foiled due, in large part, because of the nanotransmitters which I had implanted in some of the terrorists' teeth. That was my invention!

I shouldn't take all of the credit for the invention of the nanotransmitters. In fact, the brilliant scientists at CIA's Langley headquarters came up with the working model. I just had the idea. To date, a couple of dozen transmitters had been implanted at my Dubai dental clinic. The CIA had installed facial recognition software with an encrypted satellite uplink in my office. Any and all patients that entered the Dubai clinic were captured on video which was scrambled, encrypted and sent thousands of miles around the world to observers in the United States. These observers monitored the signals from Langley, Virginia, and they let me know which of the Arabs that came to me for care was a good candidate for the nanotransmitters.

Three of the nanotransmitters had stopped functioning. This indicated dead terrorists because none of the transmitters had any type of mechanical issues since they were first implanted within the last year. It was a good design!

I finished my coffee and thought about how good the last year had been to Becky and me. Enough of the reflecting…it was time to focus on the now!

CHAPTER TWO

MY WIFE, BECKY, and I had met four unique people and we had become good friends with these two couples. I had worked closely with Ashonte' and Lance on our last endeavor, which we had coined the name, The Saudi Oil Gambit. Ashonte' shared my love for flying and we had spent hours together in the Avanti II that the CIA had delivered to Dubai for my personal use. Lance had nearly lost his life to an American mercenary on a rooftop in Washington, D.C. Becky, Grace and Cyndi had become good friends.

At the end of our mission to save America from a terrorist plot we all decided that it was worthwhile to stay in close contact and work together. Therefore, Lance had left his CIA post, Ashonte' left his dojo in Colorado Springs and the two couples had moved to be near us on Palm Jumeirah Island in Dubai.

Becky and I put up the initial money to get them settled near us. There were homes that had become available on Frond M, which were close to our home on Frond L. These properties had originally carried price tags in the millions of dollars, but we were buying at the right time. Both properties were secured for only a million and a half dollars each. There were many high rise options along the Jumeirah Beach Residences, but Becky wanted the girls to be closer to her.

The three men had also decided that the wives had valuable skills to contribute to I.N.C.I.S.O.R. The wives also became an integral part of our small group. The six of us were now a team.

Our own government's CIA and the friendly foreign governments around the world had received prospectuses which contained our skills and services that we could provide. We were receiving calls that involved everything from kidnapping plots to coup d' états from around the world. It was looking like the world was ready for I.N.C.I.S.O.R. We knew that we had to limit the number of cases that we could tackle. Becky and Cyndi were the most skilled at divining where our particular set of skills would do the most good in the world.

Our group chose, for the time being to office out of Becky's and my home. A spare bedroom was turned into a high tech office. The CIA was willing to part with expensive, state of the art electronics from the phone and fax system to the latest in visual touch screen computer modeling boards that were mounted on two of the walls in the office. Satellite encryption was a must and also provided by the American government, as an incentive to continue with Project Loudmouth. The room was made to be eavesdropping-proof also with the help of CIA contractors. I.N.C.I.S.O.R. had the most secure and technologically advanced office in all of the United Arab Emirates. I'd even put our 'safe' room up against the U.S. Embassy in Abu Dhabi and the new Consulate Compound built in Bur Dubai adjacent to the Dubai Creek and the Consulates of Saudi Arabia and Qatar!

The wives walked together every morning which gave them time to talk through our new endeavor. Lance, Ashonte' and I knew that the three of them would have to agree on this new plan and embrace it of their own accord. Grace was a budding artist who was put to work immediately designing a logo and artwork for I.N.C.I.S.O.R. Cyndi had the memory of an elephant. She remembered everything and never forgot anything. Becky had developed interpersonal communication skills that made anyone she talked with feel like her new best friend.

I had brought over to Dubai from America two young dental associates. Each worked three days a week in the dental clinic. My partner, Jim Bobb Mulheran seemed to live on the golf course. When he wasn't on the golf course he could be found at a local tavern, sipping a scotch and regaling the women visiting on holiday with his stories of practicing dentistry in the Middle East. Jim Bobb had even witnessed a stoning and a beheading during his time in Saudi Arabia! Good stuff for story-telling. He hadn't been in the clinic in months. His partnership checks were being deposited, and not returned to me. Sometimes that was the only way I knew that he was still alive!

I made a token appearance one day a week to work on the more extensive cases that my young associates couldn't handle. The rest of my time was focused on the growing pains of I.N.C.I.S.O.R.

What an amazing whirlwind of a year it had been. New friends, new home, living in a new country, new plane and now a new career. What was I doing chasing bad guys? What training or experience did I have to place on a resume' for a modern day 'secret agent'? I had been a dentist for over thirty years! Well, at least Lance and Ashonte' had a wealth of knowledge and experience about espionage and spy stuff which, hopefully, some would rub off on me. If nothing else, I could fly the plane and be a glorified bus driver!

I knew that Lance and Ashonte' were to arrive shortly to discuss our next case and debrief with Cyndi about our case that we had just completed two days before.

The Italian aristocrat that had been returned to his family unharmed. He was kidnapped in a manner reminiscent of the kneecappings which were popular in Italy in the late 1970's and early 1980's.

Back then a Marxist group named the Red Brigade, or Brigate Rosse, terrorized Italy with kidnappings tied to kneecappings (shooting the victim through the patella and crippling them for life) or murder if there was no ransom. The Red Brigade used these techniques to raise money in support of their cause…to undermine the Italian state and pave the way for a new Marxist regime headed by a revolutionary proletariat. After a decade or so most of the members were captured, killed or just melted into the back streets of the Italian underground. The failure of the Soviet Union left the Red Brigade without a cause.

Now, thirty years later it appeared that terrorists with ties to the extinct Brigate Rosse had resurfaced. No new techniques and the identical methods of operation as were being followed that were used three decades earlier. The difference now was in a device that I.N.C.I.S.O.R. was instrumental in turning into a reality.

A newer version of the original nanotransmitter used against the Saudi Arabian terrorists had been developed. This tiny item had the ability to provide for passive GPS tracking. The listening devices used in project Loudmouth actively sent out digital signals which were picked up by listening posts on the ground and then transmitted to communication satellites to be routed to one of the computer farms in Virginia. The new device was only activated remotely by satellite if a problem developed such as the wearer becoming lost in the woods or being the victim of a kidnapping, or any other reason that they would go missing. GPS devices were readily available around the world. From OnStar to Garmin to most cellular phones global positioning devices had become commonplace. Identification chips were being implanted in favorite pets so that, if said pet went missing and surfaced as a stray in some veterinarian's office, the chip could be scanned for identification. The concept wasn't new.

What was unique about our device was its miniscule size spawned by the same nanotechnology which the CIA developed for Project Loudmouth. And the passive nature of the device. It sounded less intrusive for the private lives of the purchasers of the nanotransmitters that they had to be activated remotely to receive a signal. Actually, it was the limited battery life available in a device so tiny that required activation only when necessary. No matter. They were selling like hotcakes!

The techies at Langley had nicknamed the first nanotransmitters as PC's because they were placed like Post and Cores in endodontically treated teeth. They now had come up with a cute nickname for the new transmitters; 'minis'.

"Like the car?" I asked.

"No, it's because they are miniscule!" the two techies replied.

"Okay," I responded while thinking these guys needed to stop with the pet names for their devices. These same 'techies' had divined the name, "PC" for the first nanotransmitters that were being placed in teeth. I hadn't reacted well with their first nickname a year ago, and I know I didn't when they explained to me the name of this device. I don't have what you would call a good poker face! My being 'non-plussed' with what the 'techies' considered to be an inventive name hurt their feelings once again! They just 'huffed off' to their lab once again to soothe their hurt feelings.

The new device had opened up a large and extremely lucrative side business for I.N.C.I.S.O.R. because the tiny transmitter could be embedded in items as small as a belt buckle or the heel of a shoe. The extremely wealthy from around the world that feared for their lives every day as a consequence of their wealth, and certain unprotected politicians paid handsomely to have access to these transmitters. The developers within the CIA allowed I.N.C.I.S.O.R. the exclusive right to market the tracking devices as a partial reward for our involvement in the successful location of the nuclear bomb in Arctic National Wildlife Refuge, and my continued placement of the listening devices in the root canalled teeth of certain Arab persons of interest.

Our particular Italian Aristocrat, Adamo, had flown to Dubai just a few months earlier. He met with Becky and was immediately stunned by her kindness and compassion for his predicament. He felt as if he had known Becky for a long time. Becky fell in love with his Italian accent, and admitted that he wasn't all that bad looking!

Meanwhile, Cyndi performed a background check that showed that this Italian man was exactly what he professed. She contacted the Consulta Araldica (College of Arms) that governed Italian heraldic matters up until 1948. In general, heretofore unrecognized noble families, whether titled or not, were required by law to petition for recognition of their ranks or titles by the Crown if such was desired. The names of the heads of these families were inscribed in the Libro d'Oro della Nobiltà Italiana, a series of large, handwritten registers maintained at the offices of the Consulta Araldica. (This should not be confused with the Libro d'Oro published by the Collegio Araldico today; the Collegio Araldico is a private heraldic society, not a governmental entity, and its Libro d'Oro, though reasonably reliable, includes many fantastic histories and, particularly in cases of alleged untitled nobility, dubious claims to aristocratic lineage.)

Cyndi discovered a direct tie to the Grand Duchy of Tuscany. Tuscany (Italian: Toscana) is a region in Central Italy. It has an area of 22,990 square kilometers and a population of about 3.7 million inhabitants. The regional capital is Florence which is where Adamo resided. Our prospective client was an extremely wealthy man who lived off of a trust provided by an aristocratic family. Old money with ties to ancient Italian royalty. And he was very vulnerable. He always traveled with a bodyguard, which made him long for a more private life. He was the ideal candidate for the GPS locator device.

Becky explained to Adamo how the device worked and the different locations where it could be hidden. Our client chose to have it placed in the heel of his Bruno Magli loafers which looked to be a special order and must have cost $1,400.00. Once the device was placed, Becky explained that because of its passive nature no body scans or other devices would pick it up. The device was tested and recorded into the computers at I.N.C.I.S.O.R. Our Italian gentleman and his bodyguard concluded their business with Becky by handing over a check for $100,000 and signing a document stating that an additional $500,000 would be paid if the device was ever activated and our people became involved in the rescue.

CHAPTER THREE

I T WAS ONLY three days ago that we received a frantic call from Italy. Our client's car was found riddled with bullet holes and his lifeless bodyguard was found behind the steering wheel. Our client was nowhere to be seen and as yet there had been no ransom calls or any other form of contact. The local police in Florence had no leads or clues about what might have happened to our client.

Ashonte' immediately connected our computers through a secure, encrypted connection to the tracking computers at Langley. He punched in the identification of the GPS device and in less than one minute had the location pegged to a villa on Lake Como in northern Italy.

Lake Como, or Lago di Como in Italian, is a lake formed by the runoff from the glaciers found in the limestone and granite mountains of the Italian Alps which surround the lake to the north. The lake is located in Lombardy, Italy in the northern confines of Italy's 'boot'. The lake is the third largest lake in Italy, stretching twenty nine miles in length and over two miles wide. At over 1320 feet deep it is one of the deepest lakes in Europe and the bottom of the lake is more than 656 feet below sea-level.

Lake Como has been a popular retreat for aristocrats and wealthy people since Roman times, and a very popular tourist attraction with many artistic and cultural gems. Lake Como is widely regarded as being one of the most beautiful lakes in Italy.

Upon further study the villa was identified as Villa Oleandra, the former residence of the Heinz family and now owned by George Clooney.

Villa Oleandra is located in the town of Laglio on the western shore of the south-western branch of Lake Como.

The device was 'pinging' the satellite from within the structure. Cyndi went to work, discovering what she could about the villa from her research on the internet. She prepared to brief the group on the layout.

Our team discovered that the villa had fifteen bedrooms which wouldn't be a concern because the hidden device would lead us exactly to within three feet of our client. Pictures and schematics of Villa Oleandra were downloaded from the internet and placed onto the wall of computer screens to be studied. Cyndi also confirmed that George Clooney was not in Italy at the time and that the villa was unoccupied except for a skeleton maintenance crew.

An agreement was reached between Ashonte', Lance and me that we should move now. While they studied the Villa and surrounding area, I prepared a flight plan and route, and checked on the weather.

I phoned out to the Execujet FBO at Dubai International Airport and asked them to pull out the Avanti II and make sure that the fuel tanks were both topped off. The first leg of our journey was quite long and would have the plane "sucking on fumes". I needed every ounce of Jet A for this first leg of our expedition.

Lance and Ashonte' quickly packed bags with the necessary supplies and joined me in the garage to load up the BMW 760Li which I had already started remotely. The air conditioner was cooling down the interior nicely. The growl of the twelve cylinder engine sounded powerful and was reassuring as I got behind the wheel. We were soon speeding along the Sheikh Zayed road to the airport. I am amazed every time I travel along this fabulous seven lane highway, remembering back to the 1980's when development in Dubai had not yet begun. Now, everywhere you glanced was a spectacular high rise project!

The Avanti II was all set to depart, and Ashonte' and I performed our preflight walk around while Lance stowed the luggage on board. Ashonte' and I took our seats in the cockpit after satisfying ourselves that the moving surfaces looked good. I contacted Ground Control at 118.35 MHz for permission to taxi to the active runway after Ashonte' retrieved the current ATIS information and designation. We taxied to runway

30L and contacted the tower. We were cleared onto the runway for an immediate departure.

I moved the throttles forward to their takeoff detent and felt the rumble of the Pratt and Whitney engines as they powered up and began to thrust the aircraft down the runway. I held my feet against the brakes to let the engines spool up. When the brakes were released, she shot down the runway, pinning us to the seats. When we reached rotation speed, I eased back on the yoke and the Avanti leapt into the air. This bird loved to fly! I adjusted the heading bug and aimed the plane toward Cairo's airport which lay 1,500 miles to the northwest. The Avanti II had a maximum range of 1800 nautical miles with VFR (visual flight rules) reserves. I chose a flight level below 18,000 feet to avoid filing an IFR (instrument flight rules) flight plan. IFR requirements allowed us only 1,300 nautical miles, keeping the proper IFR fuel reserves, and would have required us to add another leg to the trip.

Once we were at altitude, Ashonte' left his co-pilot seat and joined Lance in the cabin to pour over the computer images of the villa and plan their rescue. The computers in the cabin were in contact with our base computers and Lance checked with Becky for any updates or changes. There were none. We had one huge advantage. The kidnappers had yet to make any contact or demands. They did not know about the mini. They had no idea that we knew where they were.

Four hours later we were cleared to land on runway 23R at Cairo's International Airport. Ground control directed us to the local FBO (fixed base operator) where we cleared customs and immigration, refueled the Avanti II and availed ourselves of their facilities. We had a light meal of sandwiches and Cokes. The personnel at the FBO also restocked the onboard refreshment center with drinks and fresh fruit. After just thirty minutes we were refreshed and ready to embark on the next leg of our journey.

This time we headed north, across the Mediterranean Sea with the airplane aimed at Rome's airport. This leg was a little over 1,300 miles but didn't feel any shorter to the three of us. By the time we made our approach into Rome's Leonardo da Vinci Airport Ashonte' and Lance had devised a plan and practiced it mentally and verbally several times. They were ready to extract our client from the kidnappers.

After refueling and some nourishment in Rome, I headed the Avanti north toward Milan's Malpensa Airport. This leg was just a little over 300 miles. The airport is located twenty five miles northwest of Milan and Lake Como is a short forty five minute drive from the airport. Upon landing I parked the Avanti II at Universal Aviation at Terminal 2. I arranged for the plane to be refueled and ready to go within the hour. Lance took care of renting a Land Rover and loading it with the equipment we brought in the airplane from Dubai.

We all piled into the car with the understanding that Lance and Ashonte' were the operatives on this mission. My role was to drive the car. After a short drive we found the location of the Villa Oleandra in the town of Laglio. Laglio only boasted 900 inhabitants and all was quiet this late afternoon. We all donned our communication gear and moved toward the Villa. Lance and Ashonte' studied the Villa from two different aspects, while I watched the surrounding area for any auto or pedestrian traffic.

I heard Lance say into the headset, "It looks like we caught them sleeping."

Ashonte' then spoke, "I see one eating at the counter in the kitchen, and no activity on the second or third floors."

"I concur," Lance responded, "Subject seated in the living room."

"No cars or traffic approaching," I whispered, "daylight starting to fade."

Lance and Ashonte' made a stealthy approach to the kitchen window. Lance then took two steps back and took a running leap at the glass window. The glass gave way and shattered with a loud crash. The kitchen inhabitant was stunned and raised up to see the commotion. At that moment Ashonte' raised his weapon and fired one round into the kidnapper's forehead. A silencer muffled the shot which didn't matter after the crashing of the broken glass window had disturbed the surrounding silence.

Lance had rolled on the kitchen floor and came to his feet with his weapon drawn. He observed the dead kidnapper and moved to confirm that he was dead. As he felt for a non-existent pulse, Lance listened for any other activity. When he was sure that the Villa was quiet, he turned and offered Ashonte' a hand to help him through the window. They both waited without breathing to hear if there were any other sounds in the Villa. All was quiet.

Ashonte' moved to the living room and freed our client from the plastic ties that bound his hands and feet. He removed the gag from Adamo's mouth and quickly explained that we were from I.N.C.I.S.O.R.

Our client's eyes became wide as he exclaimed about the rapid rescue. Other that muscle stiffness from being confined and a handful of bruises from his capture, he was fine and healthy. Lance kept his weapon trained on the stairway. When Ashonte' and the client appeared, the three men exited the Villa through the front door and quickly made their way to our rented car. When they were all on board and the car doors were shut I gunned the Land Rover and headed back the way we had come to Malpensa Airport. We made a clean getaway and nobody followed us.

It was decided that we would fly to Amerigo Vespucci Airport in Florence. Our client phoned his family from the Avanti II and announced to the three of us that they would be waiting at the airport. As we landed night was steadily overtaking the daylight and the local police surrounded the plane and whisked our client inside to the loving arms of his waiting family. Although badly shaken, he was unhurt. We quickly debriefed with the police, giving them the location of the villa and notifying them of the one dead kidnapper. Adamo's family was so appreciative that we had returned him to them that they showered us with offers of food and respite, but we decided to continue our trek back to Dubai.

We chose to fly through the night and complete our journey in one day. I let Ashonte' and Lance sleep in the comfort of the Avanti's spacious cabin. Both were awake by the time I landed in Cairo. Refueling, customs and immigration and a pit stop and we were ready for the last leg of the journey to Dubai. This leg Ashonte' flew with Lance as his co-pilot while I enjoyed a Crown Royal on ice from the refreshment center and then slept in the back. I felt dead tired once the adrenaline had drained from my body. All I did was watch, but I still got pumped up. I awoke when I heard the engine speed reduce for the approach into Dubai International Airport.

Ashonte' taxied the aircraft and parked outside of the front of the hangar. We exited the plane and stowed our gear in the trunk of the BMW. After a brief talk with the attendant we headed home. The mission took us just under twenty four hours…one day…and a payoff of $500,000. Not bad!

All of that action had happened two days ago. Yesterday I had heard that the Italian police had apprehended fifteen members of a terrorist cell who were linked to the kidnapping of our Italian client. We were extremely lucky to have only encountered the one soul at the Villa. AP News, in today's paper stated that," Police conducted raids across northern Italy on Monday, breaking up a leftist militant group that was allegedly planning kidnappings or kneecappings of victims to finance its plots, Milan prosecutors said. Police said they arrested 15 suspects in Milan, Turin, Padua and other northern Italian cities." No mention of the kidnapping of our Italian client or his rescue. That was just fine with me. The less press and notoriety the better.

Becky escorted Lance and Ashonte' out onto the patio. Hellos and hugs went around and they joined me at the table. Becky disappeared inside and returned shortly with a tray of mugs and coffee.

"Did you see the paper?' Lance asked.

"Yeah, we were lucky and stupid to try that by ourselves," I replied.

Ashonte' then added, "I don't know…what would have happened if we hadn't moved so quickly? He really could have been kneecapped…or worse."

Lance and I shook our heads in agreement. I added, "We would have sought out help from the local constabularies if we had encountered more kidnappers at the Villa, right?"

Lance and Ashonte' shared a glance that let me know that they were prepared for much, much worse than the local cops could have handled, and I needed to shut up.

"I've already given Cyndi my debriefing and told her all that I contributed to the mission. Now it is both of your turns," I stated and moved inside to be with Becky. Cyndi overheard me and moved out to the patio with her recording device to pick Lance and Ashonte's brains. Becky called out as I entered the office that a very grateful Italian family had wired a half a million dollars into I.N.C.I.S.O.R.'s Swiss bank account. Also, we were receiving calls from other Italian families who had heard from Adamo's family and wanted to procure minis for their own protection.

When Lance and Ashonte' completed their debriefings I suggested that we take the day off and get ready for a spectacular dinner outside the Dubai Mall. Madeleine Café was located on the second level across from the Star

Atrium and sported the largest outside terrace in the mall with great views of the Dubai Fountain and the Burj Khalifa. We had a table for six and watched the crowds gather below for the computerized water cannons to perform their magic on the thirty acre lake at the base of the Burj Khalifa.

The Dubai Fountain doesn't sound like much until you see and hear this wonderful spectacle. Designed by the same California firm that is responsible for the water display at the Bellagio in Las Vegas, the fountain is over nine hundred feet in length and shoots water almost five hundred feet into the air. That's fifty stories high! The extreme shooters that are capable of blasting the water that high are rarely used in the daily choreographed displays that occur every half hour from six at night to ten o'clock. There are over six thousand lights and twenty five color projectors that help the water look like it is dancing to the music being played.

We had a wonderful time experiencing the French cuisine. The only missing ingredient for me was the wine. A quirk of the United Arab Emirates is that alcohol is allowed only in restaurants that are in hotel properties. The cafés in the mall are all 'dry'. Finishing the meal with Madeleine Café's version of Crème Brûlée made for a wonderful dinner and we continued talking into the night. I asked the others to join me for a walk through the mall, past the aquarium that is so large that you can rent scuba equipment and dive with the fishes, to a corridor that led to the base of the Burj Khalifa. Becky and I had travelled up to the observation deck once before, but this was a new experience for the two other couples, and I surprised them with tickets for the ride up.

The elevator takes you up to the 124th floor which houses the observation deck for the Burj Khalifa, the tallest building in the world! The Khalifa is one hundred and sixty stories tall, meaning that there are thirty six floors above you when you stand on the observation deck. The elevator car is so well constructed that its occupants fly up to the observation deck in thirty seconds with no sense of movement, watching a video about the building! I was truly amazed. They are the world's fastest elevators, travelling at forty miles an hour.

We all looked out through the glass windows at the city lights below and were lost in our own thoughts. On our way around the observation deck I saw a real first for me…a gold vending machine! Really! You can buy gold ingots or coins right out of a vending machine. And the vending machine didn't take US dollars!

Becky and I left the two other couples to wander the Dubai Mall and waited for the valet to bring up our car. Cyndi and Grace were wanting to see the Olympic style ice rink that is part of the Dubai Mall. They were even talking about getting Lance and Ashonte' to strap on skates and move to the disco music! That almost made me want to stay to observe my two friends and their wives try to manage on ice skates!

Driving out to Palm Jumeirah Becky asked if we could park and take the monorail out to Atlantis. She wanted a late night drink on the sand while listening to the DJ play tunes while we lounged on the beach. I suggested that we just take the tunnel underneath the water out to the protective manmade reef where the hotel sits. This beautiful and very pink hotel boasts a five star rating and a huge Aquaventure Theme Water Park. We were just there for a nightcap, so we parked in the west parking lot, ambled by the tennis courts, circled around the pool and out onto the manicured white sand beach.

The DJ was playing songs he called Jukebox Gold from the '60's and '70's. My kind of music. Becky and I found a couch on the sand, ordered drinks and looked out at the skyline of Dubai. The skyline had three distinct high rise building areas and reminded me of Manhattan's skyline, only much bigger!

Becky nestled her head on my shoulder and whispered to me that she had had a wonderful evening. It was good to be out with our friends, but also good to be alone like this. She placed her hand on my thigh and my whole body started to tingle. I still get aroused when Becky touches me…even after twenty years! I hurried through my drink and willed her to finish hers. I had to be patient…she was calling the shots…but I knew there'd be a 'Happy Ending'.

CHAPTER FOUR

ASHONTE' MADE THE decision to complete his private pilot's license when he sold the dojo in Colorado Springs and made working for I.N.C.I.S.O.R. his full time occupation. Ashonte' was already familiar with Flight Safety in West Palm Beach Florida. Shortly after the CIA had purchased an Avanti II for my personal use Ashonte' and I spent two fabulous weeks at Flight Safety's facilities on Southern Boulevard. I was there to attend a pilot recurrency and upgrade program to get my type rating for the Avanti II. Ashonte' took the company's 'pinch hitter' course where he learned to operate the radios, basic flying maneuvers and how to land the plane if something were to happen to me.

Since he attended that training over a year ago, Ashonte' had logged more time in the Avanti II than most corporate pilots and copilots who fly similar aircraft. I had spent hours with him going over the various redundant systems, and the beauty of the design of a canard wing aircraft with pusher prop power plants and three lifting surfaces. I often let Ashonte' pilot the plane when the two or three or six of us went flying. We loved to fly over to Abu Dhabi for a quick meal and then head the aircraft back to Dubai. Abu Dhabi was only a forty five minute drive from Dubai, but we always pulled the plane out to make the trip. Ashonte' had learned the feel of the aircraft from its stalling characteristics to its handling in a steep turn; from a short field takeoff to a power off approach to a landing. He had also seen me perform a maneuver which saved us from a missile shot at us by a Russian hit squad when I had flown into Oman for a quick extrication of Lance and Ashonte' and their terrorist prisoner as the hit squad was closing in on them. An Immelmann turn at the end of the runway made the missile overshoot. His love for the Avanti II soon rivaled mine.

It made perfect sense for Ashonte' to revisit Flight Safety and spend the hours in the simulator and in actual flight to receive his private pilot's license. He learned all of the FAA regulations (known as the FAR's) and studied the Airman's (or Aeronautical) Information Manual to learn the rules of flight. He completed his dual training, working with the instructor both in the simulator and in the air. Ashonte' then completed his solo work, including a cross country solo flight. He took his written test and then scheduled his flight exam and passed them both with flying colors! He received his private pilot, multi-engine rating and the type rating for the Avanti II.

While Ashonte' was in Florida he also procured his Third Class Medical Certificate. First Class Medical Certificates were held by the 'big boys'… the commercial pilots flying for the major airlines. They had to be renewed every six months. Second Class Medical Certificates were issued to non-airline commercial pilots…like the corporate pilots…and are good for a year. The Third Class Medical Certificate is for all of the other pilots…like me…and is renewed every two years. (It's good for five years if you're under forty). I almost didn't bring that up…forty was a long time ago!

All that was left for Ashonte' to hold the same ratings as I did was to work on his instrument rating at some point in the future.

When Ashonte' returned to Dubai after completing his pilot studies he came by the house one evening with Cyndi and suggested that we needed a name for the Avanti II. Many pilots chose female names for their aircraft because, in a sense, these planes played the role of 'mistress' to them. Much of their free time was spent either flying, or caring for their airplane.

The two wives thought that Ashonte' had a great idea. We all agreed to write down names and have a get together with the six of us to decide on a name. I called Lance to let him know about the contest and we set a time for the dinner in one week. We would each pick two favorite girl's names. So there could be twelve names to pick from if there weren't any duplicates.

We all sat down to what I thought was a spectacular dinner. I grilled fat, juicy steaks on our outside grill while Becky put together a fabulous salad.

I had previously made up my recipe for Crème Brûlée which had become famous among our friends, both in the States and Dubai. In fact, Ashonte' had blamed my concoction for turning him into a diabetic. Several bottles of Turn 4 Cabernet Sauvignon later, the meal was concluded.

I went into the office and pulled out a white board and some markers. It was time to write down our names. I had really struggled with this project of finding two feminine names to bring to the table tonight. The two most important women in my personal life were Becky and Shawn. I didn't feel that either of those inspired the sultry, seductive idea of the airplane as a mistress. Most of my pilot friends had picked the wives' or daughter's names for their planes. Calling the Avanti II, "Becky" or "Shawn" just didn't do it for me.

I decided on "Aurora" for the beautiful lights we had observed in the northern sky while Ashonte', Lance and I were in the Arctic National Wildlife Reserve hunting for a buried nuclear warhead that an Arab terrorist cell had procured illegally from Russia and threatened to destroy The United States oil reserves. I also chose "Bianca", just because. The name had no significance to me…I just liked it. I wrote my two names on the board, and gave my explanation to the other five friends watching me write. I didn't see any immediate signs that any of them was 'grabbed' by my two nominations.

Becky chose to go next. Her two choices came from names of employees in the dental clinic. She had two favorites. "Angela" and "Arielle". She didn't have much to say in the way of a story about either name. Becky just said that they were both very special individuals and she loved their names. At this point my two favorites were "Aurora" and "Arielle", but it wasn't time to erase the other names. There were still eight others to write on the board.

Going around the room, it was now Lance's turn with his picks. I was thinking to myself that Lance would do well with our game because he was the one who had come up with Project Loudmouth for our first invention that had launched the three of us into a life of international intrigue and built some solid and loving relationships among the six of us. Lance pushed back from the table and stood in front of his chair. "The military often names their aircraft with the names of birds. I did not pick feminine names. My two nominations are "Peregrine" and "Lanner"." He took his seat and there was silence around the table.

"What!" Ashonte' exclaimed.

I spoke next, "Tell us what the names mean to you."

Cyndi looked at him and shook her head, "You always expect us to know what goes on in that brain of yours."

Lance took a deep breath, showing his frustration with all of us. He then told us about the two names.

"Peregrine and Lanner are two species of Falcons. The genus contains 37 species, widely distributed throughout Europe, Asia, and North America. Peregrine Falcons have been recorded diving at speeds of 200 miles per hour, making them the fastest-moving creatures on Earth. The Avanti II is the fastest turboprop in the world, right?"

I nodded at his correct assessment of the Avanti II.

"The Lanner Falcon is a bird of open country and the savanna. It usually hunts by horizontal pursuit, rather than the Peregrine Falcon's stoop from a height, and takes mainly bird prey in flight." Lance paused and took a sip of water before continuing. "When I look at the sleek lines of the Avanti II, I think back to the days of watching the falcons perform at halftime during the home games at the Air Force Academy. It was spectacular to watch those birds circle the stadium and dive at the twirling targets that were spun by the bird's handler on the football field. That plane reminds me of a sleek, fast bird of prey. Did you know that the falcon rates highest of all birds on the intelligence scale?"

"Okay, okay," I said. They are supposed to be girls' names. Anybody have a problem with Lance's two picks?" I looked around the table. Nobody spoke up. I added the two names to the board while thinking to myself that Lance may be on to something. I liked Lanner.

Next it was Cyndi's turn. She propped her elbows on the table with her palms up. She then placed her chin in her palms. I had come to recognize that this was her pose when Cyndi was deep in thought.

"Ursula and Leilani are my two names," Cyndi blurted while she gazed at the white board. She then continued,

"I can still remember the first time Lance and I rented the movie, Dr. No. We weren't married yet, but he had let me know that he was a huge James Bond fan. Dr. No, which came out in 1962, starring Sean Connery, was the first James Bond film. Ian Fleming wrote the book in 1958. I was watching Lance when Ursula Andress came out of the water in that bikini, carrying the conch shell, with a knife strapped to her waist. I've never seen such lust oozing out of a man. Do you remember, she played 'Honey Rider' in the movie? They had such crazy names for the females. My favorite was 'Pussy Galore'."

"How about 'Octopussy'," Ashonte' replied.

"Mine was 'Dr. Goodhead'!" I answered.

"Plenty O'Toole," Becky chimed in. "And Sean Connery's response… named after your father?"

"Everybody remembers something about James Bond movies, but what I remember was Lance's reaction. I could tell in his eyes that he had Ursula completely undressed in that scene. That's where Ursula comes from," Cyndi spoke. She then turned to Lance and said, "Do you remember that hula dancer when you took me to Maui for our honeymoon?"

Lance's eyes clouded over just briefly and then he lit up.

"Oh Yes!" he replied.

"I thought you were going to leave me right there!" Cyndi retorted, "She was so gorgeous!"

"Hey, babe…I'm not going anywhere," Lance said.

"I know, I know…but I was worried!" Cyndi finished.

"Great choices, Cyndi," I said as I wrote them on the board. We now had eight names, with Ashonte' and Grace to go. It was Ashonte's turn to speak.

"Do any of you know what my name means?" he asked.

There was head shaking around the table.

"No?" he queried.

"I bet most of us don't know what our names mean," I retorted, "I know that Nelson means 'son of Nell'…what's that?"

"Well, all I could find is 'strong African woman!" he said, "What were my parents thinking!"

Lance couldn't resist, "Okay, 'strong African woman', what are your picks?"

Ashonte' glared at Lance, then began to chuckle. We all joined in the laugh. I was thinking that Ashonte' was one of the toughest SOB's that I knew…don't be calling him a woman too terribly often!

"Here goes…I found two very special African names…Zola, which means 'love', and Tinashe, which means that 'God is with us'," Ashonte' claimed. "The meanings are quite clear. We all love this plane, and we hope that God is with us on every flight! Also, while we are on this name thing…I want you all to call me 'Ash' from now on."

I wrote the names on the board, while thinking that I can't be calling the airplane Tinashe.

"Give us some time to switch! Lance said, then added, "I like Ash."

Cyndi and Becky looked at each other and exclaimed together, "Ash, it is!"

"Grace, it's your turn," I said as I turned around.

"This may sound conceited, but how about 'Grace'? Grace means elegance, beauty, and smoothness of form or movement. Isn't that perfect for the plane?" she stated.

"Not bad," I said. "What else?"

"That's it. I only have the one name," Grace replied.

"Okay, we have eleven names on the board. Let's get a drink and move into the living room." I offered and began to wheel the white board into the next room. The others adjourned to the kitchen to drop off their dinner plates and grab new glasses for more refreshment.

Once settled into the comfortable chairs, I stated that I wanted to first eliminate the obvious names from the list. We all stared at the board in silence for a couple of minutes.

"Bianca's out. It means nothing," Lance opted.

"So's Angela, Peregrine, Leilani and Tinashe," Cyndi blurted.

"Everybody okay with that?" I asked, and there was only silence. "They're gone!" I said as I erased the names. "Six to go, any other obvious deletions?"

"I really like Lanner, but it's not really a name for a mistress," Lance opined, "Also Zola sounds like a name for a striptease dancer."

"Two more down?" I asked the group. Not hearing any objections, I erased the two names. "Any more to cross out?" I asked.

The group was quiet. I then rewrote the four names: Aurora, Arielle, Ursula and Grace.

Ashonte' spoke next, "My favorite is Aurora. Reggie you were right about the beautiful northern lights when we were in Alaska."

"Let's do this," I suggested, "Everyone write down their favorite name from the list and we'll count the ballots." I passed out paper and Becky got pens from the office. Once everyone had finished, Becky collected the papers and handed them to me. I unfolded each sheet and placed a mark by the name. By now, I recognized most of the writing.

"Aurora one," as I opened the first sheet, "Grace one; Aurora one; Ursula one; Arielle one; Grace one." "There's a tie," I spoke as I erased Ursula's and Arielle's names from the list. "Do we vote again?" I asked the group of good friends.

Lance spoke up, "I'm bored with this. We're wasting good conversating time bothering with this. I like Aurora. All in favor?" Four hands went up. "Okay, Aurora is it. Let's go out on the patio and enjoy this night air!"

Just like that it was done. My plane would now be called Aurora. It was one of my picks, so I'd better get used to it!

While my wife and our good friends refreshed their drinks and moved outside to the patio, I wheeled the white board back into the office. I stood back and studied the name. "Aurora".

I moved to the computer and typed in Aurora on the Wikipedia site. I quickly discovered that Aurora was also the goddess of the dawn in Roman mythology. I liked the name even more! I am a 'morning person' and love to watch the sun rise. I also downloaded a picture of the Aurora Borealis that caught my eye from the many pictures posted on the internet. The Northern Lights were really spectacular in all of their glory, but this one picture really moved me. I thought to myself, "What a great paint job that would be for 'Aurora'."

I left my thoughts in the office and moved to join the party.

CHAPTER FIVE

LANCE, ASHONTE' AND I had driven out to the Dubai Airport to do some polishing and waxing on "Aurora". The high gloss shine on the interior woodwork and metal fixtures needed constant attention. Every fingerprint showed. All of the smudge marks were also evident after a flight. The polishing work was a labor of love for Ashonte' and me. Lance went along so that he could hang out with us. We weren't flying anywhere today, just enjoying the ambience of the interior of the Avanti's cabin and each other's company.

We had also turned on the swiveling monitors that were mounted between the four back chairs that faced each other. This type of arrangement is called club seating and is very popular among executive aircraft. The fold out tables were both out and being restored to their glossy finishes. We had the sound turned down so that we could talk with each other and not have to yell.

Lance was offering up a ribald story from his time as a young marine. He was telling Ashonte' and me of the tight harnesses that he had to wear as a paratrooper, and how they cinched him down so tight that he couldn't walk to the plane with an erect posture. He was so hunched over that he looked and moved more like a crab. This, by the way, reminded him of a young South Korean girl that resided in one of the brothels just outside his military base outside of Seoul. "You Numba One GI!" she would say to every man in a uniform. Lance always had stories of female conquests before he met Cyndi. And he loved to tell those stories to us!

Lance was just returning his story to present day and the awful times he is experiencing with hemorrhoids because of his days jumping out of perfectly good airplanes and many harder than ideal landings when I held up my hand to stop him. Lance ceased speaking immediately, wondering what was up. I turned to face one of the monitors and turned up the volume. All three of us stopped our chores and watched the breaking news story.

"We interrupt our regularly scheduled broadcast to bring you this breaking story out of the Middle East," the Fox announcer was saying. "We go now to Greg Palkot reporting live from Saudi Arabia."

"There has been an explosion of enormous magnitude in Iran." Greg began. "Shock waves are being felt here in Riyadh, Saudi Arabia, four hundred miles southeast of the blast." After a pause as Greg looked to the northwest and the camera shook erratically, he faced the camera again, "We have no confirmation…but it is feared that the explosion is from the nuclear facility at Bushehr on the Persian Gulf." He listens into his earpiece, holding his hand over the device. The picture returns to the Fox anchorman as he says, "We now go to The White House."

"Hey guys," Lance opens, "Aren't we about the same distance from Bushehr?"

Ashonte' had already switched the other monitor to the internet and was calling up a map of the Middle East. "You're right! We are almost the same distance from Bushehr as Riyadh. But we're to the southea…"

Just then the ground began to rumble. It felt to me like the occasional earthquake that I had felt as a young boy, growing up in Colorado.

Lance was the first one out of the plane as he sprinted for the open doors of the hangar, with Ashonte' close on his heels and me bringing up the rear. Once outside and clear of the hangar buildings we stopped to catch our breath.

"Don't trust this Arab construction," Lance opined.

"Hey, you remember the Burj Khalifa?" I said, and then continued, "That was a Chicago architect and a South Korean contractor. The Emirates use expatriates for all that stuff! I'm sure that our hangar will be okay."

The rumbling soon subsided as we glanced around to see many individuals out on the tarmac running to open spaces away from the various airport buildings. I looked to the tower which I assumed was the most susceptible structure at the airport, and it seemed to be intact. I wondered about any aircraft that may be on approach or landing while the ground was shaking. As a pilot, I was prepared for high crosswind landings, and even icy landings. There was nothing in the Airman's Information Manual about the ground shaking during landing! I wondered if the men in the tower stayed at their posts or if they skedaddled for the stairs! Who was monitoring the skies around the airport?

Ashonte' dashed back into the hangar. Lance and I were less enthusiastic as we followed Ashonte' and headed back to the hangar.

"What about aftershocks?" Lance asked to no one in particular.

The hangar seemed to have withstood the onslaught without any overt damage. We got to the main cabin door entrance to Aurora and could hear Ashonte' banging away on the keyboard to the monitor that was online.

"First, we heard possible nuclear blast from Bushehr, right?" he quipped.

"Then it feels like an earthquake, here!" he continued.

"We need to assume the worst for now until we are sure what happened. We're only four hundred miles from the blast site. I'm checking on the prevailing winds," Ashonte' said, "Map shows winds mainly travel to the northeast in this region, and we are south, southeast of Bushehr...should be okay from any radiation fallout."

"Gosh," I blurted, "How do you think of this stuff? Let's get the wives called."

I noticed Lance and Ashonte' reach for their cellphones as I pulled mine out of my breast pocket. I quickly dialed the house and heard a 'busy' signal. As I hung up, my phone rang with Becky's custom ringtone, 'Pretty Woman'. I immediately answered with, "I'm okay...everything alright there?"

"I'm pretty shaken up, no pun intended," Becky replied. "Do they have earthquakes in this part of the world?"

"Don't know," I spoke into the phone, "I don't think it was an earthquake. Do you have a TV on?"

"No, I've been working on all of the new Italian accounts for the 'mini'," she said.

"Turn one on...I'm heading home RIGHT NOW!" I emphasized.

The other two had the same reaction and we all headed for our cars. I noticed thousands of people standing outside their various structures with dazed looks as I drove home. They were all just milling about. No one seemed to know what to do next after they were shaken from their daily routines. Cars were abandoned wherever they had halted…many right in the middle of the road! I had seen this happen when it was prayer time. Muslim drivers would just stop their vehicles wherever they were and run to a mosque. First time I saw that I thought these people were nuts! Now I've gotten used to it. Dubai even has little 'mini mosques' at the gas stations to use if you're filling up at prayer time.

It made the drive home quite dicey. Half an hour later I pulled into our garage. I noticed that many of the boxes that I had stored in the garage were littered on the floor. I could hear the television as soon as I turned off the car. I opened the door and Becky flung herself at me. It was a desperate grasp. She was sobbing.

"They say it was a nuclear blast from somewhere in Iran," Becky blurted out between sobs. "What is happening? Are we in danger? Where should we go? I'm really scared."

"It'll be alright," I said as I stroked the back of her head. I knew that I had to attempt to calm her, even though I didn't have a clue as to what was happening.

I escorted Becky back into the living room and we sat on the sofa. Becky had the television tuned to CNN. It surely was not my first choice of news channels because of the station's liberal bias, but their world coverage was probably the best of all of the international channels. As we watched, Wolf Blitzer had assumed the anchor desk and was trying desperately to pull together all of the intelligence that was flooding his newsroom. The 'ticker tape' was scrolling across the bottom of the screen. I noticed that the digital video recorder was not on and reached for the remote. We immediately began to record the broadcast.

As Wolf was attempting to make contact with an AP reporter stationed in Egypt, the 'ticker' scrolled that more than one million lives were feared lost in the disaster. I looked up to the ceiling and closed my eyes, "Oh God," was all that I could pray. I felt a huge knot welling up in my stomach. I had only experienced a feeling like this three times in my life while watching television. The first time that I had cried during a newscast was when it was announced that Princess Diana was killed in that horrible car accident in Paris. That was two people who died. The second time was the horrible destruction of the World Trade Center and all of the lives lost in that devastation. That was a little over three thousand lives lost. Becky and I had lost a good friend when the northern building collapsed. I had that same feeling inside me now, but also knew that I had to keep it together for Becky who was now sobbing uncontrollably. Over a million lives lost? Unbelievable!

I freed myself from her death grip just for a moment and went into the bedroom to turn on the Fox network and hit record on the digital video recorder in that room. I then returned to Becky and held her closely.

The immediate reports seemed to be clear on only two points. There was a nuclear explosion, and it was located in Iran. I made the assumption that the location was Bushehr because that was where Iran placed their first nuclear reactor, and it was now functional. There were other locations in Iran where uranium was being refined and processed, such as the facility at Natanz, but it seemed to me that all of the rhetoric from the United States and Israel against the nuclear development of Iran was aimed at the nuclear reactor in Bushehr. Israel had all but promised not to allow the reactor to become active.

CNN took a break from attempting to sift through all of the reports that were flowing into the station to rebroadcast the President of the United States' one minute statement about the disaster. I remembered that the President was just getting ready to speak when the ground began to rumble at the airport and we had all run outside. The President's message was terse, almost to a fault. He stated that there had been an explosion in the Middle East and that the explosion may have been from a nuclear reactor. There may be many deaths and the hearts of all Americans were with those who may have perished. The message then ended abruptly, and Wolf Blitzer took over with a ten minute commentary about what the President said.

Washington, D.C.

President John James finished his message to the American people and shooed the camera and sound crew out of his office. His National Security Director was waiting in the wings as the film crew beat a hasty retreat.

"What's up?" President James asked.

"Our satellite tasked for Iran has gone offline. We assume it is due to EMP from the blast site. That confirms it was a nuclear explosion. We will have another satellite in position within twenty minutes," the Director replied.

"EMP? That's Electro Magnetic Pulse, right?" the President asked.

"Yes sir, happens when there is a high energy explosion which causes damaging electrical currents and voltage surges. Basically, everything electric fails." The Director responded.

"Did Israel do this without our knowledge?" the President asked, "I hate getting caught with my pants down around my ankles. I told that Prime Minister not to take any action without me knowing."

"I've called Tel Aviv," the Director responded. "They say they know nothing!"

"The sergeant Schultz response, again?" President James groused. "Israel better not be behind this disaster!"

"Get me Netanyahu on the phone immediately!"

Dubai, U.A.E.

It felt to me like Becky and I had been glued to the television for hours, and yet the reports remained sketchy and inconclusive. Becky had regained her composure and moved to the kitchen to begin dinner. Her actions were almost 'robot-like'. Neither of us was hungry or would be able to eat. While she worked, Becky called out, "Do we have to worry about radiation or a nuclear cloud like Chernobyl or Japan?"

"No," I replied, "Ashonte' already checked a map of the prevailing winds. Any damaging radiation or nuclear particles from the fallout will be carried to the north and east, away from Dubai."

"What about the Persian Gulf?" she countered.

"We'll have to wait and see what this will do to shipping in the area," I answered. I moved to the office to check in on our companions. Ashonte' and Lance were with their wives, also glued to their televisions. After brief conversations and assurances that the four of them were alright, I asked the two couples to join Becky and me in the morning to observe how the world's reaction to this apparent disaster would unfold.

Normally, Becky and I would have drinks on the patio, followed by our meal. Tonight we ate inside. We had very little to say to each other as we continued to watch the TV. I know that I was lost deep in my own thoughts. I walked around the house after dinner making a mental note that all of the windows and doors were shut tight. I felt just a little bit paranoid. Sleep did not come easily that night. Becky awakened me at one point when she was in the throes of a horrifying nightmare. She actually screamed out in the darkness which scared the living daylights out of me.

By mid-morning the six of us, I.N.C.I.S.O.R.'s team, were gathered around our living room. The women were seated on the couch watching the latest from CNN. Ashonte', Lance and I were huddled around a card table. Lance had been able to make contact with Langley after hours of trying unsuccessfully to find an open band on the communications satellite. Like the regular phone lines, all of the available bandwidth for satellite communications was either occupied or had been closed down.

Langley confirmed to Lance that it was the nuclear reactor at Bushehr. A Lacrosse radar imaging satellite had been tasked to take up a position over the Persian Gulf. The satellite was chosen because it had the ability to see through clouds and smoke, and there would be much of that in the area for a good long time. The SAR imagery could provide clear imagery to one meter, far short of the ten centimeter resolution provided by the photographic satellites, but those satellites couldn't see through the clouds and dust. The first pictures were so unbelievable that some interpreters claimed that there was a problem with the cameras. There was nothing but scorched earth for a ten mile radius around where the town of Bushehr had been. The coastal town just wasn't there anymore. Not even evidence of any man-made structures. The town had been on the coast of the Persian Gulf. The nuclear reactor was located southeast of the town. The devastation reached outward to the north and west in a semicircular pattern that reminded one analyst of a concert in the park. There were no towns or structures to the southeast of the reactor facility. At least not close enough to be in harm's way from the explosion.

Satellite images of the sea lanes in the Persian Gulf showed the hulls of five super cargo ships that had found themselves too close to the blast to survive the shockwave that upended the vessels, killing all on board and sending their loads of containers to the bottom of the Gulf. The size of the tidal waves that took out these mighty ships must have been immense… and terrifying for the crews to observe coming.

Experts were saying that the 'dead zone' from such a blast would stretch out twenty miles from the epicenter. One hundred percent of life in that zone was, or would be soon, eliminated. Sixty five percent of life out to thirty miles would also be annihilated. Beyond thirty miles the devastation would be mild to moderate with very little loss of life.

There were calls into Russia's Atomstroyexport. They were the main contractor involved with finishing and bringing the reactor online. The CIA needed to know what type of plutonium rods had been supplied to the nuclear reactor at Bushehr. With that knowledge the specialists at the Global Nuclear Security Technology Division at Oak Ridge would be able to assess the present and future dangers of travel into and around the area.

Another team of analysts were poring over the satellite images received immediately before the first spy satellite went inactive. There had been attempts to communicate with the satellite by the controllers at Peterson Air Force Base in Colorado Springs…but all they got was static. There was one blurred photograph that showed what may have been a missile entering one of the buildings at what once was the Bushehr Nuclear Power Plant. Evidence of a missile was not present on any of the preceding photographs. Was it a missile? Too soon to tell for sure!

Teams of nuclear experts were being hastily assembled for the long flight from the United States to the Middle East.

Iran was screaming that it had been attacked by basically everybody. Right now they were placing blame on any object and all of the countries outside of their own borders. Allies and foes were named. Russia to the United States; Iraq to Israel. No country escaped the vitriol flowing out of Tehran. But no 'mea culpa's'. The Iranians were convinced that it had to be an outside destructive force. The nuclear facility was the safest in the Middle East. That was an easy claim because it was the only nuclear facility in the Middle East. Nothing could have gone wrong within the facility. As of yet, the ruling leaders in Iran were not requesting any help. Just a lot of posturing on television and videos showing the activation of their military forces. Actually, not a major change in how Iran's political and military process operated.

All air and sea travel into or out of the Middle East had been halted. The United States was working hard to assess the size of the radioactive cloud that was moving toward Turkmenistan and Uzbekistan. All of the

Middle Eastern countries had closed down their borders and all of the military bases had been placed on high alert. Tensions were extremely high, not just within the region, but all over the world.

There was also widespread panic among the people of the Middle East. Ashonte' had been able to discern from the internet that the prevailing winds at our latitude and longitude moved to the northeast. Therefore any radioactive cloud would be carried away from our locale. Others who either didn't have access to the internet or were not computer 'savvy' were panicked about the chance that a cloud of deadly and unseen gasses could descend upon them at any time. As is typical with hysteria, rather than lock themselves within their homes, they wanted to run. Immediately all land routes were overwhelmed with desperate people trying to escape what they knew nothing about. Thanks to Chernobyl for all of the graphic photographs and descriptions of the effects of radiation on animal and plant life.

While we huddled together trying to put all of the pieces into some sense of cogent order, the phone rang. Becky quickly got up from the sofa and moved into the office. I watched her walk across the living room and instantly felt the pang of desire that I so often felt when I saw her move. Over twenty years of marriage and I was still so in love with her. I returned to my discussion with Lance and Ashonte'.

Becky came out of the bedroom/office with a shocked look on her face. "It's the Prime Minister of Israel!" "On the phone!" "It's Netanyahu!"

In an instant the room became devoid of all conversation. Cyndi reached for the remote and muted the television. All eyes were on me. I slowly glanced around the room at all of the individuals that had become the I.N.C.I.S.O.R. team. I had a feeling in my gut that it was time for all of us to go to work. My gaze came to rest on Ashonte'. "Good friend," I said, "Can you get on the line in the kitchen?" Ashonte' headed for the kitchen as I headed to the office.

"Becky, you know that Netanyahu is not the Prime Minister now," I admonished.

"No, No, No! He's been elected, again. The Likud Party is back in power!" Becky replied in a huff. "Don't keep the man waiting!"

I headed to the office and picked up the receiver. "Good morning Mr. Prime Minister, this is Dr. Nelson speaking. I have Ashonte' Black on the other line."

Tel Aviv, Israel

"Dr. Nelson, Mr. Black; shalom…I am Benjamin Netanyahu," the Prime Minister stated. "The recent events in the Middle East have found me on the phone for hours with your State Department. A contact at the CIA recommended that I give you a call. I, or rather Israel, find it necessary to hire I.N.C.I.S.O.R. How soon can you make a trip to Cairo?"

Dubai, U.A.E.

"As soon as the travel restrictions are lifted, we're there!" I replied. "Why don't we plan for a week from today? Can you have your office get back to me with a location?"

Tel Aviv, Israel

"Someone from my office will call back within two days," Mr. Netanyahu responded, and hung up the phone.

Dubai, U.A.E.

I held the receiver to my ear for a moment, listening to the static on the line. I really didn't think that Mr. Netanyahu would come back on the line, but I was enjoying the moment. Israel's first Prime Minister who had been born in Israel (actually, their ninth Prime Minister) had just had a conversation with me! And Israel wanted to employ I.N.C.I.S.O.R.! I wondered briefly what was up, but knew that I would find out shortly in Egypt. Why Egypt?

I returned to the living room and Ashonte' had already rejoined the group. He had a big smile on his face, and I noticed the Lance was glancing at him with a quizzical look. Cyndi was the first to speak, "What was that about?"

CHAPTER SIX

Dubai, UAE

AS THE WORLD'S mass hysteria over first the nuclear disaster in the Middle East, and then everyone's own dread for their safety began to wane, the six I.N.C.I.S.O.R. members spent the majority of their time at Becky's and my home.

The discussion moved from updates about the explosion…to planning for the meeting with Israel…and then back to the explosion…as news of the devastation trickled in.

I knew that America and Russia would have teams in the area of Bushehr with their protective suits and monitoring equipment attempting to make some sense about what had happened to the reactor and the town. There must have been extremely tight security around these teams, because there was no mention of them on Fox or CNN.

The local news broadcasts seemed to be filled with ranting Iranians from the head Abdullah to anybody who was allowed in front of a camera screaming and gesticulating that justice must be done…that revenge must be accomplished…someone must pay! It looked like this craziness was limited solely to the Iranians. There seemed to be calmer heads speaking from the other Middle Eastern countries.

While we were discussing the latest world events, the phone rang. I moved to the office and answered, "Reggie Nelson, how can I help you?"

"Dr. Nelson, this is Dr. Suttmiller with FRMAC," came the terse response.

"Excuse me, but what?" I replied.

"Sorry, let me explain," he answered, then continued, "FRMAC is the anagram for the Federal Radiological Monitoring and Assessment Center. We are a highly sophisticated, but little known, operation that is critical in the event of a nuclear disaster. In the event of a nuclear accident or terror attack, similar to what the United States government thinks has happened in Iran, FRMAC is the first line of defense, in a sense. Our team members have sprung into action, grabbed their gear, and were airborne in an instant, ready to monitor the radiation and assess what should be done next. It is our team that is in country and making their way to Bushehr."

"I have never heard of you folks!" I exclaimed.

"No one else in the world has our kind of expertise," Dr. Suttmiller continued, "no matter what the scenario or where, ground zero for the responders is Las Vegas. This is where the emergency response starts. The thousands of people who drive past the north end of Nellis every day have no idea what's just beyond the fence in our non-descript beige building. The only outside hint is the sign. When the unthinkable happens, this is the nerve center; the eyes, ears, and brain for emergency responders and policymakers who need to know as soon as possible how bad things are on the ground. The central mission is to coordinate data that is measured in a radiological release and get it to the right people at the right time."

"And you said that you are in Las Vegas?" I asked.

"The reason we're in Las Vegas is simple -- the decades of real life experience and hands on expertise emanating from the Nevada Test Site," he continued, "FRMAC was created in the aftermath of the Three Mile Island power plant incident in March, 1979 and became more urgent after the attacks of 9/11."

"I remember the Three Mile Island disaster!" I exclaimed, "That happened when I was a senior at Dartmouth College. In fact, our college president, John G. Kemeny, chaired the President's Commission on the Accident at Three Mile Island, created by Jimmy Carter in April 1979. I remember that when president Kemeny returned to Dartmouth College, he addressed the students. When asked what caused the meltdown, he replied that the proximate cause would probably never be known. I seem to remember that it was a stuck valve or something like that."

"Your memory is right on," Dr. Suttmiller continued, "Intelligence experts say there is no question that terrorists are trying to obtain nuclear materials for a bomb. It could be when, not if."

"The worst case scenario has to be a nuclear detonation, by far. Every other nuclear accident pales in comparison. With a nuclear detonation, hundreds of thousands or more may die. So it's just enormous in scale," said Dr. Suttmiller and he continued, "Our teams train constantly, similar to war games. They make projections about what would happen if a bomb went off, say, near the White House, where the radiation would spread, what areas would need to be evacuated, how long the region would be contaminated."

"The news is claiming that more than a million souls have perished!" I lamented.

"Yes, and here's why…Inside this area around Bushehr, unless people got into prominent shelter, survival is unlikely," said Dr. Suttmiller, "In 50 years, you still have to worry about the fallout. Our teams were in the air within two hours, in aircraft packed with the most sensitive radiation detection gear in the world. Any radiation that could pose a threat to the public will be found by our aerial sensors and sent back here to Las Vegas in real time. We are known as the 'Home Team Room'. This is the heart of the operation until the radiation monitors arrive at the scene. Our people will analyze the situation and feed information to local agencies in Iran and throughout the Middle East."

"How can I be of service?" I queried.

"We received special permission to land at Imam Khomeini International Airport outside of Tehran. The ground teams have been dropped off there and the plane has made its first pass over Bushehr. The data we are receiving is depicting a full scale nuclear explosion. The worst disaster scenario that we could imagine," Dr. Suttmiller continued, "The ground teams are in the process of securing transportation to head toward Bushehr."

"What can our team do to help?" I asked.

"There are very few American assets in the region. I understand that you are in Dubai," he stated.

"Yes, we are about four hundred miles southeast of where Bushehr was," I remarked.

"Do you have any form of air transportation?"

"Yes, I have a private plane, but all flights into and out of the region have been grounded!" I exclaimed.

"We may need your help…if necessary, we will deal with the flight restrictions," Dr. Suttmiller stated and then asked, "What type of payload can you carry?"

"The plane is an Avanti II. It is configured to carry seven plus the pilot and copilot. The maximum take-off weight is 12,100 lbs. The useful load is 4,150 pounds. It has a payload capacity of 1,800 pounds, or 1,350 pounds with maximum fuel," I stated.

"How easily can some of the seats be removed?" he asked.

My heart skipped a beat at the thought of stripping the gorgeous interior of my plane.

"Never been asked that question…don't know off hand," I groused.

"Can you call the manufacturer and find out?"

"Yes, I'll put in a call to Piaggio Aircraft in Italy and find out what is involved in removing some of the interior seats. May I ask why?" I asked.

"We may need your help in delivering personnel and equipment to Bushehr," he stated.

Oh swell, I thought, now I'll glow in the dark! While we talked I pulled up Bushehr's airport. The airport is located right in the heart of the city, or what WAS the city. The reactor was built eleven miles southeast of Bushehr proper. That sounded way too close for comfort to me. There is also a naval air strip, but that location is even closer to the reactor! This wasn't going to be any fun!

My thoughts then changed to remembering that the CIA had purchased the Avanti II, now proudly dubbed Aurora for my use. I was arguing with myself about doing my civic duty and helping versus the fact that I had already saved the country from one terrorist plot when Dr. Suttmiller continued, "Thanks ahead of time for all of your help while we work through this catastrophe. Can I call you tomorrow? Will that be enough time for you to check on the seats?"

"Yes, that should be plenty of time. I will make the call as soon as we're done," I claimed.

"Then we're done," Dr. Suttmiller remarked, and the line went dead.

I lingered, with the phone to my ear and stared at the computer image of the Bushehr airport layout, for a minute or so. My mind was racing with thoughts too quickly for any one thought to take shape.

Lance entered the office and observed my trance-like state. "What's up…who was on the phone?" he asked.

My reverie broken, I replaced the phone into its charger and turned to face him. "That was a Dr. Suttmiller from FRMAC."

"What is fermac? A new McDonald's burger?" he questioned.

"No, FRMAC, the Federal Radiological Monitoring and Assessment Center in Las Vegas, Nevada," I replied.

"Never heard of them…do they want something from I.N.C.I.S.O.R.?"

"They may…we'll have to see…I need a drink!"

"Well, let's all get one and you can brief us on your call!" Lance opined.

We joined the others in the living room and I explained about the call. The discussion evolved from talking about this unheard of federal agency to focusing on the dangers of being around radiation, its effects, and possible exposure. It became painfully clear that none of us were able to speak with any knowledge other than what we had seen on television. All that any of us knew was that radiation was unseen and really scary! We could all agree that an unseen threat was the worst kind.

The group broke up for the day with the other two couples leaving for their own homes and thoughts.

I returned to the office and placed a call to Piaggio Aero in Genoa, Italy. I discovered that the seats can be removed with a little effort, but that the removal should be performed by a certified airframe and power plant mechanic. The company was willing to fly someone down to Dubai to assist with disassembly of the cabin. I let them know that I would call back if their help would be necessary. I really didn't want to face this. Aurora was just fine the way she was!

Becky had dinner ready when I was done. My thoughts were so far away that I was bad company and I ate with no taste for what she had prepared. I apologized for being such a schmuck and headed to the bedroom. I felt exhausted for no good reason and knew that I had to get horizontal. Maybe sleep would help put the day behind me. The radiation thing was really beginning to bother me…and they were going to 'jack' with my plane! No good!

Tehran, Iran

Jack Mast was joking with his teammates as they sat in a non-descript building next to the tarmac at the Imam Khomeini International Airport. Their team had deplaned about an hour ago and the plane refueled quickly and departed Tehran heading for Bushehr to retrieve the first high altitude data from the site of the nuclear disaster.

"No, No!" he exclaimed, "Pull up your chairs around me!"

The eleven team members each had already arranged the chairs in a circular pattern around Jack. One of the team told him to look up.

"Oh!" Jack remarked, "You're already here! Okay, this is what you do… take out a piece of paper and write down your first pet's name that you can remember or your favorite pet if you can't remember the first one. Then write down the name of the first street you lived on…or the first street that you can remember."

Jack gave the team a minute to write down their names.

"Okay," he claimed, "This is the best way to come up with names for porn stars! Let's go around the circle…I'll start…My name would be Ginger Gaylord!"

"Is that for a male or a female?" one exclaimed and got an immediate laugh from the group.

"Could go either way, huh," Jack replied, "You're next!" He pointed to the young man who had asked the question. As he looked around the room at his team members, Jack felt proud to be with this group. These were the top scientists and technicians who worked with radiation in the United States. There were four women and eight men, including Jack. Jack was the oldest team member and had become the self-elected 'mother hen' for the group. Some of the faces looked so young that Jack wondered if they had really finished high school. He knew that they all had college degrees and that there were six along with doctorates in nuclear physics.

Also, Jack thought about the irony of the group's current situation. Here, in this room, was a brain trust that included more years of information about nuclear radiation and disasters than could be assembled anywhere in the world. He knew that the Russians also had years of experience in dealing with nuclear disasters.

But, he also knew that a number of their first response scientists, some men that he had come to know through international conferences, to the Chernobyl Nuclear Reactor Number Four meltdown in the town of Pripyat on April 26, 1986 were not protected properly and had perished at too early an age. Fifty deaths, all among the reactor staff and emergency workers, were directly attributed to the accident. It is estimated that there may ultimately be a total of 4,000 deaths attributable to the accident, due to increased cancer risk. What was just amazing to Jack was the fact that despite the accident, Ukraine continued to operate the remaining reactors at Chernobyl for many years. The last reactor at the site was closed down in 2000, 14 years after the accident.

The Russian team which was descending on their location, probably as he had the thought, would be made up of a much younger brain trust than the American team. Also, Jack expected, there would be one or two on the Russian team from Atomstroyexport, the company that had finished the Bushehr reactor for the Iranians. These men would be worthless…their interest would lie in protecting the company…and not in gathering solid, unimpeachable information. Jack was proud of his team! He would be suspicious of the Russians.

Back to the game, Jack thought, and refocused on his team. Matt was just starting to speak, "My favorite pet was a dog named Duke, and I grew up on Golden Staff Road."

"See what I mean," I began, "Duke Staff! Great porn name! Next?"

The game continued until all twelve team members had listed their first or favorite pet's names and the first street name they could remember living on. One of the team members also volunteered Jack's name for the list! Jack had never thought much about his name, but the young member was right…Jack Mast would be a great porno name! The team came up with a fun list of names to send on to Hollywood, but the purpose, Jack knew, was to kill time and keep the group entertained while they awaited the cars and trucks that would form the caravan to carry them southeast toward Bushehr. Only God knew what they were getting in to. He knew that all of the equipment had been checked recently and Jack willed it to be in top working order!

An Iranian airport worker appeared at the door with a cart full of food and drinks for the team. Jack noticed a large bowl of fruit which contained plums, pomegranates, quince, prunes, apricots, and raisins. All of the local fruit was represented here. There was also a large platter containing chelo kabab, which is a rice dish served with roasted meat. The meat looked to Jack to be lamb. He also knew from his studies of Iran, and before that, Persia, that the local chefs were experts in the use of seasonings. To achieve a balanced taste, characteristic Persian flavorings such as saffron, dried limes, cinnamon, and parsley are blended with the meat and rice. The aroma from the cart was fabulous and immediately beckoned the ravenous team closer to the door.

The food and utensils were arranged on the table closest to the door while the team watched, and then the Iranian worker grabbed the cart, turned heels and left without a word. The twelve members formed a line, grabbed plates and silverware and filled their plates with food. Jack only took some of the fruit. He had, in his past travels to third world countries, many bouts with diarrhea similar to Montezuma's Revenge, which is so common in the United States from travelling to Mexico.

The drink was a steeped Persian tea blend, which Jack deemed was safe since the water had been boiled.

As the team enjoyed their meal, Jack saw that the platter and fruit bowl had been wiped clean. "A hungry group!" Jack thought. He also hoped that there wouldn't be a run on the bathrooms soon, or that there wouldn't be more serious complications from the food being devoured.

As he was contemplating the gastronomy of his team members, the door opened again. This time in marched eight men all in jumpsuits. Jack recognized the symbols on the left sleeves of the jumpsuits. This was the Russian team. A man that Jack assumed was the leader of the team walked up to Jack and clicked his heels together. He then bowed slightly toward Jack with his hands clasped tightly behind his back and said, "Viktor Spasky at your service! You are Jack Mast? Yes??"

The man was too stiff and formal for Jack to be comfortable. 'Viktor' knew who he was but he had no clue who this man in front of him was. His command of the English language was far superior to Jack's command of Russian. He thought about saluting the Russian in his own language, but chose to let the conversation continue in English. Jack offered his hand, "Jack Mast at your service."

Viktor did not shake Jack's outreached hand. Jack withdrew his hand awkwardly and said, "You just missed the meal."

Viktor replied, "Food is of no consequence to us…when do we depart?"

Jack thought, "What a prick." "Don't know," he said, "It's all up to the Iranians…they are probably having some trouble finding drivers willing to head toward all that radiation!"

"Don't they know that we have monitoring devices? Don't they know about our protective gear?" Viktor questioned.

"Can't help you, Viktor, but I'd suggest that you take a chill pill. These people are highly superstitious and I wouldn't expect the drivers to be very highly educated. I have also learned that in this part of the world they will move at their own pace and that pace will be much slower than we'd like it to be!" Jack replied.

"Chill pill! What's that? I'm not hot. Oh, you mean take it easy…need to get going soon!" Viktor said.

"We go when we go," Jack announced and turned to sit with his team.

The Russians gathered around a table on the other side of the room. Jack thought as he watched their group how strange it was that after this many years that there was still this high level of distrust between the Americans and the Russians. He thought back to what had led to the feelings of mistrust.

The USSR or The Union of Soviet Socialist Republics, and for short known as the Soviet Union or Soviet Russia, was a socialist state that existed on the territory of most of the former Russian Empire in Eurasia between 1922 and 1991. The United States and the USSR were allies as recently as World War II. Still the level of mistrust was high and continued to worsen. The Soviet Union and its satellites from the Eastern Bloc were one of two participating factions in the Cold War, a prolonged global ideological and political struggle against the United States and its Western Bloc allies. The Soviet bloc ultimately lost, however, having been hit by economic standstill and both domestic and foreign political unrest.

In the late 1980s the last Soviet leader Mikhail Gorbachev tried to reform the state with his policies of Perestroika and Glasnost, but the Soviet Union collapsed and was formally dissolved in December 1991 after the abortive August coup attempt by hard line members of the Communist Party. The coup d'état only lasted two days and then Gorbachev was returned to government. This unrest is blamed for the destabilizing the Soviet Union and for its eventual dissolution. Since then the Russian Federation has been exercising its rights and fulfilling its obligations.

The USSR bankrupted itself over many issues, and over many years. Star Wars was only one facet of the equation that led to the downfall of the USSR. The myriad of causes of their demise included a corrupt, inefficient internal mechanism that sold goods to its people at a price that had no relationship to the cost of development, manufacture and distribution.

Jack was a young adult during the time that President Reagan beat communism with capitalism. The United States was simply able to outspend the USSR on the Space Defense Initiative. To Jack, the idea of a space-based umbrella over the United States seemed ludicrous when 'Star Wars' was first announced to the American people. He never thought that a satellite defense system would actually be able to stop the tens of thousands of Intercontinental Ballistic Missiles, or ICBM's, that the USSR had aimed at the United States. But later, upon the collapse of the Soviet Union, Jack was able to see the brilliance of the former US President's plan. Capitalism vs. communism…just spend them into oblivion!

Now, over twenty years later there was still a strong undertone of distrust and loathing from the Russians about the Americans. Jack knew that most of these types of opinion came from the ignorance of the Russian people…and that most of that ignorance came at the hands of the Russian state who taught their people that Americans were lazy and filled to the gills with debauchery. Jack also knew that it was too soon for the people of Russia to forget that they were once a superpower, and that now only the United States remained with that title. Maybe their time working closely with the Russians on the disaster at hand would quell some of the Russians' fears and reshape their thoughts.

As Jack was contemplating his knowledge of the USSR and Russian history, a convoy of a dozen vehicles pulled up outside of the building. All of the team members, both American and Russian, heard the commotion and arose from their tables. Soon, an Iranian captain (Jack assumed from his military garb and the bars on his lapels) entered the room and announced that it was time to depart. His English was passable and Jack approached the officer.

"What do you expect our travel time to the area to be?" Jack enquired.

"The distance from Tehran to Bushehr is around eight hundred kilometers, or five hundred of your miles. We expect the journey to be slow going due to congestion on the roads leading out of the area. It will be three days before we arrive at the site. Tonight we will encamp outside of Qum," the Captain spoke.

Jack had a wry smile on his face. "Qum, you said? Oh, I apologize, I am Jack Mast. I head up the American delegation. The Russians are over there," he said, pointing to the group on the other side of the room. Viktor strolled up at this point and clicked his heels, again.

"Viktor Spasky, head of Russian team," he announced.

"Capitan Ahmad Jafar at your service. We must leave now!" the Iranian ordered.

The twenty people sent by their respective countries filed out of the room and into the bright afternoon sunlight that temporarily blinded the group. Jack noticed that the pile of American gear was already loaded onto one of the trucks in the caravan. He also noticed that the first two and last two trucks were loaded with Iranian troops. All had guns at the ready. A strong sense of foreboding clouded over Jack's mind. He was not expecting all of this firepower.

There were five large Suburbans for the team members to pile into. Each Suburban contained a driver and soldier riding 'shotgun'. Each of the soldiers had an AK 47 perched on their knee. They really were riding shotgun! The Americans took up the first three SUVs, and the Russians piled into the remaining two SUVs. There was a sixth SUV for the Captain and his entourage, and two trucks full of gear for the journey.

The caravan headed through Tehran and joined highway 7 heading southwest, presumably toward Qum. One of the team members in Jack's SUV asked what the destination was for tonight. Jack couldn't resist, "We are going to Qum!" he exclaimed. There were chuckles from the back seat that the two Iranians didn't understand or react to.

Highway #7 is also known as the Persian Gulf Highway, and the Qum Highway. The road is a six lane freeway and we moved easily down the road for the fairly short drive to Qum. The highway looked to Jack like it had been well built, but poorly maintained after the initial construction. He also noticed that the traffic was much lighter heading southwest than the oncoming traffic moving toward Tehran.

Jack was also amazed at the number of cars he observed stopped on the side of the highway with somebody beside the car peeing on the side of the road. The men relieving themselves did not have a care in the world about who drove past and watched. Jack had had to perform this emergency roadside task, but always had looked for bushes or trees. Then it hit him… there were no bushes or trees. This was some really desolate country!

Jack opened his laptop and Googled Qum. The city lies 97 miles to the southwest of Tehran. He discovered that the city had over one million inhabitants, and that it is the largest center for Shi'a scholarship in the world, and is a significant destination of Muslim pilgrimage. Also he found that the Fordow uranium enrichment facility was located to the north of the city, with a purported capacity of 3,000 centrifuges. Jack made a mental note about this facility and a similar facility to the southeast in Natanz, which boasted 7,000 centrifuges.

As the convoy approached Qum, highway 7 had become the Qom-Kashan Freeway and it circled the city to the east. The convoy slowed just past Engelab Boulevard and exited from the shoulder into a field which looked freshly plowed, but barren and dusty. An enclave had been hastily erected with a number of small tents placed haphazardly around a larger central tent structure. The Suburbans each headed for a small tent and the four guests of each SUV disembarked and made their way into that tent. The vehicles were then corralled at the southern end of the encampment near two tanker trucks. Jack guessed correctly that the trucks carried fuel for the caravan.

A local army unit had been tasked with setting up the camp. The main tent contained tables where dinner and breakfast meals were to be served. There was no entertainment this night. Jack wondered if belly dancers, so common in the Middle East, were allowed in Iran. He made a mental note to ask about that detail later. None of the team members were very talkative this night and all headed quietly to their cots for a fitful night of sleep.

The next day the caravan resumed its trek along highway 7, with the next stop outside the town of Natanz. Natanz was a smaller town with only about 40,000 souls. But, here again was a location that housed a nuclear enrichment plant over twice the size of the plant in Qum. The facilities were underground and tours were not offered. Jack wondered if the location of the local garrisons had something to do with these underground facilities.

Southeast of Natanz highway 7 became known as the Ishfehan-Kashan Freeway. The caravan continued on a course to Esfahan which required exiting highway 7 and following highway 9 into the town. The convoy spent the second night in a similar encampment to the southeast of the town. The group was told the next day that it would be slow and tough going from here.

The route required the group to follow route 65 to route 55, then onto route 86, only to rejoin route 55 somehow for the final push toward Bushehr. Geiger counters, which remained on and quiet since departing Tehran now began to pick up minute amounts of radiation in the atmosphere. The smooth six lane freeways were gone. The roads became narrow, hilly and extremely tortuous with many tight hairpin curves. Once route 86 rejoined route 55 the road widened to a four lane highway which led the way into Bushehr. The team members knew that they were very close to the target, but it felt like the convoy was crawling over this last distance. There also was excited interest by the Iranian troops in the Geiger counters, which had become much more noisy of late.

The convoy came to a sudden halt just southwest of the town of Choghadak. The trucks were now within twenty miles of the city of Bushehr, and within thirty miles of the nuclear reactor, as the crow flies. The Geiger counter in the lead truck was steadily crackling away. The nuclear watch teams all knew that there was little concern for radiation poisoning this far removed from the disaster. The Iranian drivers and soldiers did not. The troops were getting noticeably worried and edgy.

Jack moved to extract his lanky frame from the rear seat of the second Suburban in the convoy. He stretched broadly beside the SUV. Upon completing his stretch he noticed that highway 55 was completely abandoned except for their convoy of twelve trucks. He thought about how eerie it was to be alone on a four lane superhighway. No traffic coming or going as far as the eye could see! He looked back toward the town… the caravan had stopped just past the 'T' where highway 96 joined into highway 55. There was no sound or movement coming from the town proper.

Jack made his way forward to talk with Captain Jafar. He was also standing alongside the road next to his vehicle.

"Captain," Jack called out, "This will be a good site for our base camp."

"What about the Geiger counters and their chatter?" Jafar asked.

"The quantity of radiation in the atmosphere here is not a concern. Protective clothing will not be required except by those that move closer toward the reactor," Jack stated.

"Okay," the Captain said hesitantly, and then to his troops, "We make camp here! Do not concern yourselves about radiation problems. I have been assured that we are safe here!" He turned to Jack for reassurance and Jack nodded his approval with a grand gesture that the troops could see. Jack saw that the trucks could stay on the highway just like they were. Who were they blocking? Again, eerie!

The Iranian soldiers went to work policing the area and setting up the tents that would be the temporary home to the radiation scientists and technicians ready to tackle the disaster zone off to the southwest. The American and Russian teams busied themselves with setting up all of the sensitive equipment and working to establish communication links with their respective home countries.

The plane that had brought the American team had made daily passes over the disaster site while the teams made their way from Tehran, and uplinked the information to Nellis Air Base in Nevada. The plane was now parked on the tarmac at the airport in Tehran.

With a link established to Las Vegas, it was time for a briefing. Jack gathered all of his team members around the television monitor and invited the Russians to join them. The first symbol that flashed onto the screen was a map of the Bushehr area with destruction rings overlaying the map. All could see that the outer ring of destruction was still fifteen miles away, and that their camp was in a safe place.

How to approach the site? How long could they be exposed? The briefing was about to begin!

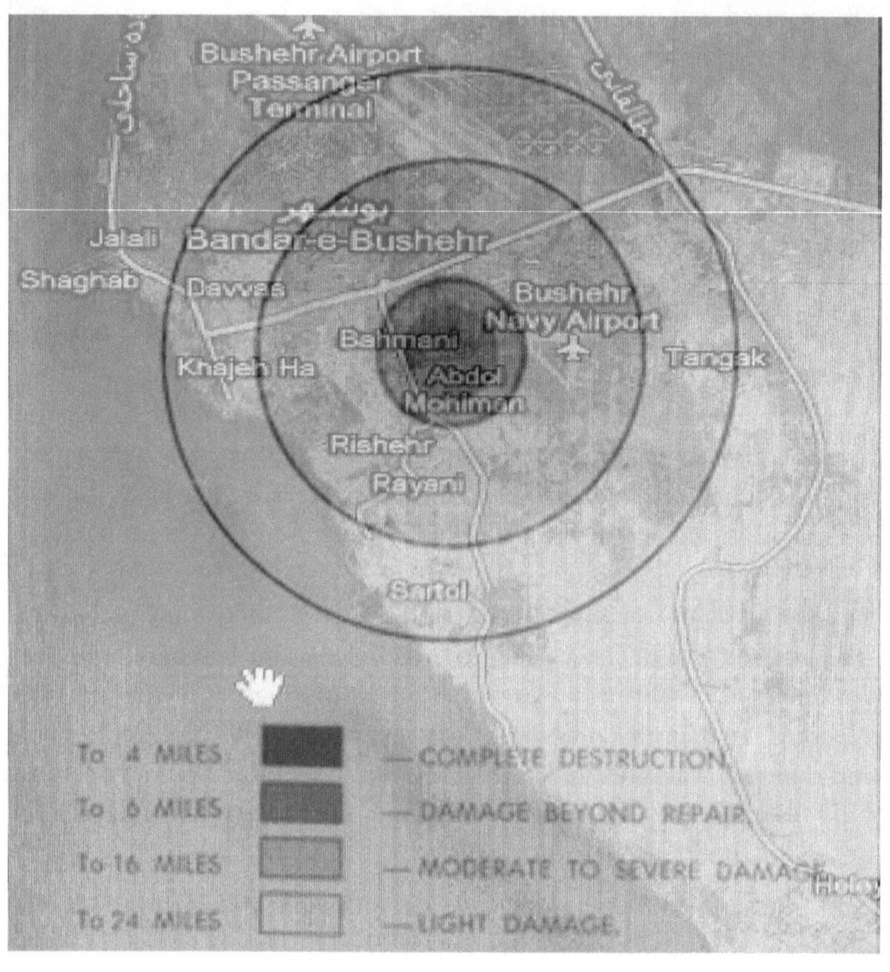
Bushehr Airport
Passanger
Terminal
Jalali
Bandar-e-Bushehr
Shaghab
Davvas
Bushehr
Navy Airport
Bahmani
Khajeh Ha
Abdol
Mohiman
Tangak
Rishehr
Rayani
Sartol
To 4 MILES — COMPLETE DESTRUCTION
To 6 MILES — DAMAGE BEYOND REPAIR
To 16 MILES — MODERATE TO SEVERE DAMAGE
To 24 MILES — LIGHT DAMAGE

CHAPTER SEVEN

Dubai, UAE

I HAD JUST RETURNED home from a morning drive out to the Dubai Airport. My mission this day was to procure a paint shop that could transform the Avanti II into her new persona, Aurora, by painting the fuselage in the color scheme that would match the picture I had of the northern lights of the Aurora Borealis. The paint scheme would have subtle and muted colors from a dark violet through the blues and greens and into yellow swirling around the body of the plane. The lines would be smooth and curving like the body of a woman. My vision was to have the sexiest plane in the sky. I already had the fastest turboprop in the air! The owner of the paint shop really liked the picture and asked if he could keep it while he designed a mockup for me to approve. I agreed and left him to his work.

Lance and Ashonte' arrived, and it looked as if they had come directly from the gym. Both were in their workout clothes and their shirts were drenched with sweat outlined by salt stains. I was surprised, as I answered the door at their appearance. I wasn't sure I wanted them to enter, dressed as they were!

They pushed their way past me and made their way to the kitchen. Becky had just finished making a pitcher of fresh squeezed orange juice, which Lance and Ashonte' attacked with a vengeance. It wasn't until they had annihilated the pitcher that Lance turned to face me. "Can we have a little 'face time' on the patio?" he asked.

Becky told me that they had called from the gym while I was driving home. She knew that they were coming over which is why she had prepared the orange juice. Becky was the one that said, "Come as you are!"

"Sure!" I replied to Lance and the three of us headed outside. Once we were seated around the table, Ashonte' opined, "You know what? We are not getting any younger. And it looks to me like I.N.C.I.S.O.R. is being positioned to have the opportunity to provide our unique set of skills and technology anywhere around the world…and maybe in several locations at once!"

"Yes, you're right, the sales of the 'minis' has increased about three fold since our rescue in Italy. The dental clinic is placing probably two 'P& C's' a week," I replied. "I've been wondering what we do if more than one 'mini' goes off."

Lance chimed in, "What immediately do we have on our plates?"

"The Israeli deal," Ashonte' offered.

"And that call from FRMAC!" I added.

"Right now we don't know what either one entails," Lance replied.

"Right on!" Ashonte' said.

"Correct!" I agreed. "We won't know until the meeting in Egypt with Netanyahu what the Israelis are after. I expect that they need something related to the Bushehr disaster. Have you been reading the papers at all?

Both nodded.

"Iran is really pushing the international community to condemn Israel for attacking the nuclear plant. And there is no proof of anything…attack or accident…that I have read." I added.

Both continued to nod.

"The guy from FRMAC, what was his name? Dr. Suttmiller! Was asking if alterations could be made to Aurora." I said.

"Aurora?" Lance asked, and then hit the side of his head. "What a dumkopf! The new name for the Avanti II, right?"

"Yep," I replied, "Just got back from the airport ordering up a paintjob to match that picture I showed you."

"You gonna wait til after these two jobs?" Ashonte' asked.

"I'd love it as soon as possible, but the paintjob will take a minimum of two weeks. I can't have the plane grounded for that long with so much going on, so it'll have to wait," I added.

"Okay, okay," Lance continued, "That's not why we're here. Ashonte' and I just came from the gym. Good workout! But we can't perform like we used to as young men. It takes much longer to recover afterwards, also! I think it is time to expand I.N.C.I.S.O.R."

Ashonte' then jested, "If Lance and I are talking like this, and just think how long it takes you to recover…you're really old!"

"Hey!" I retorted, "But I know what you mean. That Italian thing really got me thinking. The three of us have been really lucky. And Lance, you almost died in Washington, D.C.!"

"Don't remind me!" he added, as he absent mindedly rubbed the wound, "So, here's what Ash and I were talking about. Remember that Dinar revaluation that happened in Iraq?"

"Yes!" I replied, "Made a whole lot of people a whole lot of money!" I almost looked around and asked who 'Ash' was. I was still struggling with Ashonte's new abbreviated name.

"Right! And a whole bunch of them were American soldiers that were stationed in Iraq. They made out like bandits!"

I had remembered reading about Iraq and their monetary system. When Saddam Hussein was in power and was so well known as a ruthless dictator that murdered thousands upon thousands, the Dinar was trading against the United States dollar at around three to one. In other words, the exchange rate was: 1 Dinar equaled $3.20 US in 1984.

After Iraq's invasion of Kuwait and the subsequent war called Desert Storm, the Iraqi money became worthless. The Dinar fell to a low of 1 Dollar equaled 1,750 Dinars in 1994. What a meteoric plummet in value!

The United States and their allies then had to wage a second war against Saddam Hussein and occupied the country until 2011 when the troops began to withdraw from occupied Iraq and return to the United States and their families, or be redeployed to Afghanistan.

I can remember being told by a good friend to look at the investment opportunity to buy Dinar in 2010. At the time I did my research the exchange rate had improved to: 1 Dollar equaled 1,170 Dinars. There were internet websites that claimed to have the inside scoop on this investment with contacts inside of Iraq, and there were websites that called the investment a scam. I chose to pass on the investment.

The pundits were claiming that when Iraq formed their own government the Dinar would return to pre-invasion days...or maybe revalue even higher than that! I felt that the claims were too good to be true. My math work showed that if their claims proved to be accurate then a twelve thousand dollar investment would purchase ten million Dinars. The ten million Dinars valued at the Saddam day price of $3.20 would be worth a whopping $32,000,000! Thirty two million dollars made on a twelve thousand dollar investment? That was too good to be true. I chose to pass.

Well, that was the dumbest investment mistake I have ever made! The value of the Dinar, when it did revalue in 2011, exceeded everybody's expectations and approached $4.00 US in value. The wealth around the world was redistributed and many, many new millionaires were created in one day! Overnight!

"There are many, many quite wealthy United States soldiers wanting out of the military!" Lance exclaimed.

"How were they able to invest?" I asked.

"Many were stationed in Iraq and could buy Dinar at the base!" The soldiers back home that heard about buying Dinar could buy from one of the online sources. A few of the banks in the United States were also selling Dinar," Lance added.

"So, there's a huge pool of talent that we can tap into. Give them some time to get bored and realize that they have wonderful skills that we can use, and I'll bet they'll be lining up to work for I.N.C.I.S.O.R.!" Ashonte' said.

"How do we reach out to these self-disenfranchised United States soldiers?" I asked.

"Let me handle that!" Lance stated emphatically. "I still have boatloads of marine contacts."

"Sure, that's right!" I remembered. Lance had been in the military until he was recruited by the Central Intelligence Agency.

"Once a marine, always a marine! Ooh-rah!" Lance exclaimed.

"Okay, down boy!" Ashonte' interjected.

My mind raced to what I had heard about lottery winners in America. Too many times the people didn't know what to do with their new found wealth and bevvy of friends and acquaintances with their hands out. A very high percentage of lottery winners found themselves returned to their previous lifestyle in a very short period of time. I remembered reading that for many lottery winners; the reality was more like a nightmare.

There were two quotes that stuck with me…"I won the American dream but I lost it, too. It was a very hard fall. It's called rock bottom."… and…"Everybody wanted my money. Everybody had their hand out. I never learned one simple word in the English language -- 'No.'"

A newspaper article that I remembered also related a chilling incident; a brother was arrested for hiring a hit man to kill his lottery winning brother, hoping to inherit a share of the winnings.

No doubt there are crazy, sick people out in the world just waiting to pounce on the unsuspecting and ill-prepared who find themselves with new found money. I had to wonder about the soldier types that only make just above poverty wages and how they would react to the riches which had been endowed upon them. An E-1 makes $1,467 per month? Probably not a lot of cash to invest in Dinar, but what if they suddenly had thousands or millions? Might not be a good thing for many of them.

"So, what are we talking about? Two teams of three…like us?" I asked.

"Won't that depend on the business?" Lance asked.

"Yeah, but we'll have to pay them even if there is nothing going on!" I replied, "Let me have Becky look at the numbers and see what kind of money the 'minis' are bringing in…without activity. We already know what is available if one of the 'minis' is activated! Five hundred grand for a day's work for the three of us! That was nice!

Ashonte' piped in, "I like the sound of a five person strike team. Remember those FBI teams in Portland? Each team was made up of five members, each with a specific role, as I think I remember."

"Yeah, those guys were sharp!" Lance said.

"Three…five…I don't care. You two are the pros…educate me! I requested.

Lance took over at this point and assumed the role of educator. "Let me tell you first about the Navy SEALS. The SEALS are made up of…do you know what SEAL stands for?" He looked directly at me.

"No," I replied. "But I do know that they are the descendants to the UDT or Underwater Demolition Teams!"

"Right," Lance continued, "'Sea, Air and Land' is what SEAL stands for. They are the Navy's principal special operations force. The SEALS came into existence during the Vietnam War. A number of the initial SEALS were men who were on the underwater demolition teams. Men of the newly formed SEAL Teams were trained in such unconventional areas as hand-to-hand combat, high-altitude parachuting, demolitions, and foreign languages. In Vietnam, Navy SEAL kill ratio was extraordinary, with over 200 enemy dead for every SEAL casualty."

"You gunna regale us with every one of their battles, Lance?" Ashonte' chided. "We all know they're good!"

"Okay, you know I could talk about this stuff all day long. I'll get to their makeup. A SEAL Team has a Staff Headquarters element and three 40-man troops."

"I'm not hiring that many!" I exclaimed.

"No, hold on…just hold your horses…I'm about to break it down."

"Get to it, Lance," Ashonte' added.

"Here's the breakdown. Under the HQ element are two SEAL platoons of 16-20 men." Lance continued.

"Nope! Still too many!" I interjected.

"Just let me finish, Damnit! I'm getting there!" Lance pleaded. "Each Troop can be easily task organized into 4 squads or eight 4-5 man fire teams for operational purposes."

"Finally!" Ashonte' sighed. "Four to five man fire teams. That's a vote for five man teams over your three man teams, Reggie."

"I only threw the three man teams out there because of us three," I stated. "I like our team!"

Lance and Ashonte' glanced first at each other then nodded at me. I knew that they also felt a strong bond between us. The missions and travel that we had accomplished had secured that bond.

"Troop core skills consist of: Sniper, Breacher, Communicator, Maritime/Engineering, Close Air Support, Corpsman, Point-man/Navigator, Primary Driver/Navigator (Rural/Urban/Protective Security), Heavy Weapons Operator, Sensitive Site Exploitation, Air Operations Master, Lead Climber, Lead Diver/Navigator, Interrogator, Explosive Ordnance Disposal, Technical Surveillance, and Advanced Special Operations," Lance continued without responding to me. He was desperately trying to get through his story of the Navy SEALS without any further interruption!

"What? Wow! That's a lot of titles…what's a Breacher?" I asked.

"They're the ones trained in rapid entry techniques. Did you know that there is a 'breacher.com' website to train in this stuff?" Ashonte' asked.

"And the song, son of a breacher man!" I quipped.

"Next, we'll look at the Army units…" Lance began, ignoring my comment as if I wasn't even in the room!

"Aw, more?" I replied jokingly, "Can't we just agree on the five man unit?"

"This education is good for you Reggie!" Lance admonished.

"Okay, let's get to it!" Ashonte' added.

"The Army Special Forces are also known as the Green Berets. Remember that movie that John Wayne did?" Lance continued.

"Yep, loved it when I was a kid," I replied.

"They are tasked with six primary missions: unconventional warfare, foreign internal defense, special reconnaissance, direct action, hostage rescue, and counter-terrorism. The first two emphasize language, cultural, and training skills in working with foreign troops. Other duties include combat search and rescue, security assistance, peacekeeping, humanitarian assistance, humanitarian demining, counter-proliferation, psychological operations, manhunts, and counter-drug operations…" Lance attempted.

"Hey!" I interrupted. "Combat search and rescue! That's going to be great training for following up on any 'minis' that go off!"

"Please, Reggie…control yourself!" Ashonte' chided.

I could see that Lance was getting a little upset. The veins on his forehead were beginning to bulge! I chose to remain silent during the rest of his classroom training on the various elements of the armed forces of the United States.

"The Army Special Forces were formed in 1952. The Green Beret name came along in 1962.

The Army also boasts the Rangers. The term 'Ranger' was first used in North America in the early 17th century; however, the first ranger company was not officially commissioned until King Philip's War (1676) and then they were used in the four French and Indian Wars. Rangers also fought in the American Revolution, the War of 1812, and the American Civil War. It was not until World War II that the modern Rangers were born, authorized by General George C. Marshall in 1942.The first Ranger hand-picked volunteers were activated during World War II. Each Ranger battalion is composed of a Headquarters and three rifle companies. Battalions are made up of no more than 580 Rangers: Each rifle company consists of 152 riflemen, and the remaining Rangers make up the fire support and headquarters staff.

The Army also boasts the Delta Force which Chuck Norris made popular in the movies. Delta Force is the United States' primary counter-terrorism unit. Delta Force's primary tasks are counter-terrorism, direct action, and national intervention operations, although it is an extremely versatile group capable of assuming many covert missions, including, but not limited to, rescuing hostages and raids. Delta was formed after numerous, well-publicized terrorist incidents in the 1970s led the U.S. government to create a counter-terrorist unit.

Delta Force's structure is similar to the British 22 Special Air Service Regiment, the unit which inspired Delta's creator, Charles Beckwith. The squadrons are based on the organization of the SAS "Sabre Squadron" and each contains 75 to 85 operators. Each sabre squadron is broken down into three troops, one Reconnaissance/Sniper troop, and two Direct Action/ Assault troops, that can either operate in teams or in groups as small as four to six men.

The Marines have the U. S. Marine Corps Forces Special Operations Command or MARSOC. The training includes: direct action, close quarters battle, special reconnaissance, foreign internal defense, fire support, tactical casualty care, irregular warfare, survival evasion resistance and escape, and infantry weapons and tactics. They boast that the members of MARSOC fight the secret wars that never make the front page and bring the highest level of expertise to every operation they are involved in.

The Air Force's Special Tactics teams consist of airmen from three different career fields: Combat Controllers, Pararescuemen, and Special Operations Weathermen. Each of these special operations career fields requires specialized intensive training. Operating with Navy SEALs, Army Special Forces and Rangers, Special Tactics personnel are specially trained to seize enemy airfields and recover distressed personnel in hostile territory," Lance taught.

"I'm getting really bored," I added when Lance took a break. "We can see from all of these units that four to six men is a good unit size. Can we just agree now that we will put together two teams of five men?" I said.

Ashonte' chimed in, "Sounds about right for me! Ten men and no wives involved, right?"

We all nodded in agreement.

"Thanks Lance for the lesson…how do you know all this stuff?" I asked.

"Right here on my EVO," he replied, "No, I knew about the individual special ops units from my Marine training…the details came via the internet."

"It seems to me that we want to seek out ex-military men that have already been trained and have obtained these skills. Why reinvent the wheel, so to speak." I opined.

"You're absolutely right, Reggie!" Lance added, "We want to recruit Green Berets, SEALS, MARSOC, Deltas, Rangers, and the Air Force guys."

"What about the foreign trained guys, like MI-6 and the SAS?" Ashonte' asked.

"All of these specially trained men are 'badasses'. But I personally don't think we'll need to reach outside of the borders of the United States. I'll find plenty of guys, well trained, and ready to become a part of I.N.C.I.S.O.R." Lance said.

"So, focus on the U.S. of A., and see what shakes loose! Are we done? I'm hungry!" I stated.

CHAPTER EIGHT

S HORTLY AFTER OUR meeting Lance and Cyndi returned to the United States on a recruiting trip. The male members of I.N.C.I.S.O.R. had come to the consensus that we would work on developing a team of five members to be stationed in Colorado. The Colorado team would procure warehouse space in close proximity to DIA, or the Denver International Airport. The warehouse space would house a state of the art gym and workout area to keep the team sharp. It would also have a communications space that would include the latest and greatest communications equipment. The CIA would see to it that we would have satellite links to wherever it was needed. There would be a highly restricted area within the warehouse where all of the assault and communications equipment would be kept. The team would have at their access all of the light arms and equipment that they would ask for.

A second team of five men would find warehouse space in close proximity to Frankfurt's Frankfurt am Main airport. The space would be equally equipped and protected as the facility in Denver.

The two teams would initially train at the FLETC facilities, housed at the former Naval Air Station in Glynco, Georgia. Lance would put together a menu of courses for the teams to complete. A two week course would be designed especially for these men who were to be drawn from the elite fighting forces of the United States. Courses such as Active Shooter Threat Training, and Commercial Vehicle Counterterrorism would be included in the training. Lance would bypass the Advanced Asset Forfeiture and Advanced Forensics training types of classes.

While Lance and Cyndi were enroute to America, Ashonte' and I placed a call to CIA headquarters in Langley, Virginia. The purpose of the call was to let our team of handlers know that I.N.C.I.S.O.R. was in the process of expanding…we were to add two teams of five operatives. The location of the teams would be Denver, Colorado and Frankfurt, Germany. The choice of the locations was in reaction to a map we had of where the 'mini' sales were concentrated.

There were many purchases of the 'minis' in Central and South America. These are lands where kidnappings had almost become a part of daily life for the wealthy families, or the large corporations that had sent employees to that part of the world to help with their development. In the years following the transitions from authoritarianism to democracy, crime and violence have become major problems in Latin America. Several studies indicated the existence of an epidemic in the region. High rates of crime and violence in Latin America are undermining growth, threatening human welfare, and impeding social development. Latin America is caught in a vicious circle, where economic growth is thwarted by high crime rates, and insufficient economic opportunity contributes to high crime. Crime and violence thrives as the rule of law is weak, economic opportunity is scarce, and education is poor. What an awful 'catch 22'.

Colorado's DIA is centrally located within the United States. If flights to Central or South America were needed, this would be their jumping off point. The team in Colorado would also be available to help the FBI if so requested. The FBI and Homeland Security had a stellar report card thwarting domestic and international terrorism inside the country, but that could change.

The Germany team would be in the center of most of the 'mini' purchases. This team would also procure an old warehouse close to the airport, which would be similarly equipped for training, communications and assault gear.

Our handlers in Langley were quite excited that there would be two more teams of well-trained ex-military types at their disposal. They understood that the teams were ours, and that command and control was to be in Dubai, UAE.

I received a call from Mr. Netanyahu's office. The flight restrictions over the Middle East had been lifted. Our Cairo, Egypt meeting was on for the first part of the following week.

Dr. Suttmiller had also placed a call that Becky had taken. FRMAC would need us to ferry equipment and supplies to their two teams which were approaching Bushehr. The materials would be arriving soon to Dubai's airport.

I would need to attend the meeting in Cairo alone because Ashonte' was needed in Dubai to help with the supplies that were arriving for FRMAC. Once I returned from the meeting in Cairo we would begin the task of dismantling Aurora's gorgeous cabin to turn the plane into a freight hauler for FRMAC.

We were to be very busy for a while…

CHAPTER NINE

Washington, D.C.

"GIVE ME AN update on Iran," President James almost bellowed. The National Security Advisor immediately began fumbling with the portfolios on his lap. "It's right here, sir," as he continued to fumble with papers.

The President of the United States immediately became irritated as he observed the seeming incompetence in front of him as he watched from behind his desk. "The fate of the world may lie in our next moves!" he was now bellowing.

"Just a moment," was the reply.

"The whole Middle East is blaming Israel!" the President's tone had now become sinister, causing the advisor to glance up into the face of President James. He felt like he was going to be witness to a volcano erupting.

"We have only one photo that was sent by the satellite that was wrecked in the nuclear blast. It was the last communication that came in from that satellite. We have worked hard to enhance the image, and it shows clearly Israeli markings on a cruise missile just as it struck the Bushehr nuclear facility. The missile was the cause of the nuclear detonation," the advisor opined.

"Old news!" the President interrupted. "We knew that within the first hour of the explosion! What about the work tracking the missile's flight path back to Israel?"

"No Intel about that," the advisor mumbled, shuffling again at the papers in his lap.

"Get out and get on it!" the President yelled. "We have constant satellite surveillance of that region…you cannot tell me that we don't know where the missile originated…where was it launched! I need that yesterday!" The President slammed both fists onto his desk, making all of the items on the desk jump.

The advisor rose, dumping the portfolios, and then kneeled down to pick up his mess.

"Get something solid or I'll find somebody who can!" President James seethed.

The advisor quickly scurried from the Oval Office.

"Israel swears that they have no involvement…who did this?" the President muttered to himself.

Tel Aviv, Israel

The Israeli Knesset had just completed a hastily called emergency session to address the explosion in Iran and the dangerous allegations being aimed at the State of Israel by their Middle East neighbors. The Israeli President moved to the podium to address the room crammed full of reporters. He glanced at the myriad of microphones shoved together on the platform and wondered to himself how they could have so many in such a small space. He cleared his throat and the room became instantly quiet.

"We must immediately let the world know that our government had no knowledge of this horrendous attack. The allegations of our involvement are baseless and false. They are the dangerous cries of our inhospitable foes who wish to bring harm to the Israeli people," he paused for effect; "Our hearts and our prayers are with the Iranian people as they face this horrible tragedy." Again a pause, "We offer up to the Iranian people all of our country's resources to help in any way we can."

The President quickly wheeled one hundred and eighty degrees and fled the podium as many of the reporters present jumped to their feet and yelled out questions.

"President James of the United States tells me there is a satellite photograph of what they believe is an ACM (Advanced Cruise Missile) with Israeli markings hitting the reactor at Bushehr!" the Prime Minister whispered to his aide as he hastily departed the newsroom. "Is it one of ours? Are we missing a cruise missile with a three thousand mile range that could hit such a target?"

The aide was scribbling as fast as he could write. Not paying attention to where he was scurrying, he clipped his shoulder on a doorway which sent his pad flying. He scrambled to pick up the pad and rejoin the President who had not lost a step when the aide crashed.

"Get my generals here now!" was the last command before the Israeli President slammed the door to his office.

Dubai, UAE

"Becky!"

"Yes, dear."

"Where's my blue tie?"

"Gave it to Goodwill!"

"They have a Goodwill over here?"

"No, but consider it gone! Take the lavender one…it looks better with your gray suit."

"How'd you know I was taking the gray suit?"

"You always wear that when you are meeting someone special."

"Netanyahu! Pretty cool, huh!"

"Just seeing Cairo this time of year would be cool enough for me."

"Yeah, but you have to 'man the ship' from here, did I tell you that I love you today?"

"Nope, or yesterday either!"

"Did I tell you that Grace is meeting Benjamin Netanyahu's wife in Jerusalem while we are meeting in Cairo?"

"Who do you think set up the travel arrangements?"

"Sorry, I should know better…you know all when it comes to I.N.C.I.S.O.R.!"

"Finish packing and get in here. Time for happy hour. You mix and I'll start dinner."

Tel Aviv, Israel

"Sara, when do you depart for Jerusalem?"

"My driver will be ready at seven. Grace Black arrives at eight to the Jerusalem airport. It's only an hour to get there. Did you say that she is an artist?"

"She calls herself a 'budding artist', but her work is pretty good…not my style, though."

"She must see the Israel Museum…I'll make sure of it! The Impressionist Gallery and the Gallery of the Americas should interest her, and I'll have lunch catered in the Art Garden."

"I'll only be in Cairo for the day. Not planning on a night in that place!"

"Where are you meeting Dr. Nelson?"

"Citystars Cairo…it's close to the airport…Dr. Nelson is staying the night and says he has points to use at an Intercontinental Hotel…there's a team there now to set up a safety perimeter…especially now!"

"What have you heard?"

"Just that when something bad happens in the Middle East all of the Arab countries look to blame Israel! I wish they would go back to warring among themselves. Israel is always the culprit when there is a problem."

"When do you depart?"

"Dr. Nelson is flying his own plane. I understand that he has a turboprop. He has to cover fifteen hundred miles from Dubai to Cairo. His departure is filed for seven in the morning so he should land at around ten o'clock. We're set to meet at eleven. I'm taking a long time to answer you…my hop is only 250 miles so we depart at ten. Breakfast in the morning?"

"Love to…"

"Can we plan a quiet night when we meet up in two days?"

"Love to…"

"I miss you already!"

CHAPTER TEN

Cairo, Egypt

I MADE MY APPROACH into Cairo's International Airport. Once the Avanti II had touched down, I steered the plane off of the active runway and followed the guidance of ground control to terminal one. As I taxied toward the terminal, I noticed a large jet with an equally large security force surrounding the plane. It was parked near the Hajj. I had read about this seasonal terminal used by Egypt Air for flights to Medina and Jeddah during Muslim holy days for the pilgrimage made by so many of the devotees. The terminal was deserted at this time of year.

A jeep cut in front of my plane and I noticed a sign on the back that told me to follow. I complied and was led to the Hajj. I was directed to park near the large jet. I shut down Aurora and moved to exit the plane. A uniformed Israeli soldier met me and escorted me to a Mercedes limo. I noticed that the security force had moved to encircle both planes.

It was a short ride to the Citystars Cairo hotel. I noticed that there was much activity at the airport. With the travel restrictions lifted on the Middle East, all indicators were that this airport was back to normal operations. The airport boasts over eight million passengers each year. It is located only thirteen and a half miles northeast of Cairo. I made a mental noted that Becky and I would have to check out this part of the world at a future date.

The Citystars Cairo Intercontinental Hotel is only four and a half miles southwest of the airport. As the limo pulled up to the grand entrance, my driver directed me to ask for the Citadel room at the front desk. I left my overnight bag with the concierge and walked to our meeting place.

There were two Israeli guards at the door. I noticed that they were so young! It reminded me of playing with my father's World War II flying uniform in the basement of our Littleton, Colorado home. The automatic weapons slung over their shoulders brought me back to reality. These were not children! I wondered if they were going to frisk me. After a cursory glance by the guards and a shrug, the doors were opened.

I walked into the room and looked about. The table and sixteen chairs were set up in a boardroom style. Mr. Netanyahu was at the bar getting a glass of water. I walked toward him. My first observation was that he was shorter than me, but not by much. He also had really gray hair! I knew that he was only four years older than me, and I made the assumption that political life had that effect on his hair. I had seen this happen to almost all of America's Presidents.

We shook hands and I was impressed by his strong grip. He asked me to help myself from the well stocked bar. I noticed that my favorite liquor, Crown Royal, was on the counter. I considered the Crown Royal for an instant, and then remembered that Mr. Netanyahu had only water. I took a glass, filled it with ice cubes and poured from the water pitcher. The room was quite large for just the two of us. Mr. Netanyahu took a seat at the head of the table. I chose the seat to his right.

"What do you know about the disaster in Bushehr?" Mr. Netanyahu asked.

"Very little. We felt the shock wave in Dubai. The nuclear disaster response team has asked us to help ferry equipment to the site," I replied.

"They all blame us!" he stated very bluntly.

"I've heard a lot of rhetoric on the news."

"Israel did not do this!" he avowed."

"Okay," was all that I could muster in front of this great man.

"Your government has shown us a satellite image of a cruise missile striking the nuclear reactor at Bushehr. There are Israeli markings on this missile!" Netanyahu added, and again stated, "We did not do this!"

I did not know what to say next, so I sat there and didn't respond.

Mr. Netanyahu then added, "We have made an initial count of our missiles and warheads. Israel does not have a single weapon unaccounted for…especially a cruise missile! This missile has to have come from your country's arsenal. I have related this fact to your President."

"I'm sure that the American authorities are looking into this," was my weak reply.

"Your President James seems like an honorable man, but I do not trust that your country won't attempt to cover up the facts."

"How do I fit into this?" I asked.

"Israel wishes to avail itself of the services of I.N.C.I.S.O.R." he stated.

"How so?" I asked.

"The Israeli defense forces have their hands tied in this matter. It will look like we wish to place blame on others, just as we suspect your country will do. Your team is American but I am requesting that you look at the information we can provide and information from your own CIA as a third party and with impartiality. I also need your team to move with great speed toward a conclusion. Time is of the essence!" Mr. Netanyahu claimed as he pounded his fist on the table.

The water glasses both jumped. This was the first time I had observed this great leader showing emotion. All of the times I had seen him on TV he had been so calm and collected.

"I wouldn't even know where to start," I mentioned.

"You will start with the information we provide you. You will start with the information your CIA provides you," he countered, "You will follow the leads wherever they will take you…and quickly!"

I sat there baffled and feeling really unsure and inadequate. How was our team supposed to solve this? Our small group did not have the resources at its disposal like Israel and America. I could not see any way that we could help. I was ready to reject his request.

Mr. Netanyahu looked into my eyes and he could see that I was wavering. He reached out and placed his right hand on my shoulder. With a squeeze he said, "We need your help. The world order needs your help. If we do not put this fire out quickly, I fear for my country's survival."

I lowered my head for a moment, then raised up and looked directly into his eyes. "We will do all that we can," I promised.

"It may take more than that," he quietly spoke.

As if by some silent cue the doors opened and in walked an Israeli officer. His hat was tucked under his left arm. He came to attention beside Mr. Netanyahu.

"This is Colonel Gary Kubetz of the Israeli Defense Forces. He is also a member of Mossad. He will give you all of the assistance that our country can muster," Netanyahu stated.

I rose and reached out my hand. Colonel Kubetz gave me a brief nod, but didn't return the handshake. I had never met anyone involved with Mossad, and knew only that it was Israel's version of the CIA.

"I will provide you with all that we know," Colonel Kubetz responded, "Here is my information and how I can be reached."

I took the folder from him and Prime Minister Netanyahu rose. He reached for my hand and bid me a warm farewell. Colonel Kubetz performed an about face and escorted his boss from the room.

I left the room shortly after their departure and headed to the front desk. I was informed that my room was ready and that my bag had been deposited in the room. I made my way to the elevators and then to my room. The bag was on the bed. I tossed the folder onto the bag and laid on my back gazing at the ceiling.

My head was spinning. How did I get us into this mess? What to do next? Netanyahu had said that time was of the essence. I had a deep suspicion that moving quickly would lead to peril. I'm a 'steady plodding brings prosperity' kind of guy. I closed my eyes and fell into a fitful sleep.

PART TWO

CHAPTER ELEVEN

Baghdad, Iraq

"WE ARE HERE today to honor and pay homage to our two martyrs, Hamid and Farroukh," Abdullah announced and prayed, "May they find all pleasures in the land of milk and honey."

Gathered in the room were the four remaining MADEI members who had relocated to Iraq from the United States, Abdullah, who had spoken so eloquently at their meeting in Phoenix, Arizona, and the two newest recruits from the back streets of Baghdad. Street urchins in the battle torn alleys of Baghdad were easy to come by. There was little in the way of education to show them a better way. Illiteracy was rampant...one in five Iraqis between the ages of 10 and 49 cannot read or write a simple statement. Twenty percent! Under Saddam Hussein Iraq had the lowest rate of illiteracy in the region. Now Iraq has the highest! Not something to be proud of… and there were no job prospects that could paint a brighter future. Unemployment rates among young Iraqi males are approaching 25%. One in four is not working. The strongest allure to this group was the religious teachings of men like Abdullah. He promised them glory and riches in the next life. All they must do is martyr themselves and destroy the infidel.

"Hamid and Farroukh have struck the death blow to Israel!" Abdullah cried out to the heavens.

"Allah Akbar," was heard from all the members gathered in the darkened room. The room had no furniture. The paint on the walls was beyond peeling and the floor was littered with debris. The stale, putrid odors assaulted all who ventured into this place. There were no windows to allow light in on this forsaken structure. A tapestry hung over the doorway through which they had entered. Each member had come alone, and had entered stealthily over the last hour, making sure that they were not followed. Now all were standing in a loose circle in the center of the room.

"We must assume that the Israeli markings on the missile and the Israeli items that will be found where Hamid was martyred will seal Israel's fate. The Arab world will bring doom and destruction down upon Israel's land!" Abdullah emphasized.

"What is to be our next attack?" asked one of the new members.

"For now, pray," Abdullah replied, "We will meet soon to discuss the next steps."

With those words, the group began to disperse. One of the new members lagged behind, wishing to speak privately with Abdullah. He whispered that he was in much pain in his mouth. Abdullah told him about an American Dental Clinic in Dubai that he knew of and had heard great stories about their care. Abdullah, himself, had been there! Although he hadn't needed any dental treatment. There were also MADEI funds available for the young recruit's travel to Dubai and for any needed dental treatment. There was nothing worse than a bad toothache!

Funding rarely was a problem for these ragtag groups. It defied all logic that terrorist groups bent on destruction and world chaos had access to limitless funds.

Cairo, Egypt

I checked out of the hotel the next morning. I had used mileage points toward the room, so there was nothing owed on the hotel bill when I left. This time there was no fancy limo to return me to the airport, so I caught the hotel shuttle bus to return to the Hajj terminal.

I settled up with the FBO operator, making sure that they had topped of the tanks with Jet A and ambled out onto the tarmac where my plane, Aurora, sat alone and waiting. I performed my preflight walk around the craft, checking to make sure I had full tanks as I was promised. I have no memory of the flight back to Dubai. I was still lost in thoughts about how to proceed with our new mission.

Washington, DC

"Israel states that they have accounted for their entire arsenal of cruise missiles and nuclear warheads," the aide informed President James, "They claim that it must be one of ours." The aide was seated on a couch across from the President in the oval office.

"Is that even remotely possible?" the President bellowed.

"Well sir, it is a possibility," the aide retorted, "We're checking our inventory now."

"Any more on that satellite photo?" President James asked.

"We have no other satellite images, but for the one. It is highly unlikely that a slow moving cruise missile could track from Israel to Iran without any of our assets in the region picking up on its movement. There are no radar or AWAC hits either. It's like the missile just appeared right before the explosion!" the aide opined.

"Leave me! I have a world to straighten out before it goes to hell in a hand basket!" President James stated, and rose to return to the safety of his desk.

Denver, Colorado

Lance glanced over at the table in his suite at the Hyatt Regency in downtown Denver. There had to be at least fifty resume's in five piles filling up the table. He was astonished that the one small ad he had placed online before leaving Dubai had garnered so much attention. He had glanced through a couple of the applications. If the others were similar, he would have a tough job picking ten new I.N.C.I.S.O.R. team members from the pile.

His task for the rest of the day was to make it through the stacks of applications, make notes and get ready for the interviews that began in the morning. Lance was optimistic that he could get through ten interviews a day and wrap up the process by the end of the week. Then he would begin the process of procuring warehouse space near DIA. Cyndi was already checking with realtors about available space that would meet the requirements.

He decided to contact Reggie to see how his meeting went...

Dubai, UAE

"Lance!" I said into the phone. "Glad you called…let me get Ashonte' on a three-way." I pressed the flash button on the handset and dialed Ashonte's home number. He picked up on the first ring.

"Ash Black…what's on your mind?"

"Ashonte, it's me and I have Lance on the line from Colorado."

"Damnit, Reggie! It's Ash!"

"Sorry friend, old habits."

"Hey guys, I called to check in before my interviews begin tomorrow. I have fifty guys to talk to in five days…that's a lot of talking for me!" Lance said. "What did Benjamin Netanyahu want to see you about?"

"I.N.C.I.S.O.R. is to help with the investigation into the nuclear explosion at Bushehr. I know you guys know that Israel is being blamed for the attack. The Prime Minister denies emphatically that Israel had anything to do with the cruise missile that was seen on that satellite photograph just before the facility exploded. Also, Israel is asking for an answer ASAP! I tried to 'beg off', but Mr. Netanyahu was so sincere and desperate for help."

"I'm working with the CIA to find out everything they know and get all of their materials sent over here," Ash added.

"Israel is doing the same," I said.

"Well, I'll be tied up here in Colorado for at least two weeks with interviews and procurement. I will get things locked up as soon as possible and make it back home," Lance stated.

I thought about Lance's statement. He was now calling Dubai home. Not long ago Colorado was home to all three of us. What interesting events life throws at us.

"How are you going to weed through all of your applicants?" I asked.

"I have come up with two key questions. These guys all have stellar records. These two questions will bring the cream to the top," Lance said.

"What are they?" Ash asked.

"I'll tell you after the interviews. See if my plan works! Say 'good night, Gracie'!"

With that the conversation ended and I hung up the phone. Ash was coming over in the morning and we would begin the task of poring over the collected documents. I thought about Becky. This might be our last quiet and calm evening for a while. Time to make the most of it!

Outside Bushehr, Iran

Jack Mast assembled both the Russian team and his own team members. Days had passed with little to do but collect data from their remote campground. Their aircraft continued to make daily flights over the stricken area. So far the radiation levels were too high to attempt any human forays closer to the town of Bushehr.

A new piece of equipment had just arrived. A remote controlled caterpillar driven apparatus with sensing equipment and data collection hardware was being readied next to the group of scientists.

Jack got everyone's attention and began,"The Israeli Defense Forces have allowed us the use of their ANDROS Mark V-A1 robot. It was originally tasked for bomb disposal work, but has been modified to help us with data collection. There are four cameras which will transmit video imagery back to us at camp. This thing weighs almost eight hundred pounds and travels at four miles an hour. It will be slow going, but it can get in where we cannot!"

"Two radiation detection devices have been added to the robot. There is a Scionex cesium iodide collimated radiation detector attached to the forward looking camera. The second radiation detector is a Ludlum G-M tube attached to the chassis. The wings you see on the sides of the robot are the sampling apparatus. The left wing carries three of the particulate vacuums, two debris bins and the holder for the smear sampler. The right wing carries two particulate vacuums, three debris bins and the GPS unit for navigation. The two original batteries have been replaced with K charge batteries to give the robot longer life. It can now travel twice as far."

"The first mission will take place today. We will send the robot down the road toward the town of Bushehr. We know that our camp is twenty miles from the town. We will run the robot at full tilt ten miles down the road, half the distance to town, gather samples and run it back to camp. This should be a five hour journey. Upon its return we will decontaminate the robot, recharge the batteries and analyze the soil samples. Any questions?"

The twenty group members looked at one another, and no hands went up.

"Then, let's get this thing fired up and on its way!" Jack stated.

Jerusalem, Israel

Sara Netanyahu and Grace Black finished a wonderful lunch at the Billy Rose Art Garden. They were surrounded by the finest collection of sculpture in the world. The guards kept a respectable distance. They had barred the entrance to the garden which was located on the west end of the museum. Only Sara and Grace were at the table. The servers waited at a distance to clear the meal.

"What a fabulous morning!" Grace opened, "You should feel very proud of the Israel Museum. I have filled up a whole sketch pad with ideas to help me create more paintings."

"Yes, we are proud of our museum. I am glad that you were able to enjoy our art," Sara replied. "What would you like to do with our afternoon?"

"I want you to take me to see the Wailing Wall!" Grace stated.

"You know that the Wailing Wall is one of the most sacred sites in Jerusalem outside of the Temple Mount itself," Sara added. "I would love to escort you there. What do you know about the Wailing Wall?"

"Only what I have read…that it was the Western Wall of the Second Temple. I think that it was commissioned to be built in 20 BC by Herod himself! It is called the Wailing Wall because Jews have come here for centuries to lament the loss of their Second Temple which the Romans destroyed in 70 AD." Grace stated.

"You are extremely well informed!" Sara replied. "I did not even remember the dates!"

"I am a devout Christian. Religious history is very important to me," Grace said.

On the way we will pass the Mahane Yehuda market! I have an idea for a gift that I would like to purchase for Benjamin. Would you be okay with a slight detour on our way?"

"Tell me about this market." Grace said.

"It is one of our most famous outdoor markets with over two hundred and fifty vendors. We call the market 'The Shuk'," Sara offered.

"Similar to the Souqs we have in Dubai? I especially enjoy my time walking through the Spice Souq…and the fabulous aromas." Grace said.

"Very much the same, even with all of the delicious smells," Sara responded.

"Then, I am fine with a detour!" Grace replied.

Sara Netanyahu signaled to one of the guards and informed him of their next destination. He spoke quietly into his sleeve and then indicated to the women that they were ready to proceed. Security was confirmed and the two women were escorted to an awaiting vehicle.

A short while later the two women began walking the narrow streets of the Shuk looking at the wares displayed before them and listening to the vendors call out their prices. The cacophony of sounds and wonderful smells was almost overwhelming for Grace. She was not one who usually chose to be in such crowded places.

At one point Grace needed to find a bathroom. She spotted one on the far side of a small square, told Sara Netanyahu about her need for a pit stop and made a beeline for the facility. There were a handful of tourist buses parked close by. As she moved around the front of the first bus a woman covered head to toe in a burka ran onto the bus and screamed, "Allahu Akbar"!

There was a sudden and intense explosion. The bus actually leapt into the air. A large fireball ascended above the scene. The sound was deafening and the unfortunate shoppers walking close to the bus lost their eardrums. Any soul within a fifty foot radius from the explosion was knocked off of their feet to the ground. Storefront windows within a hundred foot circle imploded into the buildings. Shards of glass from the shattered bus blew out in all directions and became missiles that found their way into many of the people crossing the square. The blast drove Grace twenty feet from where she had stood. Glass from the front windshield pierced Grace's body in many spots. One glass shard entered Grace's neck, severing her left carotid artery.

Mayhem ensued. Many ran toward where the blast had left the bus in a smoldering heap. The air was no filled with cries of help coming from the unfortunate who were too close to the bus. There were no cries from inside of the bus. Those souls were all dead. The ever present soldiers had their automatic weapons raised and searched for other attackers. It was a futile effort. The suicide bomber had been alone.

Israel had suffered through over one hundred and fifty such bombings since they began in the 1980's. The city of Jerusalem had not been a target for the suicide bombers since 2004. Now, in 2011 the attacks were beginning again with the bombing in March…and now this…

Sara and her guards had witnessed the blast as they watched Grace cross the square. They now ran to where she lay on the stone pavers. As they approached, Sara could see the spreading pool of blood seeping from Grace's neck. Sara ordered her guards to get help immediately and kneeled down next to Grace's head. She grabbed her tunic and ripped off a sleeve which Sara quickly wrapped around her hand. She applied pressure to Grace's neck attempting to stop the flow of blood.

Sara noticed the other wounds and whispered in Grace's ear. Grace did not respond. Sara then yelled at Grace to open her eyes. Again, there was no response from Grace. Sara felt hopeless as the blood continued to flow from Grace's neck and soaked her wrapped hand. Not knowing what else to do, Sara kept pressure on Grace's neck.

Sirens filled the air as the first responders began to arrive at the scene. Help had arrived and soon there were men flanking both sides of Grace. One touched Sara's shoulder and asked her to back off. She would not listen and kept her hold on Grace's neck. Not until he knelt down and applied his hand over Sara's did she reluctantly pull her hand away. She stepped back to allow the men to administer to Grace.

One of the men felt for a pulse. It was barely there. Grace was quickly placed on a stretcher and rushed to a waiting ambulance. A path was cleared and the ambulance raced off toward the nearest hospital.

Sara bowed her head and offered a silent prayer that Grace would pull through. Her guards waited quietly until she was done, and then whisked her away from that place. Sara ordered them to take her to the hospital.

The injury to Grace's neck was too severe. Grace died in the ambulance before it arrived at the hospital. There was just too much blood lost. The emergency personnel continued CPR for the remainder of the ride to the hospital. When the ambulance pulled up to the emergency room entrance there was a team waiting to take over for the men in the ambulance. A doctor listened to Grace's heart with his stethoscope as the gurney was pulled from the ambulance. There were no heart sounds. In a desperate move he moved the bell of his stethoscope to the right side of her neck. Nothing. He slowly rose up and looked into the anxious eyes of this well trained team. They had seen too many injuries like Grace's. He shook his head from side to side and pronounced her dead.

A sheet was pulled up over her body. The driver mused over the fact that this was Grace's last ride.

Sara's car pulled up to the emergency entrance shortly after. She was informed of Grace's passing. Sara again bowed her head…this time to cry.

One of the guards immediately contacted Benjamin Netanyahu. His jet had just touched down in Tel Aviv. He was having romantic thoughts about dinner with his wife when the call came through. Prime Minister Netanyahu's first concern was the safety of Sara. He was told that she was alright. But…Grace Black had perished. He listened quietly as the details of blast and Grace's demise were communicated.

Tel Aviv, Israel

Mr. Netanyahu still sat in his seat on the plane which was now parked on the tarmac. The engines were still spooling down. The cabin door had been opened and his security detail had disembarked. They had taken up their positions to insure his safety. He reluctantly picked up the phone and dialed Ash's number. Ash had just finished the three way call with Reggie and Lance. He was still seated at his desk next to the phone. He answered on the first ring.

"Mr. Black?" Mr. Netanyahu asked.

"Yes," Ash replied.

"I have some devastating news. There was a suicide bomber in the square in Jerusalem. Your wife, Grace, was a victim of the blast," the Prime Minister said.

"Is she all right? Where is she? Can I talk with her? Ash questioned.

"Her injuries were too severe. She has died," Mr. Netanyahu stated. "I am so sorry for your loss."

Ash sat there stunned still with the phone to his ear. A minute passed.

"Mr. Black?"

Ash heard the voice and slowly placed the handset in the cradle. He stared at the wall, not seeing. One of Grace's paintings hung above the desk. He looked at the painting and said, "Grace, I love you." Ash Black put his head in his hands and began to sob uncontrollably.

Dubai, UAE

I hung up the phone after being informed of Grace's death by Mr. Netanyahu. My first thought was to call Ash. I then thought the better thing was to get over to him. I silently moved to the bedroom where Becky was reading a new novel. Ash and I had discovered an American author that had over twenty books published. Becky was in the process of devouring one of his books. She looked up from her book and could see the devastation on my face.

"What happened?" she asked.

"Grace has died," I replied. "I need to get to Ash."

The book fell into Becky's lap. She was too stunned to ask questions. I turned away from her and left for the garage.

The drive to Ash's house was short. I used my key to unlock the front door and entered the house. I stood in the foyer and listened. Sobs were coming from the office. I moved to where Ash sat, stood behind him and placed both of my hands on his shoulders. I stood there and gave him time to collect himself. The sobbing eventually ceased and he rose up to face me. Without a word being said I gave him a hug. We stood there holding each other for a minute. Ash then pulled away and said, "She's gone, Reggie. Grace is gone."

I had no words. My throat had closed up and there were tears in my eyes. I just looked at him and nodded. I opened my mouth to speak and there was nothing. My heart was breaking for my good friend.

Ash moved into the living room and sat on the couch. I followed him and sat in the armchair facing the couch. Neither of us spoke for several minutes.

"I need to get to Israel," Ash opened.

"There isn't anything you can do there," I replied. "Mr. Netanyahu is personally seeing to the return of Grace's remains."

"I need to be with her."

"She's gone, Ash."

My best friend sat staring at me as if I were a stranger. There was not the familiar look of knowing that a good friend has when you make eye contact. Only a pleading, desperate look of a lost soul.

"I have to do something! I can't just sit here. We've got to call people. Does Lance know?"

That moved me into action. I went to the office and retrieved a note pad and a pen. I then rejoined my friend in the living room.

"Who do we need to call?" I asked.

"Lance, Cyndi, Becky."

"Becky already knows. What about Grace's parents?"

"They had both passed away before we met."

"Your parents?"

"Yes, I need to tell my mother."

Ash's father was in his mid nineties and his mother was approaching ninety. I wondered how they would take this blow. Ash came from a lineage that many of his family lived to become one hundred years old. I hoped the news would not shorten either of their lives. I remembered that they had lost a daughter and granddaughter to murder when Ash was in college. Now they had lost a daughter in law. I also remembered that Ash had a brother.

"Your brother?" I asked.

"Yep," he said.

"Did Grace have any siblings?" I asked.

"No, she was an only child," Ash replied.

"So there is nobody to contact in Grace's family?" I responded.

"Nope."

"Okay, you talk with your mother and brother. Becky and I will handle all of the other calls."

"Reggie, thanks for coming over, but I don't feel like company now. I'll call you later."

"You know that we will do whatever we can to help you through this. Our door is always open to you."

With that said, I rose and went to hug him again. Ash's shoulders straightened and his back stiffened as we made contact. His mind and soul had moved somewhere very distant from me. The coldness was very disquietening to me. I let go and left Ash to his misery.

When I got home Becky was in tears. She wanted to know all of the details. I told her what I knew. It didn't seem to be enough, but that was how Becky was. Even if I knew the whole story, it wouldn't be enough for Becky. I went into the office to retrieve the phone. It was time to call Lance and let him know what had taken place in Jerusalem.

I sat there for a moment remembering Grace. The whole time that I knew Grace I always felt that she was really close to God. She seemed to have that inner peace from knowing that God will take care of everything. She was the one who initiated a prayer before every meal we had together. When I was in Grace's presence, I felt safer…that she had some kind of inside track to God. All that was gone now…I prayed that she was now with God! I knew that she was.

CHAPTER TWELVE

Denver, Colorado

LANCE LOOKED ASHEN as he put down the phone.

Cyndi had just returned to the hotel room from a shopping spree on the 16th street mall. She was commenting about the free shuttle buses that ran up and down the pedestrian mall and all of the restaurants and shops that lined the mall. She was sunning on about the great deals she had found at a local discount store. She looked over her shoulder at Lance after she placed her bags on the hotel bed. She could tell by the look on his face that something bad had happened. Cyndi moved into the living room of the suite which Lance had set up as his office for the interviews he was conducting.

"What's wrong, dear?" she asked.

"That was Reggie on the phone. Grace was killed in a bomb blast in Jerusalem. I can't believe it! Reggie, Ash or me…yes. We are the ones who are in harm's way. Not you guys!"

"They had news about that blast on CNN. Oh no. Grace was there? My Gracie is dead?"

"While Reggie was meeting with Netanyahu in Cairo, Grace was with his wife in Jerusalem," Lance said.

"I know about her trip," Cyndi replied.

"We have to get to Dubai for the funeral…And I'm smack dab in the middle of all of these interviews!"

"Don't worry. I'll talk with Becky and take care of all of the arrangements," Cyndi replied. "How many more interviews do you have set for this afternoon?"

"One at three and one at five"

"Are you going to be okay getting through those? Maybe you should reschedule."

"No…this is important. I need to keep on track. I'll get through this."

"Alright, if you think you can. I'll be in the bedroom talking with Becky."

With that, Cyndi reached up and gave her husband a hug, moved into the bedroom and closed the door.

"What the hell!" Lance said, and bowed his head. He allowed himself a few moments of silent reflection and then he made a half-hearted effort to study the resume's on the table. Lance had seen many of his comrades in arms perish in battle. That is what happens in war. But not Grace in a terrorist bombing! What a sick world, he thought.

Dubai, UAE

It was my day in the American Dental Clinic. I didn't want to be there. Becky was handling most of the funeral arrangements and I felt like dead weight hanging around the house. I had a light day scheduled, but at least I would be out of the way and not feeling so helpless.

A young Arab entered the practice. The facial recognition software relayed his image up to an unseen overhead satellite and the on to Langley, Virginia. The on duty operator sitting at the computer console looked at the young man's image on the left half of the computer screen. Images were flashing by too quickly to recognize on the right half of his screen. There was a hit! He immediately sent a confirmation signal back to the office in Dubai. This man was a candidate for a PC!

The young Arab informed the receptionist that he had flown all the way from Baghdad, Iraq! Our clinic was well known in various circles there. He was being sponsored by Abdullah bin Abdel who would be taking care of the bill. Mr. bin Abdel had a digital chart with the practice. He would pay in cash! He had swelling on his right side and a horrible toothache.

Digital radiographs were taken of the infected tooth. The young Arab identified himself as Amjad Farresh. The tooth was savable with root canal therapy and an all porcelain crown, or it could be extracted. The options were explained to Amjad. The young man had not lost any of his teeth at this point in his life, and did not want to start losing them now! Could we begin immediately? He was in a great deal of pain.

The operatory was prepared with the proper instruments for the procedure. After placing the topical anesthetic and reviewing Amjad's medical history, I injected him with a 'cocktail' of lidocaine, articaine and marcaine. My assistant also gave him an elixir that Amjad drank. This elixir contained an oral sedative so that he could tolerate the procedure more easily.

I left him alone while the anesthetic got him numb. During that time I went to my office and retrieved one of the listening devices which I kept under lock and key in my desk drawer. I re-entered the operatory and placed the 'PC' on the bracket tray.

The root canal procedure went smoothly. I then implanted the nanotransmitter in Amjad's prepared tooth and sealed the floor of the preparation with Fuji IX, a glass ionomer. The crown of the tooth was prepared for an all porcelain restoration and imaged with a CEREC 3D bluecam. The computer, using biogeneric software, gave me a proposal for the crown and I made some minor adjustments. The crown was then milled out of a solid block of porcelain and glazed in our lab oven. I seated the crown, made a minor adjustment to the bite and bonded the crown to the remaining tooth structure.

The complete procedure took a little over two hours to complete. The restoration looked great, both in Amjad's mouth and radiographically. I still marvel at this technology! Amjad received his crown in just one visit! CAD/CAM technology has been around for a long time, but only recently accurate enough to replace human dentition.

Amjad was feeling great and also a bit loopy from the medication. I knew that I would most likely never see him in the dental clinic again. That was the nature of many of my Arab clients…they only appeared for emergency treatment. I gave him a prescription for an antibiotic to help rid Amjad's body of the infection, a prescription for pain and bade him farewell, urging him to come back for routine care and maintenance.

I had an encrypted message from the CIA waiting on my computer when I sat at my desk. I had seen the same message many times before. The nanotransmitter (the PC) was transmitting well. There had yet to be a failure in the little buggers! I pondered for a moment what I would do if I got a message that it had failed. "Oops, sorry! We need to redo your work." The next question would be, "Why? I feel great!" I was stumped as to what to say next…

Outside Bushehr, Iran

"The first mission of the Mark V-A1 was a complete success! All of the systems functioned beautifully," the technician told Jack Mast.

Jack was standing behind the technician as he studied the computer screen. At this distance, Jack could not make out the numbers on the screen, but he knew that the technician was adept at deciphering the data.

"I'll have a summary report in two hours, but at first glance, I think we can stage a forward camp five miles closer to Bushehr without jeopardizing our scientists," the technician stated.

Jack returned to his tent to ponder this new information.

Dubai, UAE

Grace's memorial service was small and intimate. There were no more than twenty people in attendance. I only cared for the remaining five that made up our core group. Lance and Cyndi had travelled a great distance to be there for Ash.

I rose to say a few words to the group. I began to speak, and then made the mistake of looking at Ash. His face was a mask of torment. My insides turned to rubber and I choked up instantly. I couldn't get the words out. I opened my mouth to speak…nothing, bowed my head, took a deep breath, swallowed, raised up and tried to begin again…I couldn't utter a single word. Thank God for Becky. She stood and moved to my side. She was able to articulate the words that I wanted to say about Grace.

A handful of others spoke, but I have no recollection as to what was said.

When the service was over, the others departed. There would be no burial here in Dubai. Ash was to fly back to Colorado Springs with the casket for burial there. He was leaving the next day to complete the process.

Ash wished to be alone, so the remaining four of us gathered at our home. There was some awkward small talk then Lance broke the ice.

"Hey…I know this isn't the right time…but when will it be. I need to tell you all about the interviews and the progress that Cyndi and I are having with the team recruitment," Lance offered.

"Yeah, you know what? We have to get back at it. I also have some news," Becky added.

"Maybe this is exactly what the doctor ordered," I said.

"Okay then, let me brief you on Denver," Lance said.

"The floor is yours!" I replied.

"First off, we had over fifty phenomenal dossiers that were submitted. I spent a solid week interviewing these guys. What a great group of men! Their training and military backgrounds were really similar and their ratings by their superiors were all superb. These men were the best of the best within the American military. I would have taken all fifty if all I had to do was study the information in their records. There were applicants from all of the branches of the military.

I was first stumped as to how to whittle the number down to ten, but then I was hit with a stroke of genius! I realized that I only had two main questions that needed to be asked to understand where these prospective operatives' minds were," Lance began.

"Two questions, huh!" I replied.

"Yup, just two…The first was, 'What did you do with your Dinar when you cashed in?' It hit me that we were after men that knew that the bundle of cash that they made on this investment was a once in a lifetime thing. I wanted the men that were astute enough to place the money in some type of investment vehicle. Especially the ones that were smart enough to place the money in an annuity and live off of the proceeds. The principle would never need to be touched!"

"The ones that took the money and made immediate life changing moves, such as new cars and houses, were the ones I wanted to avoid. When the money was gone, they would be in dire straits if they attempted to support that new lifestyle. These would be the ones that would be subject to money advances or other forms of bribery by the 'bad guys' in the future," Lance opined.

"That's a great first question. How many did that weed out?" Becky asked.

"There were only twenty of the fifty that chose to be wise with their money," Lance replied.

"So now you have to reduce the number by half. Was that the second question?" I asked.

Cyndi was nodding her head. It reminded me that she had been in Denver also. She and Lance had spent much of their alone time discussing the candidates.

"The second question also came to me as an inspiration," Lance continued. "It is another extremely simple one…'Are you coachable?' Most of the applicants had risen to become the cream of the crop in their various military circles. They were all leaders, and therefore more apt to give orders than take them. I felt that we wanted teams that all participated together, with no real leader. I wanted team members that could feed off of each other's ideas and opinions and design operation plans that would be more comprehensive and complete than the plans of just one leader," Lance said.

"That is brilliant!" I added. "Much more likely for the team to move and react as one organism than the members just following orders."

"I thought so too," Cyndi stated. She gave Lance a big smile.

"Want to know how I came up with that one?" Lance asked, and continued without waiting for a response, "I remembered reading a Tom Peters book about business management. He coined the phrase, 'skunk works' to describe all of the minds coming together and making a plan."

"So, what was the reaction?" Becky asked.

"It was a tough question for some and easy for others. Remember that these men had basically begun their military careers with a certain level of brain washing in boot camp. You've all seen those movies where the drill sergeant screams at the recruits and drives them to the point of utter exhaustion," Lance said.

The three of us nodded along with his statement. I remembered 'An Officer and A Gentleman' first, followed by 'Full Metal Jacket' and then the military spoof 'Stripes'. The military learned many centuries ago that the raw recruits had to be broken down and stripped of the outside world before they would learn the military way of following orders…even if the order made no sense at all!

"I found the ten that fit our bill the best," Lance stated.

"So nothing about their accomplishments in the Service?" I asked.

"You forget, Reggie, all fifty of the applicants were the best of the best that the American military had. All of them had skills that would 'wow' you and me! There would have been no way to find ten I.N.C.I.S.O.R. team members based solely on the merits and accomplishments made during military service", Lance countered. "I'm the one with the military background here. Trust me on this one!"

"Okay, okay. Tell us about the ten that you picked," I said.

"This is where I take over," Cyndi said as she opened a notebook. "First of all, they all are, or were officers. We have five Army guys, three Navy and two Air Force. I've made out sheets for each of you breaking down the two teams." Cyndi rose and passed out the papers. I looked at mine and couldn't believe the manly strength that just came from their names:

Team One – Denver	**Team Two - Frankfurt**
Lance Everett	Stirling Mason
Powers Hunt	Magnus Harper
Flex Lawson	Dick Becker
Max Galloway	Aaron Dekker
Duncan Trevino	Graham Sandler

"I have another sheet for you all. The ten men had dinner with Lance and me just before we left to come to Dubai. Magnus had gotten online and discovered the meaning of each of the team member's names. This is hilarious and kind of raunchy!" Cyndi exclaimed as she handed out the second sheet.

Lance – "Appears to be heterosexual, but no one's really sure"

Powers – "Likes sheep more than girls. Will probably end up married to a relative"

Flex – "What he loses in size he makes up for in enthusiasm and stamina"

Max – "Loves himself, which is just as well since everybody else hates him"

Duncan – "Hopeless ski bum, brains shot away a long time ago"

Stirling – "Thinks he's James Bond, in reality a hopeless dipstick"

Magnus – "Cute and tall, but a liar and a cheat"

Dick – "Hasn't seen his feet or his penis in years, very fat"

Aaron – "Ugly, but hung like a horse, prone to belly button fluff"

Graham – "Will screw anything that moves"

"This is incredibly funny!" I exclaimed.

"What would they do with our names?" Becky added when she finished laughing.

"Well, as it so happens…their irreverence was not just aimed at themselves!" Cyndi said, as she handed out a third sheet of paper. "Magnus had also looked up our names on the internet."

Lance – "Appears to be heterosexual, but no one's really sure"

Ash – "Hung like a slave, but secretly shy"

Reginald – "Arrogant twat who is crap in bed but thinks he is a stud"

Cyndi – "Too shy to come out of the closet"

Becky – "Likes root vegetables in every orifice"

"Okay, enough!" I interjected. "I hope at least this was a good ice breaker for the guys at your dinner."

Lance added, "You would have been amazed…it was like old home week for them and their paths had never crossed during their time in the military!"

"What other news do you have from Denver?" Becky asked.

Cyndi continued, "We have a five year lease on warehouse space very close to DIA. All ten men are working to get the space ready as we speak.

The CIA has been notified and is sending the armaments that we ordered. The space should be workable when Lance and I return."

Becky then spoke up, "Since you brought up the CIA, Cyndi, I'll make a segue into my dealings with them. We now have the satellite image that shows a missile striking the nuclear plant at Bushehr. I have been studying the image for hours upon hours. I think that there is something huge that the eyes at Langley have missed."

With that she pulled out the image and taped it to the white board. Becky then passed around photographs that she had scanned from textbooks and downloaded from the internet.

"It's now time for your missile education," Becky began.

"First a history lesson. The first cruise missile was the V-1 designed and used by Germany in World War II. The US Air Force developed the Matador in 1954. Currently the US, China, Russia, South Korea, Pakistan, Turkey, Great Britain, Germany, Sweden, France, Italy, Japan and India have developed or are developing cruise missiles…"

I whistled a low whistle. "I had no idea!" I exclaimed.

"Just wait, Reggie, there's a lot more!" Becky stated and continued. "There are many different configurations for cruise missiles. The categories to which the cruise missiles are classified are hypersonic, supersonic, long range subsonic, medium range subsonic and short range subsonic missiles. The most famous of the cruise missiles produced by the United States is the Tomahawk. It is considered a long range subsonic missile."

Becky began putting up pictures of the various missiles onto the white board.

"Now let's start eliminating possibilities. The distance between Israel and Bushehr is over eight hundred miles. At this distance we can eliminate the medium range and short range missiles. Also, the hypersonic and supersonic cruise missiles typically have a shorter range, so we can eliminate them. That leaves us with the group known as the long range subsonic cruise missiles. There are only four countries that have developed long range subsonic missiles: United States, Russia, China and South Korea."

"I have looked at the missile configurations from the other countries. This missile that struck Bushehr is American made," Becky stated as she pointed to the satellite image on the white board.

"So, now we are down to the missiles produced by the United States. There are three. The AGM-86B, the AGM-129 ACM and the BGM-109, also known as the Tomahawk.

"I then looked into the information that Israel provided to us. The only cruise missile configuration that has a distance of over 1500 kilometers in Israel's arsenal is the Harpoon." Becky placed a picture of a Harpoon missile on the white board. "Look at the satellite photo. The missile did not come from Israel, just as Netanyahu said!"

Becky then pulled down the pictures of various missiles, leaving pictures of the three American made cruise missiles on the board with the satellite image. She also made sure that the pictures we each had in front of us matched the pictures on the board. Becky handed the three of us magnifying glasses.

"First, look at the satellite image. Focus on the tail of the missile."

"Two fins and no rudder," Lance offered.

"Exactly!" Becky exclaimed. "Look at the three missiles!"

I could tell that she was getting excited.

"Two have an upper fin," Cyndi claimed.

"Again, right on!" Becky said. "There is only one possibility for what that missile could be! It is the AGM-129 ACM missile! It is the only cruise missile where the placement of the vertical fin is underneath the missile body. That is why you only see two fins in the satellite image! The satellite picture was shot down from the satellite in orbit. It is a picture of the top of the missile."

"That's great work, Becky," I said. "And Israel doesn't have this in their arsenal?"

"Not unless they are lying to us," Becky replied.

"What else do you know about this missile?" Lance asked.

"Here's the really weird part…it can only be launched from a B-52 platform!" Becky stated.

"Whoa…this is getting out of hand!" I exclaimed. "You are saying that the missile that hit Bushehr had to come from an aerial attack by the United States?"

"Yup!" Becky exclaimed.

"What does the CIA say about this?" Cyndi asked.

"I've relayed my findings to them…and as of yet have not heard a response. This info has to have them up in arms!" Becky replied.

"This just can't be!" I said. "There is no way that the United States took out the nuclear reactor at Bushehr with an aerial attack. Somebody else, the Russians and or the Chinese would have satellite coverage of such an attack. So would the US! And what about the Israeli markings on that missile? America orchestrated an aerial attack with a B-52 and chose to blame Israel for said attack! No way!"

Cyndi then asked, "Don't they have aerial defenses around a nuclear plant? I mean, wouldn't Iran have defense batteries around the facility in case of an aerial attack?"

"Didn't think of that," Becky replied. "I'll see what they have!" She wrote down a note to remind her to check on this new information.

Lance then spoke up, "Let's assume that the attack was not made by the United States. Who else would have a reason to take out the nuclear reactor other than Israel? Are there any missiles missing from the US arsenal?"

"Can't answer either question until we get more information from the CIA," Becky replied.

"If it is not the United States or Israel, somebody went to a lot of work to make the world think it was!" Cyndi added.

"Well, nothing more that we can do here except conjecture," I said. "What are our next moves?"

"Cyndi and I will head back to the States and wrap up any loose ends with the two teams," Lance stated. "What about Ash?"

"He's leaving for Colorado tomorrow. He has not said how long he will be or what his plans are after Grace is buried," I replied.

"Well, enough for now. Lance and I need to get packing for the return trip. We'll be back in a couple of weeks," Cyndi said.

We broke company at that point and Lance and Cyndi departed. Becky and I decided to put the I.N.C.I.S.O.R. business away for the rest of the day. I needed to get over to Ash's home to see if there was anything I could offer to help him get on with Grace's final journey.

Washington, DC

"What do you mean that the cruise missile was one of ours?" the President screamed. "Tell me that we didn't do this attack without my knowledge!"

"Absolutely not, Mr. President," the aide acknowledged. "We had no part in the attack."

"Did we lose a cruise missile? How is that possible?" President James asked.

"Well sir, there was one incident…"

Tel Aviv, Israel

Gary Kubetz snapped to attention as he entered the Prime Minister's office. He stood completely still until he was recognized.

"What news do you have?" Mr. Netanyahu questioned.

"I have just gotten off the phone with Becky Nelson. She thinks that the cruise missile in the satellite image was an AGM-129 ACM. The United States has not shared this missile with any of its allies."

"Fascinating!" Mr. Netanyahu stated as he rubbed his temples with both hands. "What does the US say about that?"

"No response yet, but I can't wait to hear their reply!" Colonel Kubetz replied.

"Let me know the instant you hear an answer," the Prime Minister stated.

With that, Colonel Kubetz came to full attention, performed an about face and left the Prime Minister's office.

CHAPTER THIRTEEN

Denver, Colorado

"WE'RE ALL SET here," Flex Lawson claimed.

The ten new I.N.C.I.S.O.R. recruits and Lance had just finished a grueling weight circuit which followed a ten mile run. Lance really felt out of shape trying to keep up with these young men. They were all standing in a loose semicircle around the main operations desk. They all had bottles of water to rehydrate themselves after the run. Lance looked over the group and knew that he had done well with the interviews. This was a good looking bunch of guys!

"Okay…time for the men heading to Germany to get their affairs in order. I want you there by this time next week," Lance ordered.

"Stirling, Dick and Aaron are going to head directly to Frankfurt. Magnus and I are going on a cruise!" Graham Sandler announced.

"Where are you cruising to?" Lance asked.

"This is so cool!" Magnus exclaimed. "Graham and I are flying to Dubai and boarding the Silver Wind, a Silverseas, Ltd. Ocean Liner. We then cruise to Oman and India, head south through the Indian Ocean to the Seychelles and follow Africa's coastline from Mombasa to Cape Town to Morocco. We'll disembark in Morocco and hop a flight to Frankfurt. You wouldn't believe the package deal we got, including first class airfare to Dubai!"

"How long is the trip?" Lance asked.

"Ten days total, so we'll be in Germany in plenty of time to help with the facility setup," Graham replied.

"Sounds like a great trip…you guys deserve it!" Powers added.

"Okay, we're adjourned," Lance stated.

Dubai, UAE

I hung up the phone from Lance's call and headed to find Becky. She was in the kitchen preparing a light lunch of hummus and pita bread, with a big bowl of red grapes, figs and dates. I moved in behind Becky and reached my arms around her. I gave her a big hug and said, "Really? Pita and hummus?"

"Reggie, you know you've got to get some weight off," Becky replied defensively.

"And your answer is to serve me garbanzo beans? And mashed up at that? Alright…would you like an Arnold Palmer?" I asked.

"Water's good for me, with a lemon? And just so you get it right next time, they're cooked and mashed chickpeas that are blended with tahini, olive oil, lemon juice, salt and garlic!" Becky said.

"Okay, you got me…what the hell is tahini?" I asked.

"Tahini is a paste made from ground sesame seeds," Becky replied.

"All this mashed and ground up stuff…don't these people have any teeth to chew with?" I said.

"You should know…you're the dentist to the stars over here!" Becky retorted.

"I'll get the drinks out to the patio…meet you there?" I said and headed for the refrigerator. I have enjoyed Arnold Palmers since I was a kid. I can still remember my father asking for one on a Sunday afternoon after a two hour tennis match. We were sitting in a booth at the Welshire Inn in Denver. Dad said that an Arnold Palmer was half iced tea and half lemonade. I was not an iced tea fan then, but ordered one also. The lemonade made the drink for me, cutting the bitter taste of the tea. I've been hooked ever since and I also always order this for my drink when we are out for lunch.

We positioned ourselves at the patio table so that we could both take in the afternoon sun. I loved watching the boating activity in the distance as the ships plied the Persian Gulf.

"What's the word from Lance?" Becky asked.

"He's all finished in Denver and off to Frankfurt. Should be back here in a couple of weeks," I replied.

"Have you heard from Ash?"

"Not a peep! Anything from the CIA?"

"I should get a call in the morning."

"You want a 'nooner' after lunch?"

Baghdad, Iraq

"How was your visit to the American Clinic in Dubai?" Abdullah queried.

"I feel great! The pain and swelling are all gone," Amjad stated. "All glory be to Allah!"

And to me, Abdullah thought as he looked at his young comrade. I'm the one that made this happen!

Langley, Virginia

"The newest PC is working great…just picked up a conversation in Baghdad. I think our target is talking with the guy who is head of this cell. Nothing of note just yet," the console operator remarked to her superior.

Outside Bushehr, Iran

The Iranian soldiers were putting the finishing touches on the campsite that was moved seven miles closer to the town of Bushehr. The Geiger counters were busy with an annoying array of 'ticks' to let the members of the American and Russian teams that there was still quite a level of radioactivity in the area. Each member wore a badge that turned color when the level of radiation became dangerous, and so far no badges had changed. The team members were on edge, though from the constant noise that reminded them of a hidden killer.

Jack was working with the group getting ready for the second foray of the unmanned vehicle. This trip was going to be over the desert terrain straight toward the remains of the nuclear plant, rather than heading down the road to the town of Bushehr. The going would be much slower due to the rough desert landscape. The first mission only involved driving the machine down the paved road toward the town. This mission would involve hills, valleys and other pitfalls in the way. This would be a long, arduous day.

San Salvador, El Salvador

Jose' 'Venerable' was watching the street urchins play as his black Mercedes sped down the street. Jose' knew that his driver was ex-Salvadoran military and had trained in the United States. He also knew that the driver was packing a .45 caliber Beretta. Jose' knew that it was especially dangerous to venture out after dark, but this was an emergency!

Jose's textile company was one of the major employers in San Salvador. Seventy thousand workers in the country toiled in the textile business. Jose's company was the largest single employer!

The company hired Jose' at their headquarters just outside Winston-Salem, North Carolina. His company produced Jacquard fabrics mainly for the transportation industry. Jose's language abilities (he was fluent in five languages, including Spanish) and his Masters in business administration made him a shoo in to run the factories in El Salvador. He had been in country for five months now.

Jose' was on call this night and an alarm had sounded at one of the factories. His driver was speeding to the site. Jose' was a small man, just barely five foot six with a slight frame. Some would say that he had an effeminate look. He had grown a mustache in hopes of a more macho look. He marveled at his driver's hulk as he sat squeezed behind the steering wheel. Jose' guessed that the driver had to be at least six foot six! Yep, he had to slouch to avoid hitting the ceiling panel with his head. Was this giant of a man afraid of anything?

A movement to Jose's right caused him to look that way as his car shot through an intersection. A pickup truck was moving at his car at a high rate of speed. He knew in an instant that they were going to be T-boned. He braced for the impact by tightening every muscle in his body...the worst thing he could do.

The impact shattered all of the windows in the Mercedes. The car was thrown onto the far sidewalk and spun around like a top. Jose' looked up just as his driver pulled his weapon and reached for the car door. Jose' noticed a half dozen men whose faces were covered and all carried AK 47's drawn and at the ready. Two of the assailants approached the driver's door and two quick short blasts from their weapons eliminated the driver and covered the dash with his brain matter.

The others quickly pulled Jose' from the car and roughly threw him into a waiting van. A burlap bag was pulled over his head and duct tape was wrapped around Jose's wrists and ankles. The maneuver took less than a minute and the van sped off into the night.

As Jose' lay sprawled on the floor in the back of the van he thought about the warnings that the United States Bureau of Consular Affairs had published about El Salvador. "Extortion is on the rise and U.S. citizens and their family members have been victims in various incidents. Violent, organized gangs are a major factor in the crime situation and are often behind extortion attempts. The U.S. Embassy warns its personnel to drive with their doors locked and windows raised, to avoid travel outside of major metropolitan areas after dark."

"How about within the city after dark?" Jose' mused.

The ride was long…Jose' estimated that he had been on the floor of the van for over two hours. It also became a hard, bumpy ride. Jose' thought that they must be taking him somewhere in the hilly country outside of San Salvador. His body was aching and sore in ways he had never experienced before. He listened for any communication between the men. "They must be well trained," he thought because there was not one word spoken during the journey.

The van finally ground to a halt and the men in the vehicle sprang into action. He was lifted up by his bound hands and feet and hauled inside a structure. His captors removed the bag that had been covering Jose's head. Jose' allowed his eyes to adjust to the light in the room. He noticed that the structure had an earthen floor which was covered in straw. The men stood him up and rummaged through his pants pockets. His keys, wallet and cell phone were taken. The kidnappers knew enough to remove the battery from his phone and toss it on the table with his other personal effects. The GPS feature in the phone was now worthless.

The man Jose' assumed was the leader approached him and spoke in Spanish, demanding the numbers for his family and corporate offices. Jose' was initially dazed and weary from the lengthy ride and did not immediately answer. The man clobbered him with a backhand to his temple. Jose's brain felt like it would explode as he careened to the floor.

Two of the kidnappers man handled him back into the chair. The leader immediately hit him again with a backhand to the other temple. Jose' saw a blinding white light as he fell to the floor on the other side of the chair.

"Now you will answer!" the lead captor admonished with a raised hand, ready to strike again.

Jose's mind went blank as he fought back a wave of nausea. One of the men threw a bucket of tepid water into his face which gagged and revived him.

"My family is not here!" Jose' pleaded. "They are not to arrive until next month."

"I know all about that!" the leader screamed. "Do you think we are fools? You work for Lantal, you have been in country for five months, your family is in North Carolina as is the headquarters for your company. Their telephone numbers…Now!"

Jose' had come around enough to speak and gave them the numbers. As he did he realized that this had to be an inside job…they knew too much about him for this to be a random criminal act. The staged accident…they were not just after anybody they could grab, but they had been gunning for him!

"Who are you people…what do you want with me…why am I being held captive?" Jose' asked.

"You have been taken hostage by Mara Salvatrucha. You may have heard of us, no?" the leader replied. "We are also known as MS-13 by your country's FBI. We are fifty thousand strong and have many thousands living in your country. Most are in the Los Angeles area, but there are many in Charlotte, North Carolina. That is how we know of your company and its efforts to exploit our citizens in El Salvador."

"I do not know of your group," Jose' stated flatly. "Again, what do you want with me?"

"Money…lots of money…we hold you for ransom to make your family and your company pay for raping our land!" The leader continued. "How much do you think your life is worth?"

One of the gang picked up a pair of large cable cutters from a wooden table in the room. Jose' had not noticed the table before. He first cut through the duct tape that had bound Jose's wrists. In a single move he then grabbed for one of Jose's fingers and wrenched it toward the hand with the cutters. The blades were placed against both sides of the smallest finger.

"How much for a finger?" the leader asked.

With that the kidnapper squeezed the cutter's handle together, severing Jose's finger. Jose' gave a blood curdling scream and passed out. The man with the cutters gingerly picked up the severed finger and placed it in a small box.

"Get that to the American Embassy in San Salvador. Leave it at the gate!" the leader ordered. "Make sure to call them afterward so that they will find it. Here is the note identifying this man."

"You others get that hand disinfected and bandaged. Place him on the cot and rebind his wrists. We have no more use of him at this point!" he ordered.

Jose' drifted in and out of conscience. Mostly out.

Dubai, UAE

"Just received a call from the CIA. There's been a kidnapping in El Salvador! The victim's company had purchased a 'mini'. I've activated the device and we have a good signal coming from a remote location outside of San Salvador," Becky stated.

"Let's get the Denver team on alert...where's Lance?" I asked.

"Frankfurt!"

"Let's get Max on the phone," I ordered. "I'll call Lance to give him a 'head's up!'"

Denver, Colorado

Max Galloway gathered his team members around him.

"We have our first I.N.C.I.S.O.R. mission!" He stated.

"Duncan...you're in charge of getting the weapons readied, Powers... you're in charge of Intel, Lance...you coordinate with the CIA and get us a ride, Flex and I will work on the planning," Max ordered.

The five sprung into action and within hours they were ready. The CIA had tasked a G-500 for the mission and it was enroute to Denver. The distance between DIA and San Salvador was a little over seventeen hundred nautical miles. The powerful jet travelled at Mach .885 which comes close to 600 knots per hour. A quick calculation showed that the flight to El

Salvador would take a little under three hours. The necessary armaments had been passed out and the rescue plan was taking shape. There would be two vehicles awaiting their arrival at the Comalapa International Airport thirty one miles southeast of the city of San Salvador. The airport location was close to the Pacific Ocean.

The team members would leave the airport and travel forty five minutes up route 5 into San Salvador. The CIA had a safe house awaiting the team's arrival in the city. The five I.N.C.I.S.O.R. team members would spend the night at the safe house in San Salvador, and make their final assault plans. They would travel north two hours along route 4 to the little town of Colima. The signal was emanating from a remote area outside of the town. There was an aerial photograph of what appeared to be an abandoned mill of some sort. It was situated where there was water on the north side of a small peninsula. Farmland lay to the east. The area appeared to be heavily forested, which would make access and close surveillance a breeze.

Just as the five were heading to leave their new home outside of Denver International Airport, a report came in that the Embassy in San Salvador had received a package containing a finger. There was a note included inside the package that identified the man and the gang that was purportedly holding him. The finger was on its way to Langley for testing and identification. The I.N.C.I.S.O.R. team would know more once they arrived in El Salvador. Also, information about the kidnappers would be sent to the G-500 while they were enroute.

The mission was a go!

CHAPTER FOURTEEN

Outside Bushehr, Iran

"HEY, JACK! LOOK at the screen!" the techie shouted and gestured toward his computer monitor. The monitor was broken into quadrants with four videos from the unmanned Andros Mark V-A1. The Mark V was making a beeline for the nuclear reactor site, according to its onboard GPS tracking device. The forward looking video camera had shown some interesting debris in its path. The techie had switched the screen so that this forward looking video now was displayed on the whole screen.

The Mark V-A1's progress had been halted as the camera panned the area.

"Look's like what's left of a campsite," Jack commented. "Who would camp out here?"

"All of the organic material at the site would have been vaporized in the blast, being this close to the explosion," the computer tech added.

"Let's forget the original mission and do a thorough canvassing of this site. This location in the middle of nowhere is disturbing to me," Jack said.

Watching the screen, Jack pointed over the tech's shoulder, "What is that?"

"Looks like the remains of a book," the tech replied.

"Can you grab it with the robotic arm?" Jack asked.

"We're set up for soil samples, but I'll try. That's all I'll be able to get," the tech stated.

"Record the GPS coordinates, get that book and hightail that thing back to our site for recharging and decontamination!" Jack ordered and left the computer tech to his work.

"Will do," the tech responded as he began to move the robotic arm for the recovery task.

Frankfurt, Germany

Lance finished his call from Reggie in Dubai. He was told that the Denver team was handling this latest 'mini' alert. Lance felt his stomach turn inside itself. He knew that the team was experienced and well trained, but he still had a sense that he wanted to be there to help guide them. It was tough letting go of all this!

Lance turned to Stirling, Aaron and Dick and spoke, "The Denver team has a mission to Central America. A 'mini' has been activated because of a purported kidnapping. A gang of thugs, calling themselves Mara Salvatrucha, has sent a finger and ransom demands to the United States Embassy in San Salvador."

"Never heard of these guys," Stirling responded.

"Supposedly a big gang in Los Angeles," Lance replied.

"What do we do?" Dick asked.

"Nothing for now…let's finish up with our facility here so I can get back to Dubai," Lance ordered.

Washington, D.C.

"Mr. President," the aide said as he waited for President James attention. "It is confirmed. The cruise missile that hit Bushehr was ours. In fact we have identified the missile as an AGM-129 ACM."

"What the hell is that?" the President asked.

"It is an Advanced Cruise Missile. The Air Force has four hundred and eighty of the things. They are in the process of decommissioning the missiles and eliminating them from the arsenal. There was an incident at Barksdale Air Force Base in Louisiana. A group of missiles was flown from Minot Air Force Base in North Dakota…"

"I know where the damn bases are!" President James interrupted.

"…well, they were flown from Minot to Barksdale for decommissioning. The warheads were to be removed before the flight. Six of them were not disarmed, and the warheads were officially 'missing' for thirty six hours!"

"What a bunch of incompetents!" the President yelled at the ceiling.

"Well, on top of that, when they discovered what had happened, one of the six was never accounted for!" the aide added.

"Really! Missing! How would it get off the base?" the President mused. "One of the most advanced weapons in our arsenal just vanished?"

"Get me Netanyahu. I need to let him in on this awful news." President James spoke into the phone set on the desk inside the Oval Office.

Tel Aviv, Israel

"Mr. President…I am glad to hear from you," Mr. Netanyahu said into the speaker on his desk.

"I have good news for you and bad news for us," President James spoke.

"The missile that hit Bushehr was definitely one of ours…an advanced cruise missile that the United States has shared with none of its allies. We have discovered that one is missing from our arsenal. Is your country responsible for the theft?"

"How dare you make such an accusation!" the Prime Minister replied hotly. "I have vowed all along that this attack was not from our country!"

"Well, with the Israeli markings that were visible on the satellite image…I just wasn't sure," the President countered.

"This was a well planned setup…and nothing more…Israel looks like the culprit and is being blamed for the destruction at Bushehr. We must announce this news to the world that the attack did not come from Israel!" Mr. Netanyahu claimed.

"Hold your horses, there, Ben. The world will still blame your country until we know more about the markings. All we know now is that one of our advanced cruise missiles is unaccounted for. And the missing missile is the same type that struck Bushehr. Here's another twist…this type of missile can only be launched from a B-52 platform. When news of this information gets out it will look as if the United States and your country were both behind the attack! With all of the years that our countries have postured against Iran about the development of their nuclear program… and our threats to take out the facility before it became active! We both look guilty as hell!" President James added. "We must wait until more information is gathered together before we announce anything. For now you have to stay on the 'hot seat!'"

Outside Bushehr, Iran

"That's a Torah!" one of Jack's team members exclaimed as they viewed the tattered book in the decontamination chamber. "How could it survive the blast?"

"Maybe the sand had shifted and it was covered at the time," another team member offered.

"We will send the Mark V back to the site to gather up more of the debris…We will put the radiation sampling on hold until we recover more items from that campsite. What is a Hebrew Torah doing at a campsite outside of the Bushehr Nuclear Reactor?" Jack announced. "Was this an attack by Israel? I need to communicate this info back to FRMAC…see what they want us to do."

Aboard a G-550 enroute to El Salvador

Duncan Trevino briefed the four other team members about the new Intel. The gang, Mara Salvatrucha, was claiming responsibility for the attack and kidnapping of a United States citizen. The gang originated in Los Angeles in the 1980's to protect Salvadoran immigrants from the more well established Mexican and black gangs. The National Gang Threat Assessment estimates that there are about 50,000 MS-13 gang members worldwide, with about 10,000 residing in the United States. Al-Qaeda had met with Mara Salvatrucha asking the gang to smuggle Muslim operatives into the US. This was a strong and powerful organization…funding much of their operations through kidnapping and torture of innocent victims.

The I.N.C.I.S.O.R. team needed to assume that the severed finger belonged to the victim. Triage immediately, followed by immediate medical care needed to be planned for. All of the team members knew how to treat wounds in the field and the medical supplies were part of their armamentarium.

The team also had to be aware that MS-13 would have eyes and ears…a network of gang members…throughout the country of El Salvador. The I.N.C.I.S.O.R. team's presence would be known from the moment they landed…to the arrival at the safe house in San Salvador…to their journey north. Surprise was probably out of the question! There would be no communication with the outside world from the time they landed until they were 'wheels up' and out of El Salvadoran air space for fear of any communication being picked up and intercepted. Their team communication gear was highly encrypted and state of the art! The I.N.C.I.S.O.R. team all knew that communicating among each other with this gear was safe.

Dubai, UAE

"Reggie! Take a look at this!" Becky yelled from the office.

I rushed in from the patio to see what the commotion was about.

"I was going through Grace's drawer in the desk. I knew that she was working on an insignia for I.N.C.I.S.O.R. but I had no idea what kind of progress she had made. Look at this!" Becky said as she held up the artwork.

I viewed the paper and reached to take it gingerly from Becky's hands.

"Wow, what a great legacy for her. Let's get an engraver and an embroiderer involved for shirts, jackets and hats!" I exclaimed. "Wait 'til Ash sees this! Have you heard anything from him…I haven't heard a thing."

"No calls, texts or emails," Becky replied. "He has not been in touch for awhile. You want me to call?"

"Let's leave him alone. He needs to get through whatever is going on with him about Grace's death. We can't help with that process. He has to do it on his own. We all seem to go through the same cycle of grief…with the denial…anger…acceptance stuff, but it's how long each phase takes that is the unknown. He'll be back when he's good and ready!" I finished.

"Also, take a look at this!" Becky added and showed me a diagram. "Cyndi was right…Iraq has strong missile defenses in and around Bushehr. The reactor is protected by four HAWK sites and an HQ-2 battery. The circles indicate the overlapping areas of protection. The Bushehr Air Base also has an S-200 battery."

"What's a HAWK?" I asked.

Becky looked around the office for her reading glasses.

"They're around your neck, my love," I pointed.

"I need about twenty pairs of these things the way I lose them!" Becky exclaimed.

Becky donned her glasses and read from her notes. "The HAWK is a medium range surface to air missile. It was initially designed to destroy aircraft, but has been modified to also destroy other missiles in flight."

How about that! And the HQ-2 battery?" I asked.

Again, from her notes. "HQ stands for HongQi. It is a Chinese system. It is a long range medium to high altitude surface to air missile system. The missiles are two stage rockets and it is a very old system developed in the mid '60's."

"And the battery around the air base?"

The S-200 is a Russian missile defense system. NATO calls it the SA-5 Gammon. It is a very long range medium to high altitude surface to air missile system. It is designed to defend large areas from bomber attack or other strategic aircraft. The fire control radar can be linked to other longer range radar systems. Again, developed in the mid '60's. Iran has about two hundred of these launchers," Becky read. "I have pictures too! Want to see?"

Becky handed me the photographs.

"But they'd have radar operating on all of these systems!" I said. "In fact, it just hit me…the sites should be part of a long range radar defense system. Something should have shown up on their radar!"

"Haven't heard anything from Tehran. You'd think that if they had a radar track on an incoming missile that they'd be screaming about it and using that info as proof of the attack!" Becky replied.

"Interesting. I wonder if they got any defensive missile shots off. Or were they all asleep at the wheel!"

CHAPTER FIFTEEN

El Salvador

THE FIVE TEAM members disembarked from the G-550. They had donned tourist clothes and told the airport authorities that they had come on a golf outing. The last thing these men looked like were corporate types who wanted a getaway from their wives back in the States! Even the golf disguises, including hats, wigs, sunglasses and ridiculous plaids could not hide the well muscled physiques! A trained eye would have seen through it all, but not the customs agent on duty. Anyway, it was siesta time and he was tired and bored with his job.

The two cars made their way northwest toward San Salvador and the safe house. The traffic on route five was quite congested. The distance from the airport was only twenty six miles, but very slow going. It reminded the team members of a point in their briefing…El Salvador was the smallest of the Central American countries and also the most densely populated. El Salvador is roughly the size of all of the Hawaiian Islands put together, but with a population of over six million people!

With the blackened car windows the outside traffic could not observe the men in the two cars. There was no doubt that there were cars and plants along the way following the cars to their destination. The local CIA operative had arranged a bit of a switcharoo that the I.N.C.I.S.O.R. team was unaware of…The two cars pulled into the Hilton Princess San Salvador. The brightly clad men disembarked and entered the hotel while the cars pulled into an underground garage. Two different cars were waiting to offload the luggage, as the five men took the elevator to the garage level.

The two new cars now departed the hotel property…also being watched… but the observers had no idea that the newly arrived team was on board!

The safe house was a short drive from the hotel. The cars entered a garage and the door was lowered. The five men plus the two drivers entered the house. The drivers busied themselves in the small kitchen, preparing food for dinner.

Lance Everett found a laptop in the den and began punching buttons and making sure that he was on a secure and encrypted satellite link. He checked on the latest Intel. They had not been out of communication for terribly long, but things can change. The finger had been delivered to Langley and the CIA had confirmation that the kidnap victim was one Jose' Venerable'.

Powers and Flex busied themselves with preparing the gear for the assault to begin in the morning. There were four sets of identical weaponry. The men had decided to use the same handguns and automatic assault rifles so that they could share ammunition and parts in the case of a failure. The only difference to the fifth set was a sniper rifle with a night scope.

One of the major first hurdles that the teams had to debate and decide upon was the old argument about which was the best handgun. The debate had raged on for years and still there was no clear winner. The 9mm versus the .45 caliber. The .45 caliber proponents asked the simple question, "Would you rather be hit by a golf ball or a bowling ball?" The 9mm camp states, "I feel more secure with fifteen shots than the seven to nine in the larger caliber."

The argument seemed to boil down to momentum versus kinetic energy.

Momentum is simply the bullet's mass times its velocity. A bullet's momentum can be thought of as how much 'push' or 'shove' it has. Can the bullet knock a man off his feet? None of the commonly used handguns today can knock a man off his feet.

Kinetic energy is the ability to do work based on the bullet's speed. It is defined by one half the bullet's mass times its velocity squared. A bullet's energy goes up dramatically as its speed increases. Therefore, some 9mm loads would have more stopping power that the larger .45 caliber.

The team members then discussed their combat training. The assault rifles could be fired as single shots or bursts. Handguns were different.

None of the men had been trained to fire single shots…double tap to the chest and on to the brain…three shots fired in succession.

The debate over the stopping power of a single bullet depending on caliber didn't much matter. Three shots would bring down any man! And the team members were extremely accurate!

So, the 9mm handgun won the battle for now. Fifteen rounds made more sense than seven. Five men could be taken out with one clip before the need to reload. The Glock was the weapon of choice because failures were so rare. The gun could literally be dragged through the mud and still fire! The choice was the G-17 Gen 4. This gun actually had a magazine capacity of nineteen with a reversible enlarged magazine catch which was changeable in seconds. It also accommodated left or right-handed operators. The 9 mm. ammunition was produced by Cor-Bon with 115 grains of powder and the highest velocity at 1350 feet per second. Hollow points were the bullet of choice…these were killing bullets, not stopping bullets.

The utility belts contained four extra clips, so that each man carried almost a hundred rounds.

The Special Operations Forces Combat Assault Rifle, or SCAR-H, also known as the MK 17 was the rifle of choice for the men of I.N.C.I.S.O.R. The rifle fired a 7.62x51mm NATO round and the bullets could be designed to expand, tumble or fragment in tissue to give very effective terminal performance. Four of the men on each team carried this weapon. One was designated as a sniper and carried the M 40A5 with an effective range of 1000 yards. The term 'sniper' was interchangeable among the team members as they were all excellent marksmen, and Flex Lawson had the sniper designation on this mission.

The communications gear was checked next. The men each wore an INVISIO bone conduction headset. The bone conduction microphone is located on the exact spot in the ear where the mandible meets the ear canal. This provides ultimate clarity that doesn't rely on sound directly from the mouth. Communications are possible even when the face is covered with a gas mask, respirator or re-breather apparatus. Also there is little ambient noise to interfere with communication. The Kevlar woven cables allow for an increased range of head movement.

And finally, the vests were examined. The new vests had 28 layers of Kevlar body armor. They provided level IIIa ballistic protection, level II stab protection and level II spike protection. Over the years, the weight had been reduced drastically with these vests weighing in at six and a half pounds.

Each man also sported a Blackhawk knife made famous by the United Kingdom Special Forces.

ATN PS23-4 fourth generation night vision goggles were also there for each of the team members. Each set sported a camera which would stream video back to a unit in the car.

Dinner was ready when the equipment check was completed.

The men ate in silence except for Lance's update on the new Intel. It had been confirmed by Langley that the finger belonged to the kidnap victim known as Jose' Venerable'. His picture was passed around the table. The five men committed his face to memory. The latest satellite image showed that there were five cars on the property outside of Colima. There was no way to know the number of gang members that were at the site.

The satellite photo didn't show any signs of defensive preparations being made to the site. At some point the gang members would have to expect a military assault by the El Salvadoran army. Maybe they didn't expect an assault to happen so quickly. Negotiations had not yet begun. There would be rounds of negotiation and maybe an agreed upon settlement before an attack by the military. At least that's how it happened in the movie 'Proof of Life".

The team's 'ace in the hole' was the undiscovered mini. The five men had listened intently to Lance Wood's tale of the rescue of the Italian dignitary. They heard about the quick response and only the single guard at the villa. They heard about the arrests by the Italian authorities of other Red Brigade members following the successful raid.

There were lots of areas around the property to provide cover...both for the team members and the kidnappers. The two cars would depart at 0300, and the teams would deploy under the cover of darkness at 0500.

Each man took a bed and slept the few hours before the mission was to start.

0500 Outside Colima

It looked to the five team members that they had caught the gang members of Mara Salvatrucha sleeping. The two cars did not pick up any surveillance on the two hour journey north.

The men were all dressed in black for the pre-dawn rescue. They applied black grease paint to their faces, even Powers who was already dark complected.

The men took up their initial positions around the abandoned mill. Flex found high ground for his sniper position and performed a slow sweep of the grounds with his rifle scope. He could see five sentries positioned around the entrance. Flex communicated their positions to the four other members of his team. The sentries were all stationary. Not one guard was making rounds. "What poor tactical planning!" Flex thought.

The assault team would move in slowly on the sentry positions. Stealth and night maneuvers, along with the night vision goggles were skills that would give the I.N.C.I.S.O.R. team an immediate advantage.

With knives drawn, the four men each eliminated a sentry. Flex fired one suppressed round that took out the fifth sentry. Then, they waited... and watched for movement. There were no walkie talkies or any other form of communication gear on the five sentries. Only cell phones.

The team advanced on the shed where the mini was sending out its signal, under the watchful eye of Flex from his sniper position. As they advanced, explosive devices were placed in the vehicles and other points around the compound to hinder any counterattack as they made their egress. Max and Duncan took up positions of either side of the entrance to the shed, as Lance and Powers took up flanking positions on either side of the shed. The team members had not noticed any movement or sound coming from the other buildings in the compound.

Max crouched in front of the door to the shed. He began to open it as quietly as he could. The door opened about six inches and then banged into some sort of obstacle!

"Hey!" came a shout from the other side of the door.

Max came up from his crouch and put his shoulder into the door. He crashed through the door, sending the gang member that had been sleeping in a chair just inside the door sprawling onto the earthen floor.

A quick double tap to the chest and one in the forehead silenced the gang member forever. Max rolled to his left as Duncan ran into the room and rolled to his right. The cot lay to the far side of the room. Three other MS-13 members lay sleeping on opposite walls of the room. The three had been startled out of their slumber by the shout. They were on their knees and raising their weapons.

Everyone in the compound…the good guys and the bad guys heard the gunfire. The element of surprise was definitely gone now!

Max and Duncan each took out the gang member closest to them. The third managed to fire his weapon, spraying the room with bullets. He must not have seen his assailant's locations because he fired wildly until the magazine was empty and the gun fell silent. He threw the weapon on the floor, quickly pulled out a knife and made for the cot.

Duncan reached the kidnapper first and grabbed for the knife hand while placing his other hand around the man's neck. Duncan knew that ten seconds of pressure on the carotid artery would render the man helpless, but that could be a long ten seconds! He manhandled the man's knife hand with his own superior strength and the kidnapper's elbow buckled. The kidnapper's own knife plunged into his gut and blood began spewing from the open wound. Duncan released his grip as the man crumbled to the dirt floor.

Jose' lay whimpering on the cot curled up in a fetal position with his back to the action. Duncan and Max both grabbed him and got him off of the cot. Jose's hand was loosely bandaged.

"We are here to rescue you. Can you move?" Max shouted at Jose'

Jose' nodded his head and began to teeter toward the door. Max and Duncan took up positions on either side of Jose' and helped him stagger toward the open door.

"We have the package and we're on the move!" Duncan whispered into his microphone.

Just then gunfire erupted from the building to the left of the shed. Splinters of wood scattered around the room. Max and Duncan hit the ground and pulled Jose' down with them.

"I'm on it!" Powers yelled as he began to return fire.

"Three muzzle flashes," Flex announced as he took aim from his sniper position. He let loose one round from his rifle. "Two muzzle flashes, now!" he stated as calmly as he could.

Lance moved around the shed to help Powers return fire. As he did, there was another flash of gunfire from the building to his right. Lance felt the impact on his chest and was knocked to the ground.

Powers continued to lay down cover fire and yelled for the three to get a move on!

Max and Duncan scooped Jose' up like a bag of potatoes and threw him out the door. They fired at the building to the left as they ran for cover. Powers then joined them on the retreat.

"Where's Lance?" Max asked as they ran.

"Saw him take a hit as he rounded the shed," Flex said into his earpiece. "He's still down."

"I'm on it!" Powers yelled and headed for the back of the shed. He saw the eerie glow of Lance's body as it lay still on the ground. He could not see any movement. Powers knelt down to feel for a pulse, just as Lance let out a soft moan. "Good!" Powers thought.

Lance began to stir, but the wind was gone from his lungs. He was gasping for air as Powers helped him to a kneeling position.

"You okay?" Powers asked.

"Hurts like hell!" Lance groaned. "Must have some cracked ribs…don't feel any warm, sticky stuff."

"Can you move?" Powers replied. "We must get moving!"

"Help me up," Lance grunted as his breaths began to return, although they were really labored.

Flex watched the scene unfold in his night scope. "You two move around the shed on my side…the other three are about thirty yards ahead of you…no bad guys on this side…the shed will give you some cover."

Gunfire was erupting from three of the surrounding buildings. The I.N.C.I.S.O.R. team had the advantage of the darkness and their night vision goggles, but they were clearly outgunned.

Flex saw one of the gang members move outside from the cover of the building and quickly eliminated him with a single shot.

Powers and Lance had closed the distance and rejoined Max and Duncan and the freed hostage. They used the heavy brush to aid them in their getaway. The cars were only fifty yards ahead. The MS-13 gang members were lighting up the night with their inaccurate sprays of gunfire. Tracers were seen going in all directions! Several of the gang began to creep out of the buildings and to chase after the I.N.C.I.S.O.R. team. Flex dropped one more gang member then reached for the remote control. He clicked the button six times and explosions in the buildings and cars engulfed the compound. "That should hold them for awhile!" Flex thought as he policed up his sniper position. The plan was to meet up with the escaping cars five hundred yards down the road.

With the compound in flames behind them, the five men covered the distance to the two cars in a crouching sprint. Max and Duncan placed Jose' in the back seat of one car, with Duncan joining him to provide emergency care to Jose's hand. Max got behind the wheel and started the vehicle. Powers helped Lance into the back seat and then took the driver's position and started his car. The two vehicles sped off toward the town of Colima. The darkness was giving way to a spectacular sunrise. The men shed their night vision headgear and checked their weaponry. The cars both made a brief stop as Flex joined Powers and Lance. Flex placed his sniper rifle into the trunk and picked up his assault rifle. He also grabbed the first aid kit and box of ammunition and moved to the back seat so that he could offer Lance any first aid.

As the two cars sped south toward San Salvador, the five team members took time to regroup and reload. So far, so good! They had conquered the objective and had their hostage freed and in tow. Although dehydrated and in much pain from the amputation, Jose' seemed okay. Duncan immediately gave Jose' two shots. One was a powerful antibiotic and the other a powerful narcotic for the pain. As Jose' slumped back in the car seat, Duncan gently unwrapped the filthy bandage placed haphazardly around Jose's hand and cleansed the wound. The hand was then rewrapped with sterile bandages.

They were about an hour north of San Salvador when a rag tag caravan of cars and trucks was spotted speeding north to intercept them. Max was driving the lead car and observed the gaggle of cars and trucks first.

"Trouble coming!" Max announced. The men all watched as the distance closed quickly between the northbound vehicles and their two southbound cars. There looked to be six vehicles coming at them with guns bristling from every window! There was a slim chance that they wouldn't be recognized, but their blacked out windows gave them away when they were abreast of the oncoming cars. The team members also knew that their pursuers would have called ahead with descriptions of the two automobiles.

Gunfire erupted from the cars as the drivers locked their steering wheels to the left to cross over the road and intercept the I.N.C.I.S.O.R. vehicles. The gunfire was inaccurate as the pursuing cars careened around behind them. Soon they recovered and the chase was on! Men were leaning out of the windows on both sides of the gang cars as they sped to close the distance.

Lance and Flex initially crouched low in the back seat. It wasn't long before bursts from the gunmen shattered the back window of their car. Now they sat up and took aim on the first chase car. Lance killed the driver and Flex shot out the left front tire. The car skidded sideways and then began to roll. The two men hanging out of the passenger side windows were immediately cut in half on the first roll. As the car tumbled to a halt, the car immediately behind it crashed into it. There was a massive explosion as the two cars ignited into a fireball right in the middle of the road.

The four other vehicles were slowed briefly as they picked their way around the burning hulks. The two retreating I.N.C.I.S.O.R. cars sped off to create a decent distance between the others.

"You guys okay?" Max asked as he had seen the action in his rear view mirror.

"Everybody's good," came the response from Powers.

In the early dawn the traffic was light, but picking up. They still had a half an hour to the city of San Salvador and another forty five minutes to the airport. The men talked as they sped south. The decision was made to make a beeline for the airport and skirt the city. By now every Mara Salvatrucha gang member in San Salvador was awake and gunning for them.

"Call the Embassy!" Flex said into his headset. "See if they can get the El Salvadoran Army to help out at all."

"Good idea, Flex!" Duncan replied as he pulled out his cell phone and dialed the Embassy.

"Whoa!" Powers spoke. "They're moving up on us quickly! Get ready for more action!"

Flex and Lance aimed their assault rifles out of the space where the rear window had been. The MS-13 drivers must have learned from observing the demise of the first two vehicles because they drove wildly and erratically, swerving from side to side and attempting to flank the two I.N.C.I.S.O.R. cars on the shoulder and opposite traffic lane. Route 4 between Colima and San Salvador had nice, graded and wide shoulders which proved ideal for the MS-13 gang to overtake their prey. The drivers crouched down in their seats and made for difficult targets at these speeds.

Sporadic gunfire came from the shooters in the side windows as the pursuers swerved from side to side. Lance returned fire as the cars swerved to the left, and Flex fired when they approached on the right.

At one point Powers had a thought and began to slow down and lag behind Max's car.

"What are you doing?" Flex yelled. "They're gaining on us!"

"Ever see 'Top Gun'?" Max asked. I'm sucking them in…watch this!"

A car pulled up on the left flank and one pulled onto the shoulder on the right flank. The gunmen were firing rapidly at the car. Flex and Lance returned fire. Powers yelled, "Hold on!" and first stomped on the brake pedal, downshifted and then floored the accelerator pedal. The car immediately screeched as the four tires locked, sending the pursuing cars slightly ahead of the car. The pursuing drivers both hit their brakes and began fishtailing as they lost control.

Power's car then jumped forward and just cleared the two cars on the side as they careened together with the sound of screeching metal and then split apart wildly veering off to opposite sides of the road. The car on the right smashed into a tree, killing all the occupants instantly. The car on the left barely missed an oncoming truck, hit the shoulder at a high rate of speed and flipped over.

"Two more down!" Powers yelled as he sped forward to join up with Max's car.

"How you guys doing back there?" Max asked. "You're having all the fun!"

"Want to switch?" Lance said. "Glad to share the fun."

"No, no," Powers said. "You two take care of our package! We'll continue to play your wingman."

"Not far from the north end of the city," Max replied.

"Two vehicles still left and they're coming for us," Flex said.

"Stay on it!" Duncan cheered as he watched out the rear window of the first car.

The pursuing truck got close enough to the trailing I.N.C.I.S.O.R. car to hit its bumper and left side quarter panel. This maneuver, named in police circles as the Pursuit Intervention Technique, or Tactical Vehicle Intervention, caused the car to spin wildly around so that it was facing northbound in the southbound lane. Most drivers would lose control of their vehicle, but Powers had experienced this move at FLETC while taking the Offensive Driving Course as one part of the Vehicle Ambush Countermeasures Training Program (VACTP). Before the car had reached the half turn, he had placed the gear shift into reverse and gunned the accelerator. He emptied his pistol out the open driver's door window into the truck's windshield. The front seat occupants were sprayed with his 9mm hollow point bullets and died immediately. The truck driver flung the steering wheel to the right which sent the truck rolling onto the shoulder and ejecting the six occupants in the bed.

The final car driver made a wise move and kept up the pursuit at a safe distance behind the two I.N.C.I.S.O.R. cars. He had watched many of his gang members perish in the reckless attempts to overtake them. He had also called ahead to San Salvador and knew that an ambush was hastily being assembled and that they would be ready in time!

Max's cell phone began to chirp. He looked at the screen and recognized the number of the US Embassy in San Salvador. He listened into the receiver…

"There is a roadblock set up to intercept you at Diagonal Cipactly… remember where the four lanes turned into two as you headed north?" the Head of Embassy Security said.

"Yes I do…any way around it?" Max replied.

"Yes…follow my instructions exactly…we are seeing real time images downloaded to our facility by the CIA satellite that is following the 'mini'," the Security Chief stated.

"Hey, that's pretty cool stuff!" Max exclaimed.

"You're coming up on Calle California…turn left and I'll guide you through the backstreets to hook up with route five to the airport! It'll be just like those street guidance applications in your phone in the states, but I will be the little voice telling you to turn right and left. And if you miss following my directions, I'll be the voice calling you an ass!

Also, the Army has agreed to help and is enroute to the ambush site."

"We're all yours!" Max replied.

The pursuing car observed the two I.N.C.I.S.O.R. cars exit route four onto Calle California and phoned ahead to the gang member in charge of the ambush. He began to scramble the MS-13 gang members who had set up the ambush site into their vehicles to enter the chase. Just at that moment two El Salvadoran helicopters opened fire on their ambush positions, killing many of the gang members and pinning the others down. Two trucks attempted to flee and were destroyed by air to ground missiles fired by the choppers.

Flex and Lance knew that they could not continue to have this car behind them reporting on their progress. Flex timed the pursuer's lag time and had Powers adjust his speed so that the pursuit car was four seconds behind. Flex and Lance each grabbed two M-67 grenades. These grenades had a pyrotechnic delay M 213 fuse which gave them four seconds from pulling the 'spoon' to detonation. Lance pulled the spoons on his two grenades and dropped them out of the missing back window…Flex followed suit a second later. The four grenades clattered to the pavement while the two men watched.

The grenades exploded just as the pursuit vehicle drove over them. The car leaped into the air and fell on its side. There was immediately a second explosion as the gas tank erupted and the car was incinerated.

Max followed his instructions and Powers followed as the two cars made a slow circuit through San Salvador. They entered route five without incident and headed for the airport. Duncan called ahead to alert the pilots to have the G-550 ready to go.

About halfway enroute to the airport the men noticed that they had air cover! A drab green El Salvadoran Army chopper had joined them and was providing cover. All of the men…except Jose'…relaxed, knowing that the helicopter 'had their six'. As they made their way onto the circle drive, known as the Autopista Comalapa, at the airport the I.N.C.I.S.O.R. team took note of the Army trucks parked on both sides of the airport entrance. They knew that the most dangerous leg of an escape is a shootout while the Gulfstream builds speed for takeoff. That is when the aircraft is most vulnerable. This time, the El Salvadoran army had their backs and the departure on runway 7 was unremarkable and safe.

Denver, Colorado

The Denver team members of I.N.C.I.S.O.R. had all survived their first test. The skills that they all had acquired during their time in the military had proved invaluable. The training courses at FLETC were more than they expected!

The Gulfstream had dropped the team off in Denver and was on its way to North Carolina, giving Jose' a first class ride back to his family. The men had heard that there was a slim chance that the severed finger may be able to be reattached because of their quick response time. One of the hospitals in Winston Salem had a team of surgeons ready to reunite Jose's hand and finger.

It was time for the men to let their hair down for a night of football and beers at Champs.

CHAPTER SIXTEEN

Los Angeles, California

"HOW IS THIS possible?" the MS-13 gang leader asked.

Many Mara Salvatrucha gang members had gathered in the leader's crib after hearing about the shootout in El Salvador. These thugs sported the blue and white gang colors of the El Salvadoran flag. Their upper torsos were covered in gang ink, or tattoos. It was the motliest crew ever assembled in one place. Besides having their limbs, necks and faces sporting various gang art and tattoos of violent creatures, skulls and other satanic images, the gang members donned clothing that was many sizes too large for their bodies. The pants collectively hung down below their buttocks. Some wore bandanas, others had caps worn askew.

The pants hanging low was a look that began in the prisons of America. It signified to the prison population that the particular inmate was available for homosexual sex. The prisoner was announcing that they were willing to be the 'girlfriend' for other inmates. In the mid to late '90's the released inmates continued the prison fashion on the streets. A funny walk had to be learned to keep the pants from falling down around their ankles. Kids thought it was 'cool' to sport this gangsta look. Many were just wannabes…but not this bunch.

This group had caused a progressive increase in violent crime in America and had a careless disregard for law enforcement. Many a gang member had threatened and even attacked law enforcement officials. So many of the MS-13 gang were in prisons around the country that the leaders began to think that fewer tattoos may be better so that the gang members didn't stand out so badly on the streets.

MS-13 had become the most feared gang in the United States. Their criminal activities included drug smuggling, gun running, hits for hire, people smuggling, theft, drug sales, arson and strong-arming the local merchants. They had affiliations with Mexican gangs. Many were expert in the use of the Machete and would leave dismembered bodies at the crime scene. The FBI MS-13 National Joint Task Force labeled the threat from this gang in Los Angeles to be "high". Gang members from Los Angeles had an elevated status with the other gangs around the country. The gang members actively recruited in the junior high schools and high schools. In the poor neighborhoods with both parents working, recruiting new members was relatively easy.

"We had just left the demand letter and severed finger of our hostage in El Salvador at the United States Embassy the day before. It should have taken the FBI and State Department longer than a day to verify the identity from the finger and to begin to formulate a response to our demands!" the leader continued.

There were grumblings around the room but none of the gang members articulated a verbal response.

"How is it possible that an attack team has swooped in and freed the hostage? What was his name?"

"Jose' Venerable'," the second in command replied. "He worked for that company in Winston-Salem, North Carolina. I think they have textile plants in El Salvador exploiting the cheap labor in our homeland!"

"Get that chapter in North Carolina going on what happened. With all of the men that we lost I want revenge! Find another American firm that we can hold for ransom in our homeland," the MS-13 gang leader ordered.

Colorado Springs, Colorado

It had been some time since Ashonte' Black, nee Ash Black, had said his final goodbye to Grace. He buried her alone. No family or friends in attendance. That's how he wanted it. He had been numb for so many days since the explosion in Jerusalem and news of her death.

On this particular morning Ash awakened with a newfound energy and resolve. He was going to become a new man with a new image. He began to write out a list of all of his attributes, good and bad. Ash then closed his eyes and imagined what he would become. He made a second list with these features and then set out to compare and combine the two lists.

He placed a call to Dubai. He'd be back in the game in a little while. Just needed a bit more time…

Outside Bushehr, Iran

Jack addressed the twenty scientists and some of the Iranian soldiers that gathered around him. "We have now recovered several items from the campsite. All of the items, from the Torah to this laser sighting device," he held up the piece of equipment, "are Israeli made. There is no explanation for these things being here except that this campsite was used to guide the missile attack on Bushehr. All of this evidence," he waved his hand over the table of items, "is very damning for Israel."

"Digital images have already been relayed back to FRMAC in Nevada. We have requested that a plane be sent to pick up these things and get them to the United States."

Viktor spoke up at this point.

"Russia concurs that the devices need to be analyzed by your CIA. Russia condemns Israel for their involvement in this attack!"

"We will get back to analyzing the radiation in the area," Jack continued. "Our task is nearly complete. We should be heading home within the week."

Captain Jafar then offered to drive the collected items to the closest town with an airport. "Shiraz has an airfield considered to be the second most reliable behind Imam Khomeini Airport in Tehran. It is less than two hundred miles from here…about a five hour drive."

Jack considered the offer and made the decision that he would ride along with the Iranian Captain. He wanted the items to get to the United States and not end up being cursed in some Iranian mosque. He told Captain Jafar of his decision and the Captain reluctantly agreed.

Jack placed a call to FRMAC in Nevada. Dr. Suttmiller told him that there was a plane available in Dubai. Jack told him that they would leave at first light and to have the plane there at noon. He didn't want to linger in Shiraz as he wanted to return to his scientists.

Dr. Suttmiller said that he would take care of the arrangements and also to have a jet capable of long range flight waiting at the Dubai Airport to ferry the items to the United States.

Dubai, UAE

I looked up information about the Shiraz airport when my call from Dr. Suttmiller was over. "Pretty demanding!" I thought…I had to drop everything and fly to this airport in the morning. At least it was close. This distance looked to be about 350 miles. I'd be able to get there in under an hour. With a little luck I'd be able to complete the round trip and be back for a late lunch with Becky!

I also checked the distance from Bushehr…178 miles…plenty far to be out of harm's way.

I wondered why the scientists at Bushehr were wanting items flown out of Iran and on to the United States. "Need to know," had been Dr. Suttmiller's response. He did not know that I.N.C.I.S.O.R. had been asked by Israel to help solve this 'whodunit'. I could wait to find out from the CIA what was up.

Dr. Suttmiller also informed me that my 'ferry' services were not going to be necessary after this trip. The scientists were wrapping things up and would be vacating Iran within the week. The initial reading was that the area would remain too hot or inhabitable for many, many years to come.

I told Becky about the call and my short mission the next morning. It hit me that I hadn't had the plane out since my trip to Cairo. With Ash and Lance away, and the events unfolding within I.N.C.I.S.O.R., I hadn't had Aurora out for any fun hops. I also thought about what Dr. Suttmiller had said…they wouldn't need the plane any more. Good time to get the paint job going and transform the Avanti II into Aurora from the outside! I let the paint shop know that I'd be dropping the plane off after my jaunt tomorrow. They had a great paint scheme ready, and they'd show it to me on the computer when I got back. The owner of the paint shop also said that he could put Aurora's cabin back together! That was great news to my ears.

Port Rashid, Dubai

"Look at this place!" Graham exclaimed.

Graham and Magnus had taken a taxi from the Dubai International Airport to Port Rashid where they were to board the cruise ship that was awaiting their arrival.

"I googled this place before we left, Magnus said. "Port Rashid is another man-made island that was completed in 1973. It was originally designed to handle all of the sea traffic into and out of Dubai. By the end of 2008 all cargo operations were moved to the Jebel Ali Port. Dubai then redeveloped Port Rashid to become solely a cruise terminal for the ocean liners cruising the Arabian Gulf."

"The Jebel Ali Port is the world's largest man-made harbor and the biggest port in the Middle East. It is home to over five thousand companies from one hundred and twenty countries. Jebel Ali has also become the most frequently visited port by the US Navy outside of the United States. A Nimitz class Aircraft Carrier group can be accommodated pierside!"

"This new Cruise Ship Terminal just opened in 2010," Magnus continued. "Isn't it spectacular?"

"And how about that flight over here! I've never flown first class but knew that those people got free drinks, better meals and wider seats, but that was insane! Sleeping berths! Really!" Graham exclaimed.

"It depends on who you fly. Emirates Air gets my vote for the best airline in the world! I've never been treated so well…and that A-380 Airbus! What a monster!" Magnus added.

"Twelve and a half hours…I was really dreading being on a plane that long. I was not ready for what we had! Two showers in first class! What a great treat to freshen up. Then the two lounges upstairs! I think we put a hurt on their beer supply!" Graham said.

"Then those private cabins…I figured that the seat would recline, but not change into a complete bed! Did you use the mini bar?" Magnus chuckled.

"I thought the Middle East was dry…boy was I wrong!" Graham added. "How'd we swing this deal, anyway?"

"I entered a contest on the radio. I was chosen as the caller and had like eight minutes to call in and answer their question. I got it right! The prize was this cruise for two!" Magnus said, "And here we are!"

"Beats the hell out of those military transports with those webbed seats. I hope we never have to travel that way again!"

"I feel like royalty…hope the ship is as nice…let's get on board this monster."

Graham and Magnus made their way up the gangplank and were shown the way to their cabins.

Tel Aviv, Israel

Gary Kubetz hung up the phone from a call from Becky Nelson. "She's right!" he exclaimed out loud. "Iran has an antiquated but adequate air defense system. Their radar would have picked up an incoming missile… from anywhere! Why is there nothing coming out of Tehran about tracking an inbound missile to the Bushehr reactor?"

"There is no record anywhere, or from any country about a missile being tracked from here or a United States B-52. In fact, there were no American bombers in the air over the Middle East that day. Aren't the B-52's tasked out of Aviano, Italy?" the Lieutenant asked.

"No, that's just a fighter base…don't know where they would have come from," Kubetz replied.

Baghdad, Iraq

The MADEI terrorist cell members were gathered at the same ramshackle structure in downtown Baghdad. Abdullah called the group to order with a quick prayer to Allah and once again remembering Farroukh and Hamid who were martyred in the missile attack on Bushehr.

"It is now time for planning our second attack against Israel. We will take on the persona of the Iranian terrorist organization, al-Qaeda," Abdullah began.

"But we have a strong Al-Qaeda cell right here in Baghdad," one member countered.

"Silence!" Abdullah yelled angrily. "Al-Qaeda is everywhere in the Middle East! We must make the attack look like it began with the same six Iranian members named by the United States government. He read from a Wall Street Journal article…"The Great Satan formally acknowledged the connection between the world's most dangerous terrorist group and the leading state sponsor of terrorism. In a move by the Treasury Department, six members of a terrorist network based in Iran were sanctioned for serving as 'the core pipeline through which al Qaeda moves money, facilitators and operative from across the Middle East to South Asia,' principally meaning Pakistan and Afghanistan. The leader of the group, Ezedin Abdul Aziz Khalil is a Syrian who has been operating from Iran...." Abdullah put down the newspaper. "The Great Satan has just acknowledged the connection this year. It is important that we act now and assume these identities so that it appears that Iran is retaliating against Israel's attack that we have so cleverly disguised!"

Abdullah then threw down a pamphlet onto the floor. The title read, 'Military Studies in the Jihad Against the Tyrants'. "This is al-Qaeda's manual on reconnaissance and materials best used in an attack. You will all read this! You will see that they look for buildings with much glass so that the glass becomes attack weapons when the building is blown up. Also, tires and kerosene burn extremely well and that public information can provide 80 percent of the information needed about a possible target."

"One of the cell members picked up the pamphlet and began to thumb through the pages. "I will begin to find a target in Tel Aviv on the internet. I will look for a building with many windows."

"You have one week to do your research," Abdullah commanded. "You others work on how we can smuggle materials into Israel so that we can build a car bomb that will kill and maim many. I will meet with my al-Qaeda friend and pick his brain...One week!"

Langley, Virginia

"You've got to see this transcript...we have an active cell that we did not know about before! That PC that Dr. Nelson implanted just a week ago picked up this conversation," the computer operator told his supervisor. "They are planning an attack against Israel...they want to make it look like an al-Qaeda attack which began in Iran!"

The supervisor began to read through the transcript and then jumped to his feet. He quickly reached for the phone and pressed the speed dial button for the Head of the CIA. "I need to see the Director ASAP!"

He left his post and made a beeline for the Director's office. After showing his identification badge to the secretary, he was ushered into the Director's private office. The Director, or DCI as he's known in Washington circles, did not rise to greet the supervisor.

"What's on your mind? What's so important that you had to get right down here?" the Director asked.

"This just came in," the supervisor huffed, a little out of breath. "Look at the transcript of the prayer at the beginning!"

"There is mention of the Bushehr attack," the Director noted. "What else do we have on this terrorist cell...what do they call themselves? The MADEI?"

"We have very little, sir...we just picked up this from a recently implanted PC," the supervisor answered.

"Ah yes, that's that CUSPID group in Dubai," the DCI replied.

"No, sir, it's I.N.C.I.S.O.R.!" the supervisor responded.

"Molar...incisor...I don't care! Well, let's assign a task force and open up a file on this MADEI terrorist cell," the DCI ordered.

"On it, sir...what about the Bushehr reference?" the supervisor asked.

"We've already got people working on that...I'll get this memo to them," the Director replied.

"Back to work!"

The supervisor left the DCI's office and returned to his cubicle feeling very good about himself and this new information.

Washington, DC

Mr. President, sir, we have some very preliminary information that may link a terrorist cell in Iraq to the missile attack on Bushehr," the aide spoke at the daily national security briefing.

He passed copies of the transcript around the room.

"What is this MADEI group...who are these two..." the President reread the paper..."Hamid and Farroukh?"

"We just got this in. The CIA is working on it. They may be tied to a Muslim group that operated out of Arizona. All they did were protests back then with CARAMA," the Aide replied.

"Caramel?" President James asked.

"No, CARAMA...it stands for the Coalition of Arab and Muslim Americans. They state that they are about political activism and ensuring justice for Arabs and Muslims in the community. There is a Phoenix metro chapter and there was a Hamid and a Farroukh in their membership. We have people there checking on this possible connection," the Aide replied.

"Seems like more than coincidence that these names show up in Arizona and Baghdad," the President said. "Let's move on to China...and keep me in the loop with any new Intel on this MADEI cell."

Dubai, UAE

"Hey Becky! Where are you?" I called out

"Right here, Reggie...no need to yell," Becky replied as she stepped into the office.

"That was Dr. Suttmiller...you remember, the guy with FRMAC?" I asked.

"I remember...I may not have a mind like an elephant and can remember everything, like Cyndi, but I'm not senile...yet," Becky retorted.

"He's emailing us pictures of a bunch of items that were recovered from a campsite outside of the nuclear reactor at Bushehr. He told me that it is all Israeli stuff, including remnants of a Torah. What do you make of them apples?" I asked.

"This information, plus the Israeli markings on that cruise missile that couldn't have come from Israel...unless they stole it...what if it's a setup?" Becky stated.

"Setup! Who would want to set up Israel?" I replied.

"Oh, come on, Reggie...look at all the countries just here in the Middle East that want them gone. I went to one of the schools here in Dubai recently and Israel is blacked out on the Middle East map in the textbooks!" Becky said. "That's here in Dubai, the most western leaning country in this part of the world. I was shocked!"

"And, I guess that there are a lot of other groups...like the Islamic terrorists...that want the destruction of Israel and the United States. I take back my statement. I guess the list could be pretty long!" I answered. "Did I tell you that Dr. Suttmiller told me that FRMAC wouldn't need our services anymore? The Russian and American teams of radiation specialists are packing up and pulling out of the area. I guess that part of the world will be uninhabitable for many years into the future."

"And we're really no closer to figuring out who or what attacked that reactor," Becky finished.

CHAPTER SEVENTEEN

Langley, Virginia

A JOINT TASK FORCE had been formed to pursue the perceived Israeli and United States involvement in the attack on Bushehr. The meeting was being held at the CIA headquarters. The task force consisted of American representatives who included a General on the Joint Chiefs of Staff, a White House Aide to the Secretary of Defense and the Deputy Director of the CIA. Israel also had a presence at the meeting with two of its members from the Israeli Embassy.

"Let's talk about what we know first," the Deputy Director opened.

"We know that the United States did not promulgate the attack," the White House Aide responded.

"Israel had absolutely no involvement in the attack," an Embassy spokesperson said.

"We also know that it was an American missile that struck the reactor," the second Israeli Embassy member added.

"With Israeli markings," the Deputy Director responded.

"We can confirm that one of our ACM's is unaccounted for," the General said.

"But we don't know how it went missing or who absconded with the missile," the Deputy Director added.

"So, an American missile…that can only be launched from a B-52… with Israeli markings destroyed the nuclear reactor. Also, the items recovered from very close to the reactor site are all Israeli," an Embassy member said.

"The attack was orchestrated to look like a joint United States and Israel attack…that is how all of the Middle Eastern countries are viewing this information. If we do not find out who the responsible parties are, then I fear a massive attack will be launched against Israel by Iran and any other allies it can muster in the region," the General replied.

"What else do we have?" the White House Aide asked.

"One possible lead from a listening device implanted by I.N.C.I.S.O.R. into the tooth of a suspected terrorist. A conversation was picked up from what we assume is a splinter cell in Baghdad calling themselves MADEI. There is mention of two martyred members of the cell. We are actively pursuing information about the two names. There was also discussion about a planned attack against Israel and making it look like the attack came from an Iranian al-Qaeda organization," the Deputy Director said.

"Two things," the Israeli Embassy member added. "First, Israel will do everything possible within its borders to thwart a terrorist attack. Second, as you all are aware, the United States and Israel have contingency plans for an overt attack against our small country. A massive attack by the Arab States will lead to nuclear retaliation!"

"The last thing the United States needs right now is involvement in another conflict," the General answered. "Iraq and Afghanistan have really kicked our butts!"

"The world is not ready for more war and bloodshed," the White House Aide added.

"All indications are that Iran is ramping up its military. They have sent out ambassadors to meet with the other Arab neighbors. If we do not discover quickly who was behind the attack, then it will be too late," the second Israeli Embassy member said.

"What are our next moves?" the General asked.

"We are running down the leads we have from this cell in Baghdad. There was mention of another meeting in less than a week. Israel has also asked the I.N.C.I.S.O.R. team for assistance. Let us also meet again in one week to review the new information," the Deputy Director replied.

"Same place…same time?" the General asked.

"Yes, sir."

Dubai, UAE

Becky and I were enjoying 'Happy Hour' by ourselves on the patio. She had her Cosmopolitan martini and I was sipping my Crown Royal on the rocks.

"I am going to concentrate my immediate efforts on how that ACM hit the reactor," Becky said. "There are no radar tracks of a B-52 anywhere in the region…but the US swears that it can only be launched from a B-52 platform. I have already begun discussion with the CIA about this… nothing adds up, but it must, somehow!"

"Is anybody questioning that satellite image of the missile?" I asked.

"How do you mean?"

"Nobody knows where it came from…it just appeared! Could the image have been altered?"

"How? Who could have done that?"

"Maybe the same people that made the attack," I replied.

"No, no, no…Reggie! Sometimes you are so obtuse. There is no doubt in any of the circles involved about the authenticity of the satellite photo."

"Okay, wrong track…sorry," I said.

"Let me do my thing…you focus on something else," Becky replied.

"Ash should be back tomorrow. I'm taking him to the Burj al Arab for drinks and to get reacquainted," I said.

"I don't like that place…you going to the lounge at the top?" Becky asked.

"Yes…the Skyview bar next to the Al Muntaha restaurant…did you know that means 'The Top'?

"Nope, don't care…I didn't like the atmosphere and it was way too high priced for my taste!"

"You have to admit that the views are to die for! The restaurant is almost seven hundred feet up!" I said.

"I'll give you that…don't they also have the most expensive drink in the world?" Becky asked.

"Used to…there was only one barrel of that scotch left in the world. It was a Macallan fifty five year old single malt whiskey. The Skyview Bar began selling it in April 2008. The hotel assumed that at AED 27,321 or $7,500 a drink that it would last awhile, but the scotch was all gone by December that same year! The staff is searching the world to design another such cocktail!"

"Why was it so much?"

"Extremely rare scotch, water from the lake in Scotland where the brewery was located to make the ice cubes, twenty four carat gold glass and toothpicks made from the barrel that aged the scotch."

"I hate scotch…in fact, I hate all whiskey!" Becky exclaimed.

"Not my Crown Royal?"

"That too…it's all awful! And you smell like a damn brewery when you drink that stuff!"

"But this is my signature drink," I offered. "Since before you knew me I've enjoyed my Crown Royal on the rocks with a twist."

"That doesn't mean I have to like it or your breath when you drink it!" Becky said. "You have fun catching up with Ash. Think breath mint on your way home!"

Skyview Lounge atop the Burj al Arab

I had just been seated and was awaiting Ash's arrival. I had my back to the windows and was watching the bartenders work their magic and thinking about who would pay $7,500 for a drink when Ash ambled into the lounge.

"Ash! Over here!" I yelled over the music while I waved my arm.

"Good to see you my friend," Ash said as he joined me at the table.

"What's your pleasure?" I asked. "I just ordered."

The waiter came up behind Ash to get his order.

"A Tiger Woods," Ash ordered.

The waiter took the order and headed toward the bar.

"What the hell is a Tiger Woods?" I asked.

"Half cranberry juice and half iced tea," Ash responded.

The waiter reappeared and asked Ash what was in his drink. The bar tender had never heard of the drink and it wasn't in his bar guide. He was told about the concoction and left to tell the bartender. The waiter then returned again…it seems that the bartender found a recipe for a Tiger Woods drink online that involved cranberry juice, lemon juice and vodka.

"No vodka," Ash ordered. "Half cranberry juice and half iced tea."

"No alcohol after your long flight?" I asked.

"No more alcohol," Ash said. "That is one of the things I want to talk to you about."

"Okay, what's up? How did it go in Colorado Springs?"

"Grace has been put to rest. I had some time for introspection and didn't like what I saw. Therefore what you see before you is the new Ash!"

"I don't understand," I replied.

"Grace was the love of my life and she has been taken from me. I began to feel that I had nothing left to live for and then realized that that was the wrong way to deal with this loss. So, I spent some serious time looking in the mirror and I have reinvented myself," Ash stated. "Do you notice anything about the way I'm dressed?"

"You look pretty sharp...I just thought it was about the dress code in this place," I replied.

The waiter appeared with the drinks and a tower of mixed nuts to munch on. When he left us, Ash continued, "You know that I was a 'New Balance' guy...my clothes were comfortable and off the rack. No more. My shoes are Gucci and I have found a tailor in London that I can communicate with over the internet to make my clothes. No more sweatpants and golf shirts for everyday wear. When we work out or spar at the dojo I will always be in my gi. I've even had that tailor made also."

"Wow!" I exclaimed. "Mr. GQ now!"

"Do you even know what GQ means?" Ash asked.

"Not exactly...I just know that it's how to describe a sharp dresser."

"Gentleman's Quarterly magazine. Their motto is 'Look Sharp/Live Smart. I have taken those words to heart. Therefore, no sloppy look and no alcohol. Those big steaks you make? No more red meat."

"Jesus, Ash, I thought you enjoyed my barbeques," I said.

"They'll still be okay, but I'm not putting that kind of crap in my body. This is all I've got..." he said as his hands outlined his body, "...my temple, so to speak...remember that doctor you went to in Colorado Springs?"

"Yes..." I said tentatively.

"I'm living his Green Sheet diet. I juice every morning...I run or work out every day...and I am feeling superb!" Ash stated.

"What was it that Dr. J said? Only exercise on the days that end in 'Y'," I joked.

"Yeah, and his other line was, 'you only need to work out on the days that you eat…no food intake, then no need to exercise'," Ash replied.

"Can I still join you on some of your workouts?" I asked.

"I want you at them all…but I know that is not your style. You will hear a certain amount of preaching from me when I see you put poison into your body," Ash said.

"Can't we just love each other the way we are?" I asked.

"I love you too much for that…I want you in my life for a long time. You're not going to be around much longer the way you eat and drink," Ash replied.

"Well, I guess I can say, 'thanks for caring'" I said and placed my drink on the table. I was beginning to have an uneasy feeling in my gut. Ash was a changed man and I was going to have to learn and adapt to his changes. I guess that now, when we are together, I'll be drinking my Arnold Palmer while he enjoys his Tiger Woods.

"Anything else I need to know?" I asked.

"As a matter of fact, yes," Ash replied. "I will only be dating white women from now on."

"So?"

"All of the black women I have dated and married are alpha females. And rightly so…with America's history of slavery the woman always ended up running the family. The male often times was removed from the home and sold to another slave owner or died at a young age toiling in the master's fields. We were considered as nothing more than property and therefore easy to discard. Black men could not be counted on to be the heads of the households because they were not the stable ones. So, the women took over…and it's still the way it is today," Ash instructed.

"You cannot say that all black women are that way!" I exclaimed as I pulled out my EVO and Googled 'alpha female'. "It says here that an alpha female is a powerful, assertive woman. Her confidence may be due to her good looks and/or superior intelligence. Men desire her, and girls with low self-esteem hate her." I put the phone on the table.

"That's exactly right…the problem is that that's what I have encountered in all of my relationships with black women," Ash replied.

"Okay," I said. "No black women."

"Oh, and don't be fixing me up with anyone. I am done with relationships. They hurt too much!" Ash stated. I am after one thing and one thing only…companionship. Somebody to do things with both socially and sexually. As soon as they don't meet my needs they are history."

That sounded really selfish to me, but in a sense I understood what he was saying. I knew that his pain was driving a lot of this and maybe time would change things.

"Something else," Ash continued. "I only date women who are worth more than five million dollars."

"What? This talk is sounding a little insane!" I replied.

"No, listen…I met two women while I was in the States. I call them Seven and Eleven. They both had been married to professional athletes. I'm sure you've read that those guys can't keep it in their pants. Seven was married to a professional football player and Eleven was married to a professional baseball player." Ash continued.

"Seven/Eleven like the convenience store chain?" I asked.

"Didn't think about it like that, but yeah, in my case Seven and Eleven are the amounts of their settlements in divorce court," Ash said.

"Hey, as an aside, do you know where that name came from?" I asked.

Ash thought for a minute and then said, "No."

"When the convenience store chain first opened, their hours of operation were from 7 am. to 11 pm. When they opened, those hours were unprecedented for a store being open, hence the name. It wasn't until much later that they changed to be open twenty four hours a day, seven days a week," I stated.

"Oh?"

"Yep! Now, back to the women," I said.

"These two women both had similar stories. They had been put through the wringer by their professional ball playing spouses. Talk about neglected! The abuse was really evident in these two. So, what I discovered was women that are completely self sufficient, wanted to have good times and afraid of relationships. They were both really attractive, but had been so beat up that they thought that any man who acted serious was only after their money," Ash said.

"So, this is about dating unhealthy women?" I asked.

"Get off it, Reggie!" Ash countered. "It is about having a good time and nothing else. These are the type of women who Dunn and Bradstreet their suitors. I have money…they have money…good times and no ties."

"Sounds really shallow," I replied.

"So! That's what I want. See my wedding ring? This is never coming off! I touch this and I remember Grace," Ash said as he toyed with the ring. I am done with relationships…I only need occasional companionship. And, there are lots of women out there like Seven and Eleven."

"Do they have names?" I asked.

"Of course they do but I have them categorized by the amounts in their bank accounts," Ash said. "They also won't give a second thought to the cost of a flight over here."

"That's a pretty big house for just you," I commented, not sure what else to say. I was feeling like Ash's soul was really injured. My best experiences were the ones that Becky and I shared together.

"I have that Sri Lankan house boy to keep things in order. The house will be fine," Ash answered.

"Anything else you want to tell me?" I asked.

"One last thing…I am devoting the remainder of my days on this planet to the elimination of terror in the world. And I don't mean by diplomacy. Any terrorist crosses my path…they're dead! No if's, and's or but's. They took out the wrong lady when they murdered Grace…and I am here to make them pay," Ash vowed and added, "Judge, jury and executioner…that's me! I will become their worst nightmare. Don't even act like or look like a terrorist around me."

That statement sent up many red flags in my mind. Ash may be hard to control on future missions. Well, we'd have to wait and see how things played out.

"What's the news with I.N.C.I.S.O.R.?" Ash asked.

"Anything else you want to tell me?" I asked.

"Nope…bring me up to date," Ash replied.

CHAPTER EIGHTEEN

Baghdad, Iraq

"WHAT HAVE WE found out?" Abdullah asked the group.

"We have a target...the tallest building in Tel Aviv," a cell member replied.

Another member picked up the conversation. "And almost all glass on the outside. In fact, there are forty two windows on each floor...that's what al-Qaeda looks for."

"What else do we know about this structure?" Abdullah asked.

"The top eleven floors are for residential use. There are ninety eight apartments. The bulk of the remaining floors is office space. There is a helipad on the roof. There is a fitness club and swimming pool in the car park annex. And here's the best part...there is a synagogue on the third floor for residents, office tenants and visitors!"

"How did you discover all of this?" Abdullah inquired.

"Remember the manual?" a cell member asked. "This is all from the internet...eighty percent of our research can come from the internet."

"And...what else?" Abdullah continued.

"The building is named the Moshe Aviv Tower. It is located in Ramat Gan in the Gush Dan metropolitan area east of Tel Aviv. We will be striking a blow right into their capital!"

"And what about explosives? And, how do we smuggle them into Israel? They have the most secure borders in the Middle East." Abdullah stated.

"How about we take a page directly from the al-Qaeda playbook... and fly a plane into the building?"

"And we get this plane from where?" Abdullah asked.

"Imam Khomeini International Airport in Tehran!" was the reply.

"Lufthansa has one direct flight from Frankfurt, Germany into Tehran, Iran. Other flights are connected through either London, England or Vienna, Austria. The direct flight leaves Tehran at 3:25 am. Most of the passengers will be sleeping when we take the plane. Rahim was just hours short of receiving his private pilot license in Phoenix before moving to Baghdad."

"Yes that is true," Rahim replied. "I am willing to martyr myself to strike a blow against Israel!"

Three other members of the MADEI cell spoke up, willing to join Rahim.

Abdullah thought about the plan and liked how it was taking shape. Unlike al-Qaeda having to train their hijackers how to fly, Rahim already knew how to fly. The flight would originate from Tehran's Imam Khomeini International Airport. The assumption would be that Iranians had been responsible for hijacking the plane. That would definitely stir the pot of anger and hatred in the area!

"More good news…Lufthansa also has flights into Ben Gurion International Airport outside of Tel Aviv. The airport is nine miles southeast of the center of Tel Aviv, and the building is also east of Tel Aviv. Actually northeast. And here's the best part. There is a Lufthansa flight from Frankfurt that arrives in Tel Aviv at 3:20 am. If we work to delay that flight in Frankfurt, the Israeli Air Traffic Control will not be alarmed with an incoming Lufthansa flight at that time," another cell member said.

"So, you four will work on plans to get into Iran and the hijacking of the Lufthansa flight. Do we know what type of aircraft it is?" Abdullah asked.

"A 747-400," was the reply.

"Even bigger than the planes used against the twin towers. And it will have full fuel for its return flight! This will be a spectacular blow against the Infidel! I will take the other two members to Frankfurt to begin work on delaying that flight into Tel Aviv," Abdullah stated.

"Also remember that money, fake passports…anything you need will not be a problem," Abdullah added. "Let's keep planning.

Langley, Virginia

"Did you read that transcript?' the Deputy Director asked. "This MADEI group is planning a similar attack like 9/11!"

The Deputy Director's secretary nodded as she took notes.

"Who's the team working in Phoenix? Let's get them this new name… what was it…Rahid?" the Deputy Director ordered.

"No sir…its Rahim…should also be a record of his flight training," the secretary added.

"Okay, let's get a report from the Phoenix team…I meet again with the joint task force tomorrow," the Deputy Director said.

Dubai, UAE

"Ash told me that he is going to Phoenix to help with gathering information on that MADEI group. They were part of CARAMA, right Reggie?" Becky asked.

"I don't know how connected they were…kind of like the Black Panthers were to the counterculture movement of the '60's. The movement generally was peaceful but the Panthers were not. In fact, J. Edgar Hoover called the party 'the greatest threat to the internal security of the country'," I stated.

"What are you saying, Reggie?" Becky replied. "CARAMA is generally peaceful but MADEI is violent?"

"Exactly," I said. "They are planning an attack against Israel and so far three of its members have, or had, ties to Phoenix."

"Tell me again, what does MADEI stand for" Becky asked.

"Muslim Arabs Dedicated to the Eradication of Israel," I replied.

"That sure doesn't sound like a peaceful group!" Becky exclaimed.

Phoenix, Arizona

Ash Black attended the latest meeting of the group of CIA and FBI agents assigned to track down information on the four items…MADEI and the names Hamid, Farroukh and Rahim. From the information that was gathered to date, CARAMA was still a group that was in existence, but there was no evidence of MADEI. It was suggested that maybe this was a splinter group whose members all immigrated to Iraq. Hamid, Farroukh and Rahim had all been members of CARAMA and there were records of attendance at ASU. All three names had seemingly fallen off the end of the earth a while back after a speech by a man named Abdullah. Coincidence? Or was this the same man that was head of the cell in Baghdad? There were three other names on the CARAMA membership list that were no longer around. Those names and their status had been communicated to Langley. It looked like all the other leads were dead ends and there was little else to recover at the Phoenix end.

Ash discovered that the next CARAMA meeting was to be held that night. "Perfect!" he thought. "Time for some night reconnaissance."

With the meeting completed, the main speaker and head of the Phoenix CARAMA chapter headed to his car. He unlocked the driver's door and slung his briefcase into the passenger seat. He went to reach for the ignition when he felt an immense pain spreading down both sides of his neck. He realized that someone had two thumbs up under his jaw on both sides and was applying enough pressure that it felt like his brain would explode.

He attempted to scream from the pain but no sound came out. His assailant loosened the grip just enough so that the white and red flashes of pain and fear began to subside.

"Tell me about Hamid, Farroukh, Rahim and Abdullah," came from the back seat.

"I know nothing…I have told the FBI all that I know," he pleaded.

With a single move, Ash Black took both carotid arteries between his thumbs and forefingers, grabbed hold with both hands and ripped outwards.

Death was instantaneous as the man's blood spurted out covered the steering wheel and dashboard.

"You know nothing then you don't deserve to live," Ash stated as he exited the car with the man's briefcase. "Let's see if there is anything worthwhile in here."

Ash visited three other CARAMA members at their places of residence. Nobody knew about the lost members and met with equally gruesome deaths. Ash did not negotiate or ask twice. The killings were ruthless and over the top. It looked like anyone with even loose ties to the MADEI group was going to be a very unhealthy thing.

The Phoenix Police Blotter described the vicious attacks, calling them the most heinous crimes in the city. Four Muslim men dead…no robbery, no mugging…no motive. Baffling! By the time the article appeared in the paper Ash Black had nearly completed the long flight back to Dubai.

Langley, Virginia

The joint task force was just wrapping up its meeting. There had been little to add from the Phoenix team except for the names had been tied to CARAMA and there were family ties for one of the names to a Tucson family who emigrated from Iran.

The General of the Joint Chiefs of Staff spoke, "Let's task a drone to take out this cell at their next rendezvous! Do we know when they meet?"

"No but we have a bug…that PC…that will let us know when they are talking again. Would that give you enough warning?" the Deputy Director asked.

"All I need is a half hour and we'll get one of our MQ-1 Predators up and over them and drop two AGM-114 Hellfire missiles through their front door. That should get them an immediate presence with Allah and they can soon be with their seventy two virgins. We have these Predators at the airport in Baghdad," the General stated.

"Its decided, then…we take out this cell before they carry out their planned attack against Israel," the Deputy Director said.

Washington, DC

Mr. President, the Joint Task Force has decided to eliminate the terrorist cell known as MADEI," the Aide stated.

President James rose and came out from behind his desk. "What about the ties to Bushehr?"

"Just the two names mentioned…and talk of their martyrdom…we got nothing from Phoenix," the Aide said.

"Damn, so we're no closer to knowing who was behind that attack," the President replied.

"No, Mr. President, we aren't."

Dubai, UAE

"Was the trip to Phoenix productive?" I asked as Ash and I sat down with our tea drinks.

"You don't have to drink your Arnold Palmer just because I have sworn off alcohol," Ash replied.

"I'm not, but I will honor your decision and not have any alcohol while I'm in your presence," I stated.

"Didn't learn much of anything," Ash said. "But, there are four less Muslims on the planet."

"I read about that on the internet. Sounded like the deaths were pretty gruesome. You had something to do with the deaths?" I asked.

"Guilty!" Ash said as he hoisted his glass for a toast.

"What did they do?" I replied.

"I know that they were tied in some fashion to those terrorists and I'm dedicating my life to their destruction…remember?" Ash stated.

"Yes, I remember…but these were really brutal…like it was murder," I responded.

"What was it that happened to Grace? Self defense?" Ash countered.

"Hey, look at these phones," Ash said as he pulled out the packages he had arrived with. "These are so cool!"

"I'm just getting used to my EVO," I replied. "More new technology?"

"These function just like your EVO, but the techies at Langley have added some interesting features. First, the phones will search out and find encrypted lines on any system worldwide. No concerns about who could be listening. And the encryption program only works on I.N.C.I.S.O.R. phones. These five are for us, and there are five arriving in Denver and five more for Frankfurt."

"Second, the phones are voice activated. They have like a voice recognition program in them. They only work when you talk into them. In other words, you cannot use Becky's phone and I cannot use yours… once they are set up."

"And finally, there is a charge built into the phone. If you hold down the 'nine' and 'zero' buttons simultaneously for five seconds it arms the phone. Ten seconds later…kablooey! Definitely makes for a bad day for the person holding the phone and enough of a blast to change a tight situation, if you find yourself in one."

"My phone's a weapon?" I asked.

"Now it is…so, fill me in on what's gone on around here…"

CHAPTER NINETEEN

Winston-Salem, North Carolina

A BLACK CHEVY LOW rider cruised slowly past the home of Jose' Venerable'. No one could see inside the car because the windows had received dark tinting. North Carolina law requires that the window tinting must allow more than thirty five percent of the light in. These windows were, for all intents and purposes, black. The MS-13 gang members inside the car did not worry about breaking this law. Their existence on the planet was to break laws.

The gang members were performing a drive-by to plan out their attack on the Venerable' family. They noted that the home was located in a gated community, but there was no guard on duty. It would be easy to follow behind a car whose driver knew the entrance code for the gate into the neighborhood. The gang members decided that they would hit the house that night.

Los Angeles, California

"They're hitting the house tonight esse," one of the gang members told their leader.

"They just gunna tag the house with MS-13 graffiti? Like they hit that church?" the Leader asked.

"No, homes, they gunna riddle the place."

Winston-Salem, North Carolina

The Venerable' family was just sitting down to dinner. Jose' had been home from the hospital for a few days. His hand was heavily bandaged following the surgery to attempt reattachment of his finger. It was still too soon to know if the microsurgery on his hand was successful. Jose' was still learning to eat and write with his other hand. His wife was having to help him cut up his meal. Jose' was watching his wife cut up the smothered burrito on the plate in front of him and thinking about how lucky he was to be with his family.

All of a sudden there was a loud explosion as the front picture window shattered from the automatic gunfire. Bullets were being sprayed all over the interior of the house. Some even found their way into the kitchen cabinets above the table where the Venerable's were seated.

Jose' yelled for his family to get to the floor. His wife, standing by the side of his chair stood frozen in terror. Once Jose' was on his knees he reached up and pulled his wife down. The gunfire continued for the next thirty seconds…but it felt like a lifetime.

The sound of screeching tires signaled the end of the attack. Jose' crawled to the phone and dialed 911, making sure that the family all stayed on the floor. Within minutes the family members could hear the sound of sirens as the police raced to their home.

The front door was a shambles when the police burst through it. One of the officers who had transferred down from Newark, New Jersey commented that the front of the house looked like the buildings in downtown Newark after the riots. The six days of rioting in 1967 had left twenty six people dead and over seven hundred injured. Property damage exceeded ten million dollars. The fronts of many buildings looked like Swiss cheese. And, so did the Venerable' home.

Officers rounded up the family, seated them in the family room and checked for any injuries. The family room was also in the back part of the house and was relatively unscathed. The living room looked like a war zone. It was so lucky that they had been sitting in the back of the house. "Who was it…why us?" Jose' asked.

"The same gang that kidnapped you, Mr. Venerable'…they have a chapter here in Winston-Salem. Badasses! Every one of them. We've had dealings with them before. You have anywhere you can go tonight?" an officer asked.

Dubai, UAE

"Let's get the Denver team down to Winston-Salem to provide protection for the Venerable' family," I said to Becky. "It's probably a one-time attack, but let's give them some cover just to be safe."

"Ash said that he is on his way to oversee things and to help out," Becky replied.

"God help that gang if Ash is there!" I exclaimed.

"What do you mean, Reggie?" Becky asked.

"Let me tell you about getting acquainted with the new Ash…" I said.

Baghdad, Iraq

"Are we ready for the attack?" Abdullah asked.

"Here are all of our fake passports and paperwork," Amjad said as he proudly passed around the packets to each of the MADEI cell members. He was one of the two new members and felt very important that he was made responsible for procuring the documents.

"All praise be to Allah," Abdullah prayed. "Amjad, you and Sanjar will accompany me to Frankfurt. Rahim and you three…" as he pointed to the remaining cell members…"Will make your way to Tehran and make ready for the hijacking of the Lufthansa flight."

Baghdad International Airport
(formerly Saddam International Airport)

"The MADEI cell is meeting…get that drone in the air!" the Colonel ordered.

"Already launched," the controller said. "Ten minutes to target!"

Baghdad, Iraq

"Like the first attack against Bushehr, we carry nothing that can tie back to Iraq or MADEI," Abdullah continued. "Let us check every item even down to our shoes to make sure that everything is of Iranian manufacture…"

Langley, Virginia

"There is more conversation from that cell in Baghdad. They are talking about the 'first attack against Bushehr'!" the translator told her boss.

"Get me command in Baghdad!" the lieutenant screamed into the phone. He knew that it was imperative that they find out more information about this terrorist cell and that would not be possible with all of the members dead.

Baghdad International Airport

The phone rang just as the controller announced, "One minute to target! Missiles hot!" All eyes in the room were on the wide screen television mounted on the wall above their modules.

"What?" the Colonel yelled into the phone. "Stop the attack? We're ready to light up the missiles!"

"Abort…abort…abort!" the Colonel yelled from his command post.

The controller had lifted the safety cover over the launch button and was ready to press his finger down to launch the two Hellfire missiles. He quickly pulled his hand away and the cover snapped closed.

"Launch aborted," he announced. "Recalling Predator to home base."

Winston-Salem, North Carolina

It was easy for Ash Black to discover the main crib for the Mara Salvatrucha gang in Winston-Salem. Every night for a week he made off with one gang member. Stealth was also an easy skill for Ash. He wore all black and moved like a cat. The gang members never heard his approach. Once he confirmed the MS-13 tattoos on the body of his captured gang member, the gangster was summarily beheaded. There was no talking or negotiation or pleading for their life. One swipe from his Samurai sword and the head rolled cleanly off the torso.

Ash found an abandoned warehouse and each night, in typical MS-13 style he hacked up the bodies with a machete and placed them in a neat design in the middle of the warehouse floor. When the bodies were discovered the remains spelled out MS-13 with a diagonal running from upper left to lower right through the emblem. The message was clear… Mara Salvatrucha not allowed…

Dubai, UAE

"Hey Lance, now that you're back…let's all go skiing!" I said into the phone.

"Not a bad idea…I've been dying to see that place," Lance replied.

"Let's pack up the girls and meet at the Mall of the Emirates in one hour," I said.

"Sold! What do we need to bring?" Lance asked.

"Nothing…the ticket includes Jacket, Trousers, Skis, Boots, Poles and Disposable Socks!" I answered. "And a two hour pass is only 180 dirham."

"Remind me again. How much is that in dollars?" Lance said.

"The dirham is worth a little more the twenty seven cents. 180 dirham is forty nine bucks," I replied.

"Alright…see you in an hour," Lance said and hung up the phone.

Mall of the Emirates, Dubai UAE

"This place is so cool!" Becky said as we watched through the glass windows. "How do they keep the windows from fogging up?"

"Snow skiing in the desert!" Lance said. "Too much."

"Did you guys read about this place?" I asked. They have five runs, including the world's first indoor black run! Its twenty five stories high and almost two hundred and seventy feet wide. Let's go!"

I enjoyed the black run while the other three stayed on the intermediate slope. I was amazed to see that Ski Dubai had a four person chairlift to get you up the slope. When our two hours was up it was time to enjoy some fine dining at Almaz by Momo, a gourmet restaurant featuring cuisine from the Maghreb region of Northwest Africa, west of Egypt. The restaurant is in the Mall of the Emirates which meant no alcoholic beverages. I told myself that I needed to look into this Emirates custom of only allowing alcoholic drinks to be served in bars or restaurants that are part of hotels in the region.

CHAPTER TWENTY

GRAHAM AND MAGNUS were at war...on the ping pong table. They looked like Tom Hanks playing ping pong in Forrest Gump. They were both backed up at least six feet from the table's edge and whacking the ball with all their might! The poor ball would split at the seams if this kept up much longer. Finally, Graham won the set and they placed their paddles on the table.

"Great match!" Magnus urged.

Both of their shirts were ringing wet as the bartender on the poopdeck brought them towels. A group of about thirty passengers had gathered during the match and gave them a loud applause. Graham took a bow as Magnus moved to the bar to get lemonades for the two of them. They then moved to the aft railing of the ship to relax and let their bodies recover.

While they were leaning against the railing, watching the turbulent water agitated by the giant propellers of the cruise ship, Magnus and Graham engaged in light banter about each other's ability with the ping pong paddle.

Suddenly, Graham blurted out, "See those two small craft?"

"Yep," Magnus said as he headed for the bar.

"You got any binoculars behind there?" Magnus asked the bartender.

"Here you go," the bartender responded as he gave Magnus the binoculars.

Magnus rushed back to the railing and focused the binoculars on the two approaching craft. "Two small Zodiacs...one making for starboard and one heading to port side! Looks like six men in each vessel."

Graham turned and yelled to the bartender, "Get the Captain on the horn! Any weapons on board?"

The bartender indicated that he was unaware of any weaponry aboard ship and reached for the phone to dial the Captain.

"What's going on?" the bartender asked.

"Somali pirates…I think they plan to board the ship!" Graham replied.

The cruise ship had sailed from Dubai, past Oman and was making its way southwest through the Arabian Sea toward the eastern coast of Africa. The ship was due east of Somalia.

"We've been briefed about Somali pirates and holding ships and passengers for ransom," the bartender continued. "We were told that most of the attacks occur at night, which is why the timetable was set so that we would make it well past this area during the daylight hours. There are also naval vessels on patrol in this region."

"Don't see any other ships on the horizon!" Magnus announced from the railing.

Just then the Captain of the ship and his first officer joined the men at the aft railing. Magnus handed the Captain his binoculars. The first officer had a pair around his neck. The two crew members took a moment to observe the two craft.

"Looks like they will overtake us in ten minutes," the first officer spoke.

"Who are you men?" the Captain asked. "You look like you are in the military."

"Ex-military," Graham said. "We work for I.N.C.I.S.O.R."

"What's that?"

"Suffice it to say that we hire out to the military," Graham continued.

"So, you know your way around weaponry," the Captain replied.

"Yes, sir, we do!" Magnus stated. "And if we move quickly we can repel the attack."

The Captain turned to his first officer and ordered him to take Graham and Magnus to the armory. They made their way to where the weapons were kept and the first officer unlocked the cabinet.

Graham and Magnus made quick work of checking out the locker. There were handguns, which were handed around and a few automatic rifles which they each grabbed. Magnus rummaged around in the locker and exclaimed, "Look here guys! We've got Stingers!"

The First Officer responded that the company had recently supplied their ships with these missiles, but had not instructed the crews on their use.

Graham replied, "We know how to use them…we've got this!"

Magnus grabbed up two of the missiles and slung them over his shoulder. The three then made their way to the back of the ship.

The two Zodiac craft were about one hundred yards off the aft beam of the cruise ship and closing the distance rapidly. They were close enough that the men with binoculars could make out the faces of the pirates. All were armed with AK-47's.

"They're children!" the Captain exclaimed. "Look at that one…I bet he hasn't reached puberty yet!"

Magnus moved to the port side and Graham took up a position on the starboard side. They quickly assembled the Stinger missiles.

"On my mark! Three…Two…One…Fire!" Magnus ordered.

Both Magnus and Graham pressed the launch buttons at the same instant starting a sequence of events. First, small launch rockets shot the missiles out of the launch tube to clear the two men firing them. Then the launch engines fell away and the main solid rocket engines ignited and propelled the Stingers to 1,500 mph or Mach 2.

As the missiles surged forward, the passive IR/UV sensors picked up their targets. The IR sensors picked up the heat from the two outboard motors and the UV sensors picked up the shadow of the two targets. The missile's guidance systems performed the rest of the tasks.

There was a brief moment in time as the missiles made their way toward the two craft. One of the pirates reached to the floor of his craft and hoisted up a rocket propelled grenade to his shoulder.

The Captain and First Officer were glued to their binoculars, watching the missiles track toward their targets. The Captain was the one that noticed the movement in the one craft. "RPG!" the Captain yelled.

The Stinger missiles both found their targets and the Zodiac craft disappeared with a mighty explosion. The pirate with the RPG had taken aim on the stern of the passenger ship. He launched his RPG just as the Stinger found home. He was knocked back and the rocket propelled grenade headed skyward in a lazy arc headed toward the cruise ship. The men on the ship knew that this weapon had no guidance system, so it was just a matter of where the grenade would land.

The men on the railing watched in anticipation as the grenade headed for the ship. It missed and hit the water just aft of the ship, sending a water spray onto the men.

"Holy Christ! That was close," the first officer exclaimed.

"Close is only good in horseshoes and women!" Magnus joked.

"Do we look for survivors?" the first officer asked.

"Hell no!" the Captain answered. "And full steam ahead…I want out of these waters!"

The Captain turned to Magnus and Graham and offered his sincere thanks for their help. "Please dine with me tonight at the Captain's table."

Graham and Magnus accepted the offer and helped the first officer stow the weapons away in the locker. "Let's call Dubai…Reggie will get a kick out of this!" Graham said.

Dubai, UAE

"I've done some searching on the internet," I said to Becky.

"These pirate attacks in Somalia are really something…it says that this year the pirates have broken all records with the money they get from ransoms…$135 Million so far! That's eight ships hijacked and two hundred sailors kidnapped. One in fourteen attacks is successful. The Somali pirates are holding ten large ships and more than three hundred hostages! That includes ships and sailors that are still being held from the previous year."

"We're not cruising anywhere near there, are we?" Becky replied.

"No, dear…no cruises in Somali waters!" I answered.

PART THREE

CHAPTER TWENTY ONE

Tehran, Iran

THE DELEGATES ALL began to gather in groups around the central chamber where the national assembly gathered to conduct State business. The air seemed full of electricity as the men filled the room with loud chatter. The whole assembly was dressed in their finest traditional Arab garb and the colors signifying the different tribal states of Iran added color and brightness to the large hall.

The men all knew that this was to be a historic day. Many had waited their whole lives for the upcoming vote. The men chatted and cackled like women as they awaited the call to order. The agenda had only one item for discussion…Does Iran declare war on Israel?

From the energy in the room it was obvious to the aides that were scurrying around the chairs passing out the voting papers that this would be an easy vote. Some grandstanding and posturing by the leaders of Iran's national council which would include too much rhetoric…and then the vote.

The atmosphere in the large meeting room for the national council was festive. There were banners from ceiling to floor touting Iran's rich history and huge, larger than life, posters of Iran's religious and political figureheads. The bright colors from the decorations mixed with the tribal colors of the long flowing robes worn by the delegates reminded one of a celebration rather than the task that they were facing. One almost expected balloons to be released from the ceiling!

The room was called to order and the members of parliament began to take their seats. The Supreme Leader moved onto the stage and took his seat in a chair that looked more like a throne behind the podium.

Iran has an interesting political system. The country is governed by a true theocracy.

The Supreme Leader of Iran, or Leader of the Revolution, is the highest ranking political and religious authority in this Islamic Republic. The Supreme Leader is more powerful than the President of Iran. The position was created in the constitution after the revolution and fall of the Shah.

The Pahlavi dynasty had existed and governed Iran from 1925 until the overthrow of the dynasty in 1979. In an interesting twist of fate and indicative of the sentiments of the region, the overthrow of Shah Mohammad-Reza Pahlavi came about because the Shah began a series of ambitious and bold plans to further the progress of his country and march it toward modernization. His plan was called the White Revolution.

The White Revolution was a series of economic and social reforms intended to transform Iran into a global power. The Shah succeeded in modernizing the nation and extended suffrage to women. His strong policy of modernization also included recognition of Israel. He also banned the communist party after an assassination attempt in 1949. The Shah furthermore clashed with Islamists. The socioeconomic advances irritated the clergy and Islamic leaders. They harnessed the discontent among the masses and promised to focus on a return to Islamic traditions.

The Shah was forced to flee the country and ended up in Egypt as a guest of Anwar Sadat until his death in 1980. His son, Crown Prince Reza Pahlavi succeeded him as the heir apparent and he and his wife live in Potomac, Maryland with their three daughters. Many Iranians look back on the era when the Shah was in control as a time when Iran was more prosperous and the government was less oppressive. Even the uneducated poor, traditionally core supporters of the revolution, made remarks such as 'God bless the Shah's soul, the economy was better then'.

Books about the former Shah, even censored ones sell briskly, while books of the 'Rightly Guided Path' sit idle.

There have been only two Supreme Leaders in Iran's history. The Ayatollah Khomeini held the position from 1979 until his death in 1989. The current leader has held the position since 1989.

Parliament is made up of 290 members and it looked like every one of them was in attendance today. There was not an empty seat in the hall. The Guardian Council of 12 jurists (six of the twelve were clerics appointed by the Supreme Leader) marched onto the stage and took their positions in ornate chairs on either side of the Supreme Leader. The Guardian Council must approve all legislation from Parliament. They also must approve all of the candidates to Parliament. Attendance today of the Supreme Leader and the Guardian Council assured immediate action on the vote taken today.

Did I mention that this country is run by a true theocracy? Only candidates and parties that do not oppose the religious system of the governance can participate in elections in the Islamic Republic of Iran. This is assured by the Guardian Council which vets all of the candidates.

There are two political parties in Iran. The conservative party is the only party whose members have been allowed to participate in Parliament. The reformist party members have been banned and many members have been jailed. Doesn't sound like much of a two party system!

The President of Iran appeared and moved toward the podium. Every member in attendance rose and gave him a standing ovation. The applause and shouting from the group was deafening. The President stood beside the podium and was visibly pleased as he soaked up the admiration. The ovation continued for many minutes until, finally, the President raised his arms and called for the meeting to proceed.

This President had been driving Iran toward major conflict with Israel and the United States for many years. He made statements, such as "In the world, there are deviations from the Right Path: Christianity and Judaism. Dollars have been devoted to the propagation of these deviations. There are also false claims that these religions will save mankind. But Islam is the only religion the can save mankind." He claimed that the Holocaust was a myth. He claimed that the United States was behind the attacks on 9/11. In an article that appeared in Al-Qaeda's magazine he claimed to be jealous of Al-Qaeda and their responsibility for the attack on the World Trade Center in New York.

The President also pushed ahead with Iran's nuclear programs. Bushehr was the crowning jewel of the State nuclear program. The first nuclear reactor in the Middle East! He thumbed his nose at pleas from the United

States and Israel not to proceed with their nuclear program. After threats and sanctions from both enemies, Bushehr now lay in ruins.

The President of Iran continued the country's policy of refusing to recognize Israel as a legitimate state. He had been quoted in the New York Times where he called for the "occupying regime" of Israel to be eliminated, or "vanish from the pages of time". Now was his moment to fulfill that dream.

As the room became quiet, he rose up to his full stature…and began,

"The sovereign State of Iran has suffered an immense loss of the nuclear reactor at Bushehr. While the world debates the origin of the attack, I am convinced that the occupying regime of the outlaw state of Israel was the perpetrator of the attack and the nuclear destruction in Bushehr."

There were shouts from the Parliament members followed by another standing ovation.

"It is time and we have the power to strike back against the Infidel!"

Again, applause and shouts from the members.

"It is within your power and I urge you to declare war against Israel!"

The hall erupted into shouting and dancing in the aisles. It took fifteen minutes for order to be restored.

"War…Destroy Israel…Death to the Semites!" were shouted around the hall.

"I call for a vote!" the President shouted. "All those in favor stand now and be counted."

Every Parliament member stood and shouted his affirmation. The President then turned around to face the Guardian Council and Supreme Leader. The Guardian Council all stood and bowed their affirmation to the President. The Supreme Leader slowly rose from his throne. The huge hall became so quiet that the members were unnerved and glanced around to each other.

The Supreme Leader moved to the podium.

"We are at war…death to Israel…death to the Infidel!"

The room erupted into bedlam once again…Iran was at war.

Washington, DC

President James waited in the Oval Office for the news. As he waited, he thought about the fanatical and suicidal religious regime that was meeting to condemn Israel. Netanyahu had described the Iranian President as, "the world is facing another Hitler, and this moment of decision is akin to the eve of World War II." "Iran is a threat to Israel and a real danger to humanity as a whole."

The President didn't have to wait long before the National Security Advisor rushed headlong into his presence.

"The vote was unanimous…Iran has declared war against Israel!" the Advisor almost shouted.

"Calm down, man," the President advised.

"This could be the start of World War IV!" said the National Security Advisor.

"Iran would be well advised to study their history," President James countered.

"What do you mean…what are you saying?" asked the Advisor.

President James was an avid student of world history. It was now time to educate this advisor.

"Iran has not fared well when they declare war against other countries. Look at the history of their recent conflicts…Iran had four wars with Russia. In the Russo-Persian War of 1722, Persia surrendered Derbent, Baku and the provinces of Shirvan, Gilan, Mazandaran and Astrabad to the Russians. In 1796 Persia lost control of Georgia and Azerbaijan to Russian control."

"In the Russo-Persian war of 1804, the Persian Empire outmanned the Russians five to one. Persia actually declared a holy war on Imperial Russia. The Russians once again prevailed and Persia ceded the majority of the disputed territories to Imperial Russia. The Persian Khans were decimated and forced to pay homage to Russia."

"The last Russo-Persian war occurred in 1826. Again, the Persians maintained superior numbers of troops against the Russians. Once again, the Russians kicked their Arabian butts! Iran lost more territory, including Erivan and Nakhichevan to Russian control. The Shah also granted the Russians the exclusive right to maintain a navy in the Caspian Sea. This war ensured that the Caucasus would be dependent on Russia. Eventually the modern states of Armenia and Azerbaijan would emerge on the territories conquered from Persia."

"The Iran-Iraq war was the longest conventional war of the 20th century. Over half a million Iran and Iraq soldiers perished during that conflict. The tactics used in the war mirrored World War I. Trench warfare and the extensive use of chemical weapons, such as mustard gas were used. Human wave attacks with bayonets were used to wage the war, with no gains in territory by either side. Israel actually supported Iran and supplied them weaponry during that war!"

"Iran has lost much territory and manpower with each war it wages."

"Do you remember the USS Vincennes shooting down the Iranian passenger jet? That incident occurred at the end of the Iran-Iraq war," the President concluded.

"Yes, Mr. President, I remember!" the National Security Advisor replied.

"Okay, what do we do with this news?" the President asked.

"Time for a meeting with the Joint Chiefs…we need to prepare for World conflict," the Advisor added.

Tel Aviv, Israel

"The Knesset has received word that Iran has declared war against Israel," the aide announced as he entered the Prime Minister's office.

"Call our Generals in for a briefing," Netanyahu ordered.

Prime Minister Benjamin Netanyahu was left to his thoughts. The incident of the missile attack against Bushehr was going to quickly boil into a situation that he knew could mean the end of his beloved country. He reached for the papers about Iran's military forces.

The first overview that he studied was published in Global Firepower. Israel's forces ranked tenth globally, while Iran was ranked twelfth. The population numbers showed a glaring discrepancy. Israel had a population of a little over seven million souls. Iran's population totaled more than seventy seven million. Ten times the number of his little country. He then glanced at the number of available citizens when there was a conflict. Israel had available manpower of three and a half million, of which fewer than three million were considered 'fit for service'…Iran's number was over forty six million, with thirty nine and a half million 'fit for service'. These numbers were staggering now that he was facing an armed conflict. And what about the other Arab countries?

Netanyahu knew that his country's Israeli Defense Forces were some of the most battle-trained forces in the world. There were a little less than 200,000 active military, with reserves totaling over five hundred thousand. Iran boasted an active military of almost five hundred and fifty thousand, with six hundred and fifty thousand men in the reserves. Israel could not risk a prolonged war of attrition against these superior numbers.

Israel spent the equivalent of about sixteen billion dollars a year maintaining its military. Iran's military spending amounted to only nine billion dollars each year. The Prime Minister knew that Israel possessed superior weaponry compared to its Arab counterpart. And they had nukes!

Netanyahu then glanced up at the map of the Middle East that hung on his wall. The first item that he noted was that this war would involve elements on the land and in the air. Israel's navy, as well as Iran's navy would be of little use in this conflict. Iran would have to cross the countries of Iraq, Syria and Jordan or Lebanon to reach Israel. Iran's largest western border was with Iraq. He felt that it would be unlikely that Iran would proceed through Turkey to the northwest.

The Prime Minister pondered the unrest in Syria and the instability of Iraq's fledgling democracy. Could it be possible that these countries would not allow an Iranian armed force to cross into their territories? Probably just wishful thinking, he thought. They were, at the end of the day, Arab.

Time to get on the phone to the United States President…

CHAPTER TWENTY TWO

Dubai, UAE

FOUND BECKY IN the office crunching numbers for one of her many reports. I walked up to her and gave her a big hug from behind. I leaned down with my head close to hers.

"I have a surprise for you!" I whispered in her ear.

"What? You know I don't like surprises," she responded. Becky leaned her head back against my shoulder so that she could look into my eyes.

"It's a surprise! You are dressed just right for this…just grab a coat in case it gets chilly later," I said. "It's three thirty. Our ride should be here now!"

I grabbed my coat and waited for Becky in the front foyer. Soon she joined me and I opened the front door. The secret was up at that moment because Becky saw the white Toyota Land Cruiser waiting for us at the curb in front of our villa. The placard on the side of the Land Cruiser said 'Arabian Nights'.

Becky and I had lived in Dubai for over a year now. There were many things on our 'to do' list while we were in Dubai that had not been accomplished, and one was to see the sand dunes. I had met the business development manager of Arabian Night Tours when he came to the dental clinic. We talked for a long time about his business and 'bashing' the sand dunes. His one strong recommendation was to wait for a full moon. The colors of the desert were spectacular under a full moon according to him.

And tonight there was a full moon. As Becky and I headed down the walkway toward the Land Cruiser I explained to her that these SUVs normally carried three couples along with the driver, but that I had paid for the whole vehicle…it would just be the two of us. I helped Becky into the middle seat of the Land Cruiser behind the driver and I moved around to the other side to sit beside Becky.

Our driver was delightful and his English was great. He maneuvered the vehicle through the streets of Dubai and out to the Emirates Road. As he pointed the SUV toward the northeast he explained about the picture he had hanging on the rearview mirror. I was a picture of the Sheik Zayad road in the 1980's. There was nothing there! This road is now a seven lane superhighway that leads through an amazing metropolis. What a spectacular amount of development in such a short period of time! Dubai seemed to have the biggest and best of everything…the world's tallest building, an indoor ski area in the middle of the desert, the world's only seven star hotel and malls that make the Mall of America look mundane, just to name a few.

We made our way to one of the neighboring Emirates, Umm Al Quwain, and eventually to a location where twenty five other Toyota Land Cruisers had gathered. Becky and I got out of the SUV and we quickly removed our sandals and enjoyed the feel of the warm sand between our toes. The driver proceeded to let the air out of the tires. He explained to me that the tire pressure had to be reduced to fifteen pounds per square inch so that the tires would flatten and perform better on the sand.

When all of the drivers were ready, the crowd of adventurers returned to their vehicles. We headed into the dunes. Our driver led the way which gave Becky and me a fabulous view of the sea of sand ahead of us. He began gradually heading up a gentle slope of a large dune and then floored the gas pedal while cranking the steering wheel hard to the right. I had the sense that we were surely going to roll as the Land Cruiser slid sideways down the side of the dune.

He then crashed up the next dune and we fell off to the other side. These thrilling acrobatics continued for what seemed like hours, but it was really only about forty five minutes before we stopped so that we could explore the sand dunes on foot. The driver coyly explained that he had only rolled his vehicle twice in all of his years of driving. I couldn't tell if he was telling the truth or pulling our legs! There had to be a dozen times that I was sure we were going over, and I was sweating profusely in the comfortably air conditioned SUV! Becky was rubbing the hand I had been holding…seems I was squeezing a little too hard!

I had pulled similar acrobatic maneuvers in my Avanti II. But I was at the controls! Now we were at the driver's mercy. He did a phenomenal job but it was very nerve wracking!

The full moon was up over the sand as we hiked up a nearby dune for pictures. I was struck with the color of the sand. I had seen white sand beaches and black sand beaches. I had seen various shades of tan sand in the dunes of southwestern Colorado. I had never seen red sand. Becky and I looked out on a sea of red sand! Ripples of sand created by the wind literally made it look like the sea. The moon cast an eerie glow upon the sand which made it look like it was moving. My other thought was about the vastness of the desert. We were looking east for what seemed like miles and there was nothing but the desolate red sand and an occasional small, struggling bush.

When our break to explore the sand dunes was over, Becky and I climbed back into the Land Cruiser and our driver took us to the Arabian Nights camp where they were preparing a barbeque dinner for us. He explained while we were driving that we had now entered another Emirate, named Sharjah. Umm Al Quwain, it turned out, did not allow alcoholic beverage consumption or belly dancing. Sharjah was the Emirate to the southwest of Umm Al Quwain and on the way back to Dubai. Sharjah allowed belly dancing and alcoholic consumption.

Many from Dubai would travel to Sharjah to purchase their liquor. Dubai allowed liquor purchases, but at a much higher price than the Emirate of Sharjah.

The camp at Sharjah had both! There was an open bar which was a nice treat after the sand dune bashing, and there would be belly dancing once dinner was served. Also, Becky and I experienced our first camel ride (an experience I don't want to repeat). I grabbed a boogie board and surfed down a sand dune. Not quite like snow skiing…but interesting.

In the camp there was a falcon handler. I discovered that falconry was very popular among the Bedouin tribes that traversed the sand. It reminded me of watching the falcons perform at half time during the Air Force Academy's home games. The falcon was their mascot. The birds would fly high over the football stadium and then dive down to grab a piece of meat that the handler was twirling on a rope in big circles. The bird never missed! It would grab the meat right out of the handler's hands!

I took Becky's picture with the falcon sitting on her wrist. There was a sheesha smoking station. Sheesha is simply smoking fruit in a hookah pipe. Some say that sheesha smoking is safer than tobacco, while others claim that one sheesha bowl is the same as eighteen cigarettes. Becky and I do not smoke and were not tempted to try this traditional, exotic experience.

There was an area in the camp where Becky and I could adorn ourselves in traditional Arab robes and headpieces. Dressed in the traditional robes, Becky and I also got henna tattoos. The dinner was served Arab style with the guests sitting on cushions on the hard ground. I am not the most flexible man on the planet! It was awkward for me to sit like this. The entertainment consisted of the aforementioned female belly dancer, who was followed by a male dancer who whirled around continuously. His costume was brightly colored and extended out as he whirled. He explained that the dance was a Turkish religious dance. The dancers would actually pray while spinning rapidly around. The saying was, "may you whirl to ecstasy."

After the entertainment ended, the same driver returned us to our villa on Palm Jemeirah Island. Becky fell asleep in the Land Cruiser and her head was in my lap. I had fun thoughts about what she could be doing while we drove. I thanked and tipped the driver and guided Becky into our home. I was reminded of the fact that tipping is not the rule in Dubai, although the driver did not complain or refuse the tip. The afternoon and evening was an exceptional experience and one that I would recommend to all Dubai visitors, or inhabitants like us who haven't experienced the sand dune bashing.

I filled a tumbler with ice and poured some Crown Royal into the glass. I moved out onto our patio and sipped at the drink while I enjoyed the night lights of Dubai. Becky was out to the world by the time I made it to bed. It looked like she had a smile on her face...good.

Washington, DC

President James addressed the room filled with the United States Joint Chiefs of Staff.

"I have just finished a call from Israel's Prime Minister," he announced. "Israel is readying their war plans and moving to call into service their reserve contingent."

One of the many Generals in the room began to speak, "We have drawn up plans in the past for an attack against Israel by one of its neighbors. These plans will give us a framework for a measured response against Iran."

"You men prepare for war…I am about to reach out to the Arab League to try to prevent a war," the President replied.

The President rose and left his Generals and Admirals huddled in small groups as they discussed America's readiness for this next conflict. The United States had dropped immense amounts of cash and weaponry in the not too distant past fighting against the Arab terrorists in the countries of Iraq and Afghanistan. The American people were tired of news from the Middle East. Young men continued to die and it seemed to many that the missions were pointless. Terrorism may have been stifled for a brief period, but terrorism would never be snuffed out.

President James made the walk back to the Oval Office in silence. His shoulders were hunched forward as if he were seeking protection against the wind. But there was no wind…only the heavy burden facing him as the world was at a precipice. Could he stop this war? Or had inertia taken things too far. As he walked past one of the many secretaries located outside of his office, he ordered, "Get me the Emir of Qatar!" "No, on second thought, get me Nabih Berri" No, get me both!"

The President reclined in his desk chair, waiting for the calls to be placed. He used the time to reflect upon the Arab League. He knew that the League of Arab States was formed in 1945 with six original members, Egypt, Iraq, Jordan, Saudi Arabia, Lebanon and Syria. Yemen joined the League later that same year. Now there were twenty two members representing the Arab states in North and Northeast Africa, and Southwest Asia, known as the Middle East. Their annual meeting had been held in Bagdad, Iraq which was viewed as an honor to that country as it rid itself of American occupation and became, once again, a sovereign nation.

He also knew that Iran was not a member of the League of Arab States, which he now found ironic. He was about to plea with this organization to help him avoid a world conflict, and the main fomenter of the current discord came from a country outside of their sphere of influence.

"Nabih Berri on line one," was heard over the intercom.

"Got it," President James spoke at the box as he reached for the phone.

The President hesitated for just a moment while he thought about how to address Nabih Berri. He knew that Mr. Berri was the Speaker of the Parliament of Lebanon, and also that he was the President of the Arab Parliament.

"Mr. Speaker," the President began, "We have an extremely urgent situation and I need your help." President James was not one who stood on diplomacy. He had a Cabinet Member to perform those duties. He spoke the truth and never thought much about the pleasantries of small talk.

"Mr. President…I know about your 'urgent situation'. How may I be of service?" Mr. Berri replied.

"Can you reach out to the League's Parliament and help to stop this madness?" the President asked.

"I will do what I can do, but you would be better advised to reach out to the Secretary General of the Arab League…the power is there," Mr. Berri responded.

"That's now Nabil el-Araby, right?" the President queried.

"Yes, sir, that is correct. He is Egyptian and has his hands full trying to make sense out of their revolution and the upcoming vote of the people," Mr. Berri said.

"Thanks for all that you can do," President James replied and hung up the phone.

"Mr. President, the Emir of Qatar is not available. It seems that he was on holiday, but is quickly returning to Qatar upon hearing the news of Iran," the secretary's voice said through the intercom box.

"Try Nabil Elaraby," the President ordered.

As the President waited he could feel his blood pressure rising. Reaching out to countries on the other side of the world was at best awkward. That part of the world was eight to ten hours ahead of Eastern Standard Time, his time zone. He was often waking up the leaders of these countries, or they were disturbing his sleep time.

"Mr. Elaraby on the line,"

"Mr. Secretary General," the President spoke, and was about to continue…

"I expected your call before now!" the Secretary replied.

"Oh, this isn't going to go well," President James thought.

"It's been a little hectic here in Washington," the President said lamely.

"What is it that you expect me to do?" the Secretary General asked.

"How about addressing with Syria that they not allow Iran to cross into their borders. And how about the same request for Iraq?" the President said.

"You must know that the League of Arab States has suspended Syria's membership in the League because of the atrocities alleged by the revolutionaries. We can make the request, but we have no power. Your country has decimated Iraq and made it an impotent democracy. Do you expect that they will stand up to Iran? With what Mr. President?

The Secretary General's tone was scolding and spiteful. It was clear that America's involvement in his part of the world had garnered scorn rather than compliance or generosity.

"I will do this for you…I will call an emergency meeting of the Arab League states which will convene in one month," the Secretary General offered.

"We don't have a month!" President James yelled and slammed down the handset.

"Didn't make any points with that idiot," the President thought.

"Get me the CIA!" he ordered.

Dubai, UAE

"Okay guys…time to get some plans on the table for I.N.C.I.S.O.R.'s response to this terrorist cell in Iraq," I announced.

Lance had returned from his preparations for the support facility in Germany. The men were falling into a comfortable routine after hearing many times the exploits of their two compatriots while on their cruise passing Somalia. Ash had returned from the United States after his supposed surveillance of the MS-13 group in North Carolina. The local news had reported a number of gang-related deaths while Ash was in North Carolina, and something about symbology made with hacked up body parts, but Ash seemed oblivious to any of the news reports.

"Hey, on a positive note, we now have a name for this cell…MADEI,"
I added. "There is a PC that I placed in a molar of one of their members
that picked up a recent conversation."

"Anyone know what MADEI stands for?" Lance asked.

"Nope…not yet," Ash replied. "The conversation is quite recent…the
CIA analysts are working to break down the transcript…but nothing yet."

"I just received a copy of the transcript," Becky added. "The military
was just minutes away from taking out the cell when they heard mention of
the Iran attack. They chose to halt the attack to see where this information
will lead."

Becky passed out the pages that outlined the recent conversation that
had been picked up by the PC.

The five I.N.C.I.S.O.R. members read the transcript in silence for a
few moments. There were only three pages of text, so the silence did not
last for very long.

"Sounds like this MADEI group is going to hijack a Lufthansa plane
in Iran and fly it into Israel. Any idea why?" Ash broke the silence.

"Well, I suspect that they have something in mind similar to the 9/11
attacks on the World Trade Center," Lance replied.

"But why?" Cyndi asked, then continued, "A German aircraft hijacked
in Tehran…what are they trying to do?"

"How about this," Becky replied, "What if this group did have
something to do with the Bushehr attack…the Arab world sentiment is
strongly leaning to the United States and Israel as the culprits, correct?"

Everybody sitting around our coffee table nodded in agreement.

Becky continued, "So now…what if this group plans an attack against
Israel that looks like it came from Iran…?"

The room was quiet while the group considered this opinion.

"Escalation of tensions at the very least!" I stated. "This would…"

My comments were interrupted by the phone. Becky got up to answer.
We waited for her to return from the office.

"That was the White House…Iran has formally declared war against
Israel. Israel and Washington are dusting off their war preparations for an
attack against Israel."

"So, that would halt all of the domestic flights between those two
countries," I stated.

"Yeah, nothing to hijack if they aren't flying," Ash added.

"Good point!" Cyndi said. "Did Washington say anything else?"

Becky replied, "Yes, the analysts predict that it will be weeks for Iran to gear up their military. A large part of their forces have been 'mothballed' since the Iran-Iraq war. Also, Iran has to approach Syria and Iraq for permission to cross their borders. Washington doesn't think that Iraq is a possibility to stop Iran because of our influence…Syria is the current 'hot potato' because of the civil unrest there."

"So, is it 'business as usual' until overt acts of aggression begin?" Lance asked.

"I guess so," I said. "Let's make…"

The phone interrupted me again and Becky rose to take the call while we all waited for her to return.

"This time it was Langley," Becky stated upon her return.

"What does the CIA want?" Ash asked.

"It looks like there was a previous conversation that was picked up by the PC that involved this MADEI group…the interpreters misfiled the conversation…the pages are coming over now…much more info about this planned attack," Becky said.

"The CIA has asked I.N.C.I.S.O.R. to infiltrate Iraq, make way to Bagdad, find this meeting house and capture one of the MADEI cell members," Becky added.

"Jesus Christ!" Lance exclaimed.

"Pretty tall order," Cyndi replied.

"Well, folks!" I stated, "We're back to where this conversation began… let's get some planning done!"

"I'm in!" Ash announced in a sinister voice that made the hairs on the back of my neck stiffen.

Frankfurt, Germany

Dick Becker joined the other four I.N.C.I.S.O.R. team members who were in the process of getting used to their new 'digs' in Germany.

"Hey, men…gather round!" Dick announced, "Got our first mission!"

Stirling, Magnus, Aaron and Graham ceased their various forms of weight lifting and moved toward Dick. When they had all come together, Dick continued, "Just heard from Ash Black in Dubai."

"Seems he's got a bug up his butt against this MS-13 gang from El Salvador. He wants us to eliminate any gang members that are in Germany," Dick said.

"Eliminate…as in kill?" Aaron inquired.

"That's how I heard him," Dick answered.

"That gang is not even listed as an active gang in Germany," Graham announced. He had moved to a computer terminal and was busy looking for gangs in Germany. "There are only nine gangs showing up…36 Boys, Bandidos Motorcycle Club, Black Jackets, Gypsy Joker Motorcycle Club, Hammerskins, Hells Angels, Outlaws Motorcycle Club, Sons of Silence and the Warlocks Motorcycle Club."

"But, look here!" Magnus announced. He also had moved to another computer terminal. "There are a number of You Tube videos of MS-13 in Germany."

"Well, let's get our homework done and find out if the gang exists here and where these guys are," Dick announced.

"Anybody else have a problem with eliminating these gang members when they haven't done anything?" Stirling asked.

"They have to be up to no good…after all, they are a crime gang…I bet none of them have real jobs," Aaron answered.

There were murmurs of agreement from the other team members, so Stirling made a conscious decision to leave his question until another time. All five I.N.C.I.S.O.R. team members were now sitting at computer terminals gathering what information they could about the MS-13 gang and their whereabouts in Germany.

Los Angeles, California

"Hey, homies," the MS-13 gang leader began as the ragtag group of 'tatted' men gathered around. "We have news from North Carolina… shortly after the attack waged on the home of that escapee…a number of our members were found decapitated and dismembered."

"That's our MO!" one of the gang members replied.

"What's up with that?" another shouted.

"Another gang attempting to move in on our territory?" asked another.

There were murmurs of retaliation around the room.

"Don't think so…haven't seen anything to tie the murders to anyone or anything!" the leader replied.

"In fact, we have nothing to tie these acts to any group," the second in command announced.

"Our peeps are being slaughtered and nobody knows nothing?" came from the crowded room.

"Only that it has stopped for now," the leader said.

"Where are we on the next kidnapping?" the second in command asked.

Julio stepped into the middle of the circle.

"We have another Imperialist that is exploiting our brethren in El Salvador," he announced.

The gang members listened intently as the plan for the capture and ransom demands were laid out for the group.

Denver, Colorado

"Lance!" Powers called out. "You know those PC's that Reggie is implanting in the teeth of suspected terrorists that come to his clinic in Dubai?"

"Yep, what about them?" Lance replied.

"What if we do that here…for instance…these MS-13 gang members?" Powers asked.

"Can't do it in this country…some crap about their rights…you know…the land of the free," Lance said.

"Would be cool, though…who'd ever find out?" Powers countered.

"Just what we'd need! One of the PC's being found on an autopsy or something. I.N.C.I.S.O.R. has been able to stay off the radar and we want to keep it that way!" Lance countered.

"By the way, there has been a huge increase in the minis that have been ordered for Central and South America," Flex announced. "That should continue to give us a head start in our ability to respond when we are needed."

"And we sure don't expect the attacks to stop after our one successful rescue!" Max added.

"So we can only wait to respond…can't be proactive about this," Duncan finished.

The five I.N.C.I.S.O.R. team members returned to their workout.

Dubai, UAE

"Okay, the United States Air Force is going to help sneak us into Iraq," Becky announced. "Reggie will fly Aurora into the country flying above an F-16 that will be reportedly on patrol in southern Iraq. The two planes will land simultaneously at the airport in Bagdad and Reggie will immediately steer the plane into one of the US hangars away from the public terminal. The security team at the airport will help with secrecy and keeping prying eyes away upon arrival."

I had never done any coordinated flying. I had seen the Thunderbirds and the Blue Angels perform many times since my childhood and was always 'wowed' by how close together the planes seemed to be. One time, while practicing my IFR approaches in Albuquerque, New Mexico, the tower ordered me to expedite my exit from the runway. I quickly obliged and turned my plane around to see what was up. I removed my foggles (glasses used to simulate visual access to only the instrument panel) as my instructor and I watched the runway. The Blue Angels…all six of them… landed in formation, touching down on the runway at the same time. Commercial and private airplanes have miles of separation between them. It was the coolest thing I had seen!

Now the plan was for me to perform this maneuver with an F-16? And me in the Avanti II? My throat was feeling quite parched!

The discussion continued focusing around maps of the area, the ramshackle building were the MADEI meetings had occurred, how we would get to the building and the goal of capturing one of the MADEI cell members for a 'debriefing'. Ash, Lance and I would all go in together, with me performing my typical lookout duties. I didn't hear much of these plans. I was still trying to imagine flying in close contact with an F-16!

Becky finished the briefing with, "And Reggie, the Air Force will have one of the ex-Thunderbirds here soon to work with you on your flying skills!"

"Swell," I thought. "Back to school for me."

CHAPTER TWENTY THREE

"REGGIE, YOU READY to get going to the airport?" Becky called out from the kitchen.

"On my way…what time is the ex-Thunderbird guy arriving?" I responded.

"He'll be there at the hangar once you get there," Becky called back.

"I'm leaving you!" I replied.

Ash and Lance were also coming to this meeting, more for their own peace of mind than to be involved in the briefing. I thought about them during my drive to the airport. Even with all of their exploits, they had never been concerned about the guy driving the plane…all of their pilots during their missions had been military or ex-military. Now they were to fly on a pretty hairy flight with a civilian yahoo…me!

I pulled up to the hangar where Aurora was kept out of the weather and more importantly out of the sun. Lance and Ash were talking with a young man just outside the hangar doors. I made my way toward them.

I reached my hand out to greet the new man and introduced myself, "Reggie Nelson."

"Lieutenant Colonel Clark Krum," he replied.

"Let's get inside," I offered.

We entered the hangar and I showed off the Avanti II. "This is Aurora!" I beamed.

"Gorgeous bird," Colonel Krum replied. "I have never seen a pusher prop up close and personal."

The four of us mounted the steps into the cabin. Ash and Lance took seats in the club seating area while I showed off the glass cockpit. Colonel Krum and I then joined the other two in the cabin.

"What do you know about formation flying?" he asked me.

"Absolutely nothing except what I've seen at shows," I replied.

(That wasn't exactly true…I had been online after I found out about my upcoming training and found such phrases as: formation flying demands an exceptionally high level of pilot skill; it's demanding and disciplined…and: you should also have excellent stick-and-rudder skills, a high level of flight discipline, and the ability to place trust in your leader. Just a little bit of pressure, I thought!)

"For the most part it is about changing your focus. Once you have your instruments set up, you fix your eyes on a part of the plane you are designated to follow. You set your distance, speed and altitude and just keep your eyes glued on that spot. We'll be able to practice that…the Air Force has an F-16 waiting nearby."

"Great! That will be a big help," I answered.

"Your approach over the Persian Gulf will be at five hundred feet AGL. Once you make radio contact with the F-16, he will turn north toward Bagdad. You will approach high and to his port side. A special strobe will be affixed aft of his cockpit. That light will be your focus point. Once in position, you will turn off all exterior navigation lights and your transponder. He will do the same. How are you with night vision goggles?"

"Never used them!" I replied, feeling really inadequate. I glanced at Ash and Lance but didn't see anything on their faces.

"Bagdad International Airport has two runways…one for civilian use and one for the military. You will listen to Bagdad International's ATIS on frequency 127.25 for airport conditions and barometer setting. Other than that you will maintain radio silence. You will be flying to runway 33L and following the F-16 on its approach.

"Are we doing the spiral approach that I've read about?" I interjected.

"No…that approach was developed for airliners to be safer and less prone to missile attacks…you will make your approach low and with no lights! Nobody will see or hear you until it's too late for them to make a move."

"It was sounding like a whole lot of fun…NOT!" I thought.

Colonel Krum continued, "At fifty feet AGL you will fall behind the F-16 and stay high and to its port side. The civilian runway, 33R is lighted. 33L is not. It is vitally important that you stay to his port side and above his aircraft. If you fail to do this, the jet wash from his engine will flip your plane and you will touch down on your heads."

Now I saw reactions from Lance and Ash. Lifted eyebrows was it, but I knew they were concerned. This guy was not one for small talk. I remembered the Dragnet television show with Sergeant Friday stating, "Just the facts, ma'am".

"You will follow the F-16 as it taxies off of the runway to the left and into the hangar that will be ready. We will time the arrival so that there is no civilian aircraft activity around the airport. The civilian terminal will be on your right. The ground lights from there should blind any prying eyes from that terminal. I'm glad that your aircraft...did you call her Aurora? Is not painted white."

"It's painted like a picture of the Aurora Borealis!" I beamed.

"The colors will make it harder to spot." Colonel Krum replied.

"The distance from Dubai International to Bagdad International is 746 nautical miles. That a problem?"

"No trouble with the round tri..." I began to reply.

"You will be refueled in Bagdad," he answered before I could finish.

"Boy, this guy is all business!" I thought.

Almost as if he could read my mind he said, "We can get to know each other later...now let's get into the air."

We all exited the airplane and waited for the attendant to hook up to the plane with his tractor and pull it out onto the tarmac. Time to go flying!

We all boarded Aurora, except this time Ash was not my copilot. Colonel Krum settled into that seat.

"Where do we hook up with the F-16?" I asked.

"He'll find you...just fly west out over the gulf. Fly at one thousand feet AGL. Continue west until you have cleared all terminal traffic. Turn on your auto pilot."

I followed his direction and flew west at one thousand feet over the gulf waters. I was startled as the F-16 seemingly came out of nowhere and appeared beneath Aurora. My immediate reaction was to pull back on the yoke. Luckily the auto pilot did not react as I would have.

The F-16 moved ahead and to my right, keeping slightly below us.

"See that strobe behind the cockpit?"

"Yes," I answered.

"That is your focal point…now turn off the auto pilot," Colonel Krum commanded. "You follow his lead."

Now I was sweating. Was my reaction time going to be up to par with these young pups? He seemed really close!

We went through a series of maneuvers that involved slow turns to the left and to the right. We gained altitude and then went into a shallow dive. When I noticed the F-16 moving ahead I moved the throttles forward. When the distance seemed to be decreasing I retarded the throttles. I was beginning to get a feel for formation flying! Colonel Krum was relatively quiet during the session. We did all of this with no radio communication.

The F-16 pilot broke radio silence, "Not bad, Dr. Nelson…we may be able to take your training wheels off, soon!" With that, he shot ahead and then looked like he pointed the nose of his aircraft straight up. Quickly he shot out of sight.

"Wow!" was all I could say. "Did you see that?"

It was at that moment that I noticed that Ash and Lance were on each side of the cockpit entrance. I was too busy concentrating to notice that they had left their seats and were watching the show!

"Oh, to be young and flying a twenty million dollar aircraft!" Lance exclaimed.

We returned to Dubai International Airport and parked the Aurora.

The F-16 was already parked and its pilot was leaning against our hangar. We exited the Aurora and turned her over to the attendant. We then made our way toward the relaxing F-16 pilot. He had landed his craft and made it to our hangar long before I landed back in Dubai.

"Colonel Krum!" the fighter pilot exclaimed. "What an honor to meet you!" as he snapped to attention and saluted his comrade in arms.

Colonel Krum returned the salute. "Let's get a drink!"

"Nothing here at the airport. This is Dubai!" I countered.

"We're bunked at the Hyatt downtown…there's a bar there," Colonel Krum replied.

"I can top that…please join us at my home," I answered.

"Sold! Let's get out of this heat," the Colonel said.

The two jet pilots joined me in the 760Li, while Ash and Lance followed in their car. Twenty minutes later we were seated on our patio with ice cold drinks quenching our thirst.

"Lance…get Cyndi over here, Ash…you can bring anybody you'd like…we'll do some steaks on the grill!" I announced.

Calls were made and shortly the patio was full of company and lively conversation.

Tel Aviv, Israel

Prime Minister Netanyahu addressed his liaison to I.N.C.I.S.O.R., Gary Kubetz. His Colonel had just finished a phone interview with Becky Nelson.

"What is there to report on this Iraqi group?" the Prime Minister asked.

"Very little, sir…the group was almost annihilated by a Predator drone, but the attack was halted when there was mention of the attack on Bushehr. Now the CIA has directed I.N.C.I.S.O.R. to infiltrate the group to discover more information and to thwart a planned attack against Israel!" Colonel Kubetz intoned.

"Attack against Israel? While the Arab States are gearing up for war? This is madness!" Netanyahu yelled.

"Not madness, Mr. Prime Minister…a way to make sure that calmer heads don't prevail," Gary Kubetz responded.

"What?"

"Right now, Iran is reaching out to Syria and Iraq for permission to cross their lands. Both countries are reluctant at this point. They are indicating that they do not want their lands invaded and they don't want to grant access to their airspace. Without Iraq and Syria's help, Iran can only be viewed as 'sabre rattling' while both of our countries prepare the armed forces for conflict."

"Yes, so…,"

"An overt act of aggression…vis-à-vis an attack against Israel…would incite us to respond."

"And"

"The neutral Arab States would lean more positively to Iran and support them in war!"

Washington, DC

The Deputy Director of the CIA entered the Oval Office as the President's secretary directed him inside.

"Good morning, Mr. President," he offered.

"Says who?" the President replied. "What's up with that group that we didn't take out in Iraq? Why didn't we take them out?"

"There was mention of the attack on Bushehr…this group may be involved, somehow," the Deputy Director responded.

"So, what's next?"

"We're sending in the I.N.C.I.S.O.R. team to gather information from the cell members, and…"

"Why them?" the President interrupted.

"Our assets are limited in the area after the pullout. Rather than expose them, we chose to utilize the I.N.C.I.S.O.R. group. If anything goes awry, there will be no ties to the United States."

"These guys any good?" President James asked.

"Remember Alaska…and that Italian rescue? Remember El Salvador?"

"Yeah, yeah."

"That was I.N.C.I.S.O.R."

"Alright! Righteous efforts!" the President replied. "Get on with it, then…and get out of my office!"

Dubai, UAE

Ash and I had not had any alone time since his return from North Carolina. We met at the Dojo for a needed workout and a few rounds of sparring. Once again, I got my ass whipped by Ash, but I noticed what seemed to me to be a more sinister approach to his attacks and parries. I was hurting more than usual after the workout. Ash's blows had done more damage than usual. We took a break by the water cooler and I asked, between gulps of the cool liquid, "How was North Carolina?"

"Some people died there," was Ash's response.

"I saw the news…was that you?" I asked.

"Yep," was his one word reply.

"You murder these folks?"

"Yep."

"Why?"

"Bad people."

"What about the authorities?"

"What about them?"

"Why not let them deal with that gang?"

"They still have to…just fewer of them to deal with."

"The papers said that the bodies were decapitated and dismembered."

"Yep"

"Why do all that?"

"That's the MS-13 style. I wanted them to get the message in the strongest of terms and in a language that they would understand…that they are not wanted there!"

"Do you think that you will change anything?"

"Nope, but six less scumbags in the world."

"You would not have bothered with all of this ritual and targeting people for murder before Grace died," I replied.

"I'm a changed man…and my new motto is just like AA…I'll clean up the world, one scumbag at a time," Ash answered.

"That's really twisting things."

"Don't care, anymore…bad guys die!"

"Alright, alright…time to join Lance…we have a mission to plan," I said as our conversation ended with me feeling extremely unnerved at my close friend's announcement.

CHAPTER TWENTY FOUR

Bagdad, Iraq

THE FLIGHT, APPROACH and landing at Bagdad International Airport had gone smoothly. Flying over the Persian Gulf at 500 feet above the water was the easy part of the journey. There was just a sliver of a moon which did little to light up the night sky. For all intents and purposes it was a moonless night. Aurora's navigation lights and strobes were off. We were dark as we approached the Iraqi coast. I flew over two tankers that were steaming south away from Iraq. They were the only ships that we encountered. Ash and Lance watched the ships from their starboard windows and didn't notice any untoward activity. Our approach to Iraq was unnoticed.

I made radio contact with the circling F-16 at the appointed time. He slowed his speed to match the speed of the Avanti II and turned on his navigation lights briefly so that I could position Aurora above him and slightly to his left. Then the lights went out and I had only the strobe on his backside for guidance. Both aircraft approached the Iraqi coast in tight formation.

The night vision goggles were awkward, at best, but I made do with what I was provided. We approached Bagdad International from the south and lined up for the final approach to 33L. As we began the final approach I moved out to the left and made sure to keep Aurora above the F-16's flight path. The touchdown on the darkened runway was one of the hardest I've made…I hoped that I didn't bend any parts on the landing gear. An askance look from Ash let me know that the touchdown wasn't appreciated! I also heard a "Damn!" from Lance back in the cabin.

"Sorry folks!" I announced, "Welcome to Bagdad International Airport!" I sat back in the pilot's seat and realized that I was completely soaked in sweat. "Man, I'm going to need a change of clothes before we head out!"

"Change of shorts, too?" Lance quipped.

"No, smartass! That was tough!" I replied.

Ash added his piece, "Watching you had me sweating, too!"

Both aircraft quickly exited the runway and made their way into the open hangar. It was huge and cavernous. The electric doors closed and not until closure were any lights turned on inside the hangar. There was a lot of activity as airmen scurried around the two planes to make them secure. The whine from the engines ceased as they wound down. Lance, Ash and I donned our gear and made our way out of Aurora and onto to concrete floor of the hangar. We were directed to one of the side rooms, and as we made our way we were joined by the pilot of the F-16. I was astonished to see that it was Jarod Clark, the helicopter pilot we met in Alaska!

"Lieutenant Clark! What are you doing in Iraq?" Ash asked.

"Ashonte', right?" Jarod replied.

"Just Ash…but good memory!" Ash exclaimed.

"After our Alaska venture I had the chance to step up to fixed wing aircraft…to jets!" Jarod said. and it's Lieutenant Colonel, now."

"Well, congratulations!" I said and gave him a strong handshake. I was so glad to be on the ground. Normally, I'd rather be in the air, but that flight wasn't my idea of a good time!

Ash, Lance and I went to the room that we were directed to. Lieutenant Colonel Clark headed elsewhere.

A beat up Ford sedan was parked in the hangar. We were told that it was our vehicle for the mission. They also said that the engine and tranny were sound. I doubted that from the looks of the car! The appearance of the car matched most of the other cars in Bagdad; we were told…we did not want to stand out, did we?

Our gear was checked…just side arms and knives on this trip. The three of us donned our Arab gear…the traditional white, loose, shirt-like dishdasha underneath and tan abas for our outer cloaks. The checked kaffiyeh on our heads held in place by a black cord called the agal. There were sandals for our footwear. Lance and I applied dark makeup to our faces and hands. Ash watched in amusement while we painted our faces.

Maps were checked and the route outlined to MADEI's meeting house. We loaded up with Lance at the wheel, Ash riding shotgun and me in the back seat. All three of us put on our night vision goggles.

An armored Humvee escorted our car out of the airport and through the Green Zone. It left us after the last checkpoint. We were now on our own!

The streets of Bagdad were eerily dark and abandoned. There was no curfew at the present time, but we saw no evidence of activity. Lance sped through the streets, driving erratically, which made for a rough ride. He parked the Ford just blocks from our target.

The three of us pulled off our night vision goggles and exited the car. We crept along the buildings until we could see the ramshackle dwelling… our destination.

We spent a few moments observing the structure. No activity was noticed. We made our approach.

I noticed a figure lurking outside the entrance. The figure was noticed only because he took a long draw on a cigarette, and the burning ash was visible. Otherwise we could have missed him. I indicated to the other two that I would disable the sentry. I crept forward and moved behind him. I quickly got my arm around his neck in a 'sleeper' hold. It would be only seconds before he became unconscious because of the pressure I had on his carotid arteries.

At that moment, Ash appeared in front of the sentry as I held him. He looked briefly into the sentry's eyes. I thought that it was the look of death. He had his knife in hand and speedily pulled the blade across the sentry's neck. The man crumbled in my grasp. I expected him to go down from my hold, but not that he would be dead!

I pulled the corpse off to the side of the dwelling and returned to where Ash was standing. All he did was hold up one finger…one less bad guy! My head was spinning…we needed these guys alive to get information. Dead men tell no tales.

I took up my post at the entrance and watched outside as Ash and Lance made their way inside. Soon, they rejoined me with Lance carrying a man over his shoulder. We left the location and returned to the car. Lance threw the limp body in the back seat. I had the job of riding next to this terrorist and keeping an eye on him as Lance and Ash got in the front seat. We sped off in the direction of the airport.

"What the hell!" Lance yelled, the first to speak. "You killed them all!"

Ash held up four fingers. "Four less bad guys in the world."

"Damnit! Lance said, "We are supposed to find out what they know… how can we do that now?"

"We've got one…isn't that enough?" Ash replied.

I assumed from the discourse back and forth between the two of them that there were four members of the MADEI cell inside the room, plus the one guard. And that three members plus the guard were no longer alive and well.

The trip back to the airport was made in silence. The man next to me did not stir. I checked occasionally to make sure he was breathing.

Lance pulled the car into the darkened hangar and the doors were closed behind us. The hangar was then illuminated as we exited the car with our prey over Lance's shoulder. A group of men met us and relieved Lance of his burden. They dragged the terrorist into one of the rooms, while we were directed to another room for debriefing.

The debriefing was more of a yelling match between Lance and Ash. What I gathered from their argument was that Ash had entered the room and with the speed of a Panther had moved around the room slitting throats and stabbing into the hearts of the unsuspecting MADEI terrorist cell members. None of the terrorists even had time to pull out a weapon. The one live cell member was due to Lance grabbing and pulling the terrorist away from Ash and shielding him with his body.

Ash had an icy look in his eyes that spoke loudly…'don't mess with me'. The look turned me into a mute, but Lance was not letting up. The two were now face to face. Their body language and posturing made me worried that they were going to do battle. Lance towered over Ash and I had a quick thought about who would win if they grappled. I didn't want to see this.

The agent in the room with us stood up and moved to place himself between Lance and Ash. "Halt…and back off!" he yelled.

Lance took a step back and turned toward me. "Let's get out of here," he said.

Ash was not backing down and looked ready to attack the agent.

"Ashonte'" I yelled. "Let's go."

He looked in my direction with that icy stare and I feared that I was going to be his next victim. Then his manner changed rapidly and he smiled.

"Don't have to worry about this cell anymore," he stated.

"Let's pack up and get back to Aurora," I offered.

"Off we go!" Ash announced.

We gathered up our gear and headed for the Avanti II. I was so shaken that I didn't perform my typical preflight inspection of the aircraft. I donned my night vision goggles and taxied Aurora onto the unlit runway while dialing in the GPS coordinates for Dubai International Airport. I had no concern about missile attacks or anything else. I just wanted out of there and for this to be over!

It wasn't until we were in the air that I noticed that the plane had been refueled for the return flight. Ash performed his copilot duties without discussion. We flew out of Iraq low and dark and without incident. Over the Persian Gulf I turned on the navigation lights and the transponder, and I shed the goggles.

The only conversation on the flight home was between me and Dubai Approach. The landing at home was much smoother with a lighted runway. I taxied to the hangar and left Aurora in the hands of the attendant to put her away for the night.

The three of us got into my car for a silent ride to my home. I asked Lance and Ash to meet with me in the morning and they left for their own abodes.

Los Angeles, CA

"The attack went off without a hitch!" the MS-13 gang member announced to the gang leader.

"This was pure genius!" the leader cried out. "Kidnapping the family right here in Los Angeles!"

"Esse, we got the wife and kid! They're squirreled away at one of the cribs on the east side," the gang member said.

"We change our focus to the families of people exploiting El Salvador and not the exploiters themselves!" the leader replied.

"Caught them completely unawares!"

"Any trouble with the police?"

"None—we were in and out in a flash—no security," the member said.

"And nothing on the news, yet?"

"Right"

"Let's get the ransom demand down to El Salvador," the leader ordered.

"Fingers?" That was their trademark.

"No, not yet…let's see if they go for the 'proof of life' bull first," the leader replied.

The MS-13 gang in Los Angeles had chosen to act locally with the family of an engineer who was consulting with EC Engineering, headquartered in San Salvador. It did not matter to the Mara Salvatrucha gang that this company was involved in improving the infrastructure in El Salvador. EC Engineering were not exploiters of the cheap labor that was available in El Salvador. The mantra of protecting the residents from El Salvador from this kind of abuse just was thrown out the window.

And this poor man had been hired as a consultant! He spent a month at a time in El Salvador, working with EC Engineering and helping to improve the local economy. The MS-13 gang found out about him on the company website. It did not take them long to discover where he lived in Los Angeles and stake out his residence. The wife and child were easy pickings for the gang as they hit the house when the wife arrived home from school with the nine year old daughter in tow. Six gang members poured out of three vehicles and swarmed over the minivan and their unsuspecting, innocent prey.

The ransom demand for three million dollars was delivered to the corporate offices of EC Engineering in San Salvador. News quickly made it to the consultant who immediately made flight arrangements to return to the United States.

The President of EC Engineering responded to the demand. He wrote in his response that the man in question was not an employee of EC Engineering. He only functioned in an independent contractor role, advising the company. Therefore, the company would not be honoring the ransom demands and that MS-13 would be better advised to contact the consultant directly at his Los Angeles address as that was where the consultant was returning.

When word of the response arrived back in Los Angeles, the MS-13 gang leader went berserk!

"You targeted the wife and child of an independent consultant? You idiots! Any money they have will not be enough to make it worth our while! What were you thinking? Oh, I know...YOU WEREN"T!" he yelled.

The other members cowered at the tongue lashing and stayed silent until the leader was done with his ranting.

"What do we do now with the woman and bambino?" one of the members ventured to ask.

"Kill them...kill them both!" the leader replied. "And dump their bodies on their front lawn."

The leader paced back and forth with his head in his hands. "This is so effing stupid!" he yelled. "We will have nothing but heat from this!" His pace quickened. "Get out of my face!"

The others quickly cleared the room and went to perform their leader's orders. When they arrived at the house where the wife and daughter were taped up and secured, they informed the guards that the two women were to be murdered and their bodies dumped in front of their home. One of the gang members pulled out his 9mm. weapon, and in typical gang fashion with the gun held sideways, walked up to the wide eyed girl and calmly placed the gun against her forehead and pulled the trigger.

The mother watched the horrific event and struggled violently against the duct tape that held her to a chair next to her now dead daughter. She worked her head side to side and fought valiantly with the chair. The gang member waited calmly with his gun at his side until she tired. Her head was now forward with her chin on her chest. He raised the weapon and fired again. A family destroyed for nothing.

The others gathered up the two corpses and drove to the site of the abduction. They wondered why there was still no police presence at the house. The bodies were tossed onto the front lawn and the cars sped away, unimpeded.

A few hours later, the consultant drove to his home after the long flight. Now there were police all over his street. He was first stopped at a police barricade and then allowed to proceed to his home. The bodies of his wife and daughter were draped with dark plastic but still lay where they had been dumped. He cried out and collapsed into a heap when he saw them. The police escorted him into the home.

Denver, CO

"Got another gig, guys!" Max announced when he hung up the phone.

"What's up and where to?" Flex asked.

"That same El Salvadoran gang," Max stated.

"Back to El Salvador?" Lance inquired.

"Nope...at least not at first...we're off to LA," Max added.

"Another mini?" Duncan asked.

"Not this time...gather 'round," Max ordered.

The I.N.C.I.S.O.R. team, stationed in Denver, listened intently as Max filled them in on the murders in Los Angeles.

"LA cops have asked for Federal help...and the Feds asked for us! They want to take down this gang by capturing the leader...we accomplish that and SWAT takes care of the rest. They want this guy to disappear... we bring him back to Denver with us to be interrogated, then he will be removed to Florence," Max advised.

"That's where the Super Max is, right?" Powers asked.

Lance answered, "Yup, that's right, Powers. All of the world's really badasses are kept there. They are in isolation twenty three hours a day and have no, and I mean no human contact! These are the worst of the worst. The true 'end of the line'. Ain't no getting' out of there, except feet first, and even then they incinerate them!"

"Let me tell you about Supermax!" Flex added. "This place is amazing! The majority of the facility is underground. Each cell has a desk, stool and bed which are made out of poured concrete. The shower is on a timer so it can't flood and the toilet shuts off automatically if blocked! The inmates can only see the sky through four inch windows so they can't figure out where they are within the prison. They exercise in a swimming pool like structure so they stay disoriented and have now idea where they are. Phone calls are not allowed. Reporters have remarked about the astonishing and eerie quiet in the prison. Inmates end up here who exhibit 'absolutely no concern for human life'."

"So, we bring this guy back here and he ends up in a place like that? No charges? No trial? No rights?" Powers opined.

"Not our concern…you got a problem with that?" Max asked.

"No…no, I'm good," Powers replied.

"Let's get a move on…time to pack," Max ordered, and the five I.N.C.I.S.O.R. team members sprang into action.

Dubai, UAE

Lance arrived early for our scheduled meeting. I could tell that he was really upset. His countenance always looked angry to me and I sometimes wondered if his scowl was permanent, but today was even worse.

"Did you hear that our Denver team has been called out to Los Angeles?" I asked as a way to break the ice.

"No…and I don't give a damn…I got an issue with last night…with Ash," Lance replied.

"Me, too," I began.

"No! Damnit! You don't understand!" Lance interrupted.

"I've always been okay with killing a combatant. It was them or me. It was my job…my duty. In fact, years ago I had a Pastor help me with an interpretation of the Ten Commandments when I had an issue with 'Thou Shalt Not Kill'. He explained to me that the actual translation states, 'Thou Shalt Not Commit Murder'. There is a place for killing…but what Ash did last night…that was murder! Cold blooded murder!"

I then told him about what had happened with the sentry outside the dwelling that I had attempted to incapacitate. Lance shook his head.

"I've been a soldier and an operative a long time. This isn't right and I have to stop it," Lance added.

Just then Ash came through the foyer and into the living room. He had what looked like a ream of papers under his arm.

"Ready to get after this? Reggie? Lance? You got an issue with my 'style'?" Ash began.

He took my favorite chair, leaving Lance and I to sit facing him on the couch. He threw the papers that he had brought onto the coffee table. I could see that the papers looked like clippings from various newspapers.

"Style?" Lance countered. "Style? This has nothing to do with style. You murdered those men last night!"

Lance and I sat on the edge of the couch cushions, waiting for a response.

"...Yes...and?" Ash replied.

"I.N.C.I.S.O.R. is not about murder," I said, somewhat tentatively.

"What is it about, Reggie?" Ash asked. "What are we here for? Aren't we fighting bad guys? Don't they sometimes die? And what about us? Our lives are on the line, too!"

"People die in armed conflict!" Lance answered. "And sometimes it's us against them and we hope to prevail."

"And what about Grace?" Ash retorted. "Was it her against them? NO!"

Ash smashed his fist onto the top of the coffee table. I was sure the table would shatter. He quickly rose and grabbed the papers that were strewn over the table.

"Mara Salvatrucha," Ash announced as he threw several clippings on the table. "Have you two looked hard at this gang? Yes? No?" Ash looked between Lance and me. "Here!" he said as he tossed an article on the table. "This article talks about the gang members being notorious for their use of violence and a 'subcultural moral code that predominantly consists of merciless revenge and cruel retributions'. Here!" as he tossed down another newspaper. "This one describes MS-13's 'excessive use of cruelty'. Here!" as another article was thrown onto the table. "This one addresses Mara Salvatrucha's penchant for 'beheadings and mutilations' with the use of a machete as their weapon of choice."

Lance and I sat without disturbing Ash. He was on a roll...

"This gang kidnapped one of our clients. When I.N.C.I.S.O.R. rescued him, they went after his family! The members of this Salvadoran gang show absolutely no regard for human life."

Ash sat down and gathered his thoughts.

"Terrorism. Have you looked up the definition? Here!" and he tossed another paper onto the table. "This I googled, 'the systematic use of terror, especially as a means of coercion...those violent acts which are intended to create fear and deliberately target or disregard the safety of non-combatants (civilians)'"

"Combatants," Lance interjected. "That's my point! Killing in battle is different. You MURDERED those men!"

"Did I?" Ash replied as his eyes narrowed. He stood up, again.

"Here are the articles about the bombing that killed Grace," as he tossed more papers onto the table. "Did any of those people have a chance? Did any of those DEAD people lift an arm against terrorism? Did any of those people attack the terrorist? Hell, Grace was an artist!"

"Nobody said that it was right, Ash," I replied. "It was tragic and…"

Ash cut me off. "Who goes after these scumbags? Huh? The military? These guys fight dirty. They are cowards. They take out civilians. What does I.N.C.I.S.O.R. stand for? We're the 'Civilians' for a 'Safe Society', right?"

He threw more papers on the table.

"Here! These are about the million dead in Iran. This MADEI group involved? Maybe…maybe not. But your PC, Reggie recorded a conversation that said they were involved. One million dead!"

"Ash!" Lance interrupted. "We are trying to prevent World War IV!"

"Oh, bullshit!" Ash retorted. "War is for politicians and posturing. They should just let their favorite Peacocks fan their plumes of feathers and claw themselves to death!"

I chuckled at Ash's analogy…then I thought about the millions of young men that had died because of the pride of the politicians…

Ash concluded, "I have made the world a better place by eliminating this scum. I will be accuser, jury and judge…and my sentence is death. Nobody will miss them. Nobody will mourn their 'passing'. And death is immediate. I do not torture!"

"You're the living meaning of a psychopath," Lance said.

"How's that?" Ash replied.

Lance read from the laptop in front of him, "a disorder characterized by a pervasive pattern of disregard for the rights of others…"

Ash interrupted, "I'm not pervasive…you don't have to worry…just the bad guys have to worry."

Lance continued, "a lack of empathy or remorse…"

Again, Ash interrupted, "Absolutely! I feel nothing for those dead terrorists!"

"Please let him finish, Ash!" I said.

"…false emotions, selfishness, grandiosity or deceptiveness; impulsiveness, irritability, aggression, or inability to perceive danger and protect one's self." Lance finished.

"Hey! I'm careful…to a fault!" Ash retorted. "But…if it's me against terrorists…somebody's gonna die! You two get on board or kick me out…NOW!"

"You jeopardized the mission!" Lance said.

"How? How was the mission in trouble?" Ash replied.

"We wanted information about the Bushehr attack…and the hijacking they are planning," I said.

"We got one!" Ash answered.

"Only because I kept him from you!" Lance argued.

"Call it what you will…revenge…psychopath…I'm going to avenge Grace's death and eliminate every terrorist or bad guy I can…end of story! Now, Eleven Million is in town and I'm taking her out to see the sights of Dubai and then hang a 'do not disturb' sign on the front door of my house!"

I remembered the conversation that Ash and I had in the Burj al Arab when he returned from Colorado Springs. He was only going to date white women worth more than five million dollars. That was when he told me that no more alcohol or red meat would be put into his body. I knew then that he was a changed man…now were we seeing the dark side of that change?

Ash rose to leave. "I love you guys. Please accept me the way I am."

With that he left Lance and me to our own thoughts.

CHAPTER TWENTY FIVE

Dubai, UAE

BECKY FINISHED HER call from CIA headquarters in Langley, VA. and joined me on the patio. The winds had picked up and were whipping the sand into the air. Looking back toward downtown Dubai, the sky had the look of a really bad day in Los Angeles. The temperature was warm, but not a day for the beach with the wind and the sand.

"You want the good news or the bad news first?" Becky asked.

"Good news," I replied.

"Mini sales are out of this world! That murder in Los Angeles has the existing mini owners wanting the devices for their families. We are backlogged with orders. As quickly as the CIA supplies us, the minis are activated and placed in commission."

"And the bad?" I asked.

"Your hit on the MADEI quarters in Iraq was bupkis," she answered.

"Bupkis? What does that mean?" I asked.

"Nothing…Nada…Absolutely nothing of value!" Becky replied.

"Hey! We got one out alive for the CIA to interrogate! I helped deliver him, myself," I said.

"And they did just that. Sorry to say that, due to an unforeseen heart condition, he is no longer with us," Becky stated.

"That's not our fault!" I answered, defensively.

"Whoa boy, that's not what I meant. The CIA retrieved the info they could. It turns out that the five members of the MADEI cell that you,

Lance and Ash encountered were brand new recruits. The seven other members were not in Iraq. They had split into the two groups that we knew about from that meeting that the CIA picked up from the PC you implanted. The leader and two others are either already in Frankfurt...or enroute. The four other cell members have travelled to Iran. The planned hijacking of that Lufthansa flight to Israel looks like it is still on."

"I wonder what they'll do when they find out about the attack on their cell." I muttered.

"How will they know?" Becky asked. "You killed them all!"

"Be careful with that word, 'you'!" I retorted. "I didn't kill anybody!"

"You...Lance...the CIA...Ash...what does it matter? They are all dead!" Becky stated.

I was feeling defensive, again, at the way she was talking. Then I realized that she was just telling the truth. I took a sip from the glass of Crown Royal that was sitting in front of me. Not the same pleasure that I usually enjoyed from this Canadian Whiskey.

"Put the Frankfurt team on alert!" I ordered Becky. "I'll call Lance and Ash. I guess we're off to Tehran to stop a hijacking."

"One last item," Becky added.

"Okay"

"The one captured MADEI cell member knew nothing about the attack on Bushehr. We are not any closer to solving that riddle," Becky ended.

Langley, VA

The Director of the CIA was visibly upset. News of the interrogation had filtered up to him and it was clear that they weren't anywhere closer to exposing who had commenced the attack against the Bushehr nuclear reactor. Iran had declared war against Israel. The world was preparing. The United States was preparing. "Oh, God," he thought, "I long for the days of the Cold War! We only had one opponent then."

The Director placed a call to his Deputy Director, who was overseeing I.N.C.I.S.O.R.'s involvement in the unfolding world drama.

"Sir, I.N.C.I.S.O.R. has a Frankfurt team responding. They are located at the Frankfurt Airport, so technically they are already in place. The three original members of I.N.C.I.S.O.R. are making their way to

Tehran. We have no assets on the ground there that can be of any help," the Deputy Director said.

The Director placed the phone into its cradle. "Things are really going to get dicey…if those guys can't find out something!" he thought.

Los Angeles, CA

The Denver team of five I.N.C.I.S.O.R. members was ensconced at the LA police headquarters. They were there to coordinate with LA SWAT and plan the abduction of the local MS-13 leader. The planning session had gone well. LA police had quite the dossier on this particular individual. He had come to the United States several years before. After many brutal murders of which he was accused and that could never be pinned on him, including the elimination of the previous Mara Salvatrucha leader in Los Angeles, he had assumed control of the largest Mara Salvatrucha gang in the United States.

The headquarters was well known and had been under surveillance. He never ventured out alone. The task of isolating him and taking him alive was not going to be easy. One of the SWAT team came up with a brilliant idea!

Food for lunch was often procured by the gang from a Salvadoran dive just blocks from their headquarters. A runner was sent out and returned with bags of Panes Rellenos, a warm chicken submarine sandwich. The chicken, marinated and roasted with Pipil spices, was hand-pulled and served with tomatoes and watercress.

A midnight entre' into the Salvadoran food joint was planned with the goal of poisoning the marinade with campylobacter. This particular 'bug' was chosen because it is the leading cause of food poisoning in the United States, and caused by eating undercooked chicken or food that has been in contact with raw chicken. Seventy to ninety percent of chickens are infected with campylobacter. The gang members could only assume that they had eaten some bad food prepared at that dive.

Nothing that would kill…but all of the gang members who partook the next day would become violently ill…enough so to require medical attention. The I.N.C.I.S.O.R. and SWAT teams would make their way to the closest hospital and await the gang's arrival.

Others who went to that establishment on that day would also become ill, but it was deemed that these casualties were an acceptable price for the leader's capture. Anyway, they would recover.

The night incursion went off without a hitch. The next day, teams were well hidden at the hospital. LA SWAT hid out in ambulances outside of the hospital. Lance and Powers donned white coats and tried to blend in to the emergency room as staff members. Flex and Max acted like patients who were on gurneys behind moveable curtains. Duncan hung out at the emergency room desk wearing street clothes.

It was early in the afternoon when all hell broke loose. Fifteen young men, covered in tattoos crashed through the emergency room doors. Many were doubled over with violent stomach cramps. All were sweating profusely.

"We have food poisoning!" one of the gang members yelled out to the whole emergency room.

"Have a seat and fill out this paperwork," the nurse at the desk ordered.

"We need help NOW!" another gang member cried out.

The gang leader's photograph had been disseminated to SWAT and to the I.N.C.I.S.O.R. team.

"Here we go!" Duncan announced as he spotted the leader.

The emergency room personnel had sprung into action. The facility looked to Duncan like it was in chaos…albeit controlled chaos. People were scurrying around the tatted gang members like ants discovering a morsel of food. Gurneys were pushed here and there.

Lance and Powers pushed a gurney toward the leader and helped him to lie down. He was doubled up and on his side. It reminded Powers of someone in a fetal position. They pushed the gurney into an open cubicle and closed the curtains.

"We've got him!" Lance announced.

Powers searched for a vein and started an IV drip. Lance removed a syringe from his coat and sunk the needle into the feeder tube. He quickly depressed the plunger and the solution of Propofol entered the IV tube. Lance made the immediate connection between the drug, Propofol, that he was injecting and Los Angeles. Here in LA they call the drug 'Michael Jackson's Milk', referring to the milky appearance of the liquid and his last words which were a plea for 'milk'. Within seconds, the MS-13 gang leader's body relaxed as he fell into a deep sleep. His bowels also relaxed and a horrible stench arose from his soiled trousers.

Suddenly the curtain was yanked open and another gang member stood there with a gun in his hand.

"What are you doing?" he screamed. "He is not to be alone!"

Lance and Powers raised their hands in mock surrender.

"This man is sick. We are helping him," Powers said to the gang member.

The gang member waved his gun around the cubicle and was at that moment hit by a severe abdominal cramp. He doubled over, clinging to the moveable curtain.

"Madre dios!" he cried out.

Lance and Powers both moved toward him.

"No!" he cried out.

Just then Flex moved up behind him and jabbed a needle into his neck. The gang member crumbled to the floor. Max was also now on his feet and cried out to the room, "Man down!" He wanted to stir up activity in the chaotic room. A nurse and two orderlies buzzed around the downed man and moved him away.

Powers covered the gang leader in a sheet and he and Lance began to move the gurney.

"Must get this man upstairs!" he shouted.

Several gang members attempted to accompany the gurney only to be halted by severe cramping. The entire emergency room now had a putrid smell.

"That was good stuff!" Duncan thought as he surveyed the room. He heard the groaning and noticed that several had vomited right on the floor.

Lance and Powers maneuvered the gurney out of the emergency room, with Flex and Max bringing up the rear. Max observed that none of the gang was able to move after them. In the hallway they turned the gurney and headed out a rear exit.

Duncan, after watching the clean getaway, looked around the room and then exited out the emergency room entrance.

LA SWAT had an ambulance waiting at the rear entrance to the hospital. The Mara Salvatrucha gang leader was loaded onboard and the ambulance pulled away very quietly and without flair.

Powers and Lance pulled off their white coats and threw them away. They were joined by Max and Flex as they ambled around the side of the hospital for their rental van. Duncan was at the wheel as he waited for his four teammates to settle in. Then he drove off toward LA police headquarters.

"That was too easy," he announced. It was an omen of epic proportions!

The I.N.C.I.S.O.R. team arrived at police headquarters and made their way to the squad room. The LA SWAT team that had whisked off the MS-13 gang leader was already seated in the room. The SWAT leader began the debriefing, and shortly into his talk, a Los Angeles lieutenant burst into the room.

"All hell's broken loose!" he exclaimed. The SWAT team was on their feet.

"There have to be fifty of them!" he yelled. The SWAT team and their leader were running out the door, leaving the bewildered I.N.C.I.S.O.R. team staring at each other.

"What is happening?" Powers asked the lieutenant.

"That Mara Salvatrucha gang! The gang that you just took down their leader?" he replied.

"Well, the word is out! At least fifty gang members have descended upon the hospital and the SWAT team that remained at the scene has been surrounded," the lieutenant said. "Right now it's a standoff. They are demanding the release of their comrades."

"Do they know that we've got their leader?" Lance asked.

"Not yet...the other fourteen that showed up with the leader are still inside...and very, very sick!"

"Need our help?" Max queried.

"No. Every available black and white is rolling to the scene," the lieutenant finished and abruptly left the room.

"Well, ain't that a pickle!" Duncan exclaimed.

"Our mission's over, boys...what do you want to do?" Flex asked.

"How about a little sightseeing...like the grounds around the hospital," Lance said.

"Sounds good to me!" Flex replied.

"When's our flight?" Powers asked.

"Six hours…we've got a little time," Duncan replied. Sometimes it could take three hours just to get from downtown Los Angeles out to LAX.

"Let's get a move on!" Lance announced.

Frankfurt, Germany

"Okay, what do we know?" Stirling asked.

"Three perps. The MADEI cell leader and two others," Magnus replied.

"Any names or identities?" Dick questioned.

"Yep! The MADEI leader's name is Abdullah. Who'd guess. The other two go by Sanjar and Amjad. He's the one that Dr. Nelson implanted with the PC. That's how we know what they're up to," Aaron replied.

"And these three are just here to delay the Lufthansa flight from Frankfurt to Tel Aviv?" Graham asked.

"That's what the transcript says. And there's been nothing to indicate that they are deterring from that plan," Magnus stated.

"Well, with that PC in that Amjad character, they should be easy to track," Dick opined.

"Easy, yes…in fact we've already got them at the Sheraton Hotel here at the airport," Magnus said.

"Gear check, now!" Stirling ordered.

"Hey! Do we take them out or let them do their thing?" Dick asked.

"We just watch and make sure all they do is delay that flight. Anything else and we move in," Stirling replied.

"What about that Bushehr stuff?" Aaron asked.

"Supposedly, the MADEI leader, Abdullah, has some info," Magnus said. "We're supposed to monitor their movements…maybe we'll get the chance to grab him before he can escape back to Iraq."

"Seems to me that info is more crucial than this hijacking!" Graham said.

"Not our call," was Stirling's reply.

Washington, DC

"This world is going absolutely effing nuts!" the President exclaimed. "Is there anything that can stop this?"

The CIA director leaned forward on the couch facing President James. "Teams are in place, Mr. President. We'll have news shortly."

"What news? What are you talking about?"

"We're still working that link to a terrorist cell, called MADEI, in Iraq. They are planning to hijack an airliner and fly it into a building in Tel Aviv, Israel."

"I know where the hell Tel Aviv is! What's this have to do with this damn imminent war?"

"There may be a link to the Bushehr attack."

CHAPTER TWENTY SIX

Tehran, Iran

"ARE WE READY for war?" the Ayatollah asked.

"We will be ready and operational within the week!" the army General lied.

Iran's military forces had not been at war for more than a decade. During that time, very little money had come from the government to keep up with the maintenance and upkeep required to keep the vehicles running. Even less had been spent to upgrade the equipment and allow the Iranian army to join the twenty first century.

The army boasted a tank count of over seventeen hundred tanks. The problem was that over the years since the Iran-Iraq war, many hundreds of these tanks had fallen into disrepair. Just to keep some of them running, others had to be scavenged. Parts were taken from the older tanks to repair the newer tanks. Many of the cannibalized parts were also failing. Of their impressive number of tanks, only about a third, or about six hundred tanks were battlefield ready.

Iran spent over nine billion dollars a year on the military. The government called this money a defense budget. Iran had not had to defend against an attack in decades. In fact, under the current regime, there was much sabre rattling as Iran pushed to develop a nuclear program that had Israel, most of the Middle East and a large part of the world deeply concerned. The nuclear program gobbled up a lion's share of that budget leaving little monies for the modernization of the army.

"And personnel?" the Ayatollah inquired.

"We can field an impressive force, your eminence!" the General responded. "We have over one million men ready and able to go to war."

This, again, was another lie told to the cleric that assumed command over this General and all of the armed forces of Iran. The General knew that control of the armed forces of Iran by the religious zealots who had assumed power under the Ayatollah Khomeini was a farce. But politicians all over the world were in command of the military. It made no sense to him, but that was the way he was forced to exist.

He knew that when the call went out to the over half a million reserves to become ready to fight, that only a handful of these conscripts had actually reported for duty. The army would be lucky to begin this war with a half a million souls able to enter the field.

These fighting men would be entering into war with outdated equipment. They would be travelling many, many miles in vehicles that were not reliable. They would take orders from officers that had become lazy and were not familiar with current battlefield tactics. Their last war had been fought in an old fashioned 'trench warfare' style, at a huge expense of lives lost. The officers were no more prepared to launch into this war than the Ayatollahs who had ordered them to be ready to attack Israel.

"Are we making progress with our Arab friends to the west?" asked the General.

He knew that the shortest and easiest attack route would be through Iraq, travelling just north of Bagdad, and then on through Syria, travelling just south of Damascus and on into Israel through the Golan Heights.

"There is progress being made, albeit slowly," the Ayatollah replied.

This was also a lie to the army General. Negotiations with Iraq were not going well. Although the United States had withdrawn their forces of occupation from that land, the Iraqi government was still acting as a puppet of the Great Satan. Iraq was not granting permission for the Iranian forces to cross over their land. Syria was being another thorn in Iran's side. The unrest of the Syrian people was proving to make the Syrian President impotent as he struggled with maintaining his power base within that country. He was under immense world pressure to step aside and cease the atrocities against his people. The idea of allowing the Iranian army the freedom of crossing over his land was not currently on his plate of issues.

A war was being envisioned and planned out based completely on lies. Lies from the military about their preparedness and lies from the governing body about cooperation from Iran's Middle East neighbors. Routes were being plotted that would take the Iranian army over the shortest distance into Israel. Provisions were being made for a relatively short incursion into Israeli lands. The army was only preparing to encounter resistance upon entering Israel. The true reality was that all of Iran's neighboring countries were resisting their war efforts and Iran would be completely on their own while waging this conflict.

Imam Khomeini Airport

"Hey, guys!" Lance burst out. "This airport feels like Love Field in Dallas!"

"That's because it was designed like Love Field in Dallas," I replied. "In fact, this airport was originally designed by an American firm prior to the 1979 revolution. A French firm headed up the project once it got back on track following the revolution."

"That figures!" Ash exclaimed. "The damn French always seem at the ready to come in and mess things up after us. Remember all that crap with Viet Nam? America comes in to rescue the French after they mess things up in that country, and what reward do we get? The French turn around and supply the North Vietnamese with arms! These people seem to hate us except when we have to save their asses! I've never seen a country lose as many wars as the French."

"Back on point!" Lance said. "This layout is very familiar."

"You spent any time at Love Field?" I asked.

"Yeah, since Southwest refused to switch over to DFW," Lance replied.

"Great story, huh!" I said.

"Texas did all they could to force Southwest out of there…including the Wright amendment," Lance continued. "The Texas politicians even got the FAA involved, claiming that the airport was unsuitable for future air traffic demands and withheld funding for the airport."

"What a farce that was!" I added. "Large airliners, like Southwest operates, could only fly out of Love Field to another Texas location. Only small aircraft that carried less than fifty six people were allowed out of

Love Field to fly directly to other states. Southwest, for example, had to land in El Paso before flying on to Phoenix."

"Our government at work, once again!" Ash said.

"The audacity of those that think they know what is best for us," I said.

"Isn't most of that over now?" Lance asked.

"Technically, not until 2014, but most of the restrictions have been waived. Southwest can now fly into Dallas from most anywhere," I said. "Let's get back to the mission at hand!"

"Okay," Ash replied. "This is what we have. Supposedly four members of that MADEI cell are here for the hijacking. We know what flight…the Lufthansa flight to Tel Aviv, but don't have a clue about what day they plan the hijacking. Luckily, the flight only goes once a day."

"And we don't know where these four are staying," Lance added.

"Well, we know that they aren't at any of the hotels here at the airport, and we only know the name of one of the cell members…that Rahim character, he's the pilot, right?" Ash asked.

"Pilot without complete training…like the guys with 9/11. Every time I think about it, I can't believe they weren't stopped. What idiot flight school or flight instructor would take on a trainee who didn't care to learn how to land? Can of basic stuff, if you want to live through a flight!" I said. "Someone definitely should have had a clue and said something."

"Well, once again, these guys aren't going to be landing…how do you want to play this?" Ash asked.

"You and I are both pilots. Lufthansa has agreed to let us ride in the right seat…either you or me," I said, pointing to Ash.

"I would be more comfortable with you in the cockpit and Ash in the cabin with me," Lance added. "There are more of them than us. Ash and I will be better with the numbers than you, Reggie."

"Once again, Lance is right," I said sheepishly. "I don't have the experience with the hand to hand stuff that you two have."

"What do we do? Take each of these daily flights until MADEI makes their move?" Ash asked.

"I guess so…the one PC is implanted in the terrorist that went with the MADEI leader to Frankfurt. We have nothing on these four," I replied. "We can't stake out an airport room because they are not staying there.

These MADEI characters are probably staying with al Qaeda somewhere here in Tehran."

"That flight departs at 3:25. I guess we better get ready for some flying!" Lance finished.

Los Angeles, CA

"I've never seen a firefight like that on American soil!" Powers exclaimed. After the debriefing at police headquarters, the Denver I.N.C.I.S.O.R. team had made their way back to the Los Angeles hospital where they had absconded with the Mara Salvatrucha gang leader. They watched as the armed standoff between the MS-13 gang and Los Angeles police escalated into a shootout.

The El Salvadoran gang appeared at the hospital with guns drawn and no protection, except for the cars they had arrived in. The Los Angeles police had their body armor and the aid of SWAT units with automatic weaponry. The police also had the time to stake out locations around the hospital that offered adequate cover.

The gang had demanded the return of the fifteen members who were being treated in the emergency room. They had no way to know that their leader had 'left the building'. The sick gang members inside were in no condition to leave the emergency room, most being pumped full of IV fluids to replace what had been lost out of both ends of their bodies. They had bedpans for their vomit, along with bedpans to catch the vile diarrhea that was flowing so freely from them.

The Captain of the Los Angeles police forces demanded that the MS-13 gang 'stand down and vacate the premises'.

Shots were soon fired by the gang members and the melee began. Within minutes many of the gang members were lying dead or wounded behind the fusillade of bullets unleashed by the police. Those gang members that hid behind car doors attempted to return fire. Quickly they had their hands up in surrender, as it was clear that they were outgunned by the superior LA police on hand.

In the end, five Los Angeles policemen were casualties of the conflict. Only one of the police officers was critical but expected to pull through. Fifteen of the MS-13 gang were down, either dead or wounded, and over thirty gang members rounded up by the police. Five gang members escaped into the surrounding homes.

The I.N.C.I.S.O.R. team watched the confrontation with admiration for the Los Angeles police. The men of I.N.C.I.S.O.R. wanted to be involved…to help. In the end they stayed only as interested observers.

"Let's get to LAX for our flight back to Denver," Flex Lawson said.

"Hey, what's going to happen to that guy we took out of the hospital?" Max asked the group.

"The FBI took him from LA SWAT and is turning him over to the CIA. With the terrorism laws after 9/11, I don't think we'll be hearing or seeing anything of that guy ever again!" Duncan opined.

"Won't somebody else from the Mara Salvatrucha gang just step into his place?" Lance asked.

"Yeah, but maybe this gang will think twice before they murder innocent women and children," Powers added.

The Skies over Iran

This was the third flight that Ash, Lance and I flew to Tel Aviv. I was actually beginning to enjoy my role as the First Officer and my functions in the right seat of the 747-300 cockpit. The actual First Officer rode behind me at the navigation and communications console. This was the last version of the 747 to require three crew members in the cockpit. The 747-400 and newer versions fly only with the Captain and First Officer.

I had learned much on the first two flights, following the commands from the Captain and First Officer. I could now tell the Captain when we reached V2 rotation speed and knew when and how to help clean up the aircraft after takeoff. I was becoming adept at tuning the radio gear to approach and landing channels and I was figuring out the navigation equipment. Much of the equipment was similar to the Avanti II. Just different buttons and knobs to get used to. And a much bigger cockpit!

We had just reached altitude on this third flight when an explosion rocked the cockpit. It came from behind me and blew the headphones right off of my head. I ducked down into my seat in an attempt to avoid the blast. Next thing I knew I felt a razor sharp blade at my throat.

The ringing in my ears was immense. I felt like a freight train was passing right through my skull. I was badly disoriented as I remained crouched over the yolk in front of me.

"Move and you're dead!" was all that I heard, and I remained still.

I noticed out of my left peripheral vision that the pilot was being manhandled and removed from the pilot's seat. My head was pounding as my senses began to return. The first thing that I saw was that the glass panel in front of me was in a shambles.

I was ordered to sit up as the knife blade bit into my skin, and I did as I was commanded.

I dared to glance to my left as a man moved to take the pilot's seat.

"Rahim, I assume," I said to the man on my left.

Both men in the cockpit with me were immediately startled.

"How do you know my…" was all that he said before Ash moved in.

I didn't know how, but Ash had crept into the cockpit through the hole that was left after the cockpit door had been blown away by the blast. He had followed the two terrorists when they made their assault into the cockpit. He moved quickly and quietly behind the terrorist that had the knife to my throat and buried his knife into the man's spinal cord just below the skull. The man convulsed once as his knife cut into my throat and then fell lifeless behind the copilot's seat.

Before the terrorist finished his death throes, Ash had speedily moved to the other terrorist and quickly pulled his knife across the man's throat. His action was so forceful that the man's head flopped back in the pilot's seat. His death was instant.

Ash said into his headset, "Two down Lance…how you doing in the cabin?"

"Got one…moving in on the other," was Lance's reply.

Ash turned to me and saw the blood staining the front of my shirt. He pulled off his shirt and placed it on my neck.

"You okay, Reggie?" he asked.

"No," I croaked.

He examined my wound and determined that nothing major had been severed.

"You're okay…now it's time to fly this thing!" he said.

My head felt ready to explode and I felt like I was going to throw up. I glanced around the devastated cockpit.

"What are you talking about?" I cried. "Look around…it's all blown to hell!"

Ash left me holding his shirt to my neck and went to check on the Captain and First Officer.

"They're both dead from the blast," he said when he returned and worked to pull the dead terrorist out of the pilot's seat. The seat was soaked in his blood.

"You'd better move over here," Ash said as he pulled the inert body back out of the cockpit.

I did as he told me and moved to my left. My shirt and pants were now completely covered in blood and I didn't know which was mine and which was from the terrorist or the pilot. I started to look over the smashed instruments.

Ash finished clearing the cockpit of the four dead bodies. He then took up my previous position in the co-pilot's seat.

"Two down!" Lance announced into his headset.

"Got all four, Reggie," Ash turned and told me. The terrorist hijacking attempt had ended…bad for them…well for us!

"Time to see what still works in this thing," I whispered as I checked out the equipment.

I put on the pilot's headset and placed a call to Tehran approach. Nothing but static. I tried two other programmed frequencies…nothing.

"Radio's dead," I announced.

I placed my hands on the yolk and reached to turn the autopilot off. I attempted a shallow turn to the left. The mammoth plane responded and began a turn to the left.

"The autopilot and flight controls seem to be responding," I muttered. It was really hard to talk. I wondered if my vocal cords were damaged by the knife blade.

"Can't read a heading or altitude…how can I tell where we are?" I mumbled.

Ash heard my musings and said, "Looks like these old time instruments installed here," as he pointed to the panel in front of him, "are still functioning. Looks like we're at twenty eight thousand five hundred feet on a heading of two eight zero."

"We need to get back to Tehran. Got a heading for that?" I asked of my best friend.

"Just a minute…got an idea," Ash voiced and he left me alone in the cockpit.

Soon he was back, carrying a satellite phone in his hand.

"Lance is moving the first class passengers downstairs to coach. He is trying to reassure all of them that everything is okay," Ash said upon his return.

"Everything is NOT okay!" I hissed.

"Get it together, Damnit…we're it for getting this plane down!" Ash replied.

My throat was beginning to hurt more as the throbbing in my head lessened. I thought for a moment about what I knew about this aircraft. The 747-300 had been flying since 1982 and had a top speed of Mach .85… not that that was going to matter on this flight! The plane was a monster! Its length was two hundred and thirty one feet! A damn football field! It boasted a wingspan of almost one hundred and ninety six feet! My Avanti II's wingspan was forty six feet with a length of forty seven feet! The 747 had a maximum takeoff weight of 833,000 pounds and an empty weight of almost 393,000 pounds. My Aurora weighed 7,500 pounds, empty! We sat nearly three stories high in the cockpit, when it was on the ground. I thought about that…could we get on the ground in one piece?

"Reggie! Get your cellphone!" Ash ordered.

I reached for my phone in my pants. It was covered in blood. Ash took the phone and found a towel to clean it off.

"I hope these things work when they're wet!" he exclaimed.

My brain still felt scrambled as I wondered what he wanted with my cellphone.

"It's got GPS," he said as if reading my thoughts.

Ash dialed in the program and found some tape to affix it to the glass panel.

"See…we're here with a heading of two-eight-zero…just like the instrument said! Get this plane turned around!" Ash ordered.

I began a slow turn to a heading of one-zero-zero. The aircraft was holding its altitude.

Ash was on his satellite phone and made contact eventually with an AWAKS plane circling over Iraq.

"Everybody knows that we are returning to Tehran, and that we are badly damaged and without communication," Ash announced. "Turn to a heading of Oh-eight-five degrees."

I did as I was ordered as Lance stuck his head in the cockpit.

"Holy Christ!" he exclaimed. "How are you flying this plane?"

"Controls are okay," I responded. "Just the nav and com gear is out."

"Drop to flight level one niner zero," Ash said.

I released the autopilot and lowered the nose of the Boeing. The plane went into a gentle dive and I leveled her out at nineteen thousand feet above the ground.

"Tehran is scrambling fighters to check us out," Ash announced.

"Swell," I thought. "Hope they're not trigger happy."

Within minutes we had an escort of both the port and starboard sides of the cockpit. One of the planes dipped below us and out of our sight. Soon he was back to my port side. I glanced over and saw that he gave me the 'thumbs up' sign with his gloved hand. I assumed that he was communicating to me that the outside of the aircraft was okay.

"Drop to one-zero flight level and maintain this heading. Tehran airport is three thousand feet AGL. They're clearing both runways. We make our approach to 11L," Ash said.

Lance took a look at the fighters on both sides of us and left us to get the passengers ready for landing. We had two hundred innocents with us on the flight.

"Okay, drop to five thousand feet and slow to two-five-zero knots. Turn to heading one-zero-zero," Ash ordered and continued to talk on the satellite phone.

I did as I was commanded and mentally went over the landing procedures I had witnessed on the previous two flights.

"Reggie, slow to two hundred. There's the field!" Ash announced, and pointed ahead and slightly to our right.

I looked ahead and spotted the airport. "Okay, ten degrees flaps, slowing to one eighty," I said.

Ash worked the flap lever.

"Twenty degrees flaps…"

"Thirty degrees and lower the landing gear."

The plane was low and slow and the controls felt really sluggish. The speed dropped to one hundred and sixty knots as I lined up the landing.

"Full flaps!"

"Full flaps...gear down and three green," Ash replied.

The warning horn blared that we were approaching stalling speed. Then the ground proximity warning horn began to sound.

"One fifty and thirty five hundred feet...over the threshold!" Ash said as we cleared the end of the runway two hundred feet in the air.

The behemoth plane settled into ground effect as I pulled back on the yolk to flare the nose.

"One twenty...hold it...hold it"

It still felt to me that we were miles in the air. I began to fear that we wouldn't get down in time. The runway was speeding by!

Just then the main wheels hit down and I felt the jolt. Quickly I move the yolk to lower the nose as Ash retarded the four throttles and reversed the engines. The nose wheel hit hard and I hoped that it would hold. I pressed my feet hard against the rudder pedals to apply the brakes.

The end of the runway was approaching way too fast and we were still really moving!

"Ash! Help with the brakes!" I yelled. My voice had returned!

He complied as applied his two feet to help depress the brake pedals.

Finally, the plane slowed and came to a stop. Ash reached up and shut off the engines.

"I've seen better!" Ash joked.

I couldn't get my hands to release the yolk.

Soon, there were emergency vehicles everywhere as sirens cut into the afternoon sky. Lance moved quickly through the cabin and released the emergency doors as slides began to inflate. He urged the passengers onto the slides and worked to clear the cabin.

Ash and I just sat in the cockpit without speaking. We had made it! Soon there were emergency crews scrambling over the cockpit and several worked to get me out of the pilot's seat and out of the aircraft. One was holding a pressure bandage against my neck. I was placed on a gurney and taken to an ambulance. Lance and Ash were both at my side and demanded to be along for the ambulance ride to and Iranian hospital.

"Great friends," I thought and closed my eyes. "What a great plane!"

CHAPTER TWENTY SEVEN

Dubai, UAE

I WAS CONVALESCING AT home with heavy and restricting bandages wrapped around my neck. The bandages felt like hands constricting my neck and throat. Very uncomfortable! I had seen a plastic surgeon upon my return to Dubai and he had stated that the doctors in Iran hadn't done a bad job suturing my neck wound. He would perform plastic surgery later, once the initial wound had healed. He had also recommended an acupuncturist to help with the pain in my neck. I hated taking pain medication and he felt that this would be a big help to control my discomfort.

I lay on the couch in our living room, listening to Ash and Lance fill me in on the recent history with MADEI. I knew about the goings on in Frankfurt because Becky had filled me in after Magnus Harper checked in with her for a 'sit rep'.

The German I.N.C.I.S.O.R. team had an easy go of it due to the PC that I had implanted in one of the three MADEI terrorists that had travelled to Frankfurt to insure that the Lufthansa Frankfurt to Tel Aviv flight would be delayed so that the hijacked flight could assume their spot on Israeli radar. The three terrorists had stolen baggage handler uniforms and had taken up positions on the ramp surrounding their target aircraft.

Two of the I.N.C.I.S.O.R. team members actually watched through the glass in the terminal waiting area as Abdullah, the MADEI leader damaged the small door over the plug where the APC unit was plugged into the aircraft. Once the airplane engines were spooled up and the APC was disconnected, the panel would not close properly, and a warning light would blink within the cockpit.

The engines would then have to be shut down while the problem panel was inspected. This would cause a long enough delay for the terrorist plan to take effect. Once the three MADEI members saw that the plane engines were shut down and the covered ramp was returned to the aircraft cabin, they made their getaway, shedding their uniforms and returning to their rooms at the hotel.

This was the point where the I.N.C.I.S.O.R. team jumped into action. Magnus and Stirling moved in to capture Abdullah, the leader, who had his own room. Dick, Aaron and Graham moved in on the other two. The three men were unarmed and surrendered without incident. The MADEI terrorist cell members were then quickly taken to an awaiting military transport and turned over to CIA operatives for transport to the United States.

All of this occurred while I was trying to return the damaged Boeing 747-300 to the Imam Khomeini Airport. By the time I was released from the hospital in Tehran the three terrorists were well on their way to America and the CIA. Interrogation would not be pleasant for them! Lance and Ash were regaling me with their tales of what occurred behind the cockpit door. Two of the MADEI cell members had purchased first class tickets, and therefore were seated in the upper deck behind the cockpit. The other two had seats in the business class seating forward of the economy seating in the rear of the main cabin.

At an appointed time, when the 'fasten seat belts' warning was extinguished, one of the first class members moved to the front just behind the cockpit door. The terrorist cell members knew that aircraft doors to the cockpits had been reinforced and were never opened after 9/11. They knew that the door had to be blasted open, but overestimated the amount of explosive necessary to unhinge the door.

When the blast occurred the cabin was badly shaken, but the force of the blast was directed into the cockpit. The blast was not meant to take out the flight crew or the instruments. The MADEI cell pilot was expecting full use of the instrumentation behind the glass panels of the cockpit to fly his instrument of death into that high rise in Tel Aviv.

When the blast happened, Ash rushed forward into the cockpit, while Lance slid down the straight stairway that replaced the circular stairs in previous models of the 747. As he alighted in the main cabin he noticed that two men had left their seats, one moving forward and one moving to the rear of the plane. All of the other passengers were alarmed from the explosion, but were still seated.

Lance almost collided with the first terrorist, catching him unaware, and with a quick head snap severed the terrorist's spinal cord, killing him instantly. He moved as silently as he could into the economy cabin and spied the second terrorist as that man grabbed a female flight attendant around the waist. The terrorist had a knife to the flight attendant's throat and was screaming to the cabin in Arabic.

Lance withdrew his revolver from its holster underneath his jacket… took quick aim…and fired one shot. A red spot appeared on the terrorist's forehead as blood and brain matter blew out from behind him and onto the partition separating the economy cabin from the lavatories. That was when he announced to Ash that two were down.

Ash's lethal attack on the two terrorists that had taken over the cockpit was welcomed by me. At the point when he saved my life I completely forgot about his violent manner since Grace's death. I was glad to have this man as my best friend and could care less about how many bad men were not on this earth because of him.

Lance and Ash left me with one final thought…MADEI was no more.

Langley, VA

The interrogation techniques bordered on torture, but the men in the room did not mind. The information was desperately more vital than the man who attempted to keep it from them. Abdullah did well in his attempts to fight back against their physical assault, followed by the chemical assault. In the end the drugs always win…IF the victim doesn't perish.

The interrogation group discovered that the MADEI group, with considerable funds, had hired an American White Supremacist group to steal a nuclear weapon from the waylaid B-52 during the six hour period when the weapons were technically missing. One nuclear cruise missile was spirited out of the country aboard a tanker bound for the Iraqi port of Uum Qasr. The weapon was offloaded from the tanker and driven into Bagdad.

A Russian team of scientists, again with considerable funds, was procured to modify the weapon so that it could be launched from land. Even the Americans were sure that these cruise missiles could only be launched from a B-52 platform. With extraordinary effort the ACM (advanced cruise missile) was modified so that it could be launched from any vehicle or ship with the appropriate launcher installed.

To complete the transformation, the missile was repainted with Israeli markings and designations.

Once the modifications were complete the cruise missile with the nuclear warhead was driven back to the port at Uum Qasr. A fishing boat was hired and the missile stowed on board. A small army of men swarmed over the boat removing the fishing rigging and mounting the launch platform for the missile. With the platform construction complete the missile was loaded into the launcher and covered with tarpaulins to hide it from prying eyes at the docks or prying satellites in the air.

One MADEI member named Farroukh left in the boat and headed south into the Gulf. His destination was Kharg Island, which lay some sixteen miles off the coast of Iran. Kharg Island was at one point a bustling hub of activity. It was once the world's largest offshore crude oil terminal. The heavy bombing of the facilities during the Iran Iraq war by Iraq had put it out of commission. Continuous bombardment from the air by the Iraqi air force all but destroyed most of the terminal facilities. Reconstruction of the oil terminal has been very slow, leaving most of the island dormant and inactive.

Farroukh maneuvered his craft into the Kharg Island harbor and parked it among two dozen other vessels there mainly for fishing the waters surrounding the island. He took his time securing the boat to the pier, using that time to scope out his surroundings. He saw no activity around the other boats. He made his way to one of the abandoned buildings at the airstrip and made camp.

Farroukh's compatriot in MADEI was Hamid who was making his way into Iran with a laser sighting device stolen from the Israelis and other Israeli paraphernalia. Hamid and Farroukh knew that they were on a two man suicide mission. They had committed their lives to Abdullah and the cause of destroying Israel when they had heard Abdullah speak in Phoenix, AZ.

The Kharg Island missile, stolen from the Americans and covered with Israeli markings was successfully launched and it made its way to the nuclear plant at Bushehr, destroying the facility and almost everything else for many miles around it. The shockwave reached as far out into the Persian Gulf as Kharg Island, destroying the watercraft there and any signs of life, also.

MADEI's mission was to eradicate Israel. Their plan was to make the attack look like it was performed by the Israelis, and therefore cause a strong and violent recoil by the Arab states in the Middle East. Iran had taken the bait, but was moving slowly. The hijacking of the German airliner and flying it into the tallest building in Tel Aviv was a move to incite Israel into an equally strong and violent response. This would assure that the other Middle East states would react against Israel and lead to that country's eradication. MADEI's mission would be accomplished.

One of the interrogators let Abdullah know that the hijacking had been thwarted and that the remaining MADEI cell members were no longer with us. His final thought during his stay on this planet was that his plan had failed…

Washington, DC

The President was briefed about the interrogation and about the information that the United States had discovered. "Yes," it was this missing nuke from the American arsenal. "Yes," the missile was reconfigured to imitate an Israeli missile. "Yes," the missile had been launched from a boat moored at Kharg Island. "Yes," the hijacking attempt and attack against Israel was made by MADEI and thwarted by I.N.C.I.S.O.R. "Yes," the Iraqi terrorist group, the MADEI, and all of its cell members had been eliminated.

"Get me Netanyahu!" President James ordered. "Our countries have a war to stop!"

Tel Aviv, Israel

"Yes sir, Mr. President! Yes, indeed! That IS great news!" the Israeli Prime Minister exclaimed as he hung up the phone.

Mr. Netanyahu then turned to Colonel Gary Kubetz and asked for a situation report on the Israeli Army.

Colonel Kubetz brought the Prime Minister up to date. Preparations for the upcoming war with Iran were moving forward and Israel would be ready. Israel's number of armed forces could not match Iran's, but the army sported far superior weaponry.

Every time Mr. Netanyahu heard the adage of greater numbers against superior technology and training he thought back in history to the Korean conflict. The United States had far superior weaponry, but the North Koreans had the numbers. There were many reports of waves of North Korean men thrown against the American machine gun nests. The first waves of men often carried no weapons at all. The next waves may have been lucky enough to carry pitchforks or other farm implements as weapons. The final waves were armed with outdated rifles, but at this point the American machine guns often were overheating and became useless, allowing the American positions to be overrun.

Overwhelming numbers wasn't necessarily a bad thing!

He ended his musing with, "At least we have the nukes!"

He then turned back to Colonel Kubetz and asked about the position of Israel's submarine fleet. The Colonel was taken aback by the question. Israel had only three submarines in their navy. Iran boasted nineteen subs. Israel was planning and preparing for a land war, which would include support from the air. The navy was not included in the preparations.

"The United States President wants to get a team into Kharg Island to see if any evidence can be obtained about the origin of the cruise missile attack against the Bushehr nuclear reactor. The US flyovers still measure increased radiation levels throughout much of the southwestern Iranian coast and into the Persian Gulf. The United States scientists recommend an approach to the Island by submarine to minimize radioactive exposure.

We know from that Iraqi terrorist leader that the MADEI group launched the cruise missile from a boat anchored at the pier on Kharg Island. We must attempt to discover if this in fact is true. Right now it is nothing more than our word that we did not attack Iran. That's not getting us very far these days!" the Prime Minister concluded.

Colonel Kubetz placed a call to his naval counterpart and discovered that one of Israel's three submarines was on maneuvers with the American navy in the Gulf of Aden. The submarine would detach itself from the 'hide and seek' games it had been playing with the American submarines and destroyers and make its way through the Gulf of Oman and into the Persian Gulf.

Kharg Island, Iran

The Israeli submarine actually broke the surface having glided right into the Kharg Island harbor. The harbor was man-made and deep enough to handle the hulls of much larger sea going vessels. The submarine had traversed the Persian Gulf relatively undetected…there was only one incident when the sonar operator alerted the command room that he had made contact with an underwater bogey. The computer then reacted and spit out that the contact matched the noise signal and ratio of an Iranian attack submarine. The Iranian sub was making all sorts of racket in the sonar operator's headset. The Israeli sub quickly went 'all silent' and stopped their progress. Within a half an hour the Iranian contact had travelled out of the Israelis' sonar range, heading away from the sub. The Israeli submarine then continued on its journey without any further contact.

Once the submarine had surfaced in the Kharg Island harbor a raft was quickly inflated and put over the side. A team of four commandos exited the submarine with their cameras and evidence gathering gear. They were also armed with Israeli Military Industries' Uzis, the machine pistol preferred by the Israeli military.

As the team departed, the Captain of the submarine called out to them, "We will stay on the surface long enough to recharge our batteries and then we will submerge the vessel and await your signal."

The investigation team rowed to the pier and tied up the raft. They noticed that many of the boats in the harbor were beached up on the pier or thrown onto the land. The craft were lying on their sides and looked very 'out of place' on land. The sergeant pulled out a Geiger counter from his duffle bag and listened while the device chirped steadily.

"We don't have much time, men," the sergeant announced.

The four men spread out and began to inspect the boats. Shortly, one of the commandos found scorch marks on one of the boats.

"Over here!" he yelled and waved to his comrades.

The team made its way to the vessel and began taking pictures of the craft. The deck and sides of the boat were blackened. It looked to the men as if someone had taken a blowtorch to the deck. The also noticed that the rigging appeared to be a rail system that would prove to be the launching device.

They were able to gather fingerprints from places on the boat that weren't badly charred. They also dismantled parts of the launching rig and placed them into the evidence bags.

One of the team members discovered human remains not far from the boat. The body was barely recognizable as human and too badly decomposed to gather much in the way of evidence. Pictures were taken of the body and the skeletal remains of a hand were placed in an evidence bag.

The team sergeant made the call to the sub, "Ready for pickup!"

At that moment the radar operator aboard the submarine barked over the intercom, "Con…Radar."

"Radar…Con," was the reply.

"Contact…twenty miles…moving fast toward our position!" the radar operator replied. "Turboprop…four engines…almost over the Iranian coast!"

"Damnit!" the Captain muttered. "Team stay put!" he ordered into the radio set. He then picked up the intercom and ordered, "Dive…Dive…Dive!"

The outer hull of the submarine was quickly sealed as sailors slid down the stair railings and assumed their positions inside the craft. Popping was heard throughout the hull as the ballast tanks were flooded with sea water and the submarine slipped beneath the surface.

"We've got to get out of this harbor!" the Captain said to his First Officer.

"All astern…full!" was the order.

The submarine slowly gained speed and cleared the harbor.

"Put this thing on the bottom!" the Captain ordered.

"Radar…Con"

"Con…Radar…contact five miles out bearing nine zero degrees… altitude five hundred feet…moving fast!"

"Rig for silent running!" and the submarine went quiet.

The sailors aboard the Israeli submarine waited in anticipation.

"Con…Sonar…screws in the water…it just went active!"

An anti-sub torpedo had been dropped by the aircraft overhead. Its sonar device had just gone active and was searching for a contact.

The four commandos took cover and witnessed the attack. The sergeant retrieved two hand grenades, pulled their pins and tossed them into the water. The explosions had the desired effect as the torpedo turned away from the submarine and toward the harbor.

A huge explosion at the end of the pier sent debris flying toward the men. Their cover held as the commandos hunkered down to avoid injury.

"Get us out of here!" the sub Captain ordered.

"Turn to heading one eight zero…maintain silent running!" his First Officer ordered. The Israeli submarine turned to a southerly heading and crept along the bottom of the Persian Gulf just as the Iranian Aircraft was joined by three others. The aircraft circled around Kharg Island attempting to reacquire a signal from the submarine. Sonobuoys were dropped into the water and were 'pinging' like crazy. The sonar operator's headset made a horrible racket!

The submarine soon escaped the Iranian net and headed south out of the Persian Gulf. The Israeli commandos were stranded on Kharg Island. There were two huge problems for the four men. First, all of their radiation detectors had already changed colors. They needed to get away from the radiation! Second, it would not be long before the Iranians would send their navy to investigate why a submarine had surfaced at the Island.

CHAPTER TWENTY EIGHT

Dubai, UAE

I HAD TAKEN THE morning to visit the acupuncturist, Dr. White, who was recommended by my plastic surgeon. My neck and shoulders were killing me!

Dr. White's office was just down the street from the plastic surgeon's office. This one street in Dubai housed the lion's share of the cosmetic dentists and surgeons. Their offices lined both sides of the street. I had no explanation for why they all congregated in such close approximation to each other. An Oriental restaurant that Becky and I had wanted to try was in a small shopping center directly across the street. I was going to meet Becky there when my session was complete.

Dr. White completed her evaluation and soon had needles placed into my feet, my hands and into the base of my skull. I was to lay there for fifteen minutes with these needles stuck into my body! She left me in the room, alone, announcing that she 'had to get the woman in the next operatory off'.

I chuckled to myself, thinking about the Korean massages and their 'happy endings'. I knew that Dr. White meant that it was time to get the woman off the bed that she occupied, but it still struck me as a funny expression!

When my time was up and the needles were extracted, I felt great! I had no pain! Oriental medicine was a new experience for me and I was really impressed. I was talking to the Doctor about future visits when my phone rang…

"Reggie, get home fast!" Becky urged. "We have an urgent mission!"

With that she disconnected the phone and left me wondering what was happening.

I bid my adieu to Dr. White and rushed to return home.

"What's up?" I asked when I entered our home.

"Call from the CIA…there are four stranded Israeli commandos on Kharg Island. They're asking INCISOR to retrieve them!" Becky said. "I've already let Lance and Ash know and they'll meet you at the airport."

I changed quickly and made for the garage. Becky met me in the hallway with a bag.

"Sandwich for the road…sorry about lunch," she said.

I took the bag and gave her a kiss.

"Miss you already!" I replied.

I thought about the Avanti II. It had just recently been decontaminated from a previous flight into the unfriendly skies over Iran. Now we were to enter Iranian airspace again. I had some trepidation about the Iranian missile defense system, but that paled in comparison to the exposure to radiation that came with the mission.

Ash and Lance were already at the airfield and Aurora had been towed out of the hangar. Ash informed me that he had completed the preflight operations and Aurora was ready for 'blast off'. We loaded up and headed north into the Persian Gulf. We did not have permission from Iran to enter their airspace, so I flew low to the water, just three hundred feet above the waves.

The airplane runway at Kharg Island was located on the northeast end of the island. We made our approach low over the dilapidated oil terminal and turned northwest to line up the Avanti II on final approach.

Over the oil facility Ash exclaimed that there were three boats making a high speed approach from the Iranian shore toward the island.

"That must be the Iranian cavalry!" I said.

"Don't know about cavalry, but they're in a damn big hurry!" Ash exclaimed. "Let's not dally here for too long!"

We touched down and slowed Aurora down to taxi speed and did a 180 on the runway. The abandoned terminal buildings were ahead of us and to our right. As we approached, the Israeli team rushed out of one of the buildings and made their way to the plane.

Once they were all on board, I taxied to the end of the runway and made another 180. I depressed the pedals to apply the brakes and advanced the throttles while the engines spooled up. I released the brakes and Aurora shot down the runway. We were soon in the air as Ash helped to clean up the Avanti II by raising the landing gear and flaps.

Lance had a bottle of some sort of spray solution that he was applying to the four men that had joined us. I imagined that it was some sort of decontaminant to minimize the effects of their radiation exposure.

I circled to the left to avoid the oncoming speedboats.

"You guys have a welcoming committee!" I announced to the four Israelis.

Lance and the four craned to see out the port side to watch the boats. While they watched, a missile was fired and was tracking toward us. Lance shouted again, "Missile! Missile in the air!" It seemed at the moment like deja vu.

"Not again!" I said as I dove the Avanti II toward the waves of the Persian Gulf. We were low enough to see the whitecaps as they rolled toward the island.

Lance had moved to the door and pulled it open.

"Give me a flare!" he shouted over the wind gusting into the cabin.

The Israeli sergeant quickly reached into his bag and pulled out a handful of flares. He handed one to Lance. Lance struck the flare to ignite it and yelled, "Now, Reggie...straight up!"

I pulled back hard on the yolk and the Avanti II leapt into the sky. Lance grabbed for the door opening to steady himself and tossed the flare out into the air. He then struck another flare and repeated the action. And then, once again...

The missile was tracking well until the heat from the second flare disturbed its path. The missile exploded when it met the flare and rocked the plane. I prayed that the engines were okay as I surveyed the instrument panel. Everything looked okay and then...

"We're losing fuel from the port tank!" Ash said and pointed to the fuel gauges. "The port engine is running hot!"

"One of the pusher prop turbines must have been damaged in the blast," I muttered. "We're too low to shut it down...watch the temperature...I'm going to get some altitude under us."

Lance had shut the cabin door and the men watched the boats as they shrank from view.

At five thousand feet Ash announced, "Shutting down number one."

The temperature gauge had climbed dangerously into the red. Ash killed the engine and feathered the prop. I immediately had to press heavily with my right foot to apply rudder force to counter the power from the starboard engine. Ash worked the rudder trim tab to ease my load.

"Still losing fuel," he said.

I reached for the fuel switch and turned it to feed only from the starboard wing tank. Ash had the Avanti II manual out and was performing some quick calculations.

"It's a little over two hundred and fifty miles to Dubai…we left with full fuel, right?" he asked.

"Yes…and the right gauge is showing just above half," I replied.

I didn't think that the remaining fuel would be an issue, but the Avanti II was losing altitude.

Ash must have been thinking the same thought as he stated, "We'll lose a thousand feet every fifty miles that we cover." We both glanced at the altimeter as the numbers marched lower. "We'll be on the ground before we make it to Dubai…alternate airport?"

Qatar was directly to the south and much closer.

"Get the info for Qatar," I said as I did my own mental calculations. I really wanted to get home to our own airport.

"You need to turn now, Reggie, and head for the alternate," Ash offered.

"I'm going to try to make it!" I answered.

"Really?" Ash said and then shut up.

Meanwhile, Lance had moved aft to the bathroom to check for any damage. He returned to the cockpit and stood between us.

"Hey guys!" he said. "There are two holes in the bathroom wall. The wind's really whistling back there!"

Now I had concerns about the soundness of the airframe. Would it hold together?

"Lance! Do me a favor and see what you can do to lighten our load," I asked. My right leg was feeling it now after applying pressure on the rudder pedal for so long.

Lance returned to the cabin and asked the Israeli commandos to shed any unnecessary gear. Once they had stripped off their unneeded items, Lance tossed them out of the cabin door and into the Persian Gulf.

We flew toward Dubai and continued to lose altitude. We crossed under the 1000 foot level just as the DME indicated that we were fifty miles out. I raised Dubai approach on the radio and declared an emergency. We were coming in on one engine and would only have one attempt at landing. Approach control immediately turned me over to the Dubai tower and I restated our emergency.

Ten miles out I had the runway in sight. We were coming in too low. The VASI showed only red. We were well below the glide path. Ash and I had both practiced engine out approaches, but they were performed with one of the engines at idle. Not completely out!

"We'll have to come in hot!" I announced to my friend to my right.

"No flaps and don't lower the gear until over the threshold," I added.

"Got it," he replied.

I was glad that we were approaching from the sea. We'd definitely be in trouble if there were any trees along the approach path to deal with.

I maintained speed until the last possible minute, and then retarded the one throttle.

"Now!" I said to Ash, but he was way ahead of me.

"Gear down and three green," he announced.

We hit down hard and at a very high speed. The runway was designed for much larger aircraft, so we could take a long runout. I chose not to reverse the one good engine and just used the brakes to slow us down. The Avanti II slowed and we were able to take the last exit off of the runway and onto the taxiway.

"That was close!" Ash said as we slowed.

"Too close!" I added.

We taxied to the hangar and shut down Aurora. All seven of us were glad to be on the ground. Lance opened the cabin door and he led our passengers out of the plane. Four separate ambulances were waiting and men in radiation suits swarmed over the four Israelis. Each man was sprayed down and wrapped in some type of garment. They were then led to the awaiting ambulances and rushed away.

Lance, Ash and I were left to ourselves. We all began to walk around the Avanti II. When we reached the tail I was heartbroken. The port engine nacelle looked like a sieve. The metal housing was full of holes from the missile blast. Fuel was leaking out of the left wing. There were holes in the rear of the cabin. My plane was badly damaged…but it had gotten us home. I felt tears welling up in my eyes.

"It's fixable, Reggie," Lance offered.

"Yeah, I know," I replied. His words didn't comfort me.

A second wave of emergency vehicles approached us. Men in protective suits now swarmed around us and took measurements inside and out of the plane. Lance had the most radiation exposure, riding in the cabin with the commandos. We were all sprayed with this foam stuff and then rechecked.

"Acceptable numbers for these two…take that one away," one of the men said as he pointed to Lance. "The plane needs to be decontaminated, too."

"The plane needs more than that!" I retorted as I surveyed the damage.

"Change into these overalls," he ordered, and Ash and I did as we were told.

"You're free to go," he announced.

Ash and I headed for our cars. He and Lance had come to the airport together in Ash's car. I got into my car and realized that my neck pain had returned. I needed another visit with Dr. White…pronto!

Tel Aviv, Israel

"We have received phenomenal Intel from the four commandos who were retrieved by I.N.C.I.S.O.R. from Kharg Island," Colonel Kubetz announced to the Prime Minister once he stood in front of his desk. "They have relayed from Dubai fingerprints and photographs that show definitely that a missile was launched from that location. They have recovered the skeletal remains of the possible terrorist that launched the missile. All of this information has been sent to us via the internet. They also have recovered pieces from the launch platform. They will bring those home with them when they are cleared to travel."

"Looks like we have the information we needed to absolve us of involvement in this affair," the Prime Minister replied. "This evidence, along with the testimony from that MADEI character…what was his name?"

"Abdullah, sir," the Colonel replied.

"Ah, yes…it is clear now that this group was involved with the mission of destroying Israel by implicating our country in the destruction of the nuclear facility at Bushehr!" Netanyahu added.

"Yes, sir…it does!" Colonel Kubetz beamed.

"Get this information to Washington and to Tehran," Netanyahu ordered. "Let's stop a war!"

Washington, DC

"This is great news!" the President said.

"We can now tie an Iraqi terrorist organization to the attack on Bushehr," the Deputy Director of the CIA offered.

"Let's stand down from condition Red…Leave it at Orange until we see what the Iranians will do," President James ordered.

There were five threat levels that the United States acknowledged. The levels ran from Green (which equaled a low threat) to Red (which indicated a severe risk). The colors ran from Green to Blue (guarded) to Yellow (elevated) to Orange (high) to Red (severe). The United States citizens had learned to live under the Orange threat alert since the 9/11 attacks. It was only Iran's declaration of war against Israel that had moved the threat level to Red.

"I'll get on it, Mr. President," the Deputy Director replied as he turned to leave.

"Let's get that idiot President of Iran on the phone," President James said into his intercom.

CHAPTER TWENTY NINE

Dubai, UAE

I WAS SIPPING ON a glass full of ice and Crown Royal, topped with a lemon twist, while sitting on the patio at Bidi Bondi. I appreciated that the bartender at this establishment always took the time to rub the rim of my glass with the lemon twist before dropping it into the glass. It meant that each sip of my drink had a hint of lemon. I waited for Ash and Lance to arrive at a small square table with four chairs. The table was placed close to the large earthen pots filled with dried bamboo shoots. The pots and bamboo was all that the bar had placed for outside decoration. Bidi Bondi was known around Dubai as a sports bar, but I enjoyed their small patio. There were long rough wooden tables and a few smaller ones. I occupied one of the smaller tables. The umbrella was collapsed as the afternoon sun didn't create a problem.

While I waited I studied the small establishment. They were able to serve alcohol…but were not in a hotel. How did they accomplish that? The bartender had explained to me that they were associated with the hotel next door, and that was enough. Kind of like that circular bar out on the man-made island with the Burj al Arab!

"That's the Bab al Yam, right?" I asked.

"I think that's right…I kind of new here…the one by the pool," the bartender answered.

"Okay, so you don't have to actually be inside the hotel. Just associated with it. That's pretty easy!" I said.

"Still getting used to the laws here in the UAE," the bartender replied.

I sat, absent mindedly scratching at the scar on my neck. I didn't need the bandages any more, but the damn thing itched like crazy! A table full of young women caught my attention. They were laughing and carrying on with cute little umbrellas in their drinks. "Foo—foo drinks." I thought. "Are they tourists or locals?" There weren't many tourists out here on Jumeirah Palm. Bidi Bondi was located on the 'trunk' of the island.

Lance and Ash walked through the sports bar and met me on the back patio. Lance had ordered a beer from the bartender and Ash ordered his Tiger Woods. He had to explain to the bartender what was in the concoction…and that he didn't want the alcoholic version. They settled in to the empty chairs at the table.

"What are we talking about today, Reggie?" Ash asked as he sat down.

"I want to know more about guns," I replied.

"What do you mean?" Lance asked.

"Handguns…I want a handgun, and I want to know why you guys picked the guns you have," I answered.

"Oh, God!" Lance exclaimed. "Reggie with a weapon? We're doomed!"

"No," Ash said. "WE'RE not doomed…he is!"

"Next thing we know, he'll blow off a toe!" Lance joked.

"Having fun, guys?" I retorted.

"More than you know!" Ash said. "Not often you get to be the brunt of our jokes!"

"This is fun, Reggie! By the way, what do you want with a weapon?" Lance asked.

"You two are always packing…I want a gun!" I announced. I actually felt like I was pouting. I quickly changed my tone. "Tell me about your handguns and why you picked them."

"Better order more drinks…this could take a while," Ash said.

"First of all, you two, I'm not a complete novice. I used to have a Taurus 9mm. I loved the look of that gun with its wooden grips. I only shot it once. My first wife didn't allow me to take the gun when I left. She probably thought that I would shoot her. Not a bad thought in hindsight. Would have saved me a boatload of money!" I told my two friends.

"That was back in the States, right? Was it registered?" Ash asked.

"I assume so…I bought it at a gun show," I answered.

"So, that gun is still in your name?" Lance queried.

"Never thought about it…but I guess so," I replied.

"What if it's used in the commission of a crime?" Ash stated.

"And they link it back to you…" Lance continued the thought.

"Oh man, I never thought about that!" I exclaimed. "Could I be in trouble?"

"What was that…twenty five years ago?" Ash asked.

"More or less…actually more!" I responded.

"Probably not going to be an issue after that long," Lance offered.

"Back on point!" I said. "How'd you guys pick?"

"The military had quite a bit to do with my choices," Lance said. "I started off with a .45 caliber. In 1985 the Army switched to the Beretta 9mm. pistol to be more in line with other NATO forces. They called it the M9. That .45 caliber that I started with had great stopping power, but it kicked like a son of a bitch! The 9mm. is easy to shoot but doesn't stop your opponent as well. I had one sergeant say once that he'd rather have a hatchet in intimate contact than that damned 9mm."

"The CIA has a list that we can choose from. Most of us carry Glocks, but there are a few with Sig Sauers or Berettas. Lance and I both have the Glock. Did you know that we have to purchase our weapons with our own personal funds?" Ash asked.

"No, I didn't," I replied. "Okay, I've been to the Glock website. They make .45 caliber, .40 caliber and 9mm. How do you pick?"

Lance took over at this point, "The army went 9mm.; so did we. Ash and I are trained to double tap to the chest and one in the forehead. With that, stopping power isn't so important! Our training is to kill the opponent…not stop them so that we can talk about things later. I've got the Glock 17…as the name says, I've got seventeen shots. Ash, don't you have the same?"

"Yep. And I have never had to empty a magazine. Up close I prefer knives," Ash stated with a wicked smile on his face.

"Oh! That reminds me…I have a present for you, Ash" I said and reached under the table for the package. I set it on the table and then pushed it toward Ash.

"What did you do?" Ash asked as he reached for the box.

"I found this online when I was researching pistols," I replied.

Ash pulled at the paper and then freed the cardboard flaps of the box. A pair of black leather gloves lay inside.

"Shooting gloves?" Ash asked.

"Not exactly," I replied as I reached into the box and withdrew one of the gloves.

"Feel that supple lamb's skin," I said and pushed the glove toward Ash and Lance. "Then feel this…" I twisted the glove to display a knife blade protruding from the heel of the glove. As I moved the blade it glinted in the afternoon sun. "It retracts back into the wrist, but when it protrudes, your hands are free for combat…and then with a spinning motion…" I whipped my left arm toward Lance's neck.

"Hey!" Lance reacted.

"Just a demo!" I retorted.

"These are cool," Ash said as he pulled the gloves over his hands. He worked the blades out of their housings within the gloves. He then stood and spun around just once with his right hand extended. There was not an immediate effect, but then I noticed that several of the dried bamboo shoots were beginning to topple. Lance jumped up and caught the poles before they fell on the young ladies at the next table. So much for those patio decorations!

"Sharp, like a Samurai," I exclaimed.

"Lethal…nice new toy…thanks Reg," Ash said as they both sat back down.

"Back to handguns," I said. "And you're welcome! I don't like the feel of a Glock in my hand. I understand how well it's built and that it will fire under almost any condition, including under water, but I don't need that. I liked the feel of the Taurus grip, as well as I can remember."

"Have you been on their website?" Lance asked. "They don't manufacture those handles any more. Everybody is doing the polymer grips to be like the Glock."

"In fact, I have," I replied. "More than that, I called them! Way back when I had the other Taurus, everything was manufactured in Brazil. Now, manufacturing takes place in Brazil, but distribution is by Taurus USA. Much easier now to talk with somebody who speaks English. The model I want, the PT24/7 G2. It's a 9mm. that holds seventeen plus one in the chamber. The rep that I talked to said they would replace the polymer grips with Rosewood!"

"So you already ordered?" Ash asked.

"What are we doing here?" Lance added.

"No, I wanted to talk to you two, first," I retorted. "But I think I'll go ahead with my plan. Any ranges here in Dubai?"

Lance answered, "No outdoor pistol ranges. The only thing I've found is the shooting club at the Jebel Ali Golf Club.

"Becky and I have been there for breakfast…pretty nice restaurant… we caught a seaplane ride from the marina there," I interjected.

Lance continued, "They have an outdoor trap range and an indoor pistol range. We can also go out in the sand dunes!"

"Well, I'll need some target practice once it arrives," I said and thanked my friends for their help.

I met Becky for a late afternoon picnic on the Jumeirah beach. I loved the setting here, with high rise buildings behind us and the Persian Gulf out in front of us. There were numerous restaurants close by, and the most fun of all for me, Camel rides on the beach. The idea of sunning on the beach with camels walking by always got to me as really weird.

Becky had packed a great meal. Seeing her in her swimsuit made me want to return home for a little loving.

CHAPTER THIRTY

Washington, DC

"THOSE GOD DAMNED towel heads!" the President of the United States screamed when he finished his phone call.

President James was seated at the end of a long oval table. His Joint Chiefs of Staff were all in attendance for this meeting. The room was filled with secretaries and aides standing behind their prospective bosses. The temperature in the room was stifling. Many were reaching for the water pitchers on the long table and filling their glasses with the ice cold water.

Everyone in the room waited quietly for the President to finish his call with the Iranian Prime Minister. Many were taken aback at the President's outburst at the end of the call. Only his long time contacts were used to President James' remarks.

The friends closest to him also knew that he desperately loved his country, the United States of America. President James hated the way some of the countries of the world treated the United States. He especially hated the United Nations. America had been the chief supporter of the United Nations since it began in 1945. America had provided a home for the representatives of the 193 nation members. Even the Vatican was recognized. America had supplied the majority of the funding to keep this inept group 'alive and kicking'.

The United States was the greatest country on the planet, according to President James. "Those who act either overtly or insidiously to undermine our strength are scum," he once said to a close confidant.

He was an avid student of history and had studied the irony of the Middle East. Oil was hidden below treacherous and unforgiving lands, inhabited by nomadic peoples that had been at war with each other since the beginning of time. Plopping Israel down in the middle of this hotbed absolutely made no sense to President James. These warring tribes now had petrodollars to spend on advanced weaponry and could focus their aggression on a common enemy, the Jews living in Israel, rather than the infighting among themselves that had gone on for centuries.

Their Islamic religion promoted antiquated views of women as property to be dealt with in a harsh manner instead of humans capable of equal input to their male counterparts. Women were stoned to death for having affairs with foreigners, while the men were simply sent home. Women were circumcised so that sex would not be enjoyable…even painful.

The religion of Islam was a peaceful religion. How could so many use their terrorism and assaults against civilization as backed by the religion of Islam? President James had his own personal answer to that question: keep the masses illiterate and uneducated…a much better group to believe what the Imams preached. An educated man would not fall for that crap! Islam surely isn't the only religion on the planet to be used for evil. President James didn't like man-made religion for that very reason. Words could be twisted. Lord, his words as President surely were twisted on a daily basis. He knew that he was a man of faith, and very comfortable in that faith.

President James was not a man to mince words. This often got him into trouble. He used derogatory, hateful words to describe people who hated his beloved country. The man he had been speaking with was one of those men. This man had the audacity to claim that the Holocaust had not occurred! He had the audacity to speak before the United Nations on American soil and claim that the United States was behind the attacks of 9/11.

This was also the man who wouldn't back down from his plans to wage war against Israel when the American President informed him of the new information about the attack on Bushehr. It did not seem to matter who made the attack or who was at fault. All Iran needed was a reason to declare war. They had it now and were not going to stop just because Israel was not involved.

President James slammed the receiver into its cradle and looked up to the crowded room.

"That Iranian President didn't believe a word I said!" he announced, as his shoulders slumped. Then he stood straight upright as if at attention, and said, "He called me a liar…"

Then he addressed the room.

"Ladies and gentlemen," the President began. "I must relate to you some very disturbing news. Iran does not accept our explanation about the attack on Bushehr. They completely reject the truth. I actually believe that that Iranian bozo in charge would have blown up the nuclear facility himself so that he could foment a war against Israel!"

President James turned to one of the aides and asked, "How much time does this idiot have in office?"

"Two years, Mr. President. Then his two terms will be up," the aide answered.

"That's two years too long!" the President replied.

"Well, Generals and Admirals…get your war plans ready. What assets do we have in the region?" President James inquired.

"A skeleton force, mainly of advisors, in Iraq. A fair number of troops in Afghanistan. Not much else in the region," one of the Generals answered.

An Admiral then spoke, "Two carrier task forces in the area and another in the Mediterranean Sea."

An Air Force General added, "We have lots of equipment and personnel in Saudi Arabia."

"Well, put them on alert and get them ready!" President James ordered, and then to an aide he said, "Get me the Secretary of State. We need a UN resolution pronto!"

Hills outside of Kermanshah, Iran

Iran's armed forces were massing along a two hundred mile front from the south of Lake Urmia to Kermanshah. Men and equipment were pouring into the region from all parts of Iran. The majority headed northwest from Tehran. Encampments were springing up every few miles in a rough line that mimicked the imaginary line that separated Iran from Iraq.

In a matter of days, Iran had amassed an impressive force of half a million men. The rains of fall had not yet begun to soak the ground and the heat of summer was oppressive. During the day most of the men sought whatever shelter they could find from the blazing sun and awaited their orders to attack. Some worked on the armored equipment which needed constant attention.

The Iranian Generals gathered together in the mobile command center.

Tehran, Iran

The Iranian President had just completed his morning prayers after the muzzas called the masses to prayer from the minarets around the city. He stowed the prayer rug which he kept in his office. Muslims were supposed to enter the mosques for prayer five times a day. Mosques were everywhere in that city. They even had 'mini mosques' housed in the gas stations. When the call to prayer happened, automobiles were abandoned in the streets…left wherever they were so that the drivers could scramble into a mosque. Many of the roads were impassable during prayer time. The President chose to stay in his office. A luxury he assumed as the Leader of his country.

He summoned his war council into the office. Once the men had gathered he announced that Allah had blessed their mission and that the time was nigh to begin their campaign. The Generals listened closely and then began discussions among themselves. A time was chosen and a day was picked. The attack would commence in two days. The time for the invasion was dawn. The Generals shook each other's hands and there was much back slapping. The mood was festive.

World War IV was about to begin.

Dubai, UAE

Cyndi and Becky had spent the morning together and now were sitting in our living room across from me. Becky looked really pissed off, and I hadn't seen her like that in a long time…maybe ever. I put down my copy of the latest Harlan Coben novel. I had made a trip to Magrudy's book store on Jumeirah Road to pick up the new book just that morning. I was disappointed that this book didn't focus on Myron Bolitar as its hero. I had enjoyed the series of ten books that had been written covering his life and antics.

Cyndi spoke first. "Reggie the cat's out of the bag,"

"What are you talking about?" I said, becoming defensive.

"That landing you made in Tehran? Did you not think that the media was there? You three were on CNN, Damnit!" Cyndi continued.

"Ohhhhh," I groaned as my hands went up to my temples and began to massage them. "We didn't think about that!"

Becky took over for Cyndi. "Reggie, you three have worked hard to keep I.N.C.I.S.O.R. off the radar. You have done well to maintain a quasi-secret presence. Now this!"

"I looked between the two women with a shrug and a sheepish grin. "I didn't see any cameras. Nobody came up to Ash, Lance or me asking for an interview! Hell, with their dictatorship, I wouldn't think that there would be any news crews."

"Well, it turns out that you are wrong," Cyndi said. "I just hope for all of us that you're not DEAD wrong. Strong emphasis on the DEAD."

"CNN had a team in Tehran covering the struggles of the common man since the European Union placed the latest round of sanctions on Iran for continuing with their nuclear endeavors. I watched that piece! The United States and United Nations already had sanctions in place. Now the EU. The spot on CNN said that the European Union banned the import of Iranian crude oil, and blocked trade in gold, diamonds and precious metals," Becky continued.

"Okay, I believe that you saw the piece," I retorted.

"Yeah, well CNN had the piece showing that the common man is facing increased prices by fifty percent!" Becky said. "Iran's lifeblood is their oil revenues."

"Well, if you wish to discuss that, all Iran has to do is cease their maniacal drive to procure a nuke!" I argued.

"That's not it, Reggie!" Cyndi interrupted. "That same news crew got a tip and was at the airport when you landed that 747."

"They got you on film. The bit showed in their International News segment. We saw you…and Ash…and Lance! Who else do you think watched? Only millions around the world," Becky said.

"Ohhhhh, I groaned again. Al-Qaeda has operatives there too. What if they got pictures?"

"Yeah, what if!" Cyndi said. "The way I see it all five of us are in jeopardy."

"You two weren't there…" I began.

Cyndi cut me off with, "They'll connect us. They'll piece this all together. We are no longer safe! Your antics have put us all in harm's way."

"Let's all get together to discuss this," I offered feebly.

"Yeah…thanks," Cyndi said as she rose to leave. Then she pointed at me and said, "You brought us over here. We are camped out right in the middle of the Middle East! Right in the middle of this hotbed of nasty activity."

"Well, Cyndi," I replied, "That was kind of the point in choosing this location. All of the bad stuff seems to be happening right here, but we still have the safety of the UAE."

I blame you…and you alone!" Cyndi announced pointing a straight finger at me.

With that, Cyndi stood and walked out of our home, leaving Becky and me alone.

"She's a little hot under the collar," Becky said. "She'll calm down."

"Sure, but she's right," I said. "We have to be more careful now. Can you get your hands on that CNN clip?"

PART FOUR

CHAPTER THIRTY ONE

Abu Dhabi, UAE

LANCE, ASH AND I were in the middle of what had become one of my favorite pastimes. We had flown Aurora from Dubai southeast to Abu Dhabi to patronize one of my favorite breakfast hangouts. On the flight down along the coast we had flown over the Ferrari World building on Yas Island. The huge red triangular roof covers the largest indoor amusement park in the world. One of the rides is actually the world's fastest roller coaster!

The Ferrari emblem on the structure reminded me that Aurora proudly displayed that same symbol on her tail. The Ferrari endorsement was a sign that she was the fastest turboprop in the world. This was our first flight since the missile attack had damaged her back end. The repairs had gone well. She sported a new turboprop on the port side and all of her flight surfaces were repaired and seemed to be functioning well. The rear bathroom was no longer air conditioned by the holes created by the missile shrapnel. The new paint job masked any signs that repairs had been made.

The flight to Abu Dhabi was really brief, but it was great to be in the air again. Our favorite breakfast establishment had become Mirabel, found inside the Marks and Spencer Complex on Old Airport Road. Mirabel prides themselves on being a European up-market cafe and restaurant, using the best, freshest ingredients made to the highest standards and best quality, served by impeccably dressed and knowledgeable staff.

I really enjoyed being able to relax in the restaurant's elegant atmosphere. I appreciated the cloth table covers and comfortable seating.

I always ordered the same item…the steak and eggs. The waiter knew to bring the Australian prime filet cooked medium rare. I had been ordering steak and eggs whenever I travelled since I was on road trips with my parents as a child (once my mother allowed me to!). It was really hard to come by this favorite of mine in the United Arab Emirates. The local crowd had a very different sense of what to eat at breakfast time.

Lance ordered the American Grand Slam and Ash ordered the Eggs Benedict Royale. I ordered a cup of their Illy brand dark coffee. Lance chose their white hot chocolate with the marshmallow on the side, while Ash stuck with water and lemon.

We had chosen this casual setting to go over the CNN video of the 747 rescue in Tehran and address Cyndi's concerns about our being exposed on television and the repercussions if the terrorist world should discover who any of us were. Ash had also been briefed by the CIA about the MADEI hijacking attempt and was going to share with Lance and I what he had learned. It just seemed more genteel to me that we discussed our issues over a great meal and a warm setting.

Lance had brought his laptop on the journey and set it up on the table once the waiter had left with our orders. Cyndi had downloaded the CNN clip of the rescue onto the laptop. Lance was ready for us to watch once the drink order had arrived. We had a corner table that sported a bench on one side with chairs across the table from the bench. Lance had taken the bench, so Ash and I left our chairs and joined him on the bench to be able to view the screen. He began the video.

I sipped at my coffee while I watched. I noticed on the bar at the bottom of the video that the clip was only forty five seconds long. As it began, the camera panned across the large 747 as it sat on the tarmac, surrounded by emergency vehicles. Spotlights were moving across the body of the plane as if it were the main character in a Hollywood premier movie. The camera then panned toward the ground to show a number of what were assumed to be passengers and emergency personnel milling around before it. No faces could be identified from the footage so far.

The reporter was speaking in Arabic. I didn't have a clue what he was saying.

I remarked to the others, "So far, so good."

They nodded as I spoke.

Then the camera moved to show the back of an ambulance as a gurney was being loaded. The ambulance attendants were on both sides of the gurney ready to lift it into the vehicle. I was the body on the gurney and had an oxygen mask over my face. I was covered by what looked like a sheet and the attendant's bodies blocked much of the camera's view.

There was no making out who was on the bed from this video.

"Great!" I thought to myself, and then…

The cameraman began to pull back from the tighter shot of the emergency workers…and there they were…Lance and Ash beside the gurney.

The shot of the two of them lasted maybe ten seconds. It was really quick, and then the cameraman panned back to the aircraft.

"Anybody have a translation from the clip?" I asked.

"Well, there you have it," Lance spoke.

"Yeah, anybody with facial recognition software will be able to nail us," Ash added.

"We're screwed!" Lance continued.

The three of us watched the clip one more time, and then Ash and I returned to our seats.

"How about a translation?" I asked again.

"Cyndi's working on it…" Lance began.

"Does it mention MADEI…or us?" Ash interrupted.

"Cyndi isn't done, yet, but she said there were no names…just a hijacking attempt and that all of the hijackers were killed during the attempted takeover of the 747," Lance replied.

"Hey! Fun story…before Ash fills us in on what the CIA found. You two know that I've been flying since I was sixteen. That summer I used my lawn mowing money to pay for flying lessons. I went to Star Aviation at Stapleton Airport. Back then, you could do your dual training out of Stapleton, but I had to do my solo work out of Jefferson County Airport. My flight instructors were moonlighting off duty United Airlines Pilots. The 747 had just come out and a couple of my instructors were rated for the 747.

All of the airliners up until then had a single aisle down the middle of the craft. This plane had two aisles, on each side of the plane. One of my instructors told a story of turning off the fasten seat belt sign. He felt like he was wrestling with a football field as two hundred people milled around the back of the plane! This was before our computers that we have now that trim the airplane better. The other instructor told how he was over the Grand Canyon and got on the intercom to announce that you could see the Grand Canyon out the left side of the plane. He said that he thought he would lose the plane when three hundred people moved to the left side to see the landmark! That plane was a real monster!"

"Okay…my turn," Ash said.

"Yeah, I want to hear this," Lance mumbled with his mouth full.

"Come on, Lance, try chewing your food!" I joked.

"Here's the CIA story on the hijacking," Ash continued. "You guys remember that we knew there were four of the MADEI cell members in Tehran from what was heard on the PC. And three were in Frankfurt."

"Yeah, yeah, yeah," Lance said as he reached for his white chocolate.

I was always amazed to watch Lance drink these 'foo foo' drinks, like white chocolate and Cuba Libres, when he was such a monster of a guy. Even his wife Cyndi did her Jack Daniels in straight shots with a Coke chaser. He was even enjoying the marshmallow that came with his white hot chocolate!

Ash continued, "Okay, this is what they found out from the MADEI leader that the I.N.C.I.S.O.R. team in Frankfurt grabbed.

Al-Qaeda has a huge base of operations in Tehran. In fact, they told me that Iran is the largest state supporter of terrorism in the world! Well, al-Qaeda had infiltrated two men into the ramp crew of Lufthansa in Tehran. These guys got to clean out the planes and freshen up the lavatories. The two al-Qaeda guys hid knives behind the paper towel dispensers in First Class and the Business sections of the cabin.

Al-Qaeda also housed and hid the four MADEI cell members until the appointed time for the hijacking. Their flight tickets and identification papers had all been forged in Iraq. To the casual observer these four looked like Iranian businessmen travelling to Tel Aviv.

Al-Qaeda also provided MADEI with the scientists and mechanics to modify that ACM…"

"ACM…help me," I interrupted.

"Come on, Reggie…ACM is Advanced Cruise Missile," Lance retorted. "That's the missile in the satellite image hitting the reactor at Bushehr."

"Right!" I replied. ""Continue."
"Remember what Becky told us? Ash questioned. "The Advanced Cruise Missile can only be launched from a B-52 platform. And the Israeli markings. Everything pointed to either a United States attack or an Israeli strike, or a combination of both!"

"Got all that," I said.

"Well, MADEI launched that missile from a boat tied up at Kharg Island sixteen miles off the coast from Bushehr. You don't just steal an Advanced Cruise Missile from the United States armory that can only be launched from the air, stick it on a boat in the Persian Gulf and blow up a nuclear plant!" Ash exclaimed.

"So…what you're saying is…this is much larger than just the MADEI cell," Lance interjected.

"That's exactly what the CIA is saying," Ash agreed.

"It's looking like the plan came from that Abdullah character, the currently deceased leader of the now defunct terrorist cell, MADEI. He recruited his cell members both in America and Iraq. But none of them had the expertise or access to pull any of this off," Ash continued.

Lance took over at this point. "It looks like a splinter group of a White Supremacy group in the United States is responsible for stealing the nuke when a flight of B-52 bombers went missing for six hours…"

Ash interrupted, "It was six nukes, Lance! They were missing for thirty six hours!"

"Oh…right Ash," Lance replied and then continued. "According to official reports, the pilots did not know that they carried WMD's,"

"WMD's?" I asked.

"Weapons of Mass Destruction…really Reggie…after all the Iraq stuff and Sadam Hussein?" Lance scolded.

"Right…sorry," I cowered.

"And these nukes sat on the runway in Louisiana for several hours!" Lance finished.

"When you look at the protocols and the records that have to be signed…the chain of command…it would be virtually impossible for this incident to be blamed on lax security," Ash opined. "Even a soldier signing for a weapon has a paperwork trail strictly following the chain of command."

"Yeah, all that is for the conspiracy theorists," Lance interjected. "And not for us…except that what was not in the reports was that one of those nukes was absconded with and there are no reports about that!"

"But there were initial reports of only five missiles being accounted for when they arrived in Barksdale," Ash interjected. "And why Barksdale?

"That was in '07, right?" I asked.

"Yep, a few years ago," Ash replied. "Your point?"

"No point…just clarification…took a while for it to get to Iraq, huh?" I asked. "Anything about the splinter group that stole the missile?"

"The FBI has been looking at a group in Louisiana called the White League…" Lance began.

"I remember my history," I interrupted. "The White League was around in the late nineteenth century!"

"That's right, Reggie, 1874 to be exact, but it looks like they're back… and have something to do with that character, David Duke," Lance replied.

"That idiot still around?" Ash questioned.

"Haven't heard much about him since he was released from prison in 2004," I answered.

"Well…he's still at it, including a trip to Syria in 06…a year before the nuke was stolen," Lance said.

"Back to the White League…they had affiliations with the secret vigilante groups, such as the Klu Klux Klan…ah…I begin to see the connection! David Duke founded the Louisiana chapter of the KKK!" Lance began.

"But the White League members were out in the open…they actually solicited newspaper articles and coverage…and went away, or were absorbed by the Louisiana State militia and national guard when they successfully removed the Republicans from office in that state," I said. "Haven't heard about them since!"

"Well, Reggie, 'they're back'! That was the line from Poltergeist, right?" Ash asked.

"And now they aren't out in the open…highly secret…but still affiliated with the KKK," Lance continued.

"White supremacists…working with Arab terrorists…anybody got a problem with that?" I asked. "Seems like a huge stretch to link them together."

"The FBI is working the American angle. We know that the missile was stolen in Louisiana. It's possible that it was sold several times before it ended up in MADEI's hands," Lance replied.

"Oh, got it," I said.

"I want to visit Louisiana!" Ash interjected as that evil look came over his face.

"Like North Carolina?" I asked.

"White terrorists on American soil...anybody gonna miss a few of them?" Ash replied.

I began to comment and then chose to shut up.

"MADEI, or al-Qaeda hired Russian scientists...two of them...to modify the missile. They also provided the blueprints for the rail system that the Israeli Navy commandos found on Kharg Island. Hey, Reggie... Aurora still radioactive?" Lance asked.

"She's not glowing in the dark! No, no activity on the Geiger counter last time she was checked after the repairs," I replied.

"So I can put away my lead underwear!" Ash asked jokingly.

"Did seven million like the lead underwear?" I asked.

"Oh yeah! It really turned her on! Especially the fig leaf over my genitals!" Ash joked.

"Anyway, the CIA is working with the Russians to track down these two scientists. They were able to modify a missile that our American scientists couldn't do. That's pretty big stuff!" Lance continued.

"You know what they say...necessity is the mother of all invention!" I replied.

"So, to recap," Ash began. "The MADEI cell is gone...kaput...no longer in existence. The operation was bigger than MADEI, involving terrorist groups in the Middle East and the United States. They stole a US ACM, and disguised it with Israeli markings. Israeli items were found in the desert outside of Bushehr by that FRMAC team. Those were planted by one of the MADEI cell members who worked the laser sighting device for the missile attack against the nuclear reactor."

"And...their plan worked. Iran has declared war against Israel. What did MADEI stand for, again?" I asked.

"Muslim Arabs Dedicated to the Eradication of Israel," Lance answered.

"Well? A war right now may very well accomplish that," I said.

"As far as the CIA is concerned, we did well and accomplished all that they asked of us," Lance finished.

"Let's get the check," I said. "I have an appointment with Dr. White."

"That's the acupuncturist?" Ash asked.

"More needles in the neck!" Lance interjected.

CHAPTER THIRTY TWO

Dubai, UAE

"I HAVEN'T SEEN MY sister in almost a year!" Becky exclaimed while we were sitting on the patio enjoying the afternoon sun. "I want to go to Phoenix."

"Just as World War IV begins!" I countered. "You really want to be gone now?"

"Especially now! I want to be as far away from here as possible…and Phoenix is a pretty good spot for that," she countered.

I knew better than to continue the argument. What Becky wanted… Becky got. She had even coined the phrase, "Don't ask permission…ask forgiveness." I have learned over the years that many of the things that Becky wanted, Becky got.

"When do you leave?" I asked, knowing that she had already purchased her tickets. This was Becky's MO (modus operandi). She would buy an expensive item at the store or shopping online and then tell me a story about how much she saved…or why this item was so important for us to possess, when I saw no value in whatever the item was. Whenever she had decided to visit Robyn, it was a while before I was told about it.

"Tomorrow," she replied.

"Really?" I asked, thinking this was really short notice.

"Yeah, ride to the airport?" she answered.

"Sure," I said as we sat in silence for the rest of the afternoon.

I headed inside the house. "Everything okay with Robyn?" I asked as an afterthought as I left.

"Nothing wrong…I'm just lonely," Becky finished.

Lance called when I entered the house. "Cyndi found a follow-up report on CNN about the hijacking. It's good that we chose to work only with Lufthansa and not tell the Iranian authorities. The Iranian military police are taking complete credit for thwarting the hijacking. They claim to have picked up the al-Qaeda operatives at the Khomeini Airport. They credit a Lufthansa First Officer with landing the plane. And Lufthansa security for the deaths of the four terrorists aboard the plane. Nothing about I.N.C.I.S.O.R. or us. And no more pictures of Ash or me."

"That's great news, Lance!" I replied. "So we just have to worry about that few seconds when you two were captured on film. How's Cyndi now?"

"Still pissed…and fearful," Lance answered.

"At me?" I asked.

"She blames you for this. She thinks it was your fault that we moved to Dubai. Like you 'dragged' us over here. Anyway, she wants us to move back to Denver. I'm resisting, but she's going for a visit tomorrow," Lance said.

"Becky's leaving tomorrow, also…same flights? Lufthansa to Frankfurt then on to Denver?" I asked.

"That's what Cyndi's doing…Becky too?"

"Yeah…It'll just be us three here in Dubai for a while," I finished. I hung up the phone and thought about the two wives leaving…was it coincidence? Had they talked? I knew they still walked together every day, even since Grace died. They had to have talked! Was there more to this? I gave up. Figuring out women is definitely not my strong suit!

The next evening Lance and I drove Becky and Cyndi to the Dubai airport for the 1:40 am flight to Frankfurt. The flight would arrive in Frankfurt a little before 6 am, and there was a fun little restaurant at the airport for breakfast. But the layover was very long and horrendous! The flight to Denver didn't leave until 1:30 pm…too short of a time to venture into Frankfurt and a long, long time at the airport and little to do but read books!

We left the wives to deal with immigration and security and headed back to Palm Jumeirah. Lance joined me at my home for drinks into the wee hours of the morning.

The next morning Ash appeared with news from the CIA. I called Lance to get him to join us at the house. Ash waited with the news until Lance arrived. Lance came in with a bottle of Mountain Dew in his hand. That was his sign that he was struggling with a hangover from the night before.

"Those Cuba Libres get to you?" I asked.

"Big time…Reggie, I can't go head to head with you! I have to leave that up to Cyndi. She can put any man under the table!" Lance replied. "What's up?"

Ash took over at this point. "News of a kidnapping in France. This time it's a whole family. Five of them."

"Any 'mini's on them?" I asked.

"Don't know," he replied.

"Becky's the one who monitors all of the 'mini' activity, and she's off to Phoenix. I'll see if I can figure out the program that Becky uses," I said as I moved to Becky's computer in the office. As the program appeared on the screen there was a flashing symbol on the screen. I clicked on the icon. Sure enough, a 'mini' had gone active.

"We've got a live 'mini' broadcasting from northwestern France…the Loire Valley," I told Lance and Ash.

"That's our family!" Ash exclaimed.

"What do we know?" Lance asked.

"Here's what we have from the CIA…the French police have surrounded a castle in the Loire Valley. An unknown number of men have taken the castle and are threatening to kill one member of the family, beginning with the children, every day that their demands are not met…starting in two days! That was yesterday!" Ash told us.

"Send word to the German team that we will meet them in Paris," I ordered.

"Way ahead of you, Reggie," Ash replied. "I called them as soon as I finished with the call."

"I'll call the airport and get Aurora ready," I said.

"I'll get the gear together," Lance said. "What a time for a hangover!"

Lance and Ash left quickly and I scrambled around the house gathering up my things. I thought about reaching out to Becky, but she and Cyndi were still in the air on their way to Denver and Phoenix.

We met at the hangar and parked our cars. Aurora was pulled out of the hangar and the attendant told me that she was fully fueled. Ash and I performed the preflight and manually checked the fuel tanks as Lance stowed our gear in the luggage compartment in the rear of the plane.

I had filed a flight plan to Paris and informed my friends that the trip would entail two stops…one in Cairo, and one in Rome. It was a long journey for us. Paris was almost three thousand nautical miles from Dubai, but the Aurora would still be able to make the trip and get us to Paris before any of the scheduled commercial flights out of Dubai.

We loaded up and off we went. Shortly after takeoff I turned on the autopilot and sat back to enjoy the ride. It was time for some planning!

Paris, France

Ash, Lance and I met up with the German I.N.C.I.S.O.R. team at Charles De Gaulle Airport. A short Train ride later we were attempting to figure out how to get a train south to the Loire Valley. We were at the Gare Montparnasse train station. The station was built in 1840 and rebuilt in 1969. It handled fifty million passengers each year. It was the largest train station I had been in!

The eight of us found the TGV line and purchased tickets for Tours, which lay one hundred and twenty six miles to the southwest.

"TGV stands for Train a Grande Vitesse," Dick Becker informed the team. "It is France's high speed rail service. TGV trains operate at the highest speeds of any conventional train service in the world. They regularly reach speeds of three hundred and twenty miles per hour!"

"Man, that's fast!" Aaron Dekker answered and we all nodded our heads in agreement.

"We cover the distance between Paris and Tours in thirty five minutes. It's a two to three hour car ride," Dick continued.

"What do we do in Tours?" Stirling Mason asked.

"Pick up a slower train for the short ride to Montrichard," Dick answered. "Tours to Montrichard is twenty four miles and the train takes twenty eight minutes."

"The same, almost, as Paris to Tours!" Graham Sandler commented.

"Well, let's all get loaded aboard," Lance ordered.

Montrichard, France

Two hours later the eight of us were waiting at the Montrichard train station awaiting our ride. The CIA contact met us with a van, or small bus was actually more accurate, and drove us to the Chateau Hotel de Chissay. The Chateau was a short ride west from Montrichard.

The agent announced as we disembarked that this would be our base of operations. The local constabularies were aware of the presence of the CIA, but not of I.N.C.I.S.O.R. "What did INCISOR stand for?" he asked.

"**IN**ternational **CI**vilians for a **S**afe Society **OR**ganization," I answered. "We are civilians, who work internationally, with an identity that is separate from any specific government. We work on issues to restore law and order to the world's society, as we know it."

"A shadow group of the CIA?" he asked.

"No…we are completely autonomous…but we help out when we can," I replied.

"Cool," he remarked. "The Chateau is yours…I've rented bikes for you to tour the region. Chateau de Chenonceau is a short ride from here."

"What's that?" Magnus asked.

"Oh, sorry…that is the castle that is under siege," he replied. "I'll brief you all in one hour, once you're settled. We'll meet in the restaurant. It's called 'la table du Roy'. Just cross the courtyard past the fountain and you're there."

We all checked in with the reception desk and I was given the room that was called the 'Room Jacuzzi'. There was a tiny elevator that could only take two of us at a time, along with our gear, up to the rooms. My room was on the top floor of the Chateau. I opened the door to my room and immediately saw why the room was named the way it was. There was a large round Jacuzzi tub right in the middle of the floor!

I threw my bag on the bed and explored the room. The slanted ceiling and exposed wooden beams created a lot of character. I could see Becky and me enjoying this room for a week, while we biked to explore the local vineyards. I then went into the bathroom. The toilet was placed in such a way that, because of the slanted roof, I couldn't stand before the toilet to relieve myself. I either would have to stand at an angle…or sit like a girl. There was no shower. I guessed that I was to shower with the hand-held nozzle attached to the tub. There were no shower curtains around the round tub. I stood in the tub and grabbed the shower wand. It only reached up to my chest. I'd have to kneel in the tub and hold this thing to get a shower! Well, a new experience for me.

Our CIA contact had great pictures of the Chateau de Chenonceau castle. It was a popular tourist spot and was widely photographed. He gave us a brief history about the castle. It was built in the eleventh century on the site of an old mill near the town of Chenonceau. The original manor house was torched in 1412 to punish the current owner. He rebuilt the castle in the 1430's. That castle was destroyed and rebuilt between 1515 and 1521. The Chateau was seized by the crown in 1547 for unpaid debts. Henry II offered the Chateau to his mistress, who became fervently attached to the property and surrounding area. This mistress, Diane de Poitiers, oversaw the construction of the arch bridge across the Cher river, and the extensive flower and vegetable gardens set along the banks of the river in four triangles.

Henry II's widow, Catherine de' Medici, kicked out the mistress after his death in 1559 and dedicated the grand gallery, which extended along the existing arch bridge to cross the entire river in 1577. Chenonceau became Catherine's favorite residence.

Catherine died in 1589 and the chateau went to her daughter-in-law. In 1624 King Henry IV had another mistress inhabit the castle. It was uninhabited and abandoned for more than a hundred years until it was bought by the Duke of Bourbon in 1720. He sold off all of the castle's contents and statues, many ending up at Versailles, and then sold the estate itself to Claude Dupin.

Claude's wife was credited with saving the chateau from destruction during the French Revolution because it was the only bridge across the river for many miles. In 1864 Chateau de Chenonceau was sold to a Scottish millionaire. In 1891 it was sold to a Cuban millionaire. In 1913 it was sold to the Menier family who still own the castle. The castle and its gardens have been open to the public and, next to the Royal Palace of Versailles, Chenonceau is the most visited chateau in France.

He then put up an aerial map of the estate and showed where the French police were staked out around the castle. I was sure that the police were trampling many of the gardens around the property. The CIA had no idea how many kidnappers were involved. Each family member could be seen standing before the large windows in the gallery which spanned the river.

"What about the family?" Stirling asked the CIA operative.

I took over the discussion at this point. "The head of the family is a wealthy French industrialist. His company purchased the 'mini' just six months ago. According to his secretary, he was on holiday in the Loire Valley with his family for one month. They were making their way slowly through the valley visiting castles, wineries and vineyards. Here is his picture." I passed the photograph around the room.

"What is a 'mini'?" the CIA operative questioned.

"Something you guys designed for us at Langley," Ash replied.

"It's an incredibly small nanotransmitter that only goes active…and therefore is undetectable…when there is a problem…like now. It is also extremely accurate. Better than GPS. We can pinpoint which room the 'mini' is in in that castle!" Lance added.

"I guess Langley doesn't inform you guys of everything that's going on. What's the line? 'Need to know'?" I said.

"I didn't know about you and your team until yesterday," the CIA operative replied.

"And the wife and kids?" Dick inquired.

"Two girls and a boy. The boy is the oldest. He is ten. The girls stair step down from him every two years. They are eight and six," I added.

"He's pretty good looking," Stirling said. "Any pictures of the rest of the family? Is the wife a porker?"

"Stirling, you can have the good looking guy!" Aaron joked. "Not my type anyway…I'll get the wife…no matter how big she is!"

The team all had a good chuckle which broke up the tension in the room.

"No other photos of the family at this point," I concluded.

"Let's use those bikes. Time for a look around the area," Dick suggested.

"Just ride west along the Route de Tours…the road in front of the Chateau. Shortly you'll come to Chateau de Chenonceau. Just look for the police barricade," the operative joked.

Washington, DC

"I cannot stop this thing," President James mused to himself. "I cannot get the damned Iranians to listen to the facts…to reason. They know that Israel was not behind the attack at Bushehr and yet they continue with their war preparations. It is madness."

Loire Valley, France

"How's this for a plan?" Magnus began. "The kidnappers don't know that we're here. Neither do the police. As we saw, any access from land to the castle is blocked by all of the police blockades. And the only entrance into the castle is across the moat through that narrow bridge. Easy to defend. So we come from the water…the Cher River."

"The kidnappers will see us approaching from a long way away!" Lance exclaimed. "And we'll be sitting ducks on the river."

Stirling continued, "We use small subs…"

"Those two man subs?" I interrupted. "We'd need a ton of them to affect a rescue!"

"Hold your horses, Reggie…and listen!" Aaron retorted. "Please continue, Stirling."

"Thanks, we've spent the afternoon looking into this. International Venture Craft Corp. has a six person sub. We'd only need three to get in and out undetected. That's the problem…finding three quickly. U.S. Submarines makes the Discovery which can hold up to ten people. We'd only need two…still a problem to find with so little time. They also make a Nomad 1000 that can hold all of us…our team of eight plus the five family members plus the pilot of the submarine. And the good news is that there is a Nomad in St. Tropez! I've taken the liberty of contacting the CIA and they made the necessary calls to get the sub delivered to Montrichard by morning. Quite an undertaking, but they came through. The Nomad is being loaded on a flatbed and secured as we speak. The truck will take almost ten hours to get here from there!"

"And a pilot?" Lance asked.

"Flying in from the United States. He'll also be here in the morning," Dick answered.

"Tomorrow's the day that this group of kidnappers has threatened to start killing the children," I added. "We're cutting it pretty close!"

"So we make a stealth approach from the Cher River. Underwater? Is the river deep enough?" Ash asked.

"Already checked on that. The Cher River is a tributary of the Loire River. It is deep enough and wide enough. We'll have plenty of room to maneuver," Graham replied. "Also, the Nomad 1000 runs on batteries when submerged, so our approach will be silent. The river is murky enough to mask any signs that we are approaching."

"And finally, the Nomad 1000 runs on diesel engines on the surface if we need a speedy getaway," Dick added.

"And once we're under the arched bridge?" I asked.

"Rappelling gear…up both sides…rescue the family and get out the way we came," Dick answered.

"You've looked at the stone walls?" Lance questioned.

"Yep…with the rough stone blocks and all of the adornments, it'll be easy to scale. All five of our team will go up…one for each family member. You three old timers will cover our asses!" Stirling joked.

I turned to Ash. "I'm getting tired of all this 'old timer' crap!"

"Me too…we'll have to kick some young butt in the ring when all of this is over!" Ash replied.

"Our ring in Frankfurt is open to you old geezers at any time," Magnus retorted. "Bring it on!"

"Weapons?" Lance asked.

"We go in with silenced machine pistols…and our knives. Some concussion grenades if necessary. You guys will have the heavy equipment on the river bank," Aaron continued.

"Kidnappers inside? How many?" Ash asked.

"No clue," Dick added. "We assume from what the CIA has been able to glean from the police reports that some are watching the family upstairs in the Gallery. That is where the family is displayed in the windows. There must be others guarding the main entrance to the castle on the main floor. We're guessing that most of the kidnappers will be watching the police."

"Do we involve them?" I asked.

There was a resounding chorus of 'NO'!

"Not even for a diversion?" Lance added.

"This is the French. We've trained with their military on several occasions when we were in the service. Not good!" Graham replied.

The CIA operative had attended our planning session. He now added, "I'll hang out with the police. They know me. If you need a distraction, I'll figure out how to create one!"

"Perfect!" I replied. "We've got both ends covered.

"You guys any good with a gun?" Dick joked. "You know you have our backsides!"

"We'll have you covered…now you young pups get to bed. Big day tomorrow and you know how you are without your beauty rest!" Ash ordered.

CHAPTER THIRTY THREE

Iranian Headquarters in Mahabad, Iran

THE GENERAL AROSE from his kneeling position and still faced southwest toward Mecca. He had completed his morning prayers. And now it was time…

He turned to his Chief of Staff and gave the most devastating order of his career. "Give the order to fire up the tanks. We move west in one hour!"

The Chief of Staff rushed out of the tent with the General's orders. Today was the day!

The General moved to the tent where all of his commanders had gathered. They all rose and saluted as he entered. He moved to a makeshift platform in the front of the tent. A huge picture of the Ayatollah Khomeini hung behind him as he faced his men.

"We launch our attack in one hour. We travel across Iraq along a front that reaches almost two hundred miles. With our main attack force stretched over so vast a distance, constant communication is mandatory!"

Murmurs could be heard from the leaders gathered in the room.

"We do not have permission from Iraq or Syria to cross their lands. Resistance from their militias may be met but our intelligence declares that the resistance will be light with 'minimal casualties."

The murmuring became louder at the prospect of resistance from their own Arab people. Especially Iraq…there were many in the room who had fought in the Iraq-Iran war.

"We have eight hundred miles of rough terrain to cross. To maintain our lines we will move at a conservative thirty miles an hour!"

Now the murmurs became a quiet rumble. Thirty miles an hour was definitely possible on the roads, but not in open country. How could they do this?

"If your men meet any resistance…deal with it…overcome it…and march on. You will have air cover only when requested, except for reconnaissance aircraft. We will be on the move seven hours a day…or travel the equivalent of about two hundred miles a day. This plan will allow stragglers to catch up and for the line to remain strong!" the General continued. "This will also allow for plenty of rest for your men and for the resupply lines to catch up to you."

"We will take four days to cross our two neighbors to the west and then we will gather at the base of the Golan Heights to mount our attack against Israel!"

Now there were cheers throughout the room…and chants like 'death to Israel'.

"See you all in four days…now move!"

Under the thundering from the hundreds of tank engines being revved up, the order to move was given. With a jerky start the tanks, their support vehicles and the armored personnel carriers began to move west.

Iran began her attack of Israel.

Montrichard, France

The same small bus that delivered us to the Chateau Chissay had returned to take us to the awaiting submarine at the bridge over the Cher River in Montrichard. We all left the bus on a side street close to the river bank. Only the hatch cover of the submarine rose above the water.

The long truck that had brought the submarine from St. Tropez was nowhere to be seen. It had arrived in the wee hours of the morning and offloaded the sub into the river quietly and without disturbing any of the slumbering townspeople. That maneuver, alone, was quite a feat! There were no crowds gathered around the banks of the river to see the strange submarine that had appeared during the night.

The pilot, a Navy SEAL himself, greeted us all warmly on the moist grass covering the gently sloping bank down to the water. We stowed our gear on board the sub and scrambled into the dark confines within.

It was quite cramped inside the sub and I immediately felt claustrophobic. I could tell from the eyes of the men around me that they were having a similar reaction. Looking out the porthole glass it was evident that this would be no sightseeing journey! The water was so murky that I wasn't sure that the pilot could find his way.

The cover was sealed and we were off! By the time we had passed under the bridge at Montrichard the submarine was completely submersed…and invisible to all of the hikers and bike riders moving along the banks of the Cher River at this early hour.

The submarine moved noiselessly through the water with the current to help with its progress. We had about five miles to cover under water… and one bridge to clear at Chissay, along with the ancient Fort at Port Le Cher to maneuver around.

Working blind and with only his instruments to navigate through the muddy waters, the pilot covered the distance in less than two hours. He then moved the submarine downstream of the castle and turned the craft around in the middle of the river. He then approached the arched bridge over the river from the far bank of the castle proper with the sub's nose pointing upstream in the direction of our escape.

The submarine pilot worked to raise the submarine so that the hatch cover was above the water level. When the pilot gave the word, Ash popped the hatch, grabbed his duffle bag containing his sniper rifle and moved quickly out of the sub and onto the shore. He noticed that the pilot had placed the submarine hatch perfectly under the arches. None of the occupants of the castle could see us. Ash moved upstream and found cover along the bank. Lance was out next with his bag of weaponry and moved downstream to find cover.

I was out next, and as was typical for these missions, I moved up the bank to position myself next to the arched bridge and even with the first floor of the castle. I had no view of the castle windows were the hostages were displayed. I just stared at a stone wall! About as much out of harm's way as possible.

Ash and Lance both reported that they could see figures in the windows. At this sharp angle they could not make out if the figures were friend or foe. The windows closest to the castle proper were the ones that were occupied…on both sides of the Gallery. The five members of the

Frankfurt I.N.C.I.S.O.R. team poured out of the submarine and gathered under the arch along the far bank. They readied all of their gear and then swam into positions under the closest two arches to the castle keep. The information from Ash and Lance told them which windows they were to approach.

The five worked first to scale up the sides to a position above the arches. Then, grappling hooks were shot onto the steep roof. All five hooks could be seen sliding down until they attached themselves to various parts of the dormer windows on the floor above the Gallery. We all waited and observed…did the scraping sounds alert anybody inside?

The five men moved up the sides of the arched bridge almost in unison! Ash and Lance watched in admiration. I couldn't see anything but listened to the progress on my headset. When each was in position, glances were stolen through the windows.

"I've got the dad," Stirling announced.

"Mom's with me," Magnus added.

"I've got the boy," Dick said.

"The older girl is here," Aaron added.

"And I've got the little one," Graham finished.

"What about bad guys?" Lance asked.

"I've got one with the dad," Stirling replied.

They all continued with their findings.

"Confirmed, five bad guys at the windows," Ash said. "Any others?"

"Can't see anything else from here," Magnus answered.

Ash and Lance trained their rifles on the closest windows.

"Ready!" Ash whispered.

"Ready here," Lance added.

"Go in five!" Dick ordered.

I raised my weapon at the stone buttress, feeling kind of stupid that I was taking aim at a bunch of rocks.

"Four…Three…Two…One!"

At once the team crashed through five of the windows simultaneously. In the process, knocking down the five family members. The five kidnappers guarding the family at the windows had no chance. Silenced pistol shots eliminated them.

Each of the I.N.C.I.S.O.R. team crouched over their family member to assure them and attempted to explain about the rescue. Language was getting in the way and translating was proving difficult.

The mother and children began screaming immediately. The children calmed down quickly while the mother remained hysterical. There was a loud clatter of approaching footsteps on the stairway. Men were coming! They had to move quickly now!

A French gendarme was enjoying a leisurely walk through the beautiful gardens and looked up to see the men swing through the windows as the commotion began. He stood in awe as the attack commenced, surprised that the police would move in without his knowledge. He then looked to the police positions on either side of the bridge across the moat. The men were relaxed and smoking their cigarettes. Now he was puzzled. Why weren't they ready? He began to move quickly back to his position when he stopped suddenly and peered hard at the river. What was that metal thing sticking out of the water under the arch?

He then turned and sprinted out of sight!

"The French police know," I announced into my headset.

"Got it covered," came over our headsets from the CIA operative.

I heard two separate explosions from my position.

"Wow!" Ash exclaimed. "Two police vehicles just blew up!"

"It's mayhem out front!" Lance added.

Inside the Gallery, two men had burst through the entrance spraying their automatic weapons wildly around the room. Glass shattered and plaster exploded from the walls.

The INCISOR team and the hostages were crouched down and close to the floor. The bullets sprayed over their heads. All five immediately returned fire and eliminated two more of the kidnappers. There was more racket on the stairs. Dick and Aaron each pulled out a flash bang grenade and lobbed them toward the stairwell. The men covered their ears and closed their eyes tightly.

The concussion was immense and blew out any remaining glass in the windows of the gallery. Immediately the men were up and affixing their assigned family members to the rappelling gear. Magnus was the only one in trouble…the woman was still screaming hysterically and uncooperative, writhing around on the floor of the Gallery. He finally slapped her on the temple, rendering her unconscious. He grabbed up the limp body and struggled with her dead weight as he moved to the window.

All five exited in unison, almost like a Circ du Soleil performance! They quickly descended down the ropes and landed in the water. They now moved toward me, working against the current to stay abreast of my position. I urged them forward and watched for any activity on the far bank of the river.

There was now automatic gunfire from the windows of the gallery. The kidnappers were hanging out of the windows attempting to shoot down at the rescuers. Lance and Ash returned fire and eliminated that threat. Next, there were men at the windows shooting at Lance and Ash's positions! Leaves and branches were exploding off of the shrubs around them. As bullets peppered the shoreline, clods of dirt were flying everywhere. I saw Ash and Lance scramble for cover. "How could I help?" I thought.

I crept out from behind the far wall of the bridge, stuck my head out one side and glanced upward. All I could see were the arms of one of the hijackers holding and firing a weapon at Ash. I took aim and fired at his hand. Nothing! Missed!

"What did they tell me?" I asked myself.

"Breathe out…exhale…aim…and fire," I remembered and followed the mantra, firing again.

I heard a scream as the butt of the gun exploded. I moved over the river bank under the arch to the other wall and took aim at the man firing at Lance. This time I got it right on the first try! The weapon exploded and then there was no one at the window.

The five family members had been helped inside the submarine. The five I.N.C.I.S.O.R. members had scrambled inside. Ash and Lance were moving toward me from their positions and clambered into the sub. I climbed up the side of the craft and began to descend into the chamber. I noticed that the man who spotted the submarine from the garden had returned to the garden and was waving wildly on the far bank. He actually pulled out his revolver and fired at the submarine!

"Hey!" the pilot exclaimed. "This ship is not armored!"

I slammed the hatch closed. "Get this boat out of here!" I ordered.

Without the need for any more encouragement the pilot submerged the craft and made for the middle of the river. We were now proceeding against the current which would slow down our return to Montrichard.

The husband and three children were hugging their rescuers and jabbering in French like fools. The wife was beginning to come around and panicked again at being in the submarine. One of the children announced that she was like this when she was not on her medication.

Besides some cuts and scrapes…and sore eardrums…all of us were unharmed…except for Magnus who had been wounded by the woman's razor sharp nails! He had cuts all over his neck and cheeks.

Lance radioed the CIA operative who had caused the commotion in the parking lot of the castle. He let the operative know that we were away and had all five family members in tow. The CIA man made a stealthy retreat and his presence at the police standoff went unnoticed.

Lance then had an idea.

"Let us off at the bridge at Chissay," he said to the pilot. He then radioed the CIA man to meet us there.

We made it to Chissay unimpeded. The submarine surfaced and the entire I.N.C.I.S.O.R. group made their way out of the sub. The bus was there to pick us up and we returned to the Chateau Chissay.

The submarine continued on to Montrichard travelling on the surface with the use of its diesel engine. When it pulled to the river bank a horde of police appeared with weapons drawn and covered the craft. Several police climbed up to the hatch cover and helped the family exit the sub. The pilot was the last to leave the boat.

The family and pilot were quickly removed from the area and escorted to the local police headquarters.

After dropping us off at the chateau, the CIA operative made his way into Montrichard. He would do his best to answer questions and placate the local constabulary. His job wouldn't be too hard. The family was rescued and all were unharmed…except the wife. She had a tremendous headache!

Iran/Iraq Border

"Entering Iraq now, sir," the lead commander reported back to the General.

"Proceed!" the General ordered.

Hundreds of armored vehicles along a huge front stormed into Iraqi territory. A huge cloud of dust trailed the lead tanks and covered over the vehicles that followed. An American Predator flying over the border caught the incursion on video as it flew north.

"Wow! Look at this!" the man piloting the drone claimed from the hangar at Bagdad International Airport. He flashed the video onto the large main monitor in the room. Many gathered around to watch as Iran invaded Iraq.

Up until this point the Iranian army had met with no resistance. Not even the occasional nomad had fired upon them.

Washington, DC

"Mr. President?" the Deputy Director of the CIA began.

President James had his head in his hands and really did not want to be interrupted.

"What? What is it, man?" the President replied.

"The Iranian army has entered into Iraqi territory!" the Deputy Director announced. He moved to the television in the Oval Office and turned it on. The President watched the same video that was being displayed in the hangar at Bagdad.

"Holy Christ!" the President exclaimed. He then bowed his head. A horrible headache was beginning at the base of his skull and working its way up to the President's temples. President James began to absently rub the sides of his head and then sat bolt upright.

"Get the Joint Chiefs together…Now!"

The Deputy Director quickly left the Oval Office to do as he was commanded, and wondered what was up with the President.

Chateau Chissay, Loire Valley

The eight I.N.C.I.S.O.R. members were having a raucous party on the patio overlooking the pool. Dozens of bottles of champagne were in ice buckets in various locations around the patio. Corks were popping and the atmosphere was boisterous.

Magnus had been cornered by his teammates who were in the process of pouring bottles over his head. He had the distinction of being the most injured member of the team…and this was his reward…a champagne shower!

Ash, Lance and I sat at one of the tables and watched the antics of our young warriors. We toasted to another I.N.C.I.S.O.R. victory. I finished my glass of the bubbly and then switched to my standard drink. The Crown Royal felt great as it warmed my insides.

The CIA operative joined us as the festivities were winding down to a more manageable level. Several tables had been pushed together so that we could all sit together. Magnus was soaked from head to foot! Many of the others had wet shirts.

Things had gone well in Montrichard, we were informed. The submarine was already out of the water and onto the flatbed truck that brought it up from St. Tropez. The driver was about to depart for the journey back to the south of France. The submarine pilot had been released by the police. They had bought his story that all he did was transport the family up the river. Crazy that the police accepted his story! He was on the train for Tours and then on to Paris.

After the two car bombs had exploded outside of the castle, the police made a move on the castle. An armored car approached the castle on the bridge over the moat. It rammed the front door to the castle and the French equivalent of our SWAT swarmed inside. They were met with light resistance and killed four of the kidnapping gang that fired upon them. The police found two injured hijackers with shattered hands, and a number of dead men upstairs, which they couldn't understand at first. The Chenonceau castle had been secured and the two living hijackers had been removed to Paris for future interrogation.

The CIA operative sold a story to the local constabularies that the father had overwhelmed one of his captors and freed his family. He used the hijacker's weapons to return fire as the family climbed out of the windows to safety. Really far-fetched! The husband and father was backing up the story, mainly by staying mute, as we had requested of him. The wife was a basket case and the police were leaving the children alone. They were all being driven back to Paris under police escort.

The incident at Chateau Chenonceau had ended and all was well. The CIA operative left us to arrange transportation back to Paris for our team.

That was the last any of us saw of him. He vanished into the dusk as the sun was setting to the west, almost like a bad western movie.

I called Becky once I was back in my room. She was spending her days in Phoenix consoling her sister Robyn. A long term romance that had been on and off again over the years…was off. This time Robyn was sure that it was over and was very despondent. Becky was trying to help by wining and dining her…and of course, shopping.

I listened with only half and ear. This kind of stuff seemed so trivial to me right now. I hung up the phone amazed that Becky had not even asked me how my day was! Well, she'd just have to wait to hear the story until later.

CHAPTER THIRTY FOUR

Denver, CO

"LANCE, HONEY…I'M NOT coming back. I'm done with the Middle East.

"But Cyndi," Lance protested from three thousand miles away. "This is our home now."

"No, Lance, we have a home here, too…remember?" Cyndi replied.

Cyndi was calling from their home in Denver, Colorado. She was enjoying a beautiful spring afternoon. White puffy clouds dotted the crystal blue sky. The temperature was comfortably warm and her iced tea was cold. Cyndi had forgotten how safe it felt to be in the United States. After the events which took place over the recent weeks, she was positive that she didn't want to ever leave her beloved country again!

"But Cyndi…"Lance pleaded. "You are my wife!"

"Yes…and I'll stay your wife…but here in the states!" Cyndi retorted.

"But…" Lance was really searching for words. This had hit him out of the blue. He remembered that Cyndi had been upset after the 747 rescue in Tehran. Yes, it was his and Ash's faces on that CNN newscast, but no names had been used and there weren't any interviews. There was also no mention of Ash or Lance or I.N.C.I.S.O.R. in the follow up piece, and the I.N.C.I.S.O.R. team had discovered that the CNN bit had appeared only on their Middle East news…not even shown in the United States. "What about your I.N.C.I.S.O.R. duties?"

"Most of what I do is on the computer…and I can do it just as easily from our home here in Denver as being in that ridiculous part of the world where I have to fear for my life…and yours with every turn I make!" Cyndi stated.

"What about you and Becky?" Lance tried.

"Lance! I cannot go back there!" was Cyndi's reply.

Cyndi knew this man well. Lance was the most intimidating looking man that she had ever known. He was large and stocky. Still sporting the military haircut, Lance had a huge head…and no discernible neck! He had kept himself fit and trim. Cyndi knew that there was no extra fat on his body. Lance was all muscle. He was also intelligent, and they had spent many long evenings in discussion about world politics and other subjects.

Cyndi also knew Lance's heart. He was like a big, cuddly animal. She knew that he would do or say anything for her. On the occasion when they argued, all Cyndi had to do was appear at the top of the stairs dressed in one of Lance's tee-shirts. That was all she had on! Cyndi had learned over the years that this look turned Lance into Jell-O. Lance would immediately forget whatever the argument was and would fold on any topic as he mounted the stairs to join her in the bedroom.

But this was big! Cyndi had never told Lance that she would not be willing to join him on an adventure. She had moved with Lance to wherever the CIA had stationed him. Of course, there were missions that her husband attended to without Cyndi being with him. But all of the spots where she was allowed to join him, Cyndi did. And now she was telling him that she would not live with him…at least in the Middle East!

Lance had nothing more that he could think of to say. He was devastated when he realized that his wife was giving him an ultimatum. As long as he continued to live in Dubai…he would do so without her. How would this work…long term? He muttered some words that were supposed to be a goodbye. As he hung up the phone, he thought, "I've got to talk to Reggie!"

Louis Armstrong Airport, Louisiana

Ash Black walked through the terminal looking like the hundreds of other travelling souls in the airport. He approached the passport control agent and stood behind the line on the floor. When the agent signaled that he should move forward, Ash moved to the agent's cubicle and handed her his passport.

"You've been in France recently," the agent said.

"Yes, Ma'am, I just came from Paris," Ash replied.

"And you currently live in Dubai?" the agent queried.

"Yes,"

"Are you here on business…or pleasure?" was her next question.

A huge smile appeared on Ash's face. He thought about Eleven Million arriving here in two hours. Then he thought about those White Supremacists.

"Pleasure!"

Washington, DC

The room was full with all of the Joint Chiefs in attendance, along with their trusted support staff. They were all talking among themselves, and the topic was Iran and its incursion into Iraq. The room fell immediately silent as the President of the United States entered. He took his place at the head of the long table with rounded ends. All of the men and women in the room stood up, with many at attention as the President moved into position.

"I have a plan…," President James began. "…to slow down or halt Iran from its military advances to the west."

All eyes in the room were glued on the President. A handful of the aides in the room were writing furiously while watching the President. Was he about to suggest that the United States become involved in another conflict in the Middle East?

"It is clear to me that our's and the United Nation's efforts at diplomacy have failed…and failed miserably! Iran has not listened to reason. They have also not listened to the truth. The entire world now knows about the attack on Bushehr. It was an attack made by an Arab terrorist group. Their goal was to incite the Arab world against Israel. Well, ladies and gentlemen, their plan has proven successful…at least for this one powerful country. Also, there are no other Middle East nations that are willing to stand up against Iran."

The President paused to allow his comments to register with the people in the room. This was a momentous time for the United States. Her military and the citizens were growing weary of all the world conflicts that the United States felt they had to police. The majority of the population was also growing impatient with an inept United Nations and their inability to do relatively anything!

"My plan is this…we pull all of our forces in Afghanistan out of their bases spread around that country and have them march toward the Iranian border to their west. We amass all of our forces that are in country along the Afghanistan-Iran border. How long is that border between those two countries?" the President asked as he turned to the Defense Secretary.

"A little over four hundred miles, Mr. President," the Defense Secretary answered after conferring with an aide.

"And how many troops do we have in country?" President James asked.

Again, a brief conference and then, "A little over one hundred thousand…closer to a hundred and ten thousand troops."

"Okay, that's plenty of troops to make quite a racket along the border!" the President exclaimed. "Iran is rolling through Iraq with an army that our analysts believe is about all they could muster in men and equipment. They are showing limited air support for the invasion. Our Predators monitoring their progress display countless breakdowns in equipment which is stalling their progress. The United States does not expect Iraq… or Syria for that matter to mount any counter offensive which would slow Iran down."

"Israel is moving its forces into the Golan Heights. Their people feel that Iran will try to capture this high ground and mount its attack on Israel from that point. Israel has considerable resources, but it is such a tiny country. If Iran can take the Golan Heights, I am afraid to inform you that Israel may cease to exist without a massive commitment from the United States."

There was murmuring around the room as the President's statements sank in.

"Back to the plan…we amass our troops along Iran's eastern border with Afghanistan. Iran is not ready or equipped to wage a war on two fronts. This is what the United States and Russia did to Germany in the Second World War…back when we were allies with the Russians!" President James continued. "I think that Europe, including England might be speaking German today if Germany had only to concern itself with the European theater. Having to maintain two fronts killed Hitler's plans to dominate Europe."

"Same concept here. We make the Iranians believe that they are vulnerable on their eastern front. They will have to pull resources away from their army that is moving through Iraq as we speak, to defend against this possibility! The action may slow them down…it may halt them…it may get them to see the error of their ways and turn around and go home! At the very least Iran will have to commit some of their forces to protect against a threat from the east. This will weaken the army that is advancing against Israel," President James concluded. "What do you think?"

While the men and women in the room discussed the President's plan, President James sat down and thought about his Joint Chiefs. These senior uniformed leaders of all of the military branches within the Department of Defense advise the Secretary of Defense, the Homeland Security Council, the National Security Council and President James about military matters. Since 1986 this group held no operational command authority. The buck fell on the President alone, with his chain of command being first the Secretary of Defense and then to the Commanders of the Unified Combatant Commands.

The Joint Chiefs had always met in the Pentagon. Logical, since the Pentagon housed the operations for all of the military branches in the United States. "So," President James thought. "Advise me…come up with something better…or more overt…without committing any more forces to this problem."

Dubai, UAE

Lance was waiting on our front porch when Becky and I returned from a 'walk along the beach'. Actually, we had driven out to Atlantis through the tunnel that travels under the water separating the man-made palm from the out protective ring where Atlantis was built. I sat on one of the couches strategically placed along the beach and enjoyed a double Crown Royal on the rocks with a twist of lemon and watched Becky cavort in the warm waters of the Persian Gulf. It always excited me when she walked out of the water, dripping wet.

"If we had been in a more private place," I told myself, "I'd take her right here!"

She walked with such elegance and style. I noticed that many men were watching her and I'm sure had similar thoughts to mine.

I could tell that Lance was anxious to talk and invited him inside. I ushered him out to the patio and Becky poured him his signature Cuba Libre and joined us.

"Where is Ash?" Lance began. "Oh, that's right…he met Eleven Million in New Orleans after our adventure in the Loire Valley!"

"Yeah, I replied. "He flew straight from Paris to the States. I hope that he's just spending time with that woman. Ash was a little too interested in that White Supremacy group that the CIA linked to the stolen cruise missile. That group was headquartered in Louisiana, if I remember correctly."

"Becky took over at that point, "Yes, Reggie, it was Louisiana. You worried that he'll do the same thing he did in North Carolina?"

"That's it exactly, Becky. Ash has changed since Grace's death. It's not like he's become judge, jury and executioner…there's no chance for the bad guys for the judge and jury part! It's just the executioner that shows up," I replied.

"When's he coming back?" Lance asked.

"He called me from New Orleans," Becky answered. "He was only to be there for a week. We should see him in three or four days."

"I have something else that I must tell you," Lance began.

I could tell from his demeanor that this was going to be big. Lance's shoulders were slumped and he kept his eyes trained on the floor in front of him.

"What is it, dear?" Becky asked.

"I talked with Cyndi earlier…" Lance hesitated as if stifling a sob. "She told me she is not leaving Denver. She will not come over here… ever again."

"She still upset about that Tehran thing?" I asked.

"More than upset! She has had it with this part of the world. She said that she never wants to set foot in the Middle East again," Lance replied.

"Oh…let me talk with her…girl to girl. I may be able to help," Becky said.

I could tell that Lance needed some cheering up. "How about some fantastic steaks on the grill and good friends around the table!"

Lance's mood brightened at the prospect of a good meal and a hunk of great beef.

What was this news going to do to I.N.C.I.S.O.R.? What about the three of us? Hell, we were practically neighbors! I enjoyed my time with Lance and Ash. Was that about to change? I thought about all of this while I played grill master on the patio.

Northeast of Bagdad, Iraq

Major FarAz Karim heard the news report that the Iranian army was passing north of his camp. Major Karim had been a member of the Republican Guard until the invasion of Iraq in 2003 by the United States.

The Republican Guard, or the Ba'athist Iraqi Republican Guard, had been a part of Iraq's military since 1969. Its main duties were to protect Iraqi President Saddam Hussein. These were the elite troops of the Iraqi army and they reported directly to Saddam Hussein, unlike the ordinary Iraqi Army. They wore the easily recognizable red berets rather than the black berets of the regular army. These men were better trained, disciplined, equipped and paid than the regular army troops.

Major Karim was proud of his military heritage. His beloved Republican Guard had been disbanded in 2003, but he had fond memories of the glory days in the Guard. An invasion by the United States had ended all of that. Now his country was being invaded by another country! He was sick of the ineptness and infighting of the politicians that were taking responsibility to reshape his country after the departure of the American troops. There were no communiques from the political leaders about what to do with the incursion of Iran from the east.

How could his leaders not be outraged? Were they just going to allow his beloved country to be overrun…again? Well, not under his watch!

Major Karim called his mechanized unit to order. He then directed his tanks to head north and to engage the Iranian forces. The southernmost line was just about ten miles from his base. His unit sped to the north and engaged the Iranian forces.

Major Karim's forces were badly outnumbered. No matter! All of his tanks poured into battle like a street bully against the neighborhood wimp. Was this a horrible misjudgment? Was it a suicide mission? Why would the Iraqi major and all of his men commit so completely to this battle?

The answer turned out to be such a simple one…he and his men were tired. They were tired of losing battles. They were tired of being ordered around by the United States occupying forces. They were tired of the guerrilla style warfare that had been waged against them by the insurgents in his region. They were tired of their inept and incompetent government. They had a chance to make a bold statement!

The Iraqi tanks made contact and quickly disabled several Iranian tanks on the southern flank. Major Karim's unit punched through the flank and began to create havoc for the Iranians. They pushed north and engaged the Iranian front line from the rear. Several more of the invader's tanks were destroyed or disabled. His men fought fiercely. Major Karim was so proud.

Then the inevitable happened. Iran's superior numbers surrounded the Major's small cadre of men and machines. The Iraqis circled in a defensive posture. Iranian tanks began to lob shells into the circle. Soon the men and equipment were annihilated. An Iranian observer remarked that the scene reminded him of Sparta's 300 warriors surrounded by the Persians in the battle of Thermopylae. The Persians used arrows in that battle. The Iranian army used deadly explosive shells.

When the dust cleared there was no sign of life among the wrecked Iraqi armor. The Iranians moved back into position to continue their march across Iraqi territory. The Iraqi attack had caused a delay of one day in the march while the Iranian army stopped to deal with the pesky attack. Some of the Iranian tanks would need to be abandoned, but their battle line was still immense. The Iranian commanders moved more hardware to the south to reinforce that flank.

A Predator had circled around the area of Ba Qubah where the attack had occurred. The operator, sitting in a hangar at Bagdad International Airport called the other men and women in the hangar over to watch the battle on the big screen. All of the Americans felt pride for their Iraqi counterparts who had acted…and died so bravely!

Dubai, UAE

I was enjoying a day in the American Dental Clinic. It seemed as if I had not been there in weeks. I had changed into my scrubs in the private office and was sitting at the desk with one of my young associates. He was showing me a new disposable scalpel. This particular scalpel had a curved point to it and was double-sided. The blade was named the 12-B. I was 'old school' enough to always prefer a metal handle Bard Parker with changeable blades that were disposable. As I handled this new scalpel I noticed that it had a heftier feel to the plastic handle…much more like the metal grip I was used to.

As I toyed with the new blade there was a loud crash in the reception area. I'm not sure why, but I immediately slipped the disposable scalpel into the cloth waistband of my scrub pants. My associate and I both rose to check out the commotion when three heavily armed and masked men burst into the office. One of the men clubbed the associate with the butt end of his AK-47. The associate crumpled to the floor.

One of the attackers came up to me and pulled a coarse hood out of his tunic. He was shorter in stature than me. He rammed his machine gun into my stomach and I fell backwards into the chair behind my desk. As I moaned from the blow, he pulled the rough hood over my head. I then felt my hands being forced together and tied with something. The man with the hood frisked me quite thoroughly. I noticed that he had missed the front of the waistband where the cloth strap was tied to hold up the scrub bottoms.

I was muscled into a standing position and shoved and pushed out of the dental clinic. I couldn't see where I was going and stumbled many times. I heard the side door of a van slide open and I was pushed onto the floor of the van face down. I rolled on my side and rolled into a ball—a fetal position. Someone then grabbed my feet and secured them together, climbed into the back of the van and slammed the side door shut. I could hear the two front doors open and close. I assumed that there were two men in the front of the van plus the one in the back with me.

I felt every painful bump as the van bounced along the streets of Dubai. It seemed like hours before the van stopped its miserable ride. I was manhandled out of the van, and with my hands and feet tied together, I was dragged for a distance and then thrown onto a dirt floor. I heard a door close behind me…I was alone…the hood still in place…breathing dust through the burlap…my hands and feet securely bound…and afraid. I had one nagging final thought—was there a 'mini' in my tennis shoes that I wore at work?

CHAPTER THIRTY FIVE

New Orleans, Louisiana

ASH BLACK HAD enjoyed his week in New Orleans. Eleven Million turned out to be a spectacular lover. She reminded him of the Energizer Bunny. Always going…always wanting sex…insatiable! When she slept, it was the sleep of the dead. This allowed Ash to sneak out of the hotel room in the French Quarter and to dart away in the rental car. He had paid for the whole week with the car. Eleven Million commented about how wasteful that was when they rarely left the hotel room. Ash's retort was always the same about how much money she had compared to most of the rest of the world. Her comeback was also the same—her concern about stupid expenses was why she kept her eleven million dollar status alive and well!

Ash always let the argument drop at this point because of his nightly excursions. The car was being utilized much more the Eleven Million was aware of! Ash had discovered from his CIA contacts that the men being investigated for stealing the ACM 129 nuclear cruise missile were members of a white supremacy group named the White League. It was thought that the group had been defunct since shortly after the Civil War, but it turned out that they had just gone deep underground…until now.

The FBI was struggling and basically going nowhere with their investigation. They were watching some of the group but had come up with zilch. Ash felt that it was now his turn!

Every night during his stay in New Orleans he had picked a name from the White League roster. He was able to Google their addresses. Each night he would drive to a particular neighborhood, park the car blocks away, sneak up to the address and watch the residence for activity. He also watched for any outside surveillance, not that it mattered to him. But he knew that the FBI was staking out some of the White League members.

Ash was always dressed completely in black and disappeared into the night. The surrounding foliage offered him protection as he cased out the home. He used the skills he learned from the CIA to silently break into the structure. He had the stealthy moves of a big cat as he entered the residence and moved through the unsuspecting man's house. All of the men he chose were married and many had families.

Ash had chosen not to travel from Paris to New Orleans with any weapons. Knives were his first choice and therefore his first stop, once he gained entrance into the house, was always the kitchen. Many times he'd find a large wooden block on the countertops that housed impressive collections of knives. His choice was never one of the large chef's knives, but a thinner, flexible boning knife.

Ash never awakened his victims. He took the time to don a pair of gloves while he watched his prey from the bedroom doorway. He took only seconds with each victim. He moved in, clamped his free hand over their nose and mouths, and ran the blade across their neck. This motion severed both carotid arteries and cut through the man's windpipe. When the knife was extra sharp he could feel it run across his victim's spinal cord. The knife was left on the pillow next to his dying prey. He would then make his way out of the bedroom leaving his victim to die without being able to make a sound, while their blood flowed into the sheets.

Death was almost instantaneous from his attacks. Ash's movements went completely undetected by the other family members, including the spouses asleep in the bed next to his victims.

The next day, at breakfast, Ash would order the local paper along with his meal. Eleven Million and he would sit on the patio outside of their suite and enjoy the morning air. Ash would limit himself to a protein shake while Eleven Million gorged herself on eggs, sausage and breakfast potatoes. She had fresh squeezed juice and whole grain toast with each breakfast. Ash thought that maybe she felt that this was a healthy alternative, but the other ingredients in her breakfast had to have a negative effect on her arteries.

The front page of the paper would contain a brief article about his night's adventure. Distraught wives had similar stories about stirring in the morning to a sticky, wet substance soaking into their bed clothes. And their absolute dismay when they discovered their husband's heads were almost severed from their torsos. Nobody had heard or seen anything! The police reported that they had no clues and no witnesses. Initially the wives were the main suspects in the reported deaths. This suspicion ended by the third day as a pattern for the murders was evident. By the fifth day the newspaper wrote about a possible connection between the dead men and a white supremacy group.

Ash enjoyed his reading and knew that there was nothing that could lead the murders back to him. He was finishing up his protein shake on the sixth day of his stay when he received the urgent call from Lance in Dubai. Reggie had been taken by assailants who made a daring daylight raid on the American Dental Clinic.

Ash packed immediately and told Eleven Million that he had to return post haste to Dubai. She wanted to travel with him, but he refused her offer. She decided, instead to stay in the suite the two extra days that they had booked and then return to Phoenix.

Ash hailed a cab and was off to the airport. Nobody in law enforcement made the connection over the coming weeks that the killing spree ended with his departure.

Dubai, UAE

Lance had used the time while Ash rushed to return to Dubai to summon all of I.N.C.I.S.O.R.'s resources. Both the Denver team and the Frankfurt team had been summoned to Dubai and were settling into the Hilton Dubai Jumeirah Resort. The two teams were housed only minutes from Jumeirah Palm Island where the three homes of the I.N.C.I.S.O.R. leaders were located.

The twelve men and Becky crowded into the living room as they planned a response and rescue. Luckily, a 'mini' had been implanted in Reggie's sneakers that he wore at work. Becky had been able to track the signal to an adjoining Emirate, Ras al-Khaimah. The signal had been stationary for more than a day. It was emanating from an abandoned condominium project close to the Hilton Ras al-Khaimah.

It was decided that the men would all make the hour and a half drive to the neighboring Emirate and obtain rooms at that Hilton. The hotel would be used as a base for their rescue attempt. The local police in Dubai had proven inept at discovering any clues about the men who attacked the dental clinic and their escape. The dental clinic was shot up and damaged during the attack, but none of the patients or clinic team had been killed... just roughed up. It looked like the focus of the attack was Dr. Reginald Nelson. It was assumed that he would be held for ransom. The police were content to wait for contact from the kidnappers about possible demands.

Jazirat Al Hamra

I was manhandled from the floor and placed on a hard wooden chair. My hands and feet were tightly bound. The hood was removed from my head. Immediately my eyes reacted to the light in the room and I closed them tight, blinded by the light. Shortly, I could open my eyes and saw one of my attackers standing before me. I stayed quiet as my eyes adjusted. I saw two other men standing in the room. The three all had masks over their heads.

The man standing in front of me spoke. His English was excellent and I assumed from his dialect that he had trained in England. He spoke the Queen's English.

"Well, Dr. Nelson...you've been a busy man," the attacker began. "We are here to get the details of your airliner rescue in Tehran."

"Oh my God," I thought. "Cyndi was right! They know it was us."

"So, why don't you make it easy on yourself and tell us how you knew about the hijacking attempt," the attacker continued.

My mind was foggy and I was slow to think of a response.

"I need to go to the bathroom," I replied.

"Sorry, no bathrooms here," he answered. "There's a bucket for you in the corner." He pointed behind me.

I got to my feet and attempted to hop away from the chair toward the bucket. A man behind me rammed the butt of his gun into my left kidney. I hadn't thought to look behind me for other kidnappers. I saw stars and crumpled down into the chair.

"Not quite yet, Dr. Nelson," the man in front of me ordered.

I moaned as the pain knifed through my side. I wondered if that kidney would ever function again.

"How did you find me?" I groaned.

"Your hospital stay in Tehran where they sewed up your neck. Did you not think that there would be records?" he replied.

I tried to fight through the fog and focus my thoughts. It was not easy. I was disoriented and in pain. None of us had thought about the chance that there would be a record of my brief stay in Tehran.

"Now, once again…tell me why you were on that flight?" my attacker continued.

"I was just taking a flight to Israel," I groaned again.

This time my captor in front of me backhanded my temple. I saw a flash of white as it felt like my brain would explode. I slumped over to the side as I began to fade from any conscious thought. The next thing I felt was water splashed into my face. I gagged as the water entered my open mouth and found its way into my lungs. I was then yanked to an upright position which I attempted to maintain.

"You take us for fools!" the man screamed.

"Who are you?" I stammered.

"My name is Souroush," he announced. "I am a member of al-Qaeda. We were responsible for the hijacking of the Lufthansa aircraft that you interfered with."

"Al-Qaeda…oh God," I thought again. I knew about the MADEI group and their responsibility for the hijacking. The men that Ash and Lance had eliminated on the flight were MADEI cell members. Now al-Qaeda was claiming responsibility? Why not…all of the MADEI cell were dead.

"The pilot and copilot were killed," I began. "I am a pi…"

Souroush backhanded me again. This time I felt a blinding pain as I was sure that my jaw would explode. Blackness consumed me as I passed out.

Hilton Hotel Ras al-Khaimah

Two of the I.N.C.I.S.O.R. men had returned from their reconnaissance mission. They had explored the old coastal town of Jazirat Al Hamra. They studied routes to the abandoned condominium structure and possible escape routes within the small town. The two had spent the majority of their time watching for activity at the site. They had observed ten men guarding the exterior of the abandoned condominium project.

"We can assume an equal number inside," Lance spoke.

"Twenty or more against our twelve," Stirling added. "I love those odds!"

"Okay, here's how we do this," Ash said as the rescue plan was formulated.

"It is almost dusk," Graham replied. "We should move now! Tonight!"

The I.N.C.I.S.O.R. team worked with precision as they prepared the equipment for a night assault. The men all knew their assignments and had confidence that the assault would be a success. Becky had forwarded to them via the laptop set up in the hotel room the precise location of the 'mini' transmitting from inside the Al Jazirat Al Hamra complex. Blueprints were also forwarded showing the layout of the buildings.

Washington, DC

President John James found that he had a brief lull in his busy schedule. He moved from behind the desk in the Oval Office and laid down on one of the couches. He closed his eyes and began to muse about the people of his beloved country. The country that he had dedicated his life to steering through such troubled times. He crossed his arms behind his head and let his thoughts drift.

The President's first thoughts were about a poll that revealed disagreements between the feelings of the American people and the people in other countries around the planet. A question was asked about whether United States policies played a significant role in fueling terrorist actions against America. Of most of the 'ordinary people' in the United States, fewer than one in five respondents said that they do. In the rest of the world, three out of five said that America's policies played a role.

Many of the Americans that were questioned wondered why there was resentment about the United States, not just in the Middle East, but Europe, Latin America and Asia. President James pondered this and came to the conclusion that Americans suffer from extremely short memories. His people forgot the consequences of the Cold War and all of the foreign interventions made by the United States. America's actions had to leave open wounds throughout the entire world.

Also, President James thought about the fact that America was the only super power that survived the Cold War. The United States, in the President's opinion, had done little to project its domestic democratic values to the world. Instead America had shown its nuclear bombs, cluster bombs and napalm bombs. Instead of choosing to be admired as one of the most progressive nations in the history of the planet, the United States had chosen to be feared. And fear does not result in respect.

President James had always maintained a 'hawkish' view on America's role in international affairs. His country's might was a strong card to play in so many of the scenarios that developed around the world. He had always hated how the rest of the countries of the world abused their relationship with the United States. He also knew that as the only super power, many of the world's despots had their aim set to bring America to its knees. Being 'numero uno' meant that many of the world's leaders were gunning for his country to try to knock it out of that number one status. Those that wouldn't face the United States on the battlefield would choose to kill and maim her citizens. What cowards they all were!

He would have to work on a campaign to remind and educate Americans about their country and its place in the world. His citizens must not suffer from the short term memory loss that seemed so rampant. If they would just remember…he hoped…they would understand and not be so quick to lose heart when a conflict lingered. President James knew that his American people wanted a strong leadership that offered them protection in the world…but they also wanted to feel good about it.

His thoughts then moved to the moral decay which seemed so prevalent in his beloved country. He was reminded of how the Roman Empire faltered and died because of the same issues that were plaguing America today. Alcoholism, drug abuse, teen pregnancy, abortion, homosexuality, violence, child abuse, pornography, rape, robbery and murder occupied most of the news headlines each day. Would this horrible trend erode the moral and political foundations of the United States?

President James was a God fearing man and his faith was strong. He knew that forces within the country plotted to systematically and incrementally remove many of the moral principles that he had honored his whole life. He thought of a quote from George Washington, who warned that '…reason and experience both forbid us to expect that national morality can prevail to the exclusion of religious principle.'

What could he do? These two issues weighed so heavily on his mind. He was the country's elected leader. Was it possible to steer America onto a healthier path?

President James pondering was interrupted with a loud knock on his office door. He rose from the couch and took his seat behind the desk.

"Enter," he ordered.

"Mr. President, the head of I.N.C.I.S.O.R. has been kidnapped!" the presidential aide announced.

Border between Iraq and Syria

The military forces of Iran had reached the Syrian border. The tanks led an assault that met with little resistance from Iraq. The one attack that the Iranian forces endured had been like 'pesky ants at the picnic', as one commander had reported. That attack had the effect of slowing the invasion by a day. The Iranian force had moved across the two hundred miles of Iraq and it was reported back to Tehran that the main body was now crossing into Syria.

Tehran, Iran

"The United Nations have delivered to our embassy a demand to cease and desist," an aide to the Iranian President reported.

He then continued, "They are also prepared to issue sanctions against Iran for our aggression against Israel."

The President waved his hand as if to dismiss the UN threat and announced, "The United Nations is impotent! We will have conquered Israel before they can zip up their flies!"

"Do we respond?" the aide inquired.

"No! Absolutely not! They do not deserve an answer. We are moving into Syria now and will annihilate Israel within days!"

Jazirat Al Hamra, Ras al-Khaimah

I was roused to consciousness by another bucket of water thrown into my face. Souroush stood before me holding what looked like jumper cables attached to a battery at my feet. My scrub top had been removed and lay on the dirt floor next to the battery. My kidnappers had also discovered the hidden scalpel which also lay on the floor next to the battery.

He reached forward with the clamps and attached them to each of my nipples. I cried out as he clamped the electrodes to me.

And then he began again, "You were about to say that you were a pilot. We know that! We also know that you were in the cockpit acting as the co-pilot. Why were you on that flight? And who was with you? I want the names of your associates!"

Without waiting for an answer he turned a knob on top of the battery. Electricity shot through my chest. I felt like a fiery, red hot poker had been shoved into my heart. The pain was like nothing I had ever experienced. I was sure that my heart would stop. I tried to cry out, but could not muster up my voice. Every muscle in my body stiffened in response to the shock. Just when I was sure that I would die, he dialed back the knob and the electricity stopped.

I noticed that my crotch was wet. Had I wet myself? Was it wet from the water that had been splashed on me? Why was I thinking about that?

"Answer me now!" Souroush threatened, as he reached for the knob again.

"Yes!" I stammered. "I was the First Officer on the flight!"

"And the others?" he yelled.

Just then gunfire erupted outside the room. Souroush and the others picked up their weapons and moved toward the commotion. As they reached the door it exploded into thousands of splinters. The al-Qaeda men in the room were blown off of their feet. My chair was also blown backwards. The electrodes stayed attached to my chest. I rolled to my side and reached toward the battery and felt for the scalpel. I wrapped my fingers around the scalpel and began to work to cut through the ties binding my hands.

Five men stormed into the room and each eliminated an al-Qaeda captor. Souroush had turned to train his weapon on me just as his head exploded from the hollow point round that found its home.

Ash and Lance were on me quickly and worked to finish freeing my hands and feet. Lance then removed the electrodes and observed the nasty burn marks on my chest.

"So sorry, Reggie," he said. "Can you move?"

I attempted to stand but had no control of my legs. I melted into his arms.

"Ash! Help me!" Lance called out as they each took an arm. They dragged me out of the room that I feared would become my tomb. I recognized Dick and Powers as we moved. The other members of I.N.C.I.S.O.R. fell in behind us to provide cover.

Once outside, we moved toward awaiting vans that had been pulled up in front of the abandoned condominium project. Lance and Ash placed me on the floor of one van as gingerly as they could. Every nerve ending in my body was on fire and all my muscles would do was twitch uncontrollably.

As I lay there I watched the I.N.C.I.S.O.R. teams load another body in the van behind us. The men then piled into the vans and we made our getaway. I did not hear any more sounds of gunplay and we had soon left the town and entered onto the E-311 highway, or Emirates Road for the sixty mile journey back to Dubai.

Lance was behind the wheel and watched in the mirrors for any pursuit vehicles. None were seen and everybody in our van began to noticeably relax. My muscles began to stop their involuntary movements and I felt like I was gaining some semblance of control. Ash was trying to play the role of nursemaid. He gave me a bottle of water and I gagged as I attempted to consume too much of the liquid.

"Hold your horses there, Tonto!" he exclaimed. "Not so fast on the H_2O!"

I realized that I had not had anything to eat or drink since my capture. I didn't even know what day it was…or how long I had been held captive. I noticed that the mood of the other I.N.C.I.S.O.R. team members was somber and asked why all of them had such long faces.

I learned that the body that was placed into the trailing van was that of Max Galloway. He had fallen prey to a stray bullet during the gun battle outside of the condo. I fell silent, also, and was left to my own thoughts during the drive back to Dubai.

My right jaw and tempero-mandibular joint had slowly taken over as the most painful area of my body. I felt around the area with my hands and tongue. Several teeth were loose, but I couldn't feel any broken crowns. I also couldn't tell if the blows I had received at the hand of my captor, Souroush, had been strong enough to fracture my jaw. If it was broken. At least the pieces were in place.

CHAPTER THIRTY SIX

Dubai, UAE

THE NINE SURVIVING I.N.C.I.S.O.R. team members, four from the Denver team and five from the Frankfurt team were drinking beers on our back patio. Ash and Lance were with the men as they both celebrated my rescue and mourned the loss of their comrade in arms.

Becky and I were in the kitchen preparing burgers and dogs for the night's festivities. I had been to my physician and received a report that I was okay and that my body would recover from the electrical stimulation that it had received. The burns on my chest would heal. An MRI revealed that there were no hidden hematomas in my brain matter that had been scrambled by the blows. My partner in the American Dental Clinic venture, Jim Bobb Mulheran, had found another dental office where he could utilize their panoramic radiograph to make sure that my mandible was not fractured. It was not.

Other than aches and pains…I would survive my kidnapping. Becky moved in close and placed her arms gently around my shoulders…afraid to hug me too hard.

"Reggie," she began. "Are we safe here? Do we need to leave this place?"

"Becky, I love you," I began.

She cut me off and continued, "I know that Reggie! I'm not talking about us! I was so-o scared until I heard that you were safe. My stomach is still in knots. My fear is not going away. I don't feel safe here."

I had come to rely very heavily on Becky's gut over the years. There had been too many times that her gut feeling had been accurate. Now it was telling her that she was not safe? Not good. I held her closely for one long hug and kissed her lightly on her forehead.

"We'll deal with this when we are alone. Let's get to our guests," I said.

Becky and I both knew that she was right…and that I was stalling.

Warsaw, Poland

Mariola was enjoying her morning walk while escorting her two dogs. The dogs were a present from her father who was in love with everything Polish. The two were from the same litter…brother and sister…and Mariola had chosen Polish names for the pair to play on their relationship. The male was named Braciszek (Polish for brother). The female's name was Siostra (Polish for sister).

This Polish breed of dog was now called the Polish Hunting Dog.

"Pretty mundane name," Mariola though as 'Brat' sniffed at the base of a tree.

The breed used to be named Scenthounds. Poland had always been covered by deep forests which were full of big game. The scenthound became a precious auxiliary for the hunters in the region. Some hunters in the eastern regions still hunted with these dogs, but they were just big pets to Mariola. The dogs looked similar in coloring to their German counterpart, the Doberman Pinscher, but they were broader through the shoulders and sported a heftier hind quarter.

Her father had picked this breed for Mariola because the dogs were known to be very courageous and brave. They love to run and swim and are known for their intelligence. Mariola loved doing these same things and preferred a walk with her dogs to anything else…including time with her husband. Brat and Sasha were the nicknames that Mariola had given to the two dogs when they were puppies. They were both wary of strangers but they were calm and gentle with Mariola. They were the best guard dogs and companions for her.

As she waited for Brat to finish with his tree, Mariola glanced down the avenue. It was an early spring day. The sun was up and warming the crisp air. The trees that lined her street were in full bloom. She could smell the sweet fragrance from the blossoms. An occasional car passed by to break up the silence and her reverie.

Brat was tugging at his leash. He was ready to move to the next tree so that he could investigate the smells on its trunk. Sasha stayed by Mariola's side and watched her brother's antics with indifference. Brat, it seemed, had to leave his mark on every trunk that they passed. He would sniff… and then move into position to lift his leg. "I hope that he had enough to drink this morning!" Mariola thought. "Or else he'll run out of ammo!"

Mariola then reflected on her life. She had met her husband while at University. He was a descendent of the Radziwill family. At one time, centuries ago, the family controlled a majority of the lands and townships in Poland. The family had reached the height of importance and power during the Polish Golden Age. Much of its wealth and power was lost during The Deluge. In Poland this was called the Potop…the Swedish invasion and occupation of Poland. This had happened back in the mid Seventeenth Century.

And then there was Hitler. Germany's invasion of Poland in 1939 and the beginning of the Second World War ended what was left of the family's great fortune. But they still had much wealth. She had married well. The early years with Filip had been a dream husband. They travelled all over the world. Mariola felt deeply loved. And then she delivered a son.

Dawid was Mariola's and Filip's only child, but Filip now had a male heir. Soon after the birth, Filip turned a cold shoulder to Mariola. She was left to her own devices throughout the day and soon became depressed. Her friends did not understand…she had so much more than them… at least on the surface. She felt so alone. Filip was devoted to Dawid and spent all of his time grooming his son to be an integral cog in the family's business. Mariola found herself sleeping alone and isolated. Her two dogs became her only solace.

"How could I feel sad on such a glorious day?" Mariola thought to herself. "I am going to make this the best day!" She began to think of an outdoor café where she could enjoy a morning coffee and pastry while the dogs lounged at her feet.

Mariola paid no heed to the panel truck that had pulled to the curb. Brat and Sasha came to attention and their low growls alerted her to the truck. The back doors of the truck flew open and four men jumped out and ran toward her.

Brat reacted first, jerking the leash out of her hand and nearly pulling her arm out of its socket! Sasha then bolted toward the men. Each dog attacked, jumping on a different assailant. The two men were caught unawares and attempted to fend off the vicious attacks. Completely defensive, the two men each had raised arms that the dogs grabbed hold of with bared teeth. While the dogs ripped into human flesh, the other two men pulled out weapons from their coats and two shots rang out. Both dogs yelped in pain and released their hold. The men kicked the dogs away and they fell in lifeless heaps upon the grass.

Mariola screamed and began to run from the scene. One of the men quickly overtook her and wrestled her first onto the ground and then into the back of the panel truck. The three other attackers jumped into the truck and it sped away.

Dubai, UAE

The two teams were preparing to return to their home bases.

Lance had reviewed the dozens of resume's that he had on file from his interviews in Denver. Michael MacAteer had been chosen to fill the vacancy created when Max Galloway died on the mission to save their leader, Reggie. Michael was a thinker and constantly worked through scenarios in his head to come up with the best solution. This action often stalled a response, but Lance saw his introspection as a good thing.

Michael had flown to Dubai to join his new team. All ten of the men were bonding well.

Ash and Lance planned on a last special evening for the men in Dubai before they headed to Denver and Frankfurt. It would be a no expense spared night at Wafi Gourmet in the Dubai Mall at the base of the Burj Kalifa. They had also made reservations for the men to travel up to the observation deck on the one hundred and twenty fourth floor of the Burj.

Becky and I would join the men at the restaurant once they had all travelled to the top. Then the call came in. Another 'mini' had gone active. This time it was Poland.

I placed a call to Ash.

"Where are you guys?" I asked.

"On the observation deck! Where you sent us with all of these young pups! Lance is pointing out the sights in Dubai," Ash replied. "Hey! The cell phone reception is really good from up here!"

"Another 'mini' has gone active," I said.

"My God!" he replied. "When it rains…it pours!"

He then spoke to Lance and Lance grabbed Ash's cell phone out of his hand.

"Can't we pass on this one?" Lance asked.

"No! We cannot pass! These people have paid us. Get the teams moving. Becky is making the arrangements. Send all ten of them!" I answered, and then finished, "Sorry about dinner."

"Ash and me?" Lance asked.

"Let the men go alone. We need to talk!" I said and disconnected from the call.

Outside Umm al 'Amud, Syria

The Iranian forces had not encountered any resistance as they rolled across Syria. The tanks and armored vehicles were reuniting east of Umm al 'Amud after splitting into two main bodies to cross the Euphrates River. One force travelled to the north of the reservoir formed by the Euphrates damn. The other force moved to the south of the damn to cross the river.

The only problem that had arisen to plague the Iranian commanders' plans was the number of vehicles that had broken down during the journey. Dozens of tanks and personnel carriers seized up and were left abandoned along the drive toward Israel. The Iranian command guessed that about one quarter of the attack vehicles had been lost during the push through Iraq and Syria.

But, now they were more than three quarters of the way along their journey. Soon, the Golan Heights would be in sight. There was less than one hundred miles to cross before they reached their destination.

Bagdad, Iraq

"Look at all of the abandoned hardware!" the techie flying the Predator announced.

The commanding officer came over to look at the monitor.

"Where are they now?" he asked.

"A hundred miles or so from the DMZ," was the answer.

"Inform the UN Command that they have two days to prepare!" the officer ordered. "And let them know about the strength of the Iranian forces...with all of their losses."

Warsaw, Poland

The ten men of I.N.C.I.S.O.R. had gathered in the terminal at Warsaw's Chopin Airport. Powers and Stirling had gone to retrieve the two rental vans that were waiting for the teams. Even though the men were dressed in civilian clothing, the group stood out like a sore thumb among the patrons of the airport. Several security guards had stopped to take a closer look at the group, but had chosen not to engage them.

Magnus had his laptop up in the front seat of the forward van. Becky, once again, had done her homework while they had been in the air. The 'mini' was transmitting from a location just north of the city of Czestochowa. Dick headed the caravan out of the airport and found signs that led him to the A-2 Autostrada. The vans headed west until they joined into the A-1 Autostrada to head south toward Czestochowa.

Flex was driving the second van and had a driving map up on his GPS. There was one hundred and twenty eight miles between the two cities. He figured that, travelling on an Autostrada, they would be at their destination within two hours. What the GPS didn't show him was that much of the National Motorway A-1 was currently under construction. The trip became slow and tedious after their long flight.

Becky had also found a hotel in Czestochowa which was located just off of the Motorway. It was named the Hotel Scout. She had booked five rooms all containing two twin beds. The men divvied up the rooms and all of them crashed onto their beds for some shut eye. They had agreed to meet in the hotel's restaurant in three hours so that they could formulate a rescue plan.

When they all came together, Aaron was making joking comments about the bidets in the bathroom. It was clear that none of the men had ever found this European custom to be worthwhile. They crowded around two large tables and began to review Becky's layout of where the 'mini' was located.

As they were working, Becky phoned to inform them that the 'mini' was on the move. She was tracking its movement northward along the A-1. Should they depart immediately and attempt to intercept? The group decision was to stay put and react when the 'mini' was stationary again. The men put the laptops away and enjoyed watching the chef toss pizza dough high into the air behind the kitchen counter.

Powers and Lance were bold enough to ask if they could try their hands at tossing the pizza dough. The chef acquiesced and gave them each a ball of dough. Powers began to work the dough and made his first toss. He was doing well with the expanding dough circle until an errant toss ended on top of the stove. Lance was laughing so hard that he forgot about his toss, which came down and covered his head! That move brought laughter from the whole restaurant!

The next morning the men of I.N.C.I.S.O.R. felt well rested, and there was news from Dubai that the 'mini' was once again stationary in the city of Gdansk. They all ate a hearty breakfast, packed up their belongings and headed to the vans for the seven hour drive north.

Gdansk, Poland

"Make sure that she is well bound," the leader ordered.

Mariola's plastic binding straps were checked and found to be secure.

"We put her…" and he pointed to Mariola, "on the yacht and she will be out to sea by tonight," the leader announced.

"What are you doing with me?" Mariola asked.

"You are to become the fourth wife for Sheik Mohmar al Ishtah," the leader replied.

"You are selling me into white slavery?" Mariola said as she bowed her head.

"No, my dear. Your husband has sold you to the Sheik. His yacht will arrive tonight," the leader of the group answered.

Mariola sat bolt upright. "My husband!" she screamed. "He would ne…"

"Oh yes he would! He's wanted you out of his life for a long time," the leader retorted and then he turned to the others. "Gag her! I don't care to hear any more."

Hotel Gniecki, Gdansk, Poland

Becky had worked her magic from afar and the ten men took up their rooms in the small, non-descript hotel. It was only blocks from the abandoned warehouse where the 'mini' signal was transmitting.

The men donned their dark clothing and rounded up their reconnaissance gear. They left the hotel as a group but quickly split into smaller teams as they moved toward the Motlawa River to spy on their prey. The men came on to Wislna Street and immediately spotted the warehouse. Three sides of the building were exposed, while the fourth side faced the river and would require a water approach. There was no activity outside of the building.

With the other men hidden around the building, Flex and Aaron crept closer to the entrance and began the slow process of peering into the building through the filthy and broken windows. They moved quietly, making sure not to disturb anything on the ground. The first three attempts to look inside revealed nothing. And then…

There she was! Hands and feet bound and her mouth was gagged. Flex counted the men in the room. There were six of them. "This is going to be a cake walk!" Flex thought as his mind did the math. Ten I.N.C.I.S.O.R. men against these six thugs.

Flex and Aaron crept away from the building to rejoin their compatriots. Once they were all together, Aaron offered, "We should take them now!"

Michael countered, "We need a plan, boys…remember the movie? 'I love it when a plan comes together.' We're not ready!"

"Let's get back to the hotel, make our plan and get back here just after dark," Powers said. "I like working in the dark!"

The men agreed with Powers and backed away from the warehouse. Back at the hotel Duncan called Becky to see if there had been any ransom demands.

"No demands," Becky said. "I find that a little bit troubling! What else could they have in mind? And why this warehouse?"

"Well, we've got 'em and will move in shortly," Duncan announced.

"God speed," Becky replied. She knew that it would do no good to ask them to be careful. She said a little prayer and then picked up the phone to call Cyndi in Colorado.

Abandoned Warehouse, Motlawa River

The twin turbines growled as the sleek yacht slowed and pulled alongside the pier that marked the warehouse's existence for the river traffic. The new, stylish fiberglass yacht glistened in the moonlight and was a sharp contrast to the dilapidated building that it was moored alongside. Men jumped onto the wharf and secured the large ropes to the pylons. With the yacht tied to the shore, the Captain cut power to the engines and the large craft fell silent.

A gangway was rotated into place so that the yacht's occupants could disembark. From within the main salon a bearded man appeared in long flowing robes. The white garments were adorned in gold lame'. His wrapped head had tassels which hung down onto his shoulders. Although it was evening, he wore sunglasses so that his eyes were hidden from view.

As the sheik mounted the gangway ornate sandals could be seen under his long robes. The sandals looked more like adornments for his feet than protection for his feet. He used his two hands to raise up his robes until he stood on the pier. His men grabbed his arms and helped him to disembark from the yacht and he was guided through the large entrance and to the inside of the warehouse. He glanced around the dilapidated and decaying facility with disdain. He hoped his business in this place would not take a long time.

Shortly men escorted a young woman and stood her in front of him. He slowly moved around her as if he were sizing up a piece of livestock. Satisfied with her outer appearance, he returned to stand before her. He reached out his hand to feel her breasts, which caused her to kick out at him. "Feisty!" he thought. "That's good to have a little fight in her. Better to tame a fierce heart than to deal with a docile creature."

One of the captors struck Mariola and she fell onto the concrete floor. She remained crumpled until two of the men grabbed her arms and jerked her into an upright stance. Her eyes were full of hatred as she looked upon this man. She would never let him touch her! Let alone lay with her! Little did she know how compliant she would become with the drugs that her handlers would inject into her veins.

"Get this one to the yacht!" the sheik ordered.

His men grabbed her up and dragged Mariola onto the craft. They dragged her into the sheik's salon and stripped off her clothing, shoes and socks. They did not touch her bra and panties which they all looked at admiringly. Mariola only bought expensive lingerie, and this matching pair was a sight to see. It was their own live version of Victoria's Secret. The men forced her onto the large bed and tied her arms and legs to the bedposts.

Mariola struggled mightily with her captors, but they succeeded in immobilizing her to the bedframe. One of the men bundled up her clothing, weighted the bundle with a large rock and took the bundle up to the ship's railing and tossed the clothing overboard into the river. He watched as the bundle quickly sank into the river.

A man entered the salon with a small black bag and moved to Mariola's side. He placed the bag on the nightstand and removed a syringe and drug vial. He moved slowly and with great precision as he lifted the drug vial, inserted the syringe needle into the vial and withdrew the amber liquid into the syringe. He wiped Mariola's arm with a sterile pad, felt for a vein and inserted the needle. She did not know it, but that amber liquid entering her body was opium. Or more accurately, heroin, the more potent derivative of the poppy plant.

Mariola struggled against her restraints but couldn't stop the man. She watched as he depressed the plunger and the drug entered her body. Her mind said to fight against the feeling, but very quickly Mariola's body went limp and she fell into a drug-induced stupor. She was left alone, tied to the large bed in the grand salon of the yacht.

Dubai, UAE

Becky placed a call to the teams moving in on the warehouse.

"The 'mini' just stopped its signal!" she reported.

"Swell, Dick replied. "So now we have no clue where she is."

"Last broadcast was from the warehouse…or more accurately, the river behind the warehouse," Becky answered. "But now you're working blind."

Motlawa River, Poland

"Signal's gone!" Dick Becker reported to the others through their headsets.

"We need to move now!" Lance ordered.

The men raced back to the warehouse and took up their positions with four men stationed in front of the warehouse, and two men on each of the sides. The final two moved to move in on the warehouse from the river side.

"We should have left someone here to keep an eye on things," Dick thought to himself.

The word was given and the four men that were placed in the front of the building crashed through the front doors of the warehouse…

Two men on either side of the doors crouched while the other two stood, using the door frame as protection. They immediately opened fire, targeting anybody that moved. Four of the kidnappers were dropped immediately, but two headed for the back door. They were dropped quickly by the I.N.C.I.S.O.R. men stationed at the dock as they attempted to exit the rear of the warehouse.

The I.N.C.I.S.O.R. team rallied near the back entrance.

"Six down and all clear! That's all of them."

"Where is she?"

The men checked all of the nooks and crannies in the warehouse. Mariola was nowhere to be seen. Flex and Michael moved to the edge of the pier. They observed running lights of a large craft turning in the middle of the river.

"She must be on that yacht!" Flex yelled.

Michael said, "Aw damn," and bolted around the side of the warehouse.

Flex yelled after him, "What the…"

Aaron and Graham saw Michael run and joined in the pursuit. Michael pulled up abruptly when he saw a small dilapidated truck parked on the side of the road that passed in front of the warehouse. He took the butt of his weapon and smashed the driver's window. Michael then brushed the shattered glass from the driver's seat and knelt to work the harness of wires under the steering wheel.

Aaron and Graham were now upon the truck and watched Michael work to hotwire the vehicle.

"I hope this thing is wired like our American cars!" Michael exclaimed.

"What are you doing?" Graham asked.

"Gotta stop that boat!" Michael replied.

Just then the truck's motor coughed once and then came to life. Michael jumped behind the wheel, revved the engine, stuck the gearshift into first gear and popped the clutch. He sped away, leaving Aaron and Graham standing in the dust.

"What's he up to?" Aaron asked.

"Must think he can ram that boat," Graham answered.

The others had joined them and watched as the truck sped away.

"We're off!" Flex ordered and the men began to run after the truck.

Shortly up the Oliwska road they spotted Michael in an empty field next to the river. He had parked the truck and had moved to the river's edge to see if he could spot the yacht. The yacht had completed its 180 degree turn in the middle of the river and was beginning to make its way out onto the Baltic Sea. It was quickly building speed.

Michael was struggling with pieces of plywood that he found in the abandoned lot.

The others saw what he was doing and ran to give assistance. They quickly formed a makeshift ramp for the truck.

"You really want to do this?" Powers asked.

"You have a better way to stop that thing?" Michael answered. "I'm all ears."

"I'm in!" Powers replied and he and Duncan jumped into the back of the truck.

Magnus got in the passenger seat. "Shotgun!"

While the other six men worked on the makeshift ramp, Michael backed up the truck and lined up his approach. The yacht rounded the bend in the river, moving slowly through the water. The men aboard the craft were unaware of the gunplay that had occurred at the warehouse after they departed. They were also unaware that they were being pursued.

As the yacht approached, Michael gunned the truck's engine and slammed it into gear. The rear wheels spun in the gravel as he floored the accelerator. The tires grabbed hold and the truck leaped ahead. Michael kept the truck on course and hit the plywood ramp doing about forty miles an hour.

"I hope this works!" Michael prayed out loud.

The truck leaped into the air as the men standing in the back bed of the truck held on for dear life…

There was a loud crashing noise as the truck smashed through the side of the yacht's steering house. The impact immediately killed the captain and two men who were standing beside him. Powers and Duncan jumped out of the back of the truck, steadied themselves after the impact and readied their weapons. Michael and Magnus were temporarily pinned inside the truck's cab.

Duncan headed aft while Powers headed to the fore deck. They dropped the men they encountered with short bursts from their weapons as they moved around the deck. Magnus had managed to crawl out the smashed front windshield and was working to free Michael from behind the steering wheel. Michael announced that his legs were broken and for Magnus to leave him alone and to move on.

Magnus left Michael and found the stairway that led to the staterooms below. The sheik's men were now alerted and had armed themselves. Magnus hid behind a bulkhead as bullets rained in his direction. Powers had found his way below decks and came at the sheik's men from behind. Powers and Magnus both opened fire from opposite ends of the hallway. Caught in a crossfire, the sheik's bodyguards were quickly eliminated. Duncan joined up with the two I.N.C.I.S.O.R. men. They then moved to check out and clear the staterooms. All were empty until they opened the door to the grand salon.

The sheik was clad only in a bathrobe. He looked like he was ready to mount the unmoving woman tied to his bed. The sheik had ripped off Mariola's panties. He was gazing upon her body as he savored the upcoming moments when he would take this woman. The door crashed open. He spun around...

Magnus was the first into the room and aimed his weapon at the sheik. The sheik's robe had fallen open and his large stomach hung over his genitals. The sheik immediately raised his hands in surrender. Powers and Duncan moved to the sides of the bed to free Mariola from her bindings. They saw immediately that she was drugged and unable to move on her own.

Magnus pulled the robe off of the sheik and placed it around Mariola. He marched the naked sheik out of the cabin and moved up the stairs. Powers and Duncan each grabbed one of Mariola's arms and moved behind Magnus and up the stairway. As they reached the upper deck they heard two rifle shots ring out...

They had not eliminated all of the sheik's men during their attack. Two had taken up positions on the main deck and were waiting to ambush the I.N.C.I.S.O.R. men when they came up from the lower deck. The sheik was shoved first up the stairway. As the sheik appeared, his men readied themselves. They did not know about the men that were on the shore.

Aaron and Dick had taken up sniper positions next to the makeshift ramp. They each fired once and the two men waiting in ambush on the boat were down.

The yacht was still moving forward and aimed for the far bank. The steering house was a shambles. The vessel could not be maneuvered from the steering house. Magnus thought for a minute and then left Powers and Duncan to guard the sheik. He ran down the stairs and found the engine room. He cut the power to the port engine. Slowly the yacht began a lazy circle to the left and headed toward the I.N.C.I.S.O.R. team that was still on the opposite shore. Once the turn was almost completed, Magnus cut the power to the starboard engine and let the craft drift.

As the yacht approached the shore Graham and Aaron jumped aboard and threw lines to Stirling and Dick. The four men worked to secure the boat.

Mariola was helped off of the boat and onto the shore. Michael was lowered onto the shore. The naked sheik was left on the deck of his craft. Sirens could be heard approaching the scene. Lance put Michael over his shoulder and Stirling did the same with Mariola. The men hightailed it from the shore and headed back to the Hotel Gniecki. The empty lot was completely abandoned by the time four police cruisers sped onto the dirt. All the police saw in their headlights was an obese naked man standing on the deck of his yacht and what looked like the back end of a truck hanging out the side of the craft.

Back in the rooms the I.N.C.I.S.O.R. teams worked quickly to inflate splints to immobilize Michael's legs. Flex then gave Michael a shot of morphine to ease his pain. Mariola was laid on a bed in another room and Dick gave her an injection of Narcan to counter the effects of the opiates in her system. She came around with a start.

"My Dawid!" she cried.

The men in the room knew from the background research that Dawid was Mariola's son. Was he with her? Did he have a 'mini' also? They tried to get Mariola to focus.

"My Dawid!" was all that she cried.

"We may have to go back," Dick said to the group.

"We can't," Graham replied. "The Gdansk police are all over that place now!"

Mariola was becoming calmer. "No," she moaned. "Dawid is with his father in Warsaw. I fear that his life may be in jeopardy also."

This statement calmed the men. They worked to make ready for their departure. Mariola and Michael were helped out of the hotel and into the two vans and the men sped south out of Gdansk.

A call was placed to Becky to let her know that the I.N.C.I.S.O.R. team had succeeded and that she should let her husband know.

Mariola moaned again from the back of the van, "No! Do not let Filip know. He's the one who sold me into slavery. He's the one who wanted to get rid of me!"

This information was relayed to Becky. She then chose to call the Polish police in Warsaw to have Filip arrested and asked that the police place Mariola's son, Dawid, in protective custody.

The men drove on to Warsaw and Mariola was reunited with her son. Dawid explained to them that his father had been picked up by the police. The men left Mariola and Dawid locked together in a long hug. They drove to a local hospital so that Michael could have his legs attended to properly. Lance stayed with Michael. The five Frankfurt team members and three remaining Denver team members then headed to the Chopin Airport for their return flights.

CHAPTER THIRTY SEVEN

Washington, DC

PRESIDENT JOHN JAMES listened to the report from his Defense Minister in the Oval Office. He maintained his silence until the Cabinet Member was finished.

"So, Iran has rolled through Iraq and Syria without anybody stepping up to stop them. These two countries had their borders violated. They had an army run through their lands…and they did nothing!" the President said.

"That's correct, Mr. President," the Defense Minister answered.

"Shut up and let me think!" President James ordered.

"Well, we're responsible for wiping out the Iraqi army and Syria is a mess right now. Guess this doesn't come as any big surprise," the President mumbled.

"That's…"

"I told you to be quiet! Damnit! Let me think!" the President yelled.

"Next up is the United Nations force in the demilitarized zone just east of the Golan Heights. What can we expect of them? The United Nations is full of a bunch of incompetents. I expect their forces will be useless due to the bungling of the UN leadership. Any progress with their damned sanctions?" President James asked.

The Defense Minister was almost afraid to speak, "The Security Council voted for the sanctions and they will be implemented within three weeks."

"See what I mean! Israel will be toast in three weeks! Get me Netanyahu on the phone…NOW!" the President ordered.

The Defense Minister turned and almost ran out of the office.

Dubai, UAE

"Hey Becky!" I yelled.

"What's up?" Becky replied.

"Let's go scuba diving! We haven't been under the water since Grand Cayman. It'll be fun!" I answered.

"Oh…and you know how much I love being under the water," Becky responded sarcastically.

"I'm not talking about travelling out into the Persian Gulf. I want to go to the Aquarium at the Dubai Mall," I said.

"And then you'll feed me?" Becky asked.

"I promise…I also want to talk about moving," I replied.

That statement floored Becky as she thought about how we had only arrived in Dubai within the last two years and I had the commitment to the American Dental Clinic. She decided to bite her tongue and wait to hear me out over dinner and went to change into her swimsuit.

We made the drive to the mall in silence and I had a valet park the Beemer. We had walked by the aquarium on other trips to the mall and stopped to watch the fish, but had never gone to swim inside the tank. As we were donning our gear, the guide explained to us that the tank was one of the largest tanks in the world. It held over two and a half million gallons of sea water and boasted the largest viewing panel in the world. There were over thirty three thousand living animals in the aquarium. Over four hundred sharks and rays were in the tank.

That got Becky's attention!

He went on to tell us that they even had a special lunar-cyclic lighting system that changed the ambience of the tank depending on the time of day.

Becky remembered how to inflate her BCD and purge her mask. We both checked our air supply gauges and moved to the diving platform. With our fins and masks in place we rolled into the tank. Even as huge as the tank was, I felt like I was in a confined space…and it was weird to be observed from outside of the Aquarium by the shoppers in the mall.

Definitely not like the open water dives that Becky and I were used to in the past. We finished, returned our diving equipment, showered and dried off and changed into our dinner clothes.

We chose the Rainforest Café next to the Aquarium. The food wasn't going to matter much as we were going to be discussing the rest of our lives.

I began with, "I've been back to the dental clinic only once since I was taken. I get really anxious when I walk through those doors."

"That's understandable, Reggie. That place holds a lot of trauma for you," Becky replied.

"Let me finish, please…I think I want out…I've talked to two of the associates at the clinic and they are willing to buy out my share. I've also talked with Dr. Mulheran and he understands. So-o-o, I think I'm done there," I finished.

"What about the CIA and the PC's?" Becky asked.

"Talked to them, also. They are okay with my decision and may decide to work with one of the young associates once they have vetted both of them," I replied. "Anyway, they've gotten good use out of the PC's that I implanted…I'm, done!"

Becky was quiet for a bit and then said, "Where will we live? Do we stay here in Dubai?"

I pulled my laptop onto the table and opened the screen. I punched a few buttons until I got to the website that I wanted to show Becky.

"What about a vineyard north of Florence in Italy?" I asked.

Becky looked at the screen and moved between the pictures. She looked at me with tears in her eyes.

"I hate this, Reggie," was all that she said.

Demilitarized Zone, Golan Heights

A forward observer sounded the general alarm as men of the United Nations peace keeping force poured out of their protective cover and climbed into their defensive positions. The UN commander soon took his place at the observation tower.

"Here they come!" he announced as he watched through his binoculars.

As the Iranian army moved ever closer the U.N. commander worried that the oncoming tanks would fire on his position. Then he worried that the Iranian army may not stop and just overrun their position. As the lead tanks approached, they did slow to a stop and…so far…no shots had been fired.

An armored personnel carrier moved in front of the parked tanks and approached the United Nations position. There was a white flag attached to an aerial antennae. The U.N. commander got down from his observation post and moved out to meet with the APC.

The Iranian commander jumped out of the vehicle and stood in front of the U.N. troop commander. The U.N. commander extended his hand in greeting…the Iranian commander chose to ignore the gesture and to raise his hand to salute.

The U.N. commander pulled back his hand and spoke first, "I have been ordered to halt your advance on Israel right here…and right now!"

"Funny, you don't look ready to stop me," the Iranian commander stated as he surveyed the United Nations forces.

The U.N. commander turned and looked over his men and then turned to face the Iranian commander once again. "I should not be telling you this but…we have been ordered to stop you…and also to not engage you. So, I guess I was supposed to scare you into turning around and running home. Listen, I am French…we have been great supporters of the Arab Nations in the Middle East. I don't give a damn about Israel. I have told you to halt. I did my duty. We will not stand in your way. Good luck and good hunting."

"What a putz!" the Iranian commander thought. "These French are just what I've always heard. Really quick to turn tail and even quicker to stab their allies in the back. I need to remember this exchange in the future!" The Iranian commander came to attention, saluted once again, and turned to mount his armored personnel carrier.

The APC returned to the Iranian front lines and the commander ordered, "Full speed ahead. These impotent troops will not engage us… next stop Israel!" With that command the diesel engines revved and the huge column began to move southwest. He then turned to his second in command, "Iran may have listened to these weak and incapable fools. We could have been stopped here, in this place, for days while negotiations commenced with the United Nations. Do you know what that idiot commander said? He told me—without prompting on my part—that he was ordered not to engage! What feeble and helpless warriors we have in front of us! Let's kick some Israeli butt!"

Washington, DC

"I know, I know," President James replied.

"Iran just pushed through the United Nations' position in the DMZ east of the Golan Heights. They will engage Israeli forces in the Golan Heights tomorrow," the Defense Secretary said.

"I said that I know! Damnit! You have anything helpful for me?" the President asked.

"No, Mr. President...except to say that I think Israel is ready for the attack," the Secretary replied.

"Oh, swell!" President James said. "This tiny country is going to stop Iran in its tracks. No effing way! And we sit here unwilling to engage? This is Bull!"

The Defense Secretary nodded in agreement and then had a thought, "Mr. President! Your tactic of amassing our Afghan troops on the Iran-Afghanistan border did have some effect. Our intelligence is indicating that at least two hundred tanks have left Syria and are hightailing it for the eastern Iranian border. That has severely limited the Iranian forces. Our analysts now believe that Israeli forces are on a pretty even ground with the Iranian forces...still outnumbered but not by much. Should be a fair fight and a tossup who will win."

"A tossup! Fair fight? What the hell are you saying, man!" President James yelled. "Israel is fighting for its life! And over nothing! We proved that Israel and the United States were not behind that attack on Bushehr. There's no sanity in that part of the world!"

"Did you know, Mr. President, that there have been some skirmishes with the Iranian troops on the Afghan border? The Iranians have actually been bold enough to move into Afghanistan and engage our troops!" the Secretary stated.

"Well, let's give them a taste of their own medicine! Order all of the Iranian positions along the Afghanistan border shelled. Order some B-52 strikes out of Italy! Let's eliminate all of their machinery that has been put along the border. Do NOT have the troops move into Iran. Just blast the hell out of their positions!" President James ordered. "Also get me Netanyahu. He needs to know about the impotent United Nations response…and to get ready!"

Dubai, UAE

Ash, Lance and I had chosen to get together for lunch and do some debriefing and talking about the future. Things had been moving so quickly with I.N.C.I.S.O.R. that the three of us had not shared any time together.

"Al-Qaeda had men on the ramp, working as plane cleaners for Lufthansa," Lance said.

He was telling me what he and Ash had found out from the investigation about the thwarted hijacking.

"That's how they hid the knives on board. They were behind the bathroom mirrors. Al-Qaeda claimed responsibility for the hijacking, even though it was planned and executed by MADEI. I guess they'll take the credit for anything bad in the world even if they had little to do with it!" Ash said.

"And the Polish incident?" I asked.

"First, it looks like Michael's off the team. Two broken legs—he's toast in terms of ever being able to engage, again," Lance began.

"And it was Mariola's husband that set the whole thing up?" I queried.

"Yeah, it's like he didn't remember purchasing the 'mini'…or he didn't think it would work…or that it could be disposed of before anybody responded," Ash offered.

"That almost happened when her clothes were tossed into the river up there in Gdansk," I said.

"I was concerned that Michael was the thinker of the group and that he'd never be able to react the way we needed him to. Boy was I wrong! The guys said that it was Michael that rushed to stop that yacht with the stolen truck. He actually moved before the others could react!" Lance added. "Now I'll be working on his replacement for the Denver team."

"Any other casualties?" I asked.

"Cuts and scrapes…nothing serious…all of the men are back in Denver and Frankfurt. Also, the Polish police don't seem to be any wiser about our rescue. Their investigation is focusing completely on Filip and his plan to sell his wife, Mariola, into slavery with that sheik. What a wild story!" Ash replied.

"And Mariola? Everything good?" I asked.

"She's with Dawid and all's well, as far as we can tell. She now has all of the family fortune!" Ash said.

"Hey, did I tell you guys? Becky bought her two puppies to replace her dogs that were killed!" I said.

"Okay, now the hard stuff," Lance began. "I know that you two know this already…but Cyndi has put her foot down and is not coming back to this part of the world. I don't know if she'll ever leave Denver again!"

"So, what are you gonna do?" Ash asked.

"Get another drink first," Lance replied. "Reggie, what is this I'm hearing from Becky? You leaving too? That kidnapping would take it out of anybody. So much for the two of us keeping you out of harm's way."

"I'm having a hard time being in the dental clinic, and yes, I've decided to sell out to two of the young associates. And…I think we, being I.N.C.I.S.O.R., are way too far up on everybody's radar. We'd be stupid if we don't assume that al-Qaeda knows who we are after that Tehran incident and my kidnapping. I believe that's how they knew to come for me!" I began.

"I do feel that the United Arab Emirates is the safest place to be in the Middle East…but maybe not for me…or Becky, any more," I continued.

"But, Italy?" Ash questioned.

"Since I first began my dental practice in Colorado in the early eighties, I've wanted to own a vineyard. There was a Denver oilman, named Jordan, who sold all of his oil holdings and bought a winery in California. I still think that the Jordan Cabernet is one of the best wines in the world!" I exclaimed. "I found a place around Florence and the property looks great on the internet photographs. I've asked Becky to come with me to take a look…and Italy's pretty central to all of the happenings around the world that I.N.C.I.S.O.R. has responded to so far."

"Except that Central America escapade," Lance countered.

"And that's what the Denver team is for!" Ash added.

"Hey guys, nothing is etched in stone, but we've got some issues to work through about our future," I said.

We were silent for several minutes while we nursed our drinks.

Ash spoke next, "I'm making a quick trip to Riyadh. Should only be gone for two days, but you won't be able to reach me."

"Isn't that where that sheik who showed up on the yacht in Poland was from?" Lance asked.

"So..." Ash began.

"Yeah, he was released by the Polish authorities. Wonder how he explained away that all the men on his boat were dead...and that truck hanging off of his boat?" I joked. "At least he had to fly back to Saudi Arabia! His yacht will be in the shop for a little while."

"And those murders in Louisiana and North Carolina? Was that you?" I questioned.

Ash Black held up his arms in mock surrender. "If it was, there is nothing to tie me to those incidents."

"Incidents! Men were systematically targeted and murdered!" I began to object.

"Bad men!" Ash countered.

"So, this isn't what I.N.C.I.S.O.R. is about," Lance interjected.

"I wasn't there on behalf of I.N.C.I.S.O.R.! I was there on behalf of Grace and the other innocent victims of the world." Ash said.

"So, now you're the savior for the world?" Lance objected.

"Just doing my little part," Ash said meekly.

This discussion wasn't going anywhere. Ash was Ash and we were going to have to accept this part of him until he got Grace's murder out of his system...if ever. I sure wasn't ready to face the future of I.N.C.I.S.O.R. without Ash and Lance. The discussion moved back to relocating.

"I'm making a trip to Denver," Lance announced. "Time to make up with Cyndi. And I'll work on Michael's replacement. I'll call you guys from there."

"Eleven Million's due here next week," Ash said. "Now we'll be pretty busy with the horizontal mambo, but I bet we could squeeze in a dinner or two!"

"Becky and I will be heading for Italy, but we'll put the trip off until after your friend's visit," I replied. "How about a name for your friend?"

"Eleven Million is just fine for now," Ash replied and held up his left hand. "And the wedding ring is still on!"

CHAPTER THIRTY EIGHT

Golan Heights, Israeli Occupied Territory

COLONEL KUBETZ WAS in the remote command trailer that had been moved up to the Golan Heights. Israel had taken the two weeks to move much of its armament up into the region. The Israeli soldiers had worked hard to dig themselves in for the imminent attack by Iran. The munitions were arriving daily and moved to the various tanks and tank busting bunkers that were strategically placed along the Golan Heights.

"Here they come!" Colonel Kubetz announced.

The Iranian army had moved to within a mile of Israel's forward positions. Almost immediately after the Colonel's announcement a barrage of the Israeli positions began. Most of the explosions were scattered and ineffective, but some of the artillery shells found their targets and there were loud explosions as tanks and munitions caught fire and were destroyed.

Colonel Kubetz radioed Tel Aviv that the Israelis were under attack. The battle had begun.

The Israeli air force had scrambled a good number of planes that now swept over the forward positions and began to methodically fire on the front lines of the Iranian advance. Smoldering wreckages could be seen in the distance as the Israeli jets loosed their Maverick air to ground missiles on their prey. The AGM-65 was Israel's best weapon to defend against armored vehicles. Many of the Israeli soldiers had nicknamed it the 'tank buster'.

Even though a great number of the Iranian tanks had been knocked out of the battle, the onslaught continued. Iranian anti-aircraft batteries had blown several Israeli jets out of the sky. Very soon the battle became tank on tank between the advancing Iranian tanks and the dug in Israelis. It soon became apparent that being able to shoot and then move to different locations was an advantage for the Iranians. Their artillery was performing well as evidenced by the large fires along the Israeli front line.

Israeli command had placed reinforced TOW missile platforms interspersed between the tanks. The TOW missile was a surface attack missile used to eliminate an armored threat. This <u>T</u>ube launched <u>O</u>ptically tracked <u>W</u>ire guided missile was extremely accurate and effective against the approaching Iranian tanks.

Colonel Kubetz scanned the battle lines and listened to the incoming reports from his officers. The battle was now scattered over a wide front as casualties mounted on both sides. Then the unthinkable occurred. The shout from inside the command center, "INCOMING". Colonel Kubetz ran for the door and jumped from the platform as the command center erupted into flames. A direct Iranian artillery hit had wiped out his command!

Colonel Kubetz lay still on the hard ground as his brain cleared from the explosion. Men had run to him and were dousing flames that were burning through his clothing. He felt a sharp pain in his left arm as he realized that part of the command trailer was embedded in his biceps muscle. He reached across his body and ripped the shrapnel out of his arm. Another soldier applied pressure to the wound to get the blood pouring out of it under control and yelled out the famous phrase on the battlefield, "MEDIC".

The Colonel's arm was wrapped in a tight bandage. He knew that he needed to get up and to continue to command the Israeli troops. He needed to get back in this fight! With a mighty struggle he found his feet, teetered for a moment until his head cleared and then ran to see what was left of his command. The answer? Nothing! It had been a direct hit. Many were dead or dying around him.

"What to do?" he thought.

Just then an APC was making its way to the front lines to reinforce the dwindling strength. Colonel Kubetz ordered the vehicle to halt and scrambled up its stairs.

"This is now my command vehicle!" he ordered.

He placed the driver's headset under his helmet and listened to the reports of destruction and the cries for help. It was becoming evident that the Iranian advance was slowing and in some areas the attack had stalled. His forces had withstood the initial attack by the Iranian army, but at great cost. The battle lulled as the Iranians seemed content with their first day's progress against the Israeli army. Artillery was being exchanged by both sides as shells fell around the Israeli encampment. Even the artillery efforts seemed to have slowed. Reserves were moving up to reinforce many of the weakened forward positions.

Colonel Kubetz knew that the opposing army was also resupplying and reinforcing their positions also. Tomorrow would be a hell of a day!

Tel Aviv, Israel

Prime Minister Netanyahu listened to the reports from the battle. He remembered back to the Yom Kippur War of 1973, when Syria and Egypt coordinated attacks against Israel. Syria moved against the Golan Heights while Egypt crossed the Suez Canal to attack Israel from the south.

His Special Forces unit made many raids against enemy positions during that war, and under his leadership a commando team penetrated deep into Syrian territory. Israel initially lost ground in the Golan Heights for the first week and then mounted a massive counter-offensive that lasted only four days and Israel took much of Syria's land.

Prime Minister Netanyahu only had one offensive to deal with this time, but a superior force than he had faced in 1973. He listened to the opinions from his army leadership and then issued the dreaded command, "Arm the nukes!"

Tehran, Iran

Parliament listened to the reports and watched the progress while it was shown on the large screens installed in their meeting hall. The mood was festive as if they were watching a ball game on the television.

The reports from the front line were mostly positive…and mostly lies. The reports prompted one of the parliament members to remark that Israel would be theirs tomorrow. How shallow and short sighted this man was. Israel was not going to roll over in two days!

Golan Heights, Israeli Occupied Territory

"It's time, sir," the aide said as he shook Colonel Kubetz awake. The Iranian troops were priming and firing up diesel engines all along the front. The Israeli troops were doing likewise as they prepared for more confrontation.

Shortly, Israeli jets were in the air carefully choosing which of their many targets they would kill with their missiles. Reports were coming in from the pilots overhead about an unusual formation taking shape among the Iranian front lines.

The pilots were reporting that the Iranians were massing in a reverse 'vee' formation…just the opposite of the wedge that is usually formed to drive through an opponent's defenses, hitting them hard in one location and driving hard to outflank the defenders before they could reinforce. This was a different attack formation…

Colonel Kubetz drank his coffee as he cleared the cobwebs from his head. His sleep was sound but way too short. His arm was throbbing under the blood soaked bandages. A medic appeared to change his dressing on the injured arm. The Colonel moved to a large white board and picked up a marker. He drew out the Iranian formation that was being relayed to him by the Israeli pilots.

"What are they trying to do?" he thought out loud. "Are they trying to herd us together in the middle?" He studied the map and the Israeli positions. And then it hit him, "No!" he yelled and bolted out of the trailer.

The Israelis had moved the lion's share of their reinforcements into the middle third of the front lines. The outer thirds would react to any attempts to flank the Israeli army. In traditional tank warfare it was too difficult for the enemy to exercise flanking maneuvers without greatly weakening their own force and subjecting it to a counteroffensive that could isolate the tanks on the sides. The classic 'divide and conquer'.

The outer thirds of the Israeli line were the weakest links. The Israelis had prepared for an aggressive frontal onslaught by the Iranians. The Iranians had worked through the night to create just the opposite scenario. Artillery was moved into the center of the Iranian front. The shelling had commenced and the effects from the artillery rounds would keep the Israelis in the middle third pinned down and unable to move effectively to reinforce the units protecting the outer thirds. The majority of the Iranian tanks had been moved to the flanks and were now attacking the weaker Israeli forces on the flanks.

It would not be long before the Iranian forces would drive through the Israelis and either surround the Israeli army or continue driving on into Israel. This move would be a death blow to Israel…and Colonel Kubetz had seen it too late…maybe.

As Colonel Kubetz made his dash to the left flank an artillery shell took out a TOW installation in front of him. He knew how to operate these missiles. The Colonel slammed on his brakes and dismounted from his Humvee. All of the men behind the reinforcements had been killed in the blast, but the hardware still seemed to be functioning after the blast.

This particular TOW missile was fired from a tripod mounting that had been secured into the hard ground of the Golan Heights. The missile was loaded and ready to fire. Colonel Kubetz took aim at an advancing Iranian tank and fired. He watched through his sighting mechanism as the missile flew toward its target with the trailing wire playing out behind it for guidance corrections. The missile flew true and impacted its target. There was a bright flash and then a delayed explosion as the sound waves trailed behind what he saw.

"One down!" Colonel Kubetz thought to himself. "They have this site targeted. I'll fire off one more missile and then I'd better move!"

He grabbed up another missile out of its protective container and secured it into the launching tube. He attached the wire to the guidance system and took aim. Another successful firing and another wonderful explosion to his ears. Just then he heard the terrifying and all too familiar sound of an incoming artillery barrage. The whistling was close! Colonel Kubetz jumped for cover…

A direct hit. The Colonel's body was vaporized by the blast. He had stopped to help defend his beloved Israel but had failed to make it to the weakened Israeli flank that was now in jeopardy of being overrun by the Iranian army.

Tel Aviv, Israel

"Mr. Prime Minister…our forces are being overrun. The battle seems to be lost. Colonel Kubetz has been killed by an artillery shell. They say it exploded right on top of him!" the Aide related to Prime Minister Netanyahu.

"Get our fighter bombers in the air. We armed them yesterday with nuclear warheads. Follow the plan…five of the planes head immediately for Tehran. Another five to lesser cities in Iran. We will take out that country and her leadership before their army can come down from the Golan Heights!" the Prime Minister ordered. "Equip our short range missile batteries with nuclear warheads. We will stop this Iranian army in its tracks!"

"What about our men?" the Aide questioned.

"We must stop this advance at all costs!" Netanyahu replied. "We must protect Israel. Also get me the President of the United States. He must know what is about to happen!"

CHAPTER THIRTY NINE

Washington, DC

"**N**ETANYAHU HAS AUTHORIZED nuclear warheads to be placed on fighter bombers that are now headed for Tehran and other areas in Iran!" President James exclaimed. "This will surely be the end of the Middle East…as we know it."

"What happened to the Israeli defenses?" the Defense Secretary asked of the President.

"An ingenious and heroic move by the Iranians found Israel's weakest areas and Iran is in the process of overrunning all of the Israeli positions in the Golan Heights," the President replied. "The Israeli Prime Minister has also authorized short range nuclear missiles to be readied to take out the Iranian army. He swore to me that Israel will not be taken by the Iranians! Call Tehran! They need to know that nuclear strikes are imminent and to stop this nonsense."

Tehran, Iran

"I do not care what that United States President says to us! We have Allah on our side!" the Parliament leader screamed into the microphone as he addressed the ruling body. "We are squashing the Israeli troops as I speak. Israel will soon be ours! Nuclear weapons or not! I am not afraid of this retaliation! Our missile defenses will bring down any intruder!"

Shouts of approval were heard around the room. And then it began as a trickle and then became a rushing torrent as the Parliament members rushed out of the room to seek shelter in the hardened bunkers that were prepared for the country's leadership. Even the speaker hightailed it out of the room to head deep underground.

Tel Aviv, Israel

"Tehran is not backing off of their attack!" the Aide exclaimed to the Prime Minister. "The Iranian leadership told the American President to 'eff' off and die!"

"Tell our fighter bombers to go 'weapons hot," Prime Minister Netanyahu ordered.

Golan Heights, Iranian Occupied Territory

The battle had become close enough that it was turning into an infantry war. The tanks and artillery on both sides were still very active. The Israeli soldiers on foot could now engage the enemy and were firing upon any moving targets as the Iranian army advanced. Their guns were becoming too hot to touch as they emptied magazine after magazine into the approaching forces.

"There are too many of them!" one sergeant yelled into his communication device. "We cannot hold out for much longer!"

The battle raged on and on. The Iranians kept up their onslaught suffering huge losses as men and equipment died on the battlefield. But... on they came. They fought like madmen as they came to within 'spitting distance' of the Israeli positions.

And then...

"What the f...!" a forward Israeli observer exclaimed. "Am I wrong, or are those Iranian tanks turning around?"

The Israeli soldiers watched in amazement as the Iranian forces turned tail and began to hastily retreat.

"Command, this is forward observation number two...the Iranian army has turned tail and is pulling back!"

The Israelis had no idea what to make of this sudden retreat. And then they saw it...

An Act of God!

A Haboob! In Arabic, Haboob means simply, 'strong wind'. In reality, it is an intense sandstorm. This freak sandstorm was overtaking the battlefield arena. A black wall of sand, dirt and debris was bearing down from the north, obliterating everything in its path. The Iranian forces which had occupied the territory beneath the Golan Heights were swallowed up immediately by the giant wall.

The swirling, biting and blinding sand worked into every opening and crevasse. It clogged everything that was exposed, rendering all of the equipment useless. Nobody could move!

"Everybody down!" came the order for the Israeli troops. The men and women that had watched in amazement as the storm approached already knew what to do and were hunkering down in their bunkers. Many, many prayers were shouted out to God for saving them before they were covered by the dust and dirt, choking off the ability to talk. Many of the soldiers began to cry. The prayers of the Israeli soldiers then continued on in silence.

In the Middle East, Haboobs can crop up at any time and sometimes they stay there for up to three months. Within minutes all progress of the Iranian troops was halted. Within hours all of the Iranian hardware... tanks, trucks, APC's...were covered in a suffocating blanket of sand. The poor exposed soldiers had nowhere to hide from the instant death that approached as they were buried alive. The men in the vehicles died a slower death as the air in their cabs became stale and starved of all available oxygen. They suffocated in agony. Some even attempted to escape their vehicles only to be swallowed up and buried as the sand filled in upon them.

Sandstorm conditions are also ideal for rain storms. The rain soon followed. The desert sands cannot soak up water quickly and the heavy rains produced flash flooding conditions quickly and without warning. The torrential rains turned the mass of sand graves into concrete tombs. The Iranian army was buried alive and then entombed forever.

Word from the Israeli positions quickly made its way back to Tel Aviv. The battle and the war were over. The Iranian army was no more…

The synagogues were soon filled to overflowing with the thankful throughout Israel offering up their prayers to God.

The Israeli command ordered the fighter bombers, carrying their nuclear armament, to return to base. The short range missile batteries, with their nuclear warheads, were ordered to stand down. The Israeli nuclear response was averted.

It would take Iran decades to rebuild and replace what had been lost at the base of the Golan Heights. Their world status as the twelfth largest army in the world was gone. There would be no aggression from this country for a long, long time.

World War IV was over.

CHAPTER FORTY

Dubai, UAE

I SAT, DEJECTED, ON the patio. I felt very lonely.

Lance was in Denver and Ash was still somewhere in Saudi Arabia. I had read in the local paper that a Saudi sheik had died in his sleep. Was this death on Ash's hands? I knew that he wouldn't confirm or deny his involvement.

Becky was in Florence. She was spending some time checking out the estate and winery I had told her about.

Cyndi was with Lance in Denver, and so far not about to leave. Lance had called and asked me to see about selling his home on Palm Jumeirah Island. With real estate in Dubai somewhat depressed, that was going to be a difficult task.

And last, I thought about Grace. She was also gone, but at least I would never forget her.

I pondered the future of I.N.C.I.S.O.R. My best friends had helped me to form this group, and the men and women of I.N.C.I.S.O.R. had performed well every time they were called upon.

Could we maintain our effectiveness if Lance, Ash and I were living apart?

I took a long, slow drink of Crown Royal and then toyed with the lemon rind.

"We all change," I thought. "The world changes. I need to go flying! I am happiest when I am in the air!"

Just then the phone rang. I rushed inside, hoping that the call was from Becky. I did not recognize the number that was displayed in the caller ID.

I picked up the phone and identified myself, "Dr. Nelson speaking... how may I help you?"

"Dr. Nelson...of I.N.C.I.S.O.R.?" the voice asked.

I became wary after my experience being kidnapped from the American Dental Clinic, but said, "Yes, who is this?"

"This is Abdiweli Mohamed Ali," the voice replied.

"Do I know you?" I asked.

"No, sir, you do not...but my country's leadership has heard about you!"

Now I was extra worried!

"I am the Prime Minister of Somalia," the man continued. "You have heard about our 'problem'?"

I thought for a moment about what I knew about that country. Honest answer was bupkis! I did not know much about this part of Africa. And a 'problem'? And then it hit me like a ton of bricks!

"Yes, Mr. Prime Minister, I have. In fact, two of my men were encountered your 'problem' while enjoying a cruise."

"My government has not handled the 'problem' well. It is growing as we speak!" the Prime Minister announced.

"And I need your help!"